Syren's Call

A FANTASY NOVEL

RICK SKOWRONSKI

Sandy,
A book you can sink your teeth into!
Rick Skowronski

First Edition

PAGE PUBLISHING, INC.
New York, NY

First originally published by Page Publishing, Inc. 2015

ISBN 978-1-63417-586-9 (pbk)
ISBN 978-1-63417-587-6 (digital)

Printed in the United States of America

by nightfall. Mother would be waiting for her. Reaching down, she organized the pile of firewood so that it balanced well on itself. That way no odd pieces would tumble out when she lifted the stack. Next, she wrapped the package, tying it tightly together by the sturdy canvas straps she had laid everything on. Once she had secured her charge, she tipped the entire collection onto its edge. Then grasping firmly onto the straps as handholds, she hoisted the heavy bundle across her shoulders, behind her head. Steadying herself for a moment against the weight of it, she started off toward the Wallgate. Placing each foot purposefully as she went so as not to stumble on a rock or trip from a ground vine and go sprawling, Syren tried to keep one eye on her progress and the other on her surroundings. It was the time of day when the deer and other forest grazers would come into the Nearwood from their hiding places, looking for food. When they did, the Hiddeans, Gremlins, and perhaps other, more perilous beasts would slink out from Stormwood, hunting for prey. She meant not to be here when they arrived. Frequently, tales of terror and mayhem would ride into town with the traveling peddlers and traders who came to sell their wares and buy curiosities and timber. Because of the settlement's remote location, civilized people usually came to Westpost as part of a caravan, with armed escorts of their own hiring. Some would occasionally arrive wounded or harried by fierce beasts or by the foul, man-like creatures that roamed the deep forest by day and stalked the open spaces at night.

Syren marched along within sight of the wall, keeping it in the darkening view to her right as she moved more or less steadily eastward. On her way, she thought about her family, about the settlement of Westpost, and about everything the wall represented, for good and for ill. Two generations ago, the western reaches of King Orman's lands were considered completely uninhabitable. The region was populated by a variety of wild and magical creatures of treacherous power, as well as by numerous bands of fierce and frightening man-beasts. These brutish but crafty beings were warlike, untamable, and bent on savagery.

In need of resources for his growing kingdom, though, the king had funded a mission to settle a sea port town on the plains of Westmarsh. That settlement became known as Ormanland, as had the region around it. The town lay several days south of where Westpost now stood, though Syren had never been there. Having been started during a time of peace in the land, the fledgling settlement of Ormanland had been well supported and heavily defended in its early years. Aided by this support, and with connection to the Centerlands by both land and sea routes, the community quickly rooted itself and blossomed, despite its remote location.

A generation later, however, the condition of the kingdom had become much different. Orman had died without having an heir or naming a successor. Into the void rushed several claimants, each striving for popular support in one way or another. Attempting to link himself to the prosperity of King Orman's time, Vice Regent Gurdred pushed to carve a new haven of civilization from the harsh wilderness of the west. A petition invited anyone and everyone to the promise of prosperity, adventure, and autonomy. Five hundred rugged and courageous settlers had responded, including Syren's mother and father. Unfortunately, the area chosen for Westpost's founding (because of its access to timber and other resources) turned out to be a decidedly harsher environment than that of its preceding neighbor. Gurdred had assigned his younger son, Prince Hallas, to oversee the project, but he proved to be a disinterested ruler at best. He ended up spending most of the meager support he was sent on maintaining his own security and comforts.

A deer bounded in front of Syren abruptly, almost crashing into her on its frantic flight past. The near collision caused her to stagger awkwardly for balance and bang painfully into a tree to keep from tipping over backward onto the large bundle she was carrying. By the time she had righted herself, the creature had disappeared into the distant underbrush. Syren paused by the tree for a minute, setting her charge down heavily, to rest. While massaging her aching neck, she studied the countryside warily in the lingering twilight. A gray gloom was starting to gather at its edges, and she noted a conspicuous quiet. The sky beyond the tree tops to the west was still a fading shade of pink, but stars were already twinkling sparsely overhead. The Wallgate was fairly close now, but darkness and danger were closing in as well. She didn't have long to go, either way.

Crouching, she hoisted the great pile of firewood again to her shoulders and, staggering briefly under its seemingly increasing weight, started off for the gate. She traveled as closely to the wall now as the Barrier, which protected its base, would allow. On her way, she thought again about her father and about the wall that surrounded Westpost. After the founding of the town, the wall had been erected to create a safe haven, a place to run to for protection in case of a crisis. Prince Hallas lived there in his palatial estate, while most villagers originally lived outside, tending gardens and livestock and gradually clearing a section of the forest. Now, nearly everyone lived inside the wall full-time, and efforts to pacify the forest had stopped. Certainly no one ever went into the deep woods. Syren's father had been a volunteer member of a militia company that was formed to drive away the terrifying and cruel forest dwellers known as the Hiddeans. On one such mission, though, his company got ambushed. Father didn't return, and his body was never recovered. As a young adult, Syren had spent much of her time searching the Nearwood for signs of her father. It was one of her two highest goals in life. Whenever she wasn't busy earning her daily bread, which took up most of her days, really, she was in the wilderness. She had already devoted many hours to tracking, looking for clues as to her father's fate, but to no avail so far. "Stormwood," she thought. "Surely, the answers must lie there."

Suddenly, she was accosted out of the darkness by three snarling figures who were brandishing short, crudely made spears. They stood more or less upright like men, but on large, wolf like feet, and with short, repulsively bald tails. Their hides were mangy and putrid smelling as if they carried some awful disease, and their heads resembled a bizarre and unnatural corruption of man and hyena. From dangerous-looking jaws sprang sharp fangs, and their eyes proclaimed a malevolent intellect. Having been taken by surprise, Syren instinctively backed away toward the wall. The maneuver kept the villains from encircling her, but as they closed in cautiously, she could see that she would soon be cornered helplessly.

As they yipped and chattered to each other, eyeing their captive hungrily, Syren knew she had only moments to decide how to save her own life. Her mind raced wildly through the possibilities. The creatures were frightening, lithe, and deadly, but they were also short of stature—maybe three feet tall. If she kept her wits about her and showed a strong face, she judged her chances good (though not perfect) of outdistancing them and reaching the Wallgate. That was assuming, of course, that she dropped the heavy bundle of firewood and ran. On the other hand, she had worked hard to find it, gather it all, and get it this far, and she was loath to leave it behind for the likes of these. Her other choice was to scream her lungs out, stand her ground as best she could, and hope that help came from the guard before she was overwhelmed and dragged off. The problem with that plan was that she was outnumbered and unarmed, and there was no assurance that the guard would come at all, much less in time.

The hideous trio were closing in on her, almost within their short reach. The real torment of her situation was realizing that, from the spot where she stood, her house was probably just behind her, on the other side of the wall, her mother quietly waiting for her return. By design, there was no way to ford the Barrier and scale the wall. As soon as she turned her back on them, the Hiddeans would pull her down from behind, and she dared not think about what would happen then. Home and hearth were just thirty feet away, but they could just as well have been thirty leagues. In a wail of anguish and frustration, Syren thrust the heavy bundle of kindling at the second of the three Hiddeans. The surprise maneuver sent all three foes dancing away to avoid being pinned, and she dashed madly toward the gate. As she passed by the first of the nasty skulkers on the way, it leapt out at her with horrifying passion, trying to seize hold and bury fetid fangs into her flesh. With a sharp cry of alarm and exertion, Syren managed to fend it off at the last moment by pure fortune, catching it alongside its mangy head with a wild sweep of her forearm. Unable to tell if she had been mauled and unwilling to look, she sprinted headlong toward the sight of the now blazing braziers that warded the Wallgate, a short ways ahead. For a handful of terrifyingly doubtful moments, she could hear the shrill, outraged chattering of the three Hiddeans close at her heels, but then her long strides and the approaching firelight left them behind.

Syren arrived at the huge wooden gate, gasping, just as the doors closed, sealing her out. She crashed straight into them to announce her presence to those who must be just inside. "Wait!" she called breathlessly, unable to shout. "Let me in! I'm still…out here. Hey!" From the other side of the doors, she heard the massive locking bar slide despairingly into place, and a single sob involuntarily left her throat. In the next moment, though, it was lifting again, a promise of rescue. Spinning around, she leaned her back against one door, uncertain if the dreaded creatures still lurked close by or if they had broken off their pursuit. When she felt the pressure of the huge portal pushing slowly toward her, she stood aside until a seam opened, and she at last stumbled in. Hauling the doors closed again behind her and lowering the locking bar were Coran and George.

"You shouldn't go out at night, Syren," Coran scolded obliviously. "You might get lost." Syren was bent over, hands propped upon her knees, sweating and breathing heavily, still reeling from her harrowing encounter and narrow escape.

"Yeah," added George pithily. "There are dangerous creatures out there, you know."

"Yeah," was all Syren could manage to say in counter to their inane remarks. There was too much.

The two stood silently for several awkward moments, scratching bug bites and looking about them aimlessly, until Coran spoke again. "Uh, did you see anything out there, Syren? Anything at all?"

From where she stood, she glared a response at him with one eye while mopping her brow with the back of her hand. They might have meant well, but just now, the puddle of their condescending ignorance was more than she could bear. Had she a copper's worth of strength or energy left, she'd have punched him hard in the stomach.

As it was, she staggered off, disheveled and grimy, torn and aching, toward home. "You have a nice night, now," George called out cluelessly from behind her.

"A nice night." Syren considered the ridiculous offer as she limped along the inner face of the town wall in the direction of her house. She began to chuckle, which grew into a kind of sorrowful, hysterical laughter and ended in sobs. "I am not crying!" she argued angrily to herself, tears streaming down hot cheeks. "I'm just...frustrated. I'm just...everything."

In the shadowed stillness that filled the space between the bustling neighborhood houses to her left and the haunting, malevolent sounds of the feral night wafting in over the wall from the woods beyond, the cool evening breeze began a work to bandage her wounds and steady her nerves. As she walked along the track beside the wall, Syren quietly contemplated her existence. Her parents had come to this region with five hundred others and devoted their lives to taming a wilderness, raising a strong family, and building a community. Now it was her community. They had passed those values on to Syren, and she wanted to see it through, make them proud.

That was the second great mission of her life, but now, years later, the reality was so much different than the dream had been. Many of her generation had abandoned the lofty goals of the founders, exchanging them for the common tasks of everyday life. Moreover, simply surviving to the next day seemed to be such a miserable exertion. Syren spent most of her days just gathering firewood. Sure, it helped the town in some small way, but at what cost? In the bigger picture, she was trading a day of her life for barely the means of scraping by to the next day. She imagined how she might one day be remembered: "Syren: She gathered sticks." "Not much of a legacy," she thought, shaking her head resignedly.

"Is this all there is?" she wondered. "Is this to be my destiny, plodding through life in submission to the tyranny of the mundane? Is there no greater call to answer, no way to honor the memory and labor of those who strove and gave all for the benefit of everyone, of me?" She ran her hand along the wall briefly, feeling its staunch immutability. The structure had been built to allow the people of Westpost to flourish, but it had become a cage and now; like everyone else, she was imprisoned by it.

Syren had finally reached the place where the community washhouses stood. Worn paths led up to the fence from various homes in the neighborhood, including hers. Sarah, one of the young wives in the quarter, was just coming out, carrying her two-year-old son. As they passed each other, she flashed Syren one glad smile of recognition, followed by one quick double take of concern over her appearance and general condition. Then she continued busily on home with little Runyon. Just as well she didn't stop. Syren was too tired to explain, in any case. Drawing some water, she carried the bucket to her house and used it to wash off the futility and disappointment of the day. Her small three-room thatched-roof house was flooded with night, and she lit a lamp to chase away the darkness for what was left of the evening. Too tired to cook, she decided to head over to the Hooded Crow and get a bite there. First, though, she would sit and have a talk with Mother. It always made her feel better. Leaving the house, she walked around the back to where she knew Mother would be waiting, by the one shade tree in the yard. Exhaustedly, Syren plopped herself down on the grass, supporting herself on the way down by resting her hand on the smooth, carved gravestone, which protruded vigilantly though the earth.

"Well, Mother," she began wearily to the dear woman she had helped lay to rest several years earlier, "it's been another day in paradise..."

CHAPTER 2

Strangers

Sunlight had not yet blanketed Westpost with its early morning delivery as it slipped speedily up the East Road on its way to the main gate of town, when Syren was already bustling through her morning tasks. Yesterday had certainly ended in a harrowing and discouraging way, but since then, she had cleaned up, dined out, and slept well, and this new day seemed cheerful enough, after all. Hard work was good for a person anyway, she thought, and despite her initial worries about the attack she had received, she had come away with nothing more than a small bruise. Life always has a broader, gladder perspective in the light of day after a good rest, she decided, and it was well to get on with it. She still longed for more purpose than just satisfying the demands of the daily grind, but life did need go on, and there were things to do. Living alone, all the chores of daily life naturally fell to her, and as there was always much to do, both to earn her keep and to spend it, she preferred to get an early start.

Breakfast had been some thistle fruit and nuts from the root cellar and tea. Normally, there would have been something heartier, like leftovers from supper the night before, but she had eaten at the tavern last night, so there were none. She might elsewise have made something fresher, like eggs and bread, but that required finding exactly what she wanted from one of the neighbors, haggling over the cost, and spending the money. While usually a pleasant social exercise on what promised to be a beautiful sunny morning, on this particular day, Syren woke up feeling pressed for time by the necessity of all the day's activities. In addition, she had of course spent money at the Crow last night and now felt compelled to save the few coins she had left.

Today was market day. The townsfolk would all be out, selling the excess of what they could make or grow or find and buying what they needed or wanted. It was important to claim a prominent spot on the Village Green so that buyers could easily find the seller—and find her rather than someone else. Syren wouldn't be the only person in town selling wood today. The smart tactic was to arrive on the Green early and stake her claim to a likely spot by setting her bundles there. This was proving an especially difficult task this morning, mostly because of the unfortunate events of last night. For one thing, she had been forced to leave one entire bundle of wood (which was no small amount) in the Nearwood when she had been waylaid by the Hiddean hunting party. That meant a smaller and less impressive-looking heap with which to justify her claim to whatever space she wanted. More importantly, though, was that binding that pile together had been her sturdy canvas straps. The only ones she owned. Without those, it was going to be difficult to transport the two piles she did have in any kind of hurry. By hand, she might spend half the morning running between her house and the Green. That would never do.

Syren quickly finished setting up for the evening cooking by dragging a sack of hard beans out of the larder and setting them in a pot full of water to soak, watering her vegetable garden from the rain barrel, and returning to the root cellar to see if she had any onion and carrots left. While she did so, she considered possible solutions to her dilemma. She might try going out into the Nearwood and looking for the missing bundle and the attached straps. If she could find it quickly, then she would have regained both the lost wood and the means of carrying it. She'd have more to sell at the market and an easy way to get it there. On the other hand, if it wasn't exactly (or very nearly) where she had thrown it, she might waste valuable time searching and end up getting nothing at all from this market day. By that plan, she stood the most to gain but also the most to lose. Instead, she could offer to pay some of the neighborhood children to help her carry what she had to the Green, and she could try searching for the missing bundle and her straps later, after the sale. This would be fast but expensive. Children don't carry much, and their feet wander as their attention does. They'd need her close supervision (which would keep her away from the Green) and she'd need a small army of them to deliver this much wood in short order.

Syren began to regret having paid what seemed now like a merchant's ransom at the Crow last night, but then she thought better of it. Yesterday had been a truly terrible day. Life-threatening, in fact! Added to the general sorrow and struggling of her circumstances, one evening at the Hooded Crow eating a hot meal over a frothy mug and some lively music had done her more good than a wagonload of alchemists, and for a fraction of the cost. No, she decided finally, it had been time and money well spent. From here, she would simply make do.

Leaving her home, belt pouch in hand, Syren began counting her coins as she made her way absently between houses toward the main road, which went both into and out of town. Before long on her way, however, she was stopped abruptly by her near collision with two of the strangest men she had ever seen. They were both clearly adults, even older adults, by their long beards, bushy eyebrows, and wrinkled complexions, yet they were scarcely four feet tall. At first glance, they were very nearly a pair, save that one was slightly taller and wider. Both were broad-chested, well built, and stocky, with large, bulbous noses, knobby cheeks, and generally oversized features, compared to their height. They wore their abundant coarse hair in long reddish tresses, the wider one being perhaps the elder, bearing streaks of gray in his hair and beard. Their two faces blinked up at Syren with dark, deep-set eyes, and they looked disoriented or perhaps confused.

Realizing suddenly that she had been gawking at the poor fellows, Syren recovered her manners and thought she had better say something. The question was, how to address them? By accounts Syren had heard while listening to travelers' tales at the tavern, these two closely resembled wild barbarians or giants, except of course that they were short and, at the moment, seemed not wild at all but rather pitiful, almost comical, really. It made her wonder why two such strangers would be aimlessly standing around in her neighborhood as if they had dropped out of the sky.

"Um...Can I help you gentlemen find something?" she offered politely, straightening herself from the collision.

Squaring themselves to face her, the younger of the pair grabbed hold of his wide belt with both hands and bowed deeply at the waist.

"Doorrrrahst," he said, rolling his *r*'s emphatically in a deep, smooth tone.

Well, that seemed friendly enough, thought Syren, but what did it mean? She could only imagine, but they seemed to be awaiting a reply of some sort, so placing her fists on her hips, she bowed back at them.

"Durast to you too!" she said, smiling. The two men turned and looked at each other silently, their confused faces blinking. When they turned back toward Syren, there was something of an awkward silence, so she decided she ought to try something else.

"My name is Syren." She explained, pointing to herself, "Syren."

After a brief pause, their faces lit up suddenly in joyful comprehension. All at once they were laughing through large, square, white teeth, tugging on each other's beards, pointing at Syren, and talking quickly to each other in rolling, throaty tones. Listening with an eager and curious grin, she thought she understood the words *Syren* and *name* and perhaps some other words as well, in their enthusiastic exchange. Then turning back, they spoke to her again.

"Durast," the shorter one said decidedly, prodding himself firmly with ten oversized fingers. "Durast name!"

"Braenog," announced the other happily, also jabbing himself in the chest with his ten fingers. "Braenog name!"

Then the first one, Durast, to indicate that he understood, stepped forward and prodded Syren similarly (but in the stomach, in her case, because of the man's diminutive stature), almost pushing her down. "Syrrin!" he mispronounced proudly, not rolling his *r* quite so much. Then while Syren regained herself from Durast's display of friendliness, they congratulated themselves with a flurry of nods, smiles, winks, and a rapid exchange of accolades.

"Yep."

"Yep, yep."

"Yep," they said.

"I am glad to meet you," Syren said to them with a chuckle as she recovered her balance, pointing first to herself and then to them.

"You are glad to meet I," they replied emphatically in unison, pointing first to themselves and then to Syren.

She took that in for a moment as they grinned at her. "Okay, we'll have to work on that part," she said more to herself than to them. Then remembering the pressing matters of the day, she excused herself from their company.

"Well, it's been good to meet you," she stressed again, "but I really must be going. Lots to be about today. Good luck to you. Market day, you see," she explained quickly over her shoulder as she left them and headed to the main road.

When she got there, she looked about for any available urchins or idle youths from the neighborhood whom she might employ to porter her load of wood to the Village Green. The road had already become a river of people flowing steadily toward the center of town, fed by the trickling tributaries of each neighborhood. Studying them, she jangled her coin purse to assess its meager weight, hoping she had enough money to inspire those she might find. Unfortunately, she soon discovered that there was no suitable labor to be had. Everyone she saw was either too young to be of use for this purpose or already engaged helping their own families.

Sighing her frustration over how next to proceed, she turned abruptly toward home only to crash again into the same two strangers she had earlier met. Apparently, they had followed her to the road, and the older one took hold of her deftly to rescue her from falling completely, lifting her with surprising strength and setting her carefully on her feet again.

"Oof! Sorry, hello, and thank you," she said absently, thinking still of her problem and how she might solve it.

"Deep."

"Heloo."

"Yep, yep."

"Sorry, good," they answered awkwardly. Then they stood quietly, shifting their weight and looking up at Syren intently, working hard to blink away the glare of the morning sun. They were evidently waiting for or wanting something from her. Just what that might be, though, was difficult to tell, and she was far too busy for all the distractions and figuring out anyway.

"Listen," she began, exasperated, "I'd love to stay around and chat, do puzzles and whatever, but I really don't have time. Today is market day. Do you understand? Market day? And the thing is, it's starting to get a bit late, you see, and I have this huge load of wood that I need to transport—" Then all at once, it occurred to her.

"Say...what are the two of you doing right now?" They gazed up at her, blinking.

"That's what I thought," she concluded. "Follow me," she instructed and strode purposefully toward her house. Turning after a short distance, though, she saw that they had not in fact followed but were instead looking uncertainly. She motioned them over emphatically as she called them, to convey her meaning.

"Durast and...and...you there. I'm sorry, what was your name again? Bargain? Uh...Brainout. Um...whatever. Come. Come and see," she insisted. On stout legs the two hustled over in her direction, and soon all three were standing before Syren's needful pile of kindling.

"Sticks," observed Durast, somewhat bewildered.

"Yes, sticks. Good!" encouraged Syren.

"Sticks, good?" inquired the other.

"Yes. Well, no, not necessarily. I mean, it all depends on what... oh, look, that doesn't matter," she said, impatiently waving her hands before them as if to erase that chain of thought and start again. Her squat companions copied the motion. Syren was beginning to feel weary, but taking a deep breath, she pressed on.

"Sticks"—Syren indicated them with her hands—"to Westpost." Here, she swept her arm broadly to indicate the town and the general direction of the Village Green. They seemed to understand, so she continued laying out her plan as clearly as she could in plain, distinct words. "Durast, and...?" She paused to ask by her expression to have the other fellow fill in his name, which worked. This might be getting easier, she thought.

"Braenog," said he.

"Right. Durast and Braenog help Syren. Carry sticks to Westpost. Yes?" She took up an armload of the wood as she spoke, to illustrate what she was saying. Then setting it back down, she grabbed up her coin purse for the next part.

"Durast and Braenog help Syren. Carry wood to Westpost. Syren give coins to Durast and Braenog. Yes?" Tipping up the bag, three small, copper coins tumbled out into Syren's hand for them to see. In an instant, Durast was studying them closely.

"Trrrreasure!" he announced loudly, rolling his *r*'s with gusto. Braenog bunched over quickly to see for himself.

"Deep treasure?" he inquired. Durast sniffed at the coins, or perhaps just snuffled, Syren wasn't sure. They seemed agreed and a little disappointed that this was not "deep treasure," whatever that was, but just then a rumble came from Braenog, probably from his stomach. It was hard to tell with these two. Syren waited anxiously as they considered. They looked back and forth between the wood pile and the coins several times before turning their attention back to Syren. They looked a little more confused than usual, or perhaps incredulous.

"Sticks...for trreasure?" asked Durast.

"Yes. Sticks for treasure. In Westpost," she confirmed. Durast turned to confer with his impromptu business partner.

"Sticks...for food?" asked Braenog, raising his hedge like eye brows hopefully. Syren laughed. They really were quite charming in their own way, these fellows.

"Quite possibly," she answered, nodding.

"Quite possibly!" Braenog echoed enthusiastically and with promise to Durast.

"Deep!" he countered.

"Good!" snapped the first, and with that, both men gave a robust cheer, tugged at each other's beards, and became a bustle of activity. Braenog worked quickly. First, with Durast hunched over slightly, he loaded a great pile of kindling onto his back, using his travel cloak as a carrier and securing the load precariously with two cords, which were tied to the back of Durast's belt and then looped around his forehead. He then stacked more logs and kindling into Durast's waiting arms until he could scarcely see where he was going. Finally, Braenog indicated to Syren that she should do the same for him. As she did so, she was astonished at the strength the two men possessed, especially for their small size and apparent age. She noticed also, now she was working somewhat closely with them, that their hands were not simply large but oversized, larger than those of any regular man. Glad for their joviality and willingness to help, she began to wonder what sort of men these were, if indeed they were humans at all. There were certainly an abundance of wondrous creatures in the world, though most, like the Hiddeans, were not of the helpful sort. It was kind of thrilling, really, to think about befriending some. She tried to picture what it might be like, the three of them working together to accomplish some higher purpose than "stick gathering," something nobler and more lasting than simply surviving to the next day.

For now, however, getting this wood to market was the thing, and it seemed they were ready. Looking at the pair of them, all loaded down with every scrap of firewood she had, they resembled two giant porcupines, but when Syren expressed her concern and asked about the weight, they both grinned broadly and said,

"Deep!"

"To Westpost!"

"Yep, yep."

"Yep."

That being decided, Syren made sure they could see her through the cover of branches and then said, "Follow me." And this time, they did.

Turning to her right at the main road, Syren made her way through the growing crowd eagerly, though not too quickly, toward town center, greeting neighbors and fellow villagers as she passed, and taking in with a measure of satisfaction the odd looks and whispers she was getting on account of her newfound friends, who waddled merrily along behind her on stubby legs while joyfully practicing their language skills.

"Sticks for food!" said one.

"Sticks for trrreasure!" came the reply.

"Yep."

"Yep, yep."

"Syren is good…Quite possibly!"

CHAPTER 3

The Baron

The Village Green was alive and busy when Syren and her two friends arrived, and hectic with the activity of various artisans and growers setting up tables, displaying wares, and greeting each other happily. Some were hanging colored streamers atop tall poles, which they had stuck in the ground to draw people's attention to their location. Mertie was setting out numerous small bunches of various herbs she had harvested in her garden, and she waived cheerfully at Syren as she walked past, taking note of the two heavily laden strangers she had in tow behind her. Mertie certainly had a green thumb. She knew a lot about plants and grew a wide variety of herbs, some for use as spices in cooking and others for medicinal purposes. Syren had learned much of what she knew about cooking from the old widow, whom she would visit occasionally just to give her some company. Many in town depended on her for medicinal remedies, and Syren had picked up some of that lore as well. Westpost had its own alchemist of course, but most folks didn't see him much. He lived at the Palace and pretty much served as the personal healer for Prince Hallas and the contingent of soldiers who protected him.

Burke occupied the area next to Mertie and was arranging the clay pots and urns he had brought for sale. Not far from there, Erwin the baker had stacks of hard crusted baguettes on a low table, and a crowd of young children had swarmed him and his cook fire, where he was frying small blobs of dough in hot oil, drizzling honey over them as they cooled.

"Sticks for food!" Syren heard Braenog announce enthusiastically to no one in particular. When she looked back, two kindling scraps sat atop the bread pile, and each of her helpers were gnawing on a baguette. Despite their arms being loaded abundantly with firewood, they had managed by some means to get the little loaves off of the table and crammed into their mouths without using their hands. Syren decided not to think too hard about how they did it. That wasn't how trading worked in Westpost, she explained to them, but the deed was done, so she moved quickly on around the Green, encouraging them to keep up.

Passing by the stands of a soap seller, a mender who was setting out his tools, several women selling produce of various kinds (where Syren had to intervene to prevent a repeat of the incident at the baker's table), and some others who were laying out shirts, leggings, or similar articles of clothing, the trio finally found themselves a spot on the Green across the road from the blacksmith's forge and workshop. Vendors greeted Syren happily as they went by, and glanced curiously at her two companions, but Durast and Braenog were quickly getting into the spirit of market day and were soon handing out happy greetings of their own to anyone they encountered.

"Deep gooood morning," they pronounced thickly at people.

"Yep, yep."

"Sticks for trrrreasure!"

Laying down their burdens roughly, they began the task of separating the whole collection into smaller piles, which Syren told them would sell individually. To their immediate left on the Green was Weldon, a tinker who was offering nails, spoons, mugs, clasps, and a variety of other household items that he had fashioned from lightweight metal. He was also assembling a small forge, in case he got opportunity to work his craft on site, repairing some item for a small fee. In need of wood for the process, he became Syren's first customer of the day, exchanging three copper coins for the wood he had selected.

To their right was Othan, who had slaughtered a cow early this morning and was now busily carving it. Market day was a good day to butcher a large animal because everyone in town would turn out, and it would be easy to sell off all the parts before it went sour. Syren knew that this would draw large numbers of flies throughout the day, but the prospect of fresh beef would also draw many buyers, so it was a handy spot for her to set up as well. Most of her patrons would be people needing wood for cook fires at home. She planned to promote the convenience of buying food to cook and wood to cook it with all in the same location.

While they were setting up, Syren was visited by her second cousin Quig. He was a thin, talkative fourteen year-old with an open face and an engaging smile that sprouted below a mop of tangled, straw-colored hair. He was carrying a basket full of cut flowers, which he was enthusiastically hawking to women who had come to the Green to buy, lavishing compliments on them as he did so. Spotting his elder cousin, he dashed over to say hello.

"A blossom, my lady?" he offered teasingly, bowing low as he did so. Syren laughed and accepted it.

"Why, thank you, kind sir," she mocked back. "Allow me the honor of presenting you this token of my appreciation." And she thrust a bundle of kindling into his arms. It was a decidedly one-sided trade, but Quig and his parents were family, the only family she had left.

"Sticks…for flowers?" Durast objected.

"*My* sticks," she asserted, "my flower." Durast harrumphed his accepting disapproval and returned to work, while Syren used the yellow petaled black-centered flower to dress her flowing black hair, by the right ear. Cocking one eyebrow, Quig jerked his head toward Durast and Braenog and looked questioningly at Syren.

"Oh, these are my…" She paused then, wondering just how to describe them. "They're friendly," she summarized. Braenog paused briefly to smile his broad teeth at Quig, then returned to his task. "They helped me carry my wood to market this morning," she finished. Quig shrugged.

"Do you have less wood than sometimes, or did you sell some already?"

"No, I lost a bundle out in the Nearwood last night," she recalled, remembering her frustration. "Hiddeans came out of the forest." Quig gasped his concern. "I made out all right," she assured him, leaving out the harrowing details for his sake, "but I had to leave the wood behind. The hard part is that those heavy canvas straps I had for carrying got left out there too. I plan to go back out and look for them when I get the chance, but I may have to get some new ones made."

"Where did it happen?" he asked.

"Someplace outside the wall, around where my house is, I think. It was pretty exciting right then, and it was getting dark, so I'm not exactly sure." Quig whistled his admiration for Syren's bravery. Then rebalancing the weight of his arm load of firewood, he bid his cousin luck on the day's endeavors and headed off home to deliver his charge.

Turning to Durast and Braenog, Syren decided to pay the two as she had promised for their work as porters and release them to their own priorities, whatever those might be. Thanking them for their help, she produced her coin pouch and pressed three copper bits into Durast's broad hand.

"Deep!" he replied, grinning broadly. Braenog, seeing the transaction, then held out his hand expectantly as well, and Syren realized that, in her haste this morning, she had been accidently vague as to whether the agreed upon sum was meant for both or for each, though they seemed clear on the subject. Not wanting to create any ill feelings, she gave Braenog the same, trying not to look (or feel) reluctant.

People were starting to gather around the Green, and Syren gave her attention to greeting passersby and people she knew in hopes of drawing them near for a sale. She could hear Durast and Braenog speaking quickly with each other where they stood. When, after a time, she turned in their direction again, she found them still standing there, looking up at her in quiet anticipation. She wondered if they were somehow confused about the nature of their working relationship.

"No more carrying," she explained, adding, "All finished now. Good day!" but the pair responded emphatically.

"Nope."

"Nope, nope."

"Durast and Braenog stay on."

"Help Syren sell sticks."

"Get trreasure for Syren."

"Quite possibly!"

They grinned eagerly, awaiting Syren's reply to their new offer.

"But don't you have someplace else to be? Other tasks to do?" she countered. Surely, she thought, she must have recruited them away from whatever it was they were doing when she first met them.

"Yep."

"Yep, yep."

"Mmm...Nope."

"Yep."

"Nope, nope."

"Nope, nope, nope," they decided, finally.

Syren thought for a moment, then sighed in hopeful resignation. "Why not?" she said with a shrug. After all, the two had so far shown themselves to be hardworking, pleasant company and something of a novelty here in Westpost. Maybe they'd turn out to be good for business. They listened carefully as Syren explained how the selling of wood was to be done, how much for how much, and so on. After signaling that they understood with a couple of "Yeps" and "Yep, yeps," they waded in enthusiastically, taking up a clutch of kindling in one oversized hand and using the other to flag in customers.

"Sticks for trreasure!"

"Deep good wood!"

"Yep, yep, yep."

"Pretty my lady, buys wood!"

"Make deep fire."

"Quite possibly!"

Apparently, they had been paying close attention to Quig's gregarious approach to salesmanship, and it combined well with their natural charisma. Soon, that section of the Green was aswarm with patrons meeting the newcomers, to the benefit of not only Syren but Weldon and Othan as well. Syren noticed at one point that Durast and Braenog were asking (and getting) a slightly higher price for the wood they were selling than Syren was and that they were keeping the difference for themselves, but the villagers didn't seem to mind, and the sale was going splendidly with their help. She decided to say nothing, determining that if the extra amount became their share at day's end, she wouldn't have to pay them from her proceeds, and they would all come out further ahead. When she later spoke with them about her observation and her idea, they seemed content with that arrangement.

During the busyness of the sale, while Syren was engaged in conversation with a probable buyer, a most disagreeable man sauntered casually up to their position. He was tall and had a thin face, narrow eyes, and pointed, smirking features. He was dressed for travel in high soft-leather boots and heavy canvas leggings. Over his linen shirt he wore a sleeveless black leather vest that protected his torso, and he had a long knife at his belt. His upper lip was failing to produce a mustache, and he engaged Durast and Braenog in absent conversation while casting his glance about skulkingly.

"And what have we here?" he asked, hefting one of the smaller fire logs in one hand.

"Sticks for treasure," Durast replied. "Pile like so for coppers, three."

"Who gave you foreigners permission to be here, making money off of us?" he accused harshly. In view of Syren's friendliness and surrounded by their success with other villagers, Westpost's newest vendors were eager to provide assurances to the man. Rather than looking subjugated or intimidated by the man's outburst, they were quick to justify their presence and activity in town by way of explanation.

"Durast and Braenog help Syren. Carry sticks to Westpost. Syren lost sticks in forest," they reported, "lost canvas straps."

"Now, why would she let a thing like that happen?" he wondered aloud, plying them for information.

"Syren says Hiddeans came. Lost sticks, lost straps in woods against Hiddeans." Braenog offered earnestly.

"Indeed." The man raised his thin eyebrows. "Where was this… attack, and when did it occur?"

"Outside of Westpost, yesternight, in the Nearwood," Durast divulged, pointing in the general direction of Syren's house. The man gazed in that direction silently, as if performing some mental calculation. The bearded pair, encouraged by their success in conversing with the man, finished their explanation. "Durast and Braenog help Syren. Stay and sell for Syren. Then Syren goes to Nearwood to find Syren's wood, find Syren's canvas."

"So you say," he expressed doubtfully, returning his attention to them and wagging the kindling he held at the two of them, "but you two watch yourselves. I attend to Syren's safety personally, and I will tolerate no threat to her well-being. Now," he commanded sternly, changing the subject, "show me the money you've gathered. Let's just make sure you aren't overcharging anyone."

Just then Syren called over while finishing her sale, irritated at the familiar man's overbearing remarks.

"Baron, what are you doing here?" she asked brusquely, "Shouldn't you be out salvaging, or slaying wild beasts or something?"

"Well, Syren." He swaggered, interrupting her conversation with Grigg the whittler and nudging the old man carelessly aside. "Fancy meeting you here. I was just forming some new acquaintances," he said, indicating Durast and Braenog absently.

"Baron?" Braenog inquired.

"He is a baron?" Durast asked Syren. For a moment, they stood more at attention.

"Not *a* baron—" Syren began.

"*The* Baron," the man finished. "The one and only Baron of Westpost. You may kiss the royal hand," he told Braenog and Durast, drawing himself up pompously and offering his hand to them. Braenog moved to comply, but Durast checked him, placing a large hand on his shoulder. Squinting suspiciously up at him, Durast looked to Syren for confirmation.

"Baron is not his title," she explained to them, "it's his name." Pursing their lips into scolding frowns, they crossed their arms over their broad chests in simultaneous refusal of his request.

"Killjoy," he scolded to Syren.

"Look, we're busy here," she said to Baron impatiently, "what is it you want?"

"What indeed?" he answered, eyeing Syren lasciviously. She exhaled in disgust. Baron continued, changing his strategy. "I heard you ran into a spot of trouble in the woods yesterday."

"Nothing I couldn't handle," Syren returned defiantly, busying herself by setting out more piles of kindling.

"You know, you really shouldn't venture into the wild all by yourself. Terrible things could happen."

"I know what I'm doing," she insisted.

"Still, you should leave that kind of thing to experts," he pressed conceitedly. "At the very least, you ought to be accompanied by someone, someone strong and experienced and brave, rather than go out alone."

"If I find anybody like that, I'll be sure to ask them," she retorted sarcastically.

"Cute," was all the reply he could manage.

"Weren't you on your way somewhere?" Syren suggested.

"Actually, I was," Baron admitted, turning to leave with firewood still in hand. "I'll see you around, Syren," he assured her, and he left in the direction of the Wallgate, twirling the wood he had taken.

"Hey," Syren called after him, "hey, you gonna pay for that?" but he waived carelessly without looking back. Syren harrumphed, exasperated, and returned to her market day mission. Durast and Braenog stood beside her, studying Baron's form seriously as it disappeared into the distance.

"Baron is not your friendly?" Durast asked Syren.

"Not my friend," she corrected. "No, he isn't."

"Not Syren's friend," Braenog acknowledged, glowering.

"Not a baron." Durast brooded.

"Topsider," Braenog concluded disgustingly. "Quite possibly."

CHAPTER 4

The Salvager and the Crow

During their time together that day, Syren's ear gradually trained itself to decipher the robust, rolling sounds her new friends made to each other by listening carefully and comparing those phrases to the way they spoke to passing villagers. She was pleased to discover that, for the most part, they were speaking the same language she was, but it was heavily accented and with a variety of their own expressions thrown in. *Topsider*, for example, was a word that Syren was unfamiliar with, though by the way it was used, it did not seem complimentary. They both also used the word *deep* to mean something completely different from the merely physical description she normally expected. She noted also that, when Durast spoke with Braenog, he didn't use his whole name but instead called him simply Nog, though Durast was always Durast.

Further, it seemed that Durast and Braenog were drawing this same conclusion, because their ability to communicate with everyone was quickly becoming more natural. They were even beginning to use *I*, *we*, *you*, and so on correctly, on occasion.

Baron's earlier conduct and conversation must have made something of an impression on Syren's small companions, because when next they found themselves with no villagers to market their firewood to, Durast asked her, "Syren, what is *salvage*?"

"Venture salvage is a pretty big business in this town," Syren explained. "It's basically going into the wilderness and bringing back items that belong to the wild races and then selling them. As I understand it, the work involves more finding than fighting, but the dangers to life and limb are very real. What gets retrieved is mostly junk and trinkets, but traveling merchants want the stuff because it sells well in the big cities. I guess risking your neck to get it is what makes it valuable. This place draws more than its share of fortune hunters. There are rumors and legends about great stores of treasure and ancient objects waiting to be found in the reckless places of the world, including, some say, in the wilds around Westpost. I don't know much about the history of all that, except what I hear told at the tavern some nights by old folks like Jack Frost. I do know that it's a risky business. Stormwood is an enchanted and dangerous place. There are not many who brave its terrors and even fewer who do it twice. There must be something to it, though, because three different venture salvage businesses operate here in town. The shops themselves are owned by local tradesmen. They're businessmen, not fighters or seekers or woodsmen. Two of them hire their own full-time prospectors, while the other simply buys what he gets offered from wandering freelancers. Mostly these people are ruffians and wildcats who come in with the traveling merchant caravans every couple of months, then stay hoping to strike it rich inside the forest.

Some never return. Others last only a short while before leaving on the next caravan, broke or broken, or both."

"And Baron?" Braenog asked.

"He was one of the lucky ones, I guess," sighed Syren reluctantly. "He came flying out of the woods one day about eight months ago with a sack full of artifacts from Stormwood and a tale of how he thrashed a pack of Gremlins single-handedly to get it."

"Artifacts?" interjected Durast. "Trrrreasure?" Syren was learning that how much treasure Durast was referring to was indicated by how long he rolled his *r*'s.

"Well, to some degree, yes. I mean, nothing of any great value," she told Durast. "Odds and pieces, mostly, but it was the kind of stuff that merchants like to buy for resale in Centerville and other places out east as curiosities to civilized folk." Despite Syren's dismissal, Durast seemed to be intrigued by the possibility that riches of any sort might simply be lying about in the wilderness, waiting for whomever might find them.

"Grrremlins?" Braenog asked for clarification, and Syren nodded. He seemed familiar with the name. For a moment, his dark eyes took on a smoldering, vengeful quality. It was rather an inward-looking expression, as if summoned from the distant recesses of bitter memory. Then remembering the present conversation, his face became a portrait of confusion.

"Baron...is deep brave?" Braenog asked, bewildered.

"I don't know," Syren answered, thinking back upon her own encounter with the three Hiddeans the prior evening. Gremlins had an even worse reputation for ferocity than they did. "Too much of his story seems hard to believe. I mean, how could he have faced a whole pack of Gremlins and come away without a scratch? On the other hand, he did bring back the head of one of them."

"Baron fights only Gremlin, perhaps?" Durast offered, not rolling his *r*.

"Perhaps," Syren conceded, "but then the salvage he returned with did suggest that it had belonged to several creatures." She shook her head. "Anyway, he became something of a local hero once people heard about the fight, the Gremlin head, and the salvage. Since then he's done comparatively little other than ride his popularity and push people around with his so-called reputation for toughness. Meanwhile, the venture salvage business is livelier than ever, in the wake of his success."

Between Syren's smaller-than-usual supply of kindling and the diligent efforts of her incidental business partners, the three of them found that they had sold all they had brought to the Green by midafternoon. This created an opportunity that Syren was hoping for.

"I need to go out into the Nearwood," she explained to Durast and Braenog. "I want to see if I can find that other wood pile and get my canvas straps back." One advantage that Syren's style of market day vendoring had over some others was the lack of anything to clean up or put away afterward. Once she had sold all her wood, she could simply leave. When she made a start toward the Wallgate, however, she was immediately accompanied by her new friends. Apparently, they had determined to become her all day companions, which was more than she had bargained for or even wanted, really, when they first agreed to help her. Still, she thought, there was a kind of merriment that came from seeing Westpost afresh through their eyes as they experienced it all for the first time. They really were quite a lively pair, and as much as she hated to admit it, Baron had been right about time spent searching the woods alone. It could be dangerous, as she well knew, and she was still just a little apprehensive in the aftermath of her most recent encounter. Syren was sure that she would get over it, but in the meantime, it might be a good idea after all to have some company, even if only as a look out in case of trouble. "C'mon," she invited as if they weren't already at her heels, "I'll show you where I saw the Hiddeans last night."

Durast and Braenog fell in step without hesitation, inquiring with great interest about the forest and those who dwelt there. Answering their questions, Syren thought it strange that two travelers would know so little about the wild. Granted, few people that Syren knew from the village would dare walk around in a woods as treacherous as this, but it was almost as if these two had never seen one. As the three of them made their way deeper into the Nearwood toward the location of last night's peril, the short pair expended no effort in being quiet, nor were they making any pretense of looking for her missing bundle of kindling. Though they were intensely watchful of their surroundings, they appeared either unaware or unconcerned about possible lurking threats to their safety. Instead, crashing about and talking in loud voices, they actually seemed preoccupied with finding the Hiddeans rather than spotting and avoiding them, to the point that they repeatedly got themselves lost from Syren or each other and had to be found and brought along.

Eventually, Syren and her company reached the spot of her conflict on the previous evening. Searching the area with the help of her two friends, however, she could find no evidence of the missing firewood, which she thought to be both discouraging and suspicious. She could only conclude that the bundle and her canvas straps had been carried off, but to where and by whom? The Hiddeans might have taken it, but would they need a pile of firewood? Living in the forest, they were surrounded by wood. Studying the ground in the vicinity, she saw no sign of the heavy pile being dragged away through the underbrush. Though vicious, the Hiddeans didn't look especially strong. If they had carried it away, it would have taken a lot of them. They did tend to hunt in packs, which is what made them dangerous.

Looking carefully about for tracks, Syren detected a variety of prints going in every direction. She was able to identify her own footfalls by matching some of yesterday's footprints to the size of the leather boots she was wearing. There were also a large number of wolf-like imprints, which might have been from actual wolves or from either a sizable group of Hiddeans moving through the area or a small band running all around. It was very hard to tell which. Those traveled to and from Stormwood, generally. There was also at least one set of large boot prints like a tall man would make. Those might have been made by members of the morning watch, but again it was difficult to know because Durast and Braenog had managed to thoroughly trample the area with their own big feet during their kindly meant search efforts.

The one unfortunate certainty was that the wood pile and her canvas straps were gone. Syren stood from where she had been crouching over some tracks to consider her options. She could follow the Hiddeans' trails, which went in the direction of Stormwood, but in doing so, she would be risking her life (and those of her friends) over two bits of canvas. She hated the idea of walking away empty-handed and letting the forest "win" again, but it did seem the wiser course, on this occasion at least. It was also possible, though, that Hiddeans had no use for firewood and had left it to be found this morning by someone from town, like the watch or another woodsman. That would be easy enough to determine. All she had to do was ask around. A bundle that size would be hard to miss. If it came to it, she'd be willing to release her interest in the wood as long as she got the canvas carriers back. Then if that hunt failed to flush out any birds, she could always reconsider a foray into Stormwood, which she could plan and prepare for.

The three of them had come out to the Nearwood late enough in the day and had been investigating the scene long enough that evening was now pressing on, and Syren encouraged that they should return to town for safety. They had learned all that ground could tell from the place anyway.

"Syren," Braenog asked purposefully, "Westpost fellows have eating when work is ended, quite possibly?"

Syren grinned. "Yes," she acknowledged, "quite possibly." Walking back toward the Wallgate, she kept a watchful eye to the north, and though she was sure there was plenty of daylight to get home by, that familiar unrest welled up inside her as she gazed in the direction of hazard's home. Stormwood. Somehow every path of Syren's life led there. One day, she promised herself, she would trace those paths to destiny's end.

Once they were back inside the protective wall of Westpost, Syren and her stocky friends returned to her house. She set wood in her fireplace, both as a ward against the oncoming chill of night and as a heat source to cook supper. When she went to her boiling kettle, however, she realized that she had soaked far too few beans. This morning, she had not expected to be cooking for three. Adding some for the possibility of cooking them the next night, she then adjusted her kindling and wood to provide a modest blaze that would simply provide a drying heat and some light to the house once darkness came.

Meanwhile, Durast and Braenog were making themselves quite at home. They handled any objects that could be lifted, tossing them (often simultaneously) between each other, inspecting them for quality and estimating their value before putting them down wherever they happened to be standing. They then both sat on every chair, apparently comparing notes as to comfort. Next, they crouched together under her table, and closely examined its quality of construction. Then when they were satisfied as to its sturdiness, the pair climbed upon it, boots and all, and joyfully engaged in a sort of contest, where each took hold of the other's hand and tried through a combination of strength and strategy to cause the other to leave his feet. Just as Syren entered the room from the cooking alcove to insist they get down, Braenog did, tumbling off the table roughly and crashing into a chair. All the items that had formerly rested on her table had been moved to the floor for the event, and they got scattered about haphazardly as Braenog fell among them. Syren's shout of protest was drowned out by Durast, who roared in delight at his victory, but as Braenog righted himself, he was laughing as well. Jumping down from the table, Durast helped Braenog to his feet, after which they congratulated each other, tugged each other's beards, and slapped each other on both shoulders. Turning gleefully, they encountered Syren, frowning and with arms crossed in front of her, and their pudgy faces produced puzzled expressions. For the sake of her housewares and because of insufficient food to feed them all, Syren recommended they dine in town at the Hooded Crow.

Across the broad dirt road that encircled the Village Green stood a ring of permanent shops. These were interrupted by just one gap, which was the only other broad road in Westpost. That way led to the barracks, which housed Prince Hallas's meager contingent of trained troops, the homes of his servants, and the Palace, where he lived. The court alchemist also lived and had his laboratory at the Palace. Everyone else lived in neighborhoods of small thatched-roof homes, which were connected not by roads but by worn footpaths. These led also to gardens and to common wells and washhouses, which were the main source of water and gossip.

Much of the usual buying and selling of daily life happened at the weekly market days on the Green, but skilled craftsmen, especially those that regularly did business with the Palace, had permanent shops to house their wares and wield their equipment. The blacksmith was on this row, along with the apothecary, Othan the butcher, Erwin the baker, and a tailor and a leathersmith. Two of the three venture salvage stores had operations here, as did one large wooden building that housed travelers, food, drink, and merriment. One of the few buildings in Westpost that had rooms above stairs, the tavern and inn promoted itself with a simple rectangular wooden shingle that hung vertically from an iron support. Carved into the weathered brown wood in blackened relief was a single crow as tall as the placard itself, facing toward the street and dressed in a hooded cape.

Walking into the Crow, Syren and her two friends found the common room alive with music, happy patrons, and a crackling fire. It had been a busy, successful market day, and people felt like celebrating. Between the entryway and the serving counter on the left, the place was crammed with jolly revelers shouting over each other's conversations and shouldering past each other in search of refills. Pushing patiently through the buzzing crowd, they managed to claim chairs at a table on the far end of the room near to where the usual group of troubadours were playing cheerfully upon flutes, lutes, mandolins, hand drums, dulcimers, fiddles, and bells of various kinds (the four of them rotating instruments as each song required). To prevent them being jostled, they played from positions upon a wooden platform raised from the floor level by a single step. Others already seated around the table were coarsely lapping up hearty-looking beef stew from wooden bowls, mopping up the savory dregs with thick chunks of bread. Braenog's stomach growled. The four grimy men cast disdainful stares at Durast and Braenog but kept eating. When they finished, they tossed their bowls into a jumble on the table, grabbed up their mugs, and moved in the direction of the counter. Syren and company took in the music and the festive atmosphere, chatting amiably about the day's events until Molly, the serving maid, bustled over with three bowls of stew, three large spoons, and a small loaf of bread.

"Five, five, five," she said hurriedly. Durast looked over at Syren, who was taking out her coin pouch.

"Food for treasure," she told him, handing coins over to Molly, who tucked them into her apron. Her friends did likewise.

"Mugs?" Molly asked quickly, brushing disheveled brown hair aside with one forearm while gathering up the empty bowls and unused spoons of that table's previous patrons.

"What do you have tonight?" Syren asked.

"We always have Garden Brew, for one bit."

"That's the local grog," Syren explained to Durast and Braenog. "It's popular, but mostly because it's cheap, one copper."

"There's still some ale in the kegs, I think, for three," Molly continued. "Caravan's due in a week or so, or there's Winyard's Well, twenty for the bottle." Braenog raised his bushy eyebrows at the price.

"Three of the three," Syren decided for all of them. Molly nodded, taking their money, and was off.

Durast and Braenog sat forward on their chairs with their chins only slightly above the table and their feet not quite touching the floor, but the posture rendered their mouths conveniently at "stew level," and they eagerly dug in, breaking the loaf in half rather than thirds. Syren, deciding not to protest about the bread inequity, was relieved to discover that her foreign friends were spoon users, and she pondered as she ate who they were, really, and what differences there were between their culture and hers. They were an endearing wonder, these two. They must surely be capable travelers and foragers, or they wouldn't have survived to come this far, yet there was a provincial innocence about them. They had been quite friendly and helpful to Syren and at the same time rather needed her guidance and company, both socially in town and when traveling in the forest. She found that being around them all day made her feel connected with the wider, wilder world. She was also rather enjoying the rare experience of being so much taller than other adults. It was fun, she realized, and she wanted more of the stuff.

Between ample mouthfuls, Durast asked, "Syren, how did Molly know our hunger or what to bring?"

"On a busy night like this," Syren explained, "it's generally understood that eaters will find a table. The muggers"—and here she indicated the many patrons who crowded the serving counter, raising tankards occasionally to indicate the need of a refill—"they tend to gather at the other end, close to the drink. What they serve for food changes from day to day, depending on what's available, but on any given day, what they make is what there is. Today it's beef stew. Remember Othan the butcher on the Green next to us?" Her friends nodded their understanding, using their bread as an edible napkin.

"Good evening, Syren," greeted a congenial voice from across the table. Looking up toward the music, Syren's gaze encountered a familiar old gentleman with twinkling sky-blue eyes, a close-trimmed and graying mustache and goatee, and time-weathered but handsomely courteous features.

"Hey, hello, Jack," she welcomed cheerfully. "Haven't seen you in a while." She indicated with a wave of her hand an invitation to sit and join them. "How've you been?"

"Quite exceedingly well, I thank you," he replied in his formal yet engaging way. The genuinely distinguished older man bowed slightly in his elegant and decoratively embroidered long robe, which was accented amiably by the bronze skullcap that fashioned his otherwise bald head. "It is good to follow one's feet," he said, sitting, "and good to follow them home again."

"So where were you off to this time?" Syren asked as Molly returned with stew and bread for Jack, a glass, and a bottle. Jack shrugged absently as he gave coins to Molly, thanking her.

"Hither and thither…and perhaps a bit further," he replied, flicking his glance at Syren's squat companions as he offered them all a taste of his bottle of Winyard. Breaking his bread, he gave a portion of it to Syren. "You've met some hungry associates, it seems."

"Oh, excuse me," Syren countered, remembering her manners. "This is Durast, and he there is Braenog. They helped me at market day today." Jack nodded his approval, eating carefully. "Durast, Braenog, this is Jack Frost, of…of…" She realized then that she wasn't quite sure where Jack was from originally. He was in Westpost as much as he was away, but despite his gregarious nature, he never spoke about his travels or history directly. For as far back as she could remember, he had been "that well-dressed old man in the tavern." Though she attributed those memories to being as a small child would have them, he always seemed to be both a member of and a visitor to their community.

"Jack Frost of Westpost and of everywhere," he finished cordially to Durast and Braenog. Then he raised his glass in salute to them and rolled a group of *r*'s enthusiastically in their direction.

Smiling broadly, they returned in kind and then continued eating. Syren was impressed and curious.

"Do you actually know these men?" she asked.

"'Know of' is more the case," he explained. "In their language, their people are known as Deepfellows, though we commonly refer to them as Stoutfellows, or just Stouts. They typically live deep in the mountains and are renowned masons, miners, and quarriers. Some, they say, wield the ancient lore of stonecrafting."

"Their language?" Syren regarded her friends with a renewed sense of wonder and excitement. "Do you have your own tongue?" she asked them distinctly. Glancing at each other curiously, Braenog turned his head toward Syren, opened his mouth widely, and protruded his tongue for her to see. Jack chuckled.

"Syren asks, have your people their own way of talking?" he interpreted.

"Ah," responded Durast. "Yep, yep, the Deepspeech. It is the words of our deep gone fellows, but it is used now only for ceremonies and other important occasions. For every other talking, we use the Allmanspeech."

"Allmanspeech?" Syren asked Jack.

"Yes. Allmanspeech is a dialect similar to what we're speaking now, the trade language used by nearly everyone, but with perhaps a few...nuances." Syren grinned appreciatively.

As she was forming her next question, the music paused in time for a mild cheer to rise up from the doorway. Looking over, Syren scowled to see Baron stride in, acknowledging the crowd arrogantly, and surrounded by a small entourage of his supporters. Swaggering over to the table nearest him, his followers handed those seated there the bowls they were eating out of, indicating with threatening glares that they should take them and be gone, which they did fearfully. Syren shifted her chair, turning her back disgustedly on the scene. Looking up from his stew, Jack furrowed his brow inquisitively over Syren's reaction.

"Not Syren's friendly," Braenog explained to Jack, nodding pointedly.

"Not friend," Durast corrected.

"Really?" Jack mused, sopping bread into his bowl. "He seems harmless enough."

"That's just it," Syren complained. "He's a complete weasel. He uses the reputation he's built for himself over nothing that really happened to bully people. He plays on their fears of the wilderness to ensure his own comforts."

"He can't be fully the charlatan if he ventures into Stormwood," Jack suggested. "How do you know he's not faced the dangers he's so fond of recounting?"

"It's because he's so fond of recounting them," Syren protested. "I see Baron around a lot, Jack. He's neither valiant nor courageous. There is no way he would face what's out there and return unscathed. He could never fight them as often as he claims, and he wouldn't come away without taking any wounds or bruises."

"The woods around Westpost are mortally dangerous," Jack conceded, then with some concern in his voice, added, "You speak as one who has seen those terrors firsthand."

Syren recalled again the shock of encountering the Hiddeans up close and unprepared. "Yes," she acknowledged, "I have." The old man waited intently while Syren sorted through her feelings on the event. Durast and Braenog listened carefully to her account.

"It was frightening," she admitted for the first time, and her eyes were far away, "to be snuck up on so abruptly by them, but I wasn't terrified exactly. I mean, my heart was racing, but so was my mind. It was not like I was in a panic or paralyzed from fear. Yet I was very frightened. Do you know what I mean?" she asked Durast and Braenog, but the Stouts blinked at her in concerned but earnest silence.

"Stouts don't normally get afraid," Jack explained. Syren looked at Jack in disbelief. "Oh, they are doubtless aware of danger," he assured her, "and would seek to protect themselves from serious harm or death, but to experience emotional fear is not in their nature." Syren paused from her story for a moment to privately admire the tenacity of the Stoutish people. It helped her, she realized suddenly, to identify the frustration of her own experience.

"You know, I think the despicable part," Syren estimated, continuing her analysis, "was the vulnerability, the thought of falling into their vile little hands, of being at their mercy and knowing there wouldn't be any." She glanced over at Baron, who was undoubtedly retelling his one tale in ever-changing and increasingly heroic fashion. "That's the thing with Baron," she concluded, stabbing the table repeatedly with her index finger. "He would crumble under that kind of pressure. He would never stand and fight. He would never want to."

"And you?" wondered Jack, who had been deftly steering the focus of the conversation the whole time.

"I feel like…" Syren leaned in at the question, emotion finding its voice. "Like, if I could meet them again on my terms, prepared…I bet I could take them. I don't like the way they threaten us, wear us down, prey upon us. In fact, I'm sick and tired of the way I and everyone in this village are imprisoned by the dread and peril of the forest, and I hate that some people are making a living by perpetuating it!"

Durast and Braenog thumped the table with their fists and rolled many *r*'s emphatically in support of their friend. Then they emptied their tankards and poured refills all around from Jack's bottle of Winyard, to his apparent surprise and mild dismay. Then as Durast turned merrily, he happened to look past Syren to Baron's table and his countenance dropped to one that balanced between astonishment and outrage.

"Syren," he asked, not taking his eyes from Baron's table, "what are these straps I look for?" Syren described them, not sure if he was using *I* correctly in that sentence or not. His gaze and then his countenance were joined by Braenog's, and in the next moment, both Stouts had hopped off their chairs and were wading purposefully through the current of shuffling patrons, toward Baron's table. After a brief exchange of quizzical glances between herself and Jack, Syren decided she had better follow them to see for herself what had drawn their attention. When she closed to within earshot of Baron's table, she could see and hear the two of them confronting him over a conspicuous pair of canvas straps.

"Do you know these little grunts, Baron?" one of his cronies was saying.

"I met them earlier today. They're Punies," he announced pejoratively, then leaning forward, he patted them both condescendingly on their heads. "Now be on your way, little ones, before you get yourselves into trouble."

Syren, outraged at the insult of her friends, formed a retort in her mind to deliver in their defense as she approached the table, but she saw Durast close one massive hand into a fist, and she began to fear delightedly for Baron's well-being.

"Straps like so belong to Syren," Durast asserted firmly.

"Is that a fact?" Baron replied derisively as ranks closed around himself and the Stouts. "And just who is it that says so?"

"Baron, what are you doing with those?" Syren interjected, breaking through and pointing at the canvas straps he was holding out of Durast's reach.

"Anything I want," he replied confidently, "they're mine."

"Since when?"

"Since this afternoon. I found them in the wilderness. That makes them salvage, and I, as everyone knows, am a salvager."

"The Nearwood is hardly the wilderness," she argued.

"Anywhere outside the wall," he corrected smugly.

"Syrrrin claims them!" Braenog pronounced, giving in to his accent in the excitement. He looked as though he expected that to either end the matter or initiate some formal challenge. It did neither. His statement was ignored as the debate raged on above him.

"Those are my straps, and you know it! The salvage laws are meant to cover long-lost items or stuff abandoned by the wild races."

"Salvage is salvage, my dear," Baron countered patronizingly. "But I'll tell you what, you may purchase them from me, if you want them so badly."

"I'm not buying my own property from you!" she shouted.

"No money again, Syren?" he taunted. "Pity. In that case, I would gladly let you have them in trade." And leaning in closely, he flicked his eyebrows at her to imply his vulgar intent.

Red-faced with anger, Syren reached out to slap away Baron's smirk, but reacting quickly, he caught her advancing hand in his. Neither wanting to give in to the other, the contest of wills became an impromptu arm wrestling match as their elbows touched down on the table. Around them, the crowd hooted and cheered wildly, mostly in support of Baron.

"Winner names the spoils," Baron leered.

"You're a pig!" spat Syren defiantly. Turning her wrist toward herself slightly, she bore down furiously against Baron's insolence. In a steady parade of moments, his arrogant grin transformed into concern, then desperation, then fear until finally he jumped up from the table, breaking off the contest before his actual defeat could be realized.

"Well, Syren," he exclaimed loudly, feigning magnanimity, "I'd love to stay and hold hands with you, but I really must be off. Some other time, I hope." Before he could move a step, however, he was confronted again by Durast and Braenog.

"Give the straps to Syren," Durast demanded sharply.

"Why sure," he complied, holding them out. "Go ahead and take them." When Braenog reached up to grasp them, however, Baron lifted them just out of the shorter man's reach. He repeated the motion each time the Stout retried, until Braenog was effectively hopping and dancing in the attempt, and Baron's friends were laughing mockingly.

"Looks like he's not quite tall enough," teased one.

"Maybe he's trying to fly," goaded another.

"Baron, stop it!" commanded Syren uselessly.

"Why don't you boys help him out?" Baron encouraged with an evil grin.

"Great idea!" called the brute nearest to Braenog, whereupon he and another man dragged him off his feet entirely, carried him to the inn's large front window, and tossed him roughly through it. Roaring in frustration, he landed coarsely onto his back, tumbling into the dirty street.

"Nog!" Syren shouted in dismay as Baron's gang laughed uproariously.

From the midst of the jumbling, mocking throng, there came a low-throated rumble, almost like the grating of heavy stones against each other. It was a sound that grew into something of a war cry, a vow that Durast and his kinsman would not go quietly into any dark realm of humiliation.

"Strong and sure, shall Deepfellows endure!" he promised aloud, then in the next moment, as rowdy hands were reaching down with ill intent to take him also, Durast drove his oversized fist deeply into the lower midsection of the scoundrel nearest him. The force of the blow doubled the man over, taking both the wind and the fight out of him. As he staggered backward to collapse gasping against the wall, a howl of collective outrage rose from Baron's dubious company, and they closed on the Stout so that he was hidden from Syren's view.

Concerned for the way he was outnumbered and outsized, Syren tried to push through the scrabbling group and rescue him from a beating by pulling him away, but the effort resulted in her and several others getting shoved roughly into the many noncombatants of that part of the tavern, and once the mugs of the well imbibed had been spilled, a general brawl ensued. Previously happy patrons became an angry mob, shouting, shoving, and landing ill-advised punches on inadvertent targets. Marley, the proprietor, hollered infuriated (and largely ignored) rebukes against the misuse and damage of the inn's furniture, windows, and trappings, while food, drink, and tableware were flung haphazardly about the room. Amid the wrestling and confusion, Syren occasionally saw Baron across the melee, exerting himself to avoid involvement in the actual fighting, while at the same time driving others into the fray. Braenog had reentered through the doorway and barreled into a group that included those who had tossed him out the window. Having knocked them asunder, he set in with his large fists to repay them for their deed while they flailed awkwardly against his determined advance.

Moving in that direction, Syren had in mind to gather her friends and escape the fighting before someone got seriously hurt, but the swell of the lurching crowd carried her to the far side of the room where, battered by a flying tankard and tipped off balance by a stumbling stranger, she fell to the floor and was trampled painfully by several others. Pressing herself angrily to a crouch, she encountered Durast, who was standing his ground against a pair of would-be skirmishers. As she rose, she noted that he seemed perfectly built for a fight of this type, in such close quarters. Being so much shorter than his opponents, they had difficulty boxing with him effectively, and both Stouts were so broad and heavy that they didn't get pushed off their feet as the swarm moved about them. At the same time, jammed together as they all were, his adversaries were unable to avoid his reach, and he was landing overhand rights and lefts with crushing effectiveness.

Before long, a contingent of Prince Hallas's personal guard arrived to restore order. They were dressed in chain mail shirts and leggings, the upper half covered by a tabard of the prince's colors. They also wore open visored helmets and carried heavy wooden clubs about the size of ax handles. Working deliberately, two of the guards would grab one brawler at random, subdue him as necessary, and throw him into the street, where the other two guards stood by to prevent his reentering the tavern. Then the process would repeat itself. Being closer to that action than Syren and the Stouts, Baron made the most of his opportunity.

"Hail, fine sirs!" he called above the din as he approached the guards deferently. "I'm so glad you've come to our rescue. Please and by all means, quell this rabble and restore order to our poor town," he pleaded dramatically. "You'll find those two," he advised, indicating Braenog and Durast, "to be especially rambunctious. I tried myself to prevent them, but they would have none of it." Then gathering up the canvas straps so that he was sure Syren would see them, he shot her one victorious smirk, turned to the doorway, and was out into the night.

The presence and actions of the guards quickly brought an end to the hostilities. Syren rose to protest Baron's remarks, but glancing about at herself and the now milling crowd, she realized that she was disheveled, drenched, dirty, and bruised, and her out-of-town companions each stood somewhat sheepishly among a small cluster of beaten and incapacitated men, most of whom were villagers. While the guards dispersed everyone to their lodgings, aggressively prodding anyone who lacked the ability or sense to comply, Marley spoke enthusiastically to the captain, registering his official complaint over the mess and damages that the inn had incurred. Syren rallied her small company to herself and tried to slip out with the others who were being herded into the street, but the guards blocked her way.

"We're detaining these two," she was told flatly.

"Please, sir," Syren answered, doing her best to look humble and vulnerable, "these men are visitors to our town. They are unfamiliar with our ways, and I can vouch for their character."

"So you are an accomplice to their actions?"

"No, sir. Rather, I dispute the report you were given. I also was an eyewitness of all the events, and I hold that they are innocent of wrongdoing."

The guard sighed in weary disgust.

"My name is Syren," she went on. "You know that I have lived here peaceably all my life. I promise that if there is to be a hearing of this matter, the three of us will appear as ordered." She described for the guard where her house was located, after which he warned them sternly not to leave town until it was decided whether or not there would be a hearing, and then he released them. They walked back to Syren's house in the dark, she patting her bruises tenderly to assess their severity, Durast straightening his belt and rubbing his fists, and Braenog picking bits of broken window out of his coarse hair and beard.

Once home, Syren set a small fire and lit the lamps, warning her guests pointedly not to climb on the furniture. It had been another long day but rather a good one, really, until the end, that is. She wanted to sit with Mother, as she often did, and tell her all that had happened and think about where it might be leading. First, though, she went to the neighborhood washhouse and returned with water for each of them to clean up with. Instead of using the water she had brought back for the purpose, though, Durast and Braenog went to the washhouse themselves and took turns dumping buckets of water on each other. Judging from the squeals of surprise from neighbors who were also wandering to the well at that time, they had apparently disrobed for the process.

Meanwhile, Syren went out to the shade tree in the backyard and stood next to the gravestone, explaining her day to Mother. About the time she was finished, she found Durast and Braenog standing quietly on either side of her.

"Syren speaks to the ground," Durast observed to Braenog as though he approved. "It is a ceremony?" he asked her.

"Sort of," she mused. "My mother and father were among the original five hundred people to settle the wilderness village of

Westpost. Now only two hundred fifty remain. They built the house behind us, the one I live in. About ten years ago there was a great sickness that swept through the town. Many villagers were very ill with it, and some died. Mother was one of those." Syren paused, still staring and the humble grave. Then she continued, "We buried her here, Father and I. He disappeared on patrol in Stormwood about two years ago, so it's just me now...and Mother. I don't really believe she can hear me. It's just a way that I honor her memory and all that she and Father strove to do. It comforts me, I guess, gives me hope for better days."

For a long moment, all three were silent, staring at the burial plot together while the Stouts tugged gently on their beards. Then Braenog reached up and carefully wrapped one great hand around Syren's upper arm. Softly and with much respect, he spoke into the silence.

"Syren is deep good fellow," he said solemnly. "Quite possibly."

CHAPTER 5

Decisions

Syren took extra time making herself ready to leave her house. After combing out her silky jet-black hair meticulously, she then braided it into a wreath behind her head and accented it with white daisies and baby's breath. She wore her finest (and only) woolen dress, a green one, which gathered at her slender waist and extended somewhat below the knee. Given the circumstances, she wished that she had something nicer to wear, made out of fine silk perhaps or even some more exotic material. Unfortunately, such amenities were expensive and hardly practical for an active sort of person like herself, who scraped her living out of the wilderness each day. No, she thought, what she had would do very well. It was pretty yet practical, which seemed to suit her. It was short enough that it wouldn't gather mud and thistle burs as she walked through town while still being long enough for her to appear sincere. After all, if she hoped to be taken seriously, she certainly didn't want to look trollopy. Her high soft-leather boots, which she had spent a solid hour cleaning the night before, rose above the hemline, covering her legs modestly but attractively. Altogether, the young woman cut a very becoming hourglass shape in the simple but formal outfit, which was just what Syren thought she needed for the occasion. Nearly three weeks had passed since the incident at the tavern, but at last she and the Stouts had been summoned to the Palace to give their account and possibly defend their actions at the grievance hearing, which had been requested by Marley, the innkeeper.

Syren waited for Durast and Nog to emerge so they could walk to the Palace together. They had been staying with her the whole time, both so she could keep an eye on them (she needed them not to get into any more fistfights until this last one was settled) and because they had nowhere else to go, really. Since that night in the tavern, the townsfolk had become wary of "the strangers" who had been so effective at defending themselves, and more so since Baron had slandered them, promoting the idea that their kind were naturally irritable and dangerous. Moreover, people were on edge because of the house that had collapsed on itself about a week ago. Rumors at the well had it that a house in one of the other neighborhoods had suddenly fallen in and buried itself in the ground during the night. People in the area were saying that they heard the commotion and muffled cries that were suddenly silenced. They also said that the most dreadful noise came from the area where the house had been. It had started with a rumbling, crumbling sound that was accompanied by a shrieking, crackling sort of devastation. Reports varied, except on the point that it was like nothing anyone had ever heard before. In response to public outcry, the prince had sent a detachment of his personal guard to secure the area and investigate. Officially, they were calling the event a sinkhole, which they said was a regrettable but natural and isolated occurrence. Syren thought it odd that no such thing had ever been witnessed before, if indeed it were "normal" to the area. Anyway, the family that lived there were missing and presumed dead, and that was making everyone feel even more vulnerable than they often felt, listening to Stormwood's eerie and threatening voice as it wafted over Westpost's protective wall at night.

Meanwhile, the Stouts had made quarters for themselves in her root cellar as they insisted on sleeping underground. She remembered that night at the Crow when she had staked her reputation and her freedom on the promise that they would appear if called to the Palace. It may have been foolish for Syren to lash her future so impulsively to a pair of relative strangers, but she had needed to make a decision on the spur of the moment. Thanks to Baron's testimony, the guards had been determined to arrest the Stouts. At that time, there had been no certainty that Prince Hallas would even grant a hearing. If he hadn't, Durast and Braenog could well have been forgotten by the prince and could languish in the Palace dungeon for years. Syren couldn't bear to think of her jolly new friends suffering a fate as harsh as that, nor did she want to have to look Baron in the face after such a victory on his part. In the end, she realized, she had given her word to the guards partly because of the friendship she had so easily developed with the two Stouts and partly as a way of thwarting Baron's smug ambitions.

As a result of everything, Syren had a vested interest in keeping the Stouts nearby. She couldn't afford the possibility that they might wander off simply because they failed to understand the importance of the promise she had made or the consequences of not keeping it. Neither could she risk them getting run out of town by an edgy crowd whose circumstances had made them suspicious of foreigners. On the other hand, she couldn't just stay home and watch over them like they were a pair of infants either. Until a hearing was announced, Syren still had to earn her daily bread, which for her meant wood gathering, and with Baron in possession of her canvas carrying straps, it made good sense to employ Durast and Nog as kindling bearers. They could help her gather and sell firewood, and she could keep an eye on them until the tavern matter was resolved. She had worked out an agreement with them to split the earnings three ways. Since she normally sold what she could gather on her own, though, this arrangement left each of them with less money than was convenient. The Stouts were good carriers and pleasant company, but Syren tended to collect less firewood when they were with her in the forest because she had to watch after them to keep them from getting lost or prevent them straying too close to Stormwood, which they were wont to do.

Their need of someplace to stay while everyone awaited the prince's pleasure on the issue of the grievance hearing was the reason Syren had invited them to stay at her house, again believing that a call from the Palace could come at any time, though it ended up taking three weeks. Durast and Braenog proved to be capable eaters and drinkers. If Prince Hallas had granted a hearing that same week as the fight at the bar, there would have been no dilemma, but now, more than a fortnight later, money and food were getting scarce, especially since the Stouts were living where Syren kept her stores.

As case in point, the two Stouts finally surfaced from their lair under Syren's house, with beards neatly combed and braided for the occasion of an audience with the prince, but also munching away contentedly as had become their custom.

"Syren is out of potatoes," announced one.

"Yep, yep. And carrots too," muffled the other through his ample mouthful.

"And apples."

"And onions and cheese."

"Yep, yep, yep, and—"

"Yes, I get the idea," interrupted Syren. "We should really be going. We mustn't keep the Palace waiting."

"Yep, yep," they agreed, and the trio walked hurriedly to the street and along it, toward the Palace.

"Syren," Durast asked as they walked briskly, "what will happen at this meeting with the prince?"

"He is really a prince?" inquired Braenog. Syren chuckled.

"Yes, Nog, he is really a prince, not like Baron. The tavern keeper wants to be paid for the damages to his place. I am going to suggest to His Highness that we should not have to be the ones to pay those damages. I also want to ask for a ruling about my canvas straps and hopefully get them back."

"Will Baron attend also?"

"I expect that he will. If I tell my side of the story and he does not show up to tell his side, then the judgment would most likely go in my favor. He doesn't want that, so he'll be there."

"What happens after? Will Syren return to Stormwood? Will she look for her father?"

"If so, Nog and Durast will help Syren," Braenog offered. "Find Father, fight Grrrremlins!" he said enthusiastically.

"Yep, yep," assured Durast decidedly.

They seemed to have discussed the matter between them already. The question made Syren consider silently as they walked the last distance along the Palace road. She hadn't given much thought to what she would do after all this recent nonsense was finally settled. It would be nice to solve the mystery of what happened to her father and to lay him to rest properly. It was also intriguing to think about discovering what secrets Stormwood was hiding—and perhaps even to strike out against the denizens of the forest, continuing the work that her parents had come here to do. Undoubtedly, such broad ambitions would require broad assistance, and these two Stouts were about as broad as they come.

Arriving at the wrought iron gate, which distinguished the Palace grounds from the rest of Westpost, Syren explained to the guards why they had come. From there they were ushered inside the Divining Hall, which they were told was the place where Prince Hallas would hear grievances and render decisions. Altogether, the Palace was an immense and imposing stone edifice of many rooms, halls, and passages, unlike any other in town for size or grandeur. High stone walls protected the living spaces and separated them from the administrative halls and rooms of state. As they approached, Syren could see the Upper Terrace, from where the prince would occasionally address the townsfolk when they were assembled for that purpose. Functional buildings, like the kitchens, storehouses, and stables, were around to one side, with the carriage house attached to the main building. Though she had never seen them, Syren understood that dark and foreboding dungeons (and perhaps even some of the more sinister chambers that accompany them) lurked somewhere beneath, among the dank foundations of the structure.

The Divining Hall itself was a fairly small rectangular room of stone block and was lit by daylight through tall thin windows on one side. A single row comprised of two low wooden benches stationed across from each other accommodated plaintiffs. In front of them was a raised stone dais, upon which stood, off to one side, a wooden chancellor's podium. Behind that was centered an ornate and cushioned throne. The entire dais and a pair of doors on the back wall occupied the far end of the space and were distanced from the visitors by a carved wooden railing. The chamber was lined left and right by half a dozen armed guards because of the occasion.

Syren, Durast, and Braenog were led by the guards to the bench that was already occupied by Baron, the two men who had thrown Braenog through the tavern window, two others from Baron's group who had been brawling that night, and three other gentlemen who had not been at the Crow, as far as Syren could remember. They were older and dressed in the fine attire of merchants. Syren recognized them but wondered why they would have any interest in these proceedings. On the other bench sat Marley, the innkeeper, by himself. Apparently, that bench was for the plaintiff and this one was for the defendants, but since the defendant's bench was full, Syren and her friends were instructed to sit on the end of the other one and wait quietly for the hearing to start.

After several minutes, during which Baron's group and Syren's group spoke among themselves in hushed tones and cast derisive glances at each other, the door on the left of the dais opened slightly, and a thin face peered out silently, perhaps making assessment of the assembly. It was several minutes more before the entire man emerged. He wore a long ornate robe of the prince's familiar blue and white colors with a wide, high collar and open sleeves that were embroidered at the cuffs with a gold filigree pattern of leafy vines. Upon his head was a broad, three-pointed hat covered in black velvet and accented with large blue and white plumes. He carried with him to the podium a collection of parchments, a quill and inkwell, a short fat candle, and a metal stamp. This was the chancellor, one of the prince's officials. Syren didn't know his name and he didn't give it. His face was stern and authoritative, and his manner was imposing. His presence made everyone quiet and still. Rather than acknowledge those in attendance, he busied himself with arranging the articles he had brought with him to the podium. Then he left the room through the door on the right, peering into wherever it led cautiously before he did so. Returning a few moments later, he crossed to the podium and addressed the assemblage.

"All rise," he instructed, whereupon Prince Hallas entered the chamber through the door on the right, crossed to the throne, and sat. He was a heavy, middle-aged man with the clean shaven face of aristocracy and curly blond hair that approached his royal collar in the back but was thinning on the top. He wore official robes of state of a design similar to those of his chancellor and bore a delicate but expensive-looking circlet upon his head. He carried with him, as an emblem of authority, a rod of ebony wood about two feet long, which was inlaid with floral designs in silver. Syren had never been this close to the prince, and the experience was kind of thrilling. The Stouts seemed preoccupied by his ornamental trappings but managed to keep their place. After His Highness had settled himself, the chancellor motioned with his hand that those summoned should sit also, which they did. The chancellor then moderated the meeting while the prince listened indifferently to everything that was said.

"This is the grievance hearing on the occasion of the commotion at the Hooded Crow tavern of approximately three weeks ago, in which an official complaint was registered by the proprietor of the inn," announced the chancellor. "Is the proprietor here?"

"I am, Your Highness," declared Marley, standing briefly and giving his name. Even though the chancellor was doing all the talking, everyone was expected to address the prince when they were invited to speak as though he were asking the questions.

"The summoned shall stand and give their names for the record," the chancellor instructed. One by one, Syren, Baron, and their companions did as they were told, except for the three gentlemen, who remained observantly quiet.

"And who are these three?" inquired the chancellor impatiently, at which point the best dressed of them rose to address the dais.

"If it please, Your Majesty," he said, "I am Berwinn Laustin. This man is Maynard Edgeworthy, and next to him is Aglar Grump. We are here to represent the interests of the venture salvage business here in town, which we believe may have some bearing on this matter." Taking a moment to write it all down, the chancellor then turned and looked to Prince Hallas, who waived his ebony silver rod once, indicating his consent.

"Very well," the chancellor acknowledged. "Mr. Marley, you may address His Majesty, briefly, with your complaint." The innkeeper's account focused on the damages incurred by his establishment as a result of the fight. It included Nog getting tossed through the window by people at Baron's table, though not why. He also asserted that flying tempers by those present at the hearing had led especially to flying furniture, food, and fists, which by the end of the matter had materially harmed his income and made necessary some expensive repairs to his place of business. Then stating his request to be compensated for the damages and loss of income, he sat down again. The chancellor hadn't written very much about Marley's story when he called on the next witness.

"Mr. Baron, what say you to these accusations?" Baron stood up.

"Your Highness, we were minding our own affairs, enjoying Mr. Marley's fine accommodations, until these foreign ruffians came over to us and started everything. After that, we were merely trying to defend ourselves." He turned then to goad Syren and the Stouts. "Syren's friends sure know how to put the *din* in *dinner*." Syren ground her teeth but couldn't reply because she hadn't been given permission to speak.

"And you 'defended yourselves' by throwing this one through a window?" the chancellor pursued coldly. Baron was forced to shrug sheepishly. "It seemed the best way at that time," he answered unconvincingly.

"Miss Syren, I have received information from the guards that you have vouched for these Stoutish...persons," the chancellor said disdainfully. He appeared unwilling to allow them to speak on their own behalf, so Syren was glad that he was going to ask her about them. "What say you, then, about the charges laid before the three of you by Marley and Baron?"

"Your Highness," Syren began, rising, "the larger part of the fight in the tavern happened by accident when some townsfolk who had taken too much to drink got themselves jostled and took offense—"

"Jostled by you," the chancellor clarified.

"By all of us, yes," she answered, indicating everyone on the bench.

"Actually, I didn't jostle anyone, Your Honor," Baron inserted, standing up.

"Silence!" the chancellor demanded of Baron, who shriveled back to his seat.

"The jostling happened," Syren continued quickly, "while I was trying to prevent these men"—and here she indicated Baron's accomplices—"from beating up Durast."

"And what had he done that caused him to need defending?" the chancellor asked insightfully. Under the weight of the chancellor's impatient glare, the whole issue seemed dreadfully trivial suddenly, but she pressed on anyway, cutting to the core of the matter.

"The whole conflict, Your Highness, stems from a disagreement I am having with Baron because he is in possession of a pair of canvas carrying straps that belong to me." Baron jumped up to protest but remembered himself and sat down again, exasperated. The chancellor did take note of the action, however. Meanwhile, Syren finished her explanation.

"Baron was seen in the Crow that night with the straps, by Durast. When he and Braenog asked Baron to return them, he refused. That's when they threw Nog out the window, and the fighting started. I realize that it isn't directly related to Marley's complaint, but I would ask His Highness to render a judgment in my favor about the straps, in the interest of preventing further public conflict over them," she concluded, sitting. Having addressed the prince so boldly, she felt inside like she had just run five miles.

The chancellor turned to get direction from the prince, who sighed in irritation, but again waved his scepter. Turning back, he addressed Baron.

"You have possession of this item?"

"Yes, Your Highness, but it is not as Syren says. I found them in the wilderness as part of my normal operations as a salvager. That makes them salvage. Aglar will vouch for me."

"Miss Syren, is this not true?"

"Well, yes, practically speaking, but, Your Highness, I was forced to leave them behind in the Nearwood as I fled from Hiddeans only the night before. Surely the salvage rules don't apply in such cases." At this point the best dressed gentlemen of the business trio stood purposefully and waited to be recognized. When he was, he made a plea of his own.

"Your Royal Majesty," he demurred, "I am certain that you are well aware of the great respect and happily generous tribute that comes to the Palace from the venture salvage business in Westpost. Indeed, the long history of venture salvage is entwined with the very success of people and Palace alike. The wresting of treasure from the savage races and their gradual withdrawal from this area are benefits to both His Highness's noble reputation and the safety of this local population. In return, the only protection we ask from the Palace is the protection of law, that those intrepid surveyors who brave the dangers of the forest be allowed the right to claim salvage over what they find. If His Majesty begins the tedious business of adjudicating exceptions to an already fine and well-functioning ordinance, will he not soon find himself in this chamber at all hours, day after day? We who support the Palace and represent venture salvage in Westpost would seek a judgment in favor of that which was wisely appointed and is already working."

Finally, the chancellor returned his attention to Marley. "Final words, innkeeper?" Marley rose to thank the prince for hearing his grievance, reminding him tactfully that the hearing was really about his request for compensation, after which everyone was told to sit and await the decision. The chancellor then went to the prince, and the two shared a quiet conversation at the throne. Try as she might, Syren was unable to tell which way the prince's favor was falling. At length, the chancellor returned to his podium and spent the next several minutes writing down the prince's decision officially as a declaration, using the candle wax and the stamp to place his seal upon it. Then he announced the results.

"His Highness Prince Hallas has decided in favor of business, which is a right and proper institution that works for the benefit of all people and must be protected. On the matter of the tavern, the prince has decided that the Hooded Crow shall be compensated. Syren, you and your associates were instigators of the disturbance, which led to the damages described. You shall submit five hundred silver coins to this office, which will then be paid to the proprietor of the inn." Syren gasped inwardly as the chancellor continued, "If you are unable to pay, your house and possessions shall be forfeited to the debt and you three shall be subject to hard labor till the remaining amount is worked off." Syren was reeling. She knew she didn't have anywhere near that kind of money, but her mind was racing, searching for possible solutions to this sudden crisis. Meanwhile, the chancellor continued with his pronouncement.

"Baron, you and your associates were agitators of the disturbance, which led to the damages described. You shall also submit five hundred silver coins to this office for the same purpose. If you are unable to comply, the same punishments will apply."

"What?" objected Baron, but the chancellor made to continue.

"As to the second matter—"

"Wait just a minute," Baron protested loudly. "This is completely unfair! I didn't throw a single punch! I'm a victim here!" With a flick of the chancellor's gaze, several guards closed on Baron and his friends and ushered them coarsely from the prince's presence while Baron struggled and objected. Then without any sign of having been inconvenienced, the chancellor finished relating the prince's decisions.

"As to the second matter, His Highness affirms the law. Items found by salvagers outside the protective wall of Westpost shall be deemed legitimate salvage and therefore belong to them for their own purposes. In gratitude for adjudicating these matters," the chancellor declared, "Baron, Syren, and the venture salvage business of Westpost agree to bring tribute to the prince in the amount of five hundred silvers each, payable to this office." Syren was reeling, feeling devastated by both decisions and by the staggering size of the financial settlements being levied upon them. Then an idea, a child born to the unlikely parents of desperation and quick thinking, formed in her mind.

"If it would please His Majesty," she pleaded, "Syren, Durast, and Braenog submit to the decrees of this hearing, but we would ask for time to raise the required amounts since we are but a humble villager and two weary travelers."

After a short pause to confer with Prince Hallas, the chancellor rendered one final judgment. "Very well," he conceded, "in his benevolence, the prince grants an extension. He will allow sixty days to comply. This hearing is now settled."

Everyone who remained stood while the prince and then the chancellor exited. Then the guards escorted them to the wrought iron Palace gate. Walking back toward home in shock, Syren was approached by Marley.

"Syren, I'm sorry," the pudgy tavern keeper pleaded earnestly. "When I made my complaint to the captain that night, I had no idea that you were caught up in this. I was angry and needed to be repaid for the damages, and I thought it had all been Baron's fault. Well, his and those bullies he roams with. He must have dragged you into it somehow when he got the summons. Then once the Palace was involved, it was out of my hands."

Despite the hopelessness of her circumstances, compassion welled up in Syren over the sincere sorrow being displayed on the old tavern keeper's face.

"It's all right," she told him, "it'll work itself out somehow." But she was far from confident.

"What will you do?" he asked, concerned.

"I don't know," she answered honestly, "I need to think on this one."

"Listen," he said, "the Crow is pretty empty right now. Come do your thinking in there. I'll buy you folks a drink. It's the least I can do."

CHAPTER 6

A New Line of Work

"The tentacles will suck out your brains!"

Syren joined her two companions in the Hooded Crow after first returning to her house to change back into more functional attire from her formal dress. Together, they sat soberly at their table, contemplating the plight of their circumstances and staring into their mugs as though the answers lay somewhere at the bottom. True to Marley's prediction, the only other customer at that time was one disheveled sot, a regular who sat at the bar obliviously, nursing his Garden Brew and mumbling forlornly to himself. Occasionally (as he just had), he would blurt out loud nonsensical warnings to no one in particular.

"A thousand silver coins," Syren stated sullenly. "A thousand," she repeated, trying despairingly to fathom the magnitude of it. "I've not seen that much money in all my years together. Now we have to raise it in sixty days."

"Syren was deep clever to ask the prince for time," Durast encouraged. Syren shrugged.

"It was something, I guess," she admitted. "I just hope we can make good use of it."

"Durast and Nog help Syren sell deep sticks for many coppers," Braenog suggested.

"Thanks, but it's no good," Syren answered. "People will only buy as much wood as they need, no matter how much we have, and they will only give these." She held up one of the small copper coins. "Ten of these is the same as one silver," she explained. "And we need a thousand silvers. Plus, remember what we already spend just to get by. No," she sighed, "we will never get that far ahead of our living expenses in two months by selling sticks, not even if we spend all our time in the Nearwood."

Durast and Nog rolled some *r*'s in appreciation of the problem. "Nope, nope," they agreed. A thousand silvers was a large sum of money.

Babbling an unintelligible dispute to a nonexistent adversary, the drunk at the bar suddenly waved his arms wildly about his head in revulsion as though something were crawling on him. The action caused him to lose his already precarious balance and tumble off his stool, landing on the floor in a heap. He lay there for a moment, cursing, as if it were the floor's fault he was injured, before trying unsuccessfully to drag himself back to his seat. Durast and Braenog watched him fall, stared at each other briefly, then looked quizzically at Syren.

"That's Stinky Joe," Syren explained. "At least, that's what most folks call him. He's in here a lot." Seeing that he was struggling and being closer to him than Syren was, the two Stouts went over and helped him back onto his perch. The assistance calmed him considerably.

"There's nowhere to hide from the tentacles," he slurred mournfully to Braenog, peering at him expressively through bulging, bloodshot, and watery eyes. The poor man's head seemed to stagger loosely upon his neck such that his coarsely whiskered, drooping face leaned so closely to the older Stout's that they nearly touched. Braenog looked over to Durast for advice on how to answer such a bizarre statement.

"He's not right in the head," he offered, suggesting that the man's comment needed no response, which proved to be the case. When they had reseated him, he leaned forward over the bar and grabbed onto his mug with both hands as though it would anchor him in place. Then they returned to their table with Syren and to the solving of their own problems.

"I suppose I could try to borrow money from everyone I know in town," Syren speculated, "though I don't know how close that would get us."

"That Jack Frost fellow," Durast observed, "seemed like he was a man of trrreasure." Syren pursed her lips in thought.

"Perhaps," she said.

"Jack Frost, Jack Frost, sends the valiant, gets them lost," piped Stinky Joe morosely to the room.

"If we see him soon, we should ask him about it," Syren agreed, "but he comes and goes an awful lot. We should be working another plan also, just in case." The Stouts nodded, refilling their tankards from a tin pitcher on the table.

"Is there other work that able folk can do?" Braenog asked. "Is that not how trrreasure be found by Westpost fellows?"

"In sixty days?" asked Syren, doubtfully shaking her head.

"Chopping tentacles is good work," Stinky Joe suggested bitterly, inserting his comments and his delusion into their conversation.

"What would Stoutfellows typically do to gain treasure?" Syren asked, hoping for some inspiration.

"Never enough tentacle choppers," Stinky Joe lamented.

"We would draw it from the deep earth," Durast replied.

"Sure, until the tentacles get you," Stinky Joe slurred derisively.

"I'm not sure that's our best option," Syren dismissed.

"Which?" asked Nog. "Tentacle chopping or—"

"Mining!" exclaimed Syren and Durast together.

"Sometimes treasure comes from battles with Grrremlins," recalled Braenog.

"Or tentacles." Stinky Joe was becoming visibly agitated.

"Or Orcs."

"Or tentacles!"

"How did he get invited to this conversation?"

"Say good-bye to your brains!"

"Stink—I mean, Joe, settle down. This isn't even any of your... Wait a minute, he's right."

"How's that?"

"His right what?"

"No, I mean he's right. That is, you guys are right. Listen, what's the biggest export business in Westpost? It's venture salvage, yes?"

The Stouts nodded. "We have heard so."

"You two have just told me what I have often heard said about the wilds around here: that the savage races keep treasure piles hidden in secret lairs that they move from place to place. It's a risky prospect, but if the three of us worked together, maybe we could find them and intercept that transport."

"We could steal from the wretch and give it to the peer!" Durast finished enthusiastically.

"And even if we only ended up with novelties, objects that belong to the wild races, say, that's the kind of stuff that sells to the venture salvage owners. That's where the money is in this town!" For the first time in a long while, Syren was feeling the exhilaration of hope. Meanwhile, Stinky Joe had continued his babbling but had also turned back to the bar for another grog, which had changed his focus and effectively removed him from the conversation.

"So how does venture salvage happen?" Durast asked. "How do we get paid for it?"

Syren thought for a moment. "We could just work it like stick gathering. You know, go out into the woods and see what we can find. The problem is that it might well be perilous, especially since we'd actually be looking for trouble. I think a better idea is to get ourselves hired on by one of the venture salvage shops."

"How would that help us?" Braenog asked.

"As I understand it, we would sign a contract, a promise, to sell what we find exclusively to that shop, and in return they would provide us with helpful equipment or perhaps a small advance so we could buy some equipment. That way we wouldn't be so vulnerable when we faced the Hiddeans or whoever."

"Strrrategy!" approved Durast.

"The idea is deep," agreed Braenog.

"Yep, yep."

"Yep."

"Okay, great! C'mon, then," Syren proclaimed, rising from the table, "let's go present ourselves to the salvagers. We're about to start a new line of work!"

Crossing the road to the Village Green, Syren considered the two venture salvage shops that were located there. Her first stop, with her Stoutish friends in tow, was Potters Pendants and Peculiary. In addition to being one of three venture salvage stores in town, the place also sold pottery, vases, and sculptures of various kinds, much of which was produced locally, and jewelry in a wide range of qualities and prices. Some of those items were produced locally, but most had come in with traveling caravans from distant, or even exotic, locales. The place had an elegant, almost aristocratic atmosphere, and there were some intriguing pieces in each category of the shop. Syren warned the Stouts not to touch anything while she waited to speak with the proprietor, but as she had suspected, Maynard Edgeworthy did not contract with salvagers. He was happy enough to negotiate for the purchase of anything they should find, but by not employing them specifically, he was also free from the obligation to outfit them. This, they learned, saved Maynard the expense of losing his equipment in the unfortunate event that salvagers who went foraging didn't return. It was a legitimate business practice but not very helpful to Syren and her companions, so they moved on.

The other shop on the Green was called Stuff Laustin Found. On the shelves were various curiosities that were supposedly wrested from Stormwood: arrowheads, bracelets made from carved bone, necklaces of similar crafting, some very old-looking coins, and a leather shirt made from some wild creature. The size of it matched Syren's memory of what would fit a Hiddean, though when she had met them personally, she hadn't bothered to take note of their taste in fashion. There were also several unusual-looking potted plants, including one that sported what looked like a fist-sized mound of moss entwined with a number of tiny barbed vines. The wooden counter top around it looked bloodstained, and a sign in drawn pictures warned against getting close to it. Syren and company found that the proprietor, Berwinn Laustin, was in.

"Good afternoon," he said. "Syren, isn't it? I've seen you around. You're that pretty little wood seller."

"Yes, thank you," she answered, ignoring his condescension for the sake of her upcoming question.

"What can I do for you?"

"We've come looking for work, actually."

"Yes, of course. You were part of that messy tavern business that we heard about at the Palace today. Beastly character, that Baron. Listen, I'm sorry that ended so expensively for you, what with the required tribute and all, but as you can see, I have a pretty small shop here. I really don't need any shopkeepers or floor sweepers or plant feeders."

"Oh, we're not seeking that kind of work," Syren explained. "We're here to hire on as salvagers." Immediately wide-eyed, the portly shop owner waved soft plump-fingered palms at them.

"No, no, no!" he rejected soundly. "That kind of thing is not appropriate for nice young ladies like you. It's much too dirty, much too dangerous."

"I have no aversion to dirt," she assured him, irritated at his patronization, "or to danger."

"The people I hire as salvagers are exclusively from out of town," he argued. "After all, what do you think would happen to me, to my business, if I took on some popular young village girl, well-known by all the local folk, and she ran right out and got herself rended or killed, hmm? I would be finished. No, no, no. Run along home, honey, you'll live a lot longer. Believe me when I tell you, I'm doing you a favor."

Checking her frustration, Syren smiled politely and exited the shop with her friends. By the time they were standing in the road, she was breathing heavily from the effort of holding back her temper.

"What now?" asked Durast.

"There is still one more place," Syren answered. "Oswald's Venture Salvage. It's on the main road, near the Wallgate." They walked together in that direction, past neighborhoods of villagers who were bustling their way through life. In a community that was only half as populated as when it was founded, there were a number of unoccupied buildings in town. One such was that of Drayton the weaver, whose vacant storefront stared forlornly at passersby, an emblem of the creeping despondency that Syren longed to vanquish from Westpost. In addition to those who, like Syren's mother, had died in the plague, many others had simply become discouraged and left. Battered by the hardships of frontier life and the dangers of the forest, they had packed up and returned with the traveling caravans to more civilized areas. Drayton had been an example of that kind of attrition.

"What if this salvage owner also won't hire us?" Braenog wondered, drawing Syren's attention back to the present problem.

"Well, in that case, I guess we're on our own, but I think he will," Syren answered. "I have seen him in the Crow from time to time, trying to recruit people into salvage."

"Why then did we not go to him first?" Durast asked.

"Partly because we were so close to the other shops. It made sense to start there. Besides that, the shop owner is not my favorite person."

"Oh?"

"I don't know him well at all, so it's just an impression, really, nothing that I can put my finger on. He just seems rather…I don't know, pushy, I guess. Anyway, we have little choice at this point. Here we are."

The sign promoting Oswald's Venture Salvage was a wooden placard portraying the now famous head of the Gremlin that had come in eight months before. Walking in, a U-shaped counter separated potential customers from shelves against the walls. On these were a variety of salvage items for sale. Behind the counter by the far wall was a lean middle-aged man with close-cropped hair that was graying around his ears. He wore a tan-colored leather vest over a linen shirt, the sleeves of which he had rolled up just past his elbows. His dark mustache was trimmed thin, and small beady eyes penetrated everything he glared at. He addressed everyone in the fast-talking, aggressive tones of a busy, important man who expected to get his way without being questioned. Examining the contents of a burlap sack that Baron had brought in and laid on the counter, he shouted a greeting past the salvager at Syren and the Stouts while he finished his trading.

"Hi, folks, have a look around, I'll be right with you. What is this stuff you've brought me, Baron? It's junk, nothing but trash. Look at this, what is this, a pile of rocks? How do you expect me to sell this stuff? I got a reputation to uphold. Tell you what, because I'm such a nice guy, I'll buy these things off you." He thrust some coins into Baron's hand.

"Three coppers?" Baron protested.

"It's a lot more than they're worth, I can't believe I'm being this generous, now get outta here. Wait, where are you going? Take this with you, now go on, and come back with some real salvage." He had tossed the burlap sack at the back of Baron's head and the material clung there briefly till he snatched it away and stomped angrily from the store. Syren's back was turned, pretending not to notice the interaction, but she couldn't help grinning at the way Baron had been set down. Before she could announce her intentions to the overbearing proprietor, however, he immediately leapt into a fast-marching parade of artificially friendly salesmanship.

"Good day to you nice people! Welcome to Oswald's Venture Salvage. What can I interest you in?"

"You are Oswald?" Braenog assumed.

"Oswald's dead. May he rest in peace." The man quickly put a hand over his heart in an obviously contrived show of respect. "I'm Aglar Grump, owner and proprietor, now what can I sell you? I've got a lot of rare and valuable artifacts in here, you know, how about one of these? It's a genuine Gremlin war club, and it can be yours for the paltry sum of fifteen silvers. What do you say?"

"It's a hunk of wood," Syren observed. Aglar immediately put it back on the shelf but rambled on, unfazed.

"What are you, an expert?"

"Actually—"

"Tell you what, I just got in a collection of arrowheads straight from the wild races of Stormwood. Only five silvers apiece. You'd be the first gal in your neighborhood to have one."

"Aren't these the stones that Baron just brought in?"

"A lot you know, these are petrified arrowheads, very old, covered in rock, but you take a hammer and a chisel, smack away the rough outer shell, the part that's not arrowhead shaped, and there you go!"

"I don't think that—"

"No? Well, how about this then, it's a real live Hiddean hunting spear. My salvager risked his very life to get it, I can't let it go for less than ten silvers."

"It's a sharpened stick," Durast observed.

"You too with the wood, eh? Look, I can see you're discerning customers, so for you, I have reserved this beauty." He pulled from another shelf a single flower in a terra-cotta pot and set it carefully before them.

"A tulip?" Syren asked doubtfully.

"That's what you think. This is a rare Stormwood poisonous tulip. Don't eat it!" He stabbed a finger at them in warning. Durast looked at Syren in confusion.

"Why would we eat a tulip?"

"How do I know what you people eat? Twenty silvers, plus you gotta sign a release. If you eat the tulip and go 'daisies up,' I'm not responsible," he crossed his arms in front of him.

"We're not here to buy anything," Syren blurted out quickly. "We want to hire on as salvagers."

"Hire on as salvagers? Why didn't you say so? Stay here." He disappeared into the back room for a moment, hollering through the open doorway. "And don't steal anything!" Braenog looked up at Syren.

"He's joking, right?" Syren shrugged. In the next moment he was returning to the counter with a document, quill, and ink flask.

"Sign here," he instructed.

"What does it say?"

"It says I'm adopting you as my children. What do you think it says? You're hiring on as my salvagers, so I get exclusive rights to the purchase of anything you find. If you sell any salvage at another shop or to anyone else, I get full recompense for the fair market trade value of the item, plus costs of a grievance hearing, as necessary."

"For how long?"

"Until you're dead, like Oswald. May he rest in peace." Aglar quickly feigned the token of respect again. "Now do you want the job or not?" Syren took the page and examined it. The terms listed on it were as he had described.

"Sixty days," Syren countered.

"What?"

"We'll sign a contract to work for you for the next sixty days—"

"Ridiculous!"

"—and we want salvaging equipment, and I want a copy of the agreement to keep for myself, signed by you."

"Outrage! I refuse to give in to such bullying."

"Have it your way. C'mon, guys, let's go offer our services to the higher-class salvagers in town. I'm sure they recognize talent when they see it." Winking at the Stouts, she turned to leave. "After all, this shop doesn't need eager salvagers like us, they have Baron."

"Blackmail!"

"I wonder what employing genuine Deepfellows and a resident from town will do to boost Laustin's popularity around the Green. Imagine the market day crowds—"

"All right, all right, all right, sixty days it is." He began scrawling on the documents, amending them to reflect the new terms. Grinning slightly, Syren, Durast, and Braenog returned to the counter, reviewed the pages, and signed one copy. Braenog's signature was not his name, but rather a design, a mark of attestation, which Syren thought was curious, but she said nothing. Then she took the copy that Aglar had signed and rolled it up like a scroll.

"All right," gruffed their new boss, "now that you've thoroughly taken advantage of this lowly shopkeeper, get out there and find me some salvage."

"Equipment?" Syren insisted, waving her copy of the agreement at him.

"Yes, yes, of course." He again disappeared into the back room and returned a moment later, tossing three large burlap sacks onto the counter in front of them.

"What's this?" she objected.

"It says *equipment*, not what kind." And he waved his copy back at her. "Now what do you think I'm paying you guys for, to stand around in the shop all day? Go on, get out there and get to work. You're salvagers now, so go salvage something!"

Syren and the Stouts stood in the road for a minute or two, burlap sacks in hand, considering their next move. They were at a crossroads of a kind. To the east, they were in sight of the Wallgate, their doorway to the wilderness and to the world. In the other direction lay Syren's house, the village, and life as it had always been. She stared in both directions. The future of Westpost was calling her, but calling her toward what? Somehow Syren knew that her next steps would shape her destiny.

Most of the day had already been absorbed by the grievance hearing, the wallowing they had done at the Crow over their circumstances, the strategy session that followed, and their hunt for employment. Now it was late afternoon. The safe course of action was to stay inside the wall until morning, but Syren had a feeling that success for herself and for the village lay on the far side of safety.

"C'mon," she said to Durast and Braenog, "we're going out toward Stormwood."

Having stopped briefly at the Wallgate to inform Coran and George of their general intentions, Syren led them on a path through the Nearwood that took them directly toward the denser, wilder forest proper. Not knowing exactly what they would find there, or if she really even wanted them to find anything, she watched carefully around her, searching for trouble with every step. As she had seen before, grazing creatures tended to come around in the early evening, and groups of Hiddeans would come stalking soon after that. On their way, they had taken note of a large hole, nearly three feet across, which descended into the ground, its curvature hiding more than a few feet of its course from sight.

"What do you suppose it is?" Braenog asked, stopping to inspect it.

"It looks like a burrowing hole," answered Syren, "but what sort of creature leaves a hole that size?"

"A large one," Braenog guessed obviously.

"Giant badger, maybe?" Syren speculated.

"Do Hiddeans live under the ground?" Durast asked.

"I don't think so," Syren replied. "At least, I haven't heard that they do."

"Snake?" wondered Braenog.

"I hope not," countered Syren, imagining the girth and length of such a beast.

In light of Braenog's suggestion, the trio decided to move away from the area cautiously. As they skirted the edge of Stormwood, Syren led the company while Durast and Braenog took positions that guarded her rear flanks on the left and right. Despite the strength and confidence of her friends, she nevertheless found herself fighting an inner battle of dread against the flashbacks of memory that were her only other experience with the notoriously cruel Hiddeans.

Some while later, and just as Syren was beginning to doubt that they would encounter anything of consequence that afternoon, a deer bounded past them from left to right a short distance away and disappeared, its natural color blending it into the forest. Syren became stock-still, holding up both hands to signal that the Stouts should do likewise. The woods around them seemed eerily quiet. Listening intently for the slightest sound, Syren realized that she had stopped breathing. Into the waiting silence, Braenog's stomach rumbled loudly. She cast a scolding glance in his direction, to which he shrugged helplessly.

"Be alert!" she whispered at them. "This is how they surprised me last time." Already, her heart was pounding at the prospect of intentionally facing the terrifying Hiddeans. The Stouts took several guarded steps away from each other to expand the perimeter of their position and gathered a large stone in each hand. Syren was unsure whether to abandon her vigil to look around her for something to use as a weapon or to keep a sharp eye out and risk facing her enemy empty-handed. For all her planning and determination, she suddenly felt very vulnerable.

"My father had a sword," she told her companions wishfully as they watched the menacing silence bear down on them from every direction. "It was a really good one, long and sharp, yet expertly balanced. It was as quick as your hand. The hilt and hand guard were decorated with braided silver. I remember how the base of the blade had a griffon carved into it on both sides. Father said it had belonged to his father. I even got to hold it once or twice…It sure would come in handy now."

"Syren will wield her father's sword again," Durast assured her. Braenog rolled a few *r*'s.

Suddenly, there was a rustling of the undergrowth around them, and a small horde of the terrible Hiddeans appeared, advancing cautiously on the three of them, snarling and circling and threatening them with crudely made but dangerous-looking spears. Syren felt a wave of panic wash over her as the fetid creatures closed in, but it was quickly replaced by concern for her friends and the jaw-clenching determination that the loyalty of their friendship should not be spent in vain. Quickly, she assessed the situation: They were outnumbered, surrounded, and much too far from the gate to make a run for it, even if she thought the Stouts could keep up. One the other hand, they probably held the advantage of physical strength. Their only chance at all, as Syren saw it, was to stay together, fight bravely, and look for an opening, to perhaps make a retreat.

"Don't let them separate us!" she called to Braenog and Durast. Then she pulled her burlap sack out from her belt, hoping it would do as a shield until she could come up with something better. In the next moment, before she could give or get any other strategic advice, the Hiddeans attacked, dashing around the sparse arrangement of trees in the area, racing past each other as they jabbed their spears at their targets, and creating a confusing, chattering melee of perilous activity. Syren used her large burlap sack and her longer reach to sweep aside the first few spear points that assailed her. She kept moving, trying to keep the trees between herself and the Hiddeans, who pressed after her. It was an effective but harmless technique, and it felt very haphazard to Syren. She knew that if she were to miss with one swipe, she would be gored, which made the tactic seem desperate and uncertain. In addition, her flailing was doing nothing to dissuade her attackers. She needed to gain some way to fight back; otherwise they would eventually wear her down.

Meanwhile, the Stouts were engaged in skirmishes of their own against multiple opponents. Durast threw both of the rocks he had at the swarming Hiddeans, but they flew amiss. The attack sent them scattering, which for the moment prevented him being overwhelmed, but it did no actual damage to the Hiddeans. Braenog, however, rather than flinging his stones into the group, took aim at one specific fiend as it charged him. The throw connected, striking the Hiddean squarely on the head and causing it to collapse into the brush a short distance away.

Spotting a long branch lying among the undergrowth, Syren raced over to it, dodging spear thrusts desperately along the way. Grabbing up one end while stomping hard on the other, a section of it broke free, and she had acquired for herself a makeshift staff. Swinging it around her kept the Hiddeans generally at bay while she looked to her companions to see how they were doing. Durast had taken the offensive and was chasing the faster Hiddeans around, angrily trying to get his hands on them as they scampered just out of his reach and poked at him with their spears. Braenog had thrown his other rock and struck another foe some distance away, in the midsection. Initially dropped by the contact, the creature popped up a moment later but fled into the forest rather than continue the attack. Altogether, the battle was a swirling, chaotic shrill in which Syren felt constantly in peril, yet rather than being paralyzed by the fear of it, the danger worked to sharpen her alertness, and she began to glance all about the scene, quickly shouting out the locations of advancing attackers in an attempt to protect the Stouts from getting blindsided.

At one point, Syren gasped in alarm as one of the creatures hurled its spear directly at Durast's throat, but the crudely made weapons were poor fliers. It embedded itself harmlessly into his beard, and he continued his pursuit, undaunted. She wanted to yell at him not to stray so far from her and Nog, but a kind of rage seemed to have come upon both of the Stouts, and she wasn't sure they would listen. Suddenly, she heard an angry shout coming from the other direction. Turning, she saw with horror that a small group of Hiddeans had leapt upon Nog from behind. His arms were too short to dislodge them, and they were biting and clawing at him savagely, trying to hold him and keep his attention, while others were closing in, in an attempt to drag him down. Without regard for her own safety, Syren charged the entire group, screaming wildly as she barreled toward them. The threat of her assault scattered the whole group save one who was attached viciously to Nog's thigh. Swinging her club vertically, she brought it down hard upon the vile creature's head, killing it.

Whirling about, she and Nog could see Durast squaring off against a single spear-wielding Hiddean. From where they stood, they could see Durast's determined but frustrated expression. Being held at spear point kept him from closing to hand-to-hand range, where Durast was at his best. In the next moment, though, doubt turned to decision on the younger Stout's face, and he stepped boldly forward against his adversary. This inspired the Hiddean to jab his spear firmly at Durast's throat. Moving quickly, Durast thrust his broad left hand forward, impaling it on the spear through the webbing between his thumb and forefinger. Growling from pain through gnashed teeth, he then grasped the spear shaft with his still stabbed left hand and jerked it toward himself. The motion hauled the Hiddean off his feet and within reach of Durast's free hand. Seizing the foul beast in midair, he dashed his surprised foe against a tree to dislodge its grip from the spear. Then turning his left hand over so that the spear tip pointed at his disoriented enemy, he finished him quickly with it.

By that time, the rest of the evil troop had fled back into the forest, abandoning their three dead and anything they happened to have dropped during the combat. Syren ran anxiously over to where Durast stood, one slender spear still embedded gruesomely through his hand and another stuck in his beard. He looked up at her and grinned painfully.

"Sticks for treasure?" he joked. The unexpected humor struck Syren in the wake of the battle, and she fell into a burst of laughter that purged some of the strain and anguish of their first real encounter with the perils of Stormwood.

"Strong and sure shall Deepfellows endure!" she heard Braenog call to his kinsman, and he rolled several *r*'s in reply while Syren addressed his wounded hand. A thin stream of blood was trickling toward his elbow, but it could certainly have been far worse. She broke off the spear as close to Durast's palm as she could, and after she did, he pulled the other end through with a grunt. Then he spat upon the wound (to Syren's dismay) and squeezing it hard with his other hand, assured her with a nod that he would, in fact, endure.

Turning back to Braenog, then, Syren could see that he was limping decidedly, so she rushed back to him.

"Nog, are you all right?" she asked, concerned.

"Yep, yep." He nodded, but it was clear to her that he was not. Crouching before him, she examined his leg. One of the Hiddeans had bitten him viciously on the thigh, and blood was welling up freely, though perhaps not too dangerously, and running over his boot.

"Hold still," she commanded him. "I need to dress this." The senior Stout made like he also intended to spit upon his wound, but Syren prevented it, probably more for her sake than for his. Instead, taking out her burlap sack, she folded it so that it was long and narrow. Because of Nog's short stature, it wrapped easily around his thigh and tied securely. When she released it, Nog pressed his wide hand over the bandaged wound to help staunch it.

"How's that?" Syren asked. Braenog nodded approvingly at the bandage, then reached out instinctively to tug Syren's beard. Realizing at the last minute that she didn't have one, he corrected himself and patted her twice on the shoulder gratefully as he often did to Durast.

A group of blackbirds suddenly scattered noisily from nearby trees, and the trio was instantly alert.

"We'd better get back to town," Syren advised, searching the distance for signs of hostile activity. "It'll be dark soon."

"Wait," countered Durast, "we must gather Hiddean trreasure."

He was right. After all, that's why they had sought the dangerous company of the Hiddeans in the first place. Quickly, Braenog and Syren gathered the bodies while Durast, still holding one hand tightly with the other, searched the open ground in the area of the fight for any wayward objects. Syren and Nog took one of the crooked wooden spears from each of the fallen Hiddeans, and Durast found two others lying among the trampled undergrowth. To their surprise, the sharpened sticks very much resembled the one they had been shown by Aglar Grump back at Oswald's Venture Salvage.

"What do you know about that?" Syren mused. "It really was a Hiddean hunting spear."

The three dead Hiddeans also wore a tunic-like garment made from the hide of some forest animal, probably a wild boar. They were cinched around the waist with a vine of some kind. The vests were somewhat bloodstained, and Syren was unsure whether that would increase or decrease their value as salvage, but they decided to take them, in any case. Searching the creatures and the battleground around them, Durast and Braenog gathered a total of seventeen silver coins. All that remained was to decide what to do with the Hiddean remains.

"Does a carcass make salvage?" Durast asked Syren.

"I wouldn't think so," she replied. "The Gremlin head that Baron brought back was much talked about, but no one kept it."

"What then? Should we bury them?" Durast wondered.

"It would seem the decent thing, to cover them somehow," Syren speculated.

"They would not bury us," Braenog reminded them bitterly. "We would be eaten, or worse."

Durast rested one hand on the older Stout's shoulder sympathetically. "We are not as they," he said resolutely. After a moment's thought, Braenog nodded his agreement, but just then, an ominous sound emanated from within the dense forest of Stormwood. A deliberate rustling advance was accompanied by a host of high-pitched yips and intermittent growling voices. It came from what sounded like a hundred places across a wide stretch of wooded cover, a looming promise of reprisal against those who had presumed to invade their territory.

"We should perhaps let their own decide what to do with them," Durast suggested as all three began to slowly back away, toward town.

"Yes, good idea," agreed Syren, nervously picking up the sack that contained their salvage items. They retreated cautiously for a handful of moments, watching the edge of Stormwood while the threat imposed itself audibly upon them in measured but increasingly bold steps.

"Nog, can you run?" Syren inquired quietly, without taking her eyes off the forest.

"Quite possibly," he answered.

"Deepfellows are able barrellers," Durast assured her.

"All right then, get ready. We should have a head start, but they may take up the chase once they see us fleeing. I told Coran and George to watch for us and hold the gate. I sure hope they're paying attention."

On Syren's signal, the three of them turned and fled toward town as fast as they could go, with Syren leading the way to give direction. At first, the Stouts proved capable runners, not fast but steady, whether they were hopping over fallen logs, dodging brush, or dashing across open ground, and the outraged shriek that arose from the impish villains of Stormwood in response to their quarry's flight was left in the distance. By the time they were halfway home, however, Braenog was slowing, and Durast and Syren had to ease their pace also or risk leaving him behind. His leg injury was clearly catching up with him, and so were the Hiddeans, but gritting his teeth, he pressed on determinedly. Darkness had mostly enveloped the countryside when they came in sight of the Wallgate, and the blazing braziers that marked its shoulders. The rabid cacophony of the angry mob close behind them combined with the nearness of walled safety just ahead to inspire a final burst of speed from all, and the trio reached the gate, panting, and slipped inside.

Thanking George and Coran for their vigilance, Syren, Durast, and Braenog walked back to Syren's house along the track inside the wall, stopping first at the neighborhood washhouse and well to clean up and rebandage. Feeling tired but exhilarated, Syren stood watch during the Stouts' turn to warn people coming to the well and prevent a repeat of last month's embarrassment. From where she was, she could hear the Hiddeans screeching in fury and throwing rocks uselessly against the protective wall of Westpost. Syren was battered, scratched, and exhausted, but this time she was not defeated. This time, with the help of her new friends, she had struck a blow against the forest, and she had won.

CHAPTER 7

Popularity

Shadows were beginning to grow long as late afternoon clasped hands once again with the early evening. Syren, Durast, and Braenog walked together down the main road toward the Wallgate, past a man who was calming a squealing, wide-eyed donkey. They had their spears in hand and burlap sacks tucked into their belts. On their way back out to the Nearwood in search of salvage, villagers who knew them would smile and wave, offering exhortations as they passed.

"Go get 'em, Syren," one would say.

"Good hunting," offered another.

"Do us proud!" was a comment they occasionally heard that puzzled Syren. She couldn't figure how her need to risk her life could possibly reflect on anyone else's reputation, but she and her companions tended to hear that from those who lived in her neighborhood. For the most part, they were just trying to raise the money necessary to pay the fines and tribute that had been imposed upon them by the Palace two weeks before at the grievance hearing.

Arriving at the gate, they explained their general plan to the gate tenders in hopes that, if something untoward should befall them, a search party would be sent out.

"Will they come for us if we don't return?" Braenog asked Syren as they passed through the gate and on their way.

"Unlikely," she answered, "but they might help out if we got into trouble and were within sight of the wall."

"A vain hope beats none at all," Durast quipped as they walked along the road outside the village. They were looking for a specific place at which to enter the woods. It was a trail that Syren said she had spotted while on their way in from their last outing, though the Stouts could not remember noticing it.

Thus far, the trio had met tentatively with success as salvagers but not to the degree they were hoping. That first chaotic encounter, in which they had slain three Hiddeans and been chased back to town, had netted them exactly twenty silver coins. Seventeen of those they had taken from the Hiddeans. The other three had been the fruit of much haggling with Aglar Grump over the total value of the salvage items they had brought back. They were, of course, under a legally binding contract to sell their findings exclusively to Oswald's Venture Salvage, and Aglar was, by that same document, legally bound to buy whatever legitimate salvage they wanted to sell. The conflict arose over how much the items in question were worth and also over what they were willing to sell out of whatever they had found. The contract had been woefully silent on these matters. Apparently, other salvagers were not inclined to keep anything they found and happy to accept whatever they were offered in payment.

Having to raise such a huge amount of money in a fairly (or unfairly) short time, however, Syren did not enjoy such a luxury. Moreover, being convinced that their employer had decidedly undersupplied them for their work, she had successfully debated with Aglar the point that, while he owned exclusive rights to whatever they sold, they were under no obligation to sell everything they found. This allowed the three new salvagers to keep back several of the spears for their own use.

In the end, Aglar's stubborn and skillful business maneuvering (and Syren's need for the money) had worn her down, and she had agreed to accept Aglar's concessions and the three silvers in exchange for the extra hunting spears and the three Hiddean vests, each of which, she suspected, Aglar would turn around and sell for ten silvers.

Nevertheless, twenty silvers for one day's work had been very promising. At that rate, Durast had projected, they would easily meet their obligation with the Palace and have a tidy sum left over. Unfortunately, the "twenty silvers per day" rate of salvaging had proved impossible to maintain. The wounds to Durast's hand and Braenog's leg, while not life-threatening, had kept them out of the forest the next two days. (With another market day approaching, they bided their time by engaging in the safer and more predictable work of wood selling, by which they raised enough copper to cover a week's worth of living expenses.) They were kept indoors the next two days after that by torrential weather. This provided a good occasion for the Stouts to finish their convalescing and feel strong again, but by the end of it all, they had only gone out once the whole first week.

"Here. Yes, this is the place," Syren assured her friends, and the three of them left the road and were soon completely out of sight from anything that looked like civilization. Syren moved deftly through the underbrush, following what she had come to recognize as the distinctive trail made by bands of Hiddeans traveling through the forest. Durast and Braenog crashed along behind her, disrupting everything in their path. Their idea of being quiet in the wilderness was to limit their conversation and to feed Braenog occasionally so his stomach wouldn't rumble. Encouraged by their early successes, though, they felt ready to take the fight to their enemy and hopefully find greater spoils. The group of Hiddeans they were tracking this time seemed different from the hunters they had encountered last week and the week before. This trail was broader and less well concealed, and Syren was both excited and nervous about what they might find at the end of it.

Determined to quicken their pace after that first week (and being pressured by Aglar to procure more salable items from Stormwood), the trio had managed two forays during the second week. On the first of those two trips, they had surprised a wild boar, and having surrounded it, they had managed to goad it to death fairly easily, though at one point it had charged through their attempts to confine it and they were forced to spend much of the afternoon tracking the wounded beast through the Nearwood. Then once they had finished it off, the process of dragging the heavy carcass back to town proved laborious. There had been two sets of tense moments on the way home when they had to defend their quarry against small bands of opportunistic Hiddeans. Syren was learning through these experiences with them, however, that the Hiddeans' main strategies were show of force (mostly through superior numbers) and intimidation and that those same tactics worked well when applied against them. She found that she was able to chase away small groups of the little fiends simply by advancing on them menacingly, even if she and the Stouts were slightly outnumbered.

Once they had dragged the boar back to Westpost, they decided to sell it to Marley at the Hooded Crow as meat, rather than offering it to Aglar as salvage. This was something of a sticky point. Technically, the beast had come from the woods and so Aglar had argued that it was salvage. Knowing that Marley would pay much more for it than Aglar would (they in fact got twenty-five silvers for it), Syren contended that consumables like meat were not salvage any more than kindling was. In the end, they agreed to disagree because neither wanted to incur the expense of involving the Palace as an arbiter over the question.

Breaking into a clearing, Syren halted the Stouts to alert them and keep them from stumbling out into the open. Her tracking of the path they were following and the experience of their second encounter with Hiddeans last week had taught her to be suspicious. The day after they had resolved the matter of the boar sale, they had returned to the Nearwood and followed a trail similar to this one, but narrower and more discrete. That trail had ended by a large rock that divided a stream. While searching the area, they had been ambushed by a small group of the fetid creatures, some hurling stones while others wielded the now familiar spears. As in their first encounter, they managed to fight them off, killing several and putting the rest to flight. The plunder and salvage from that encounter had yielded another thirty silvers and allowed them to replace their spears, which were low enough in quality that they tended to splinter after one solid impact. In the process, however, they had all been wounded severely enough to require spending the remainder of the week in town to recover. Seeing how this present situation resembled that one, Syren was determined that they should not be taken by surprise again. Turning to the Stouts, she found them blinking up at her expectantly.

"Stay here," she instructed. "I'm going to scout ahead. Quietly. I want to see if the trail picks up on the other side of this clearing or if they're still lurking around here somewhere."

Syren helped the Stouts find a spot where they would be concealed but still able to keep watch. Durast and Braenog had assumed that just being in the forest meant that they were hidden, but Syren assured them that they needed cover in order to avoid detection by creatures who were at home in the woods. They hunkered down behind a patch of tall ferns, with their backs to a wide fallen tree trunk. Satisfied that it was the best concealment they could arrange on short notice (the Stouts had suggested digging a hole and burying themselves), Syren issued final instructions.

"Don't move, don't talk, don't rumble." She poked Braenog in his round belly. He stuffed the end of a baguette into his mouth and nodded seriously. "I should be back in a few minutes. If you are discovered, holler and I'll rush back. If I get into trouble, I'll do the same."

"We will come barreling," Durast promised her. Then patting each other on the shoulders, Syren slipped off into the brush and was gone.

Stopping a short distance away, Syren took out her water skin. She was able to move through the woods quietly enough on her own by slowing her pace and stepping carefully, but she needed to go unseen as well. Pulling out some of the weeds and brambles where she was crouched churned up the dirt, and pouring water there made a slurry of mud, which she smeared over her exposed skin. Then she embedded the thorny plants in her hair and stuck them to her clothing. Having thus made her appearance less obvious, she crept around the edge of the clearing, searching for signs of the trail makers.

Her natural tendency was to watch the clearing, but she forced herself to keep a sharp eye on the underbrush that surrounded it. That, she knew, was where the Hiddeans sprang out from when they attacked. Anything coming at her from across the clearing would be detected instantly. She didn't need to watch that direction. Moving cautiously, Syren discovered a pair of large holes in the ground, burrowed into (or out of?) the loamy soil. Sloping downward at an angle and curving slightly, whatever passageways they represented were hidden from view. Syren and her fellow salvagers had seen several of these tunnels in the last two weeks as they explored the edges of Stormwood. Their origin and purpose was still a mystery, but they had learned something ominous about these holes: the Hiddeans avoided them.

Taking note of their location in this part of the forest, she wondered briefly if the creatures that made the holes might have had something to do with her father's disappearance, and she shuddered. This was no place or time for such gloomy imaginings, she told herself resolutely. One day, she would find him. For now, though, knowing that the wild and ravenous foes they already struggled against wanted no part of whatever came from the tunnels was enough to quell her and her friends' curiosity about them. Syren moved carefully on.

The wide trail they had been following picked up again on the far side of the clearing. Syren decided to follow it along for a ways without going back for the Stouts, just to see how far it might lead and to take advantage of the camouflage she had created for herself. As she traveled, she considered mudding up Durast and Braenog as well once she returned to them, but determined that the effort would prove futile since they moved too noisily through the woods to escape notice anyway. Before long, Syren could hear in the distance ahead what sounded like the raucous chattering of a large band of Hiddeans. Dropping to a crouch and searching about her anxiously, she saw a single member of the evil pack absently standing picket duty, watching the forest, its rat-like tail curling and uncurling grotesquely. Syren studied it breathlessly for several moments until it was apparent that the creature was unaware of her presence. Unlike that first night, two months ago, when she had been surprised and taken with fright, Syren had grown by experience to being confident that she could overpower the lone fiend without much difficulty. The problem was that the scuffle would likely alert the rest, and she couldn't possibly fight off the whole troop by herself.

Wanting desperately to learn more about the clamor that was going on just ahead, though, Syren lay down completely and slithered painstakingly through the underbrush on her elbows, past the picket and forward to the edge of the Hiddean encampment. From where she lay, she beheld a chaotic scene. A group of perhaps two to three dozen of the little brutes was gathered. They were chattering at each other, hopping about on their wolfish hind feet, and challenging each other with nips and shoves for possession of a variety of objects that were uncommon to the forest. Others were fighting over something they were tearing at hungrily. Across the camp from her was an overturned peddler's wagon. Syren did not recall seeing it arrive in Westpost recently, yet it didn't look especially weathered, so it seemed unlikely that it had been here in the woods for very long. Dumped onto the ground beside it was a pile of the wares that some of the Hiddeans had begun to contest each other over. Syren saw pots and pans, tableware and mugs strewn about. The cart itself was being torn apart by a small group of them.

Her attention drawn back to the cluster that was slobbishly feasting, Syren watched in horror as one separated itself from the pack, carrying a human forearm. It had been coarsely disjointed at the elbow and drooled gore gruesomely as the Hiddean gnawed upon it, pausing to screech a warning to any others who approached.

Syren assessed that most of what was happening had just begun. If they stayed after it for some while, there would be time to return here with Durast and Braenog and catch them by surprise while they were still occupied fighting over the spoils. Once they scattered back into Stormwood, this opportunity would be lost. She needed to act quickly.

Because the entire horde were so intently focused on their activities, it was not difficult for Syren to slink carefully away. Judging it an acceptable risk based on what she witnessed at the camp, she was able to sneak up behind the less-than-vigilant sentry and stab it through the throat, which slew the beast cleanly and silently. This would provide her company an access point from which to ambush the Hiddeans. She returned to find Durast and Braenog essentially where she had stationed them, and she announced herself as she approached, so they would recognize that it was her. Braenog looked up at Syren curiously.

"Syren is a bush," he stated.

"Thank you," she replied, and then she briefed them on the results of her reconnaissance. "They are not just forest dwellers and hunters," she concluded.

"They are raiders and murderers of peaceful fellows," finished Durast.

"Avenge the peddler," was Braenog's suggestion. "Rout the Hiddeans!"

"Take their trrreasure!" added Durast emphatically.

Agreeing, Syren led the company as quickly and as quietly as possible through the woods, around the clearing, and then within sight of the Hiddean camp. Many were lapping bloody jaws sickly with their long thin tongues, while others were piling plunder. The three paused briefly to consider their best next course of action.

"Barrelling in sounds good," offered Braenog. Syren was dubious.

"Against so many?"

"It worked well at the tavern," defended Durast.

"Not really," she reminded them. "That's why we're out here now. We should reconnoiter, look for an opening to strike with the most surprise."

"Stouts are not good sneakers," Durast confessed.

"Or surprisers," added Braenog.

Syren thought for a moment. For the time being, the Hiddeans were still unaware of them, but they had to act soon. Surprise was a hard thing to hold on to. Like carrying lamp oil in your hands, it tended to slip through one's fingers the longer it was held.

"Let's do both," she said finally. "I'll loop around behind that wide tree. Give me two minutes to get into position, then you can rush in." Durast nodded and Braenog grinned. "Be careful," she encouraged, and she slipped quietly away.

Syren had just reached the tree and peered cautiously around it toward the camp when she heard Durast and Braenog bellow robust war cries and saw them charge in, their short legs pounding the earth rapidly. They had gathered a heavy log, perhaps fifteen feet in length, and carrying it between them with a Stout at each end, they drove into the crowd, dividing the wicked assembly into two smaller groups, mowing down some who were caught off guard, and casting the entire horde into confusion. Seeing her chance, Syren strode out against the faction nearest her, swinging her burlap sack wildly over her head and brandishing her spear. She impaled the closest Hiddean immediately, and the effect panicked the rest. Dropping anything they were holding, they scattered and fled for the deeper forest. Syren managed to slay one of those that made an attack on her while running past.

Meanwhile, both Stouts had taken up arms, with Hiddean spear in one hand and a large rock in the other. Discord reigned among the savages, and they ran madly about, grabbing up pots, screeching threats, throwing coins and clutter at their enemies, and generally being ineffective in the defense of their ill-gotten treasures. Durast strode in against them fearlessly. Dodging a cooking pot, he gored an adversary through the midsection. Braenog was hurling stones with deadly accuracy. When one of the vile beasts tried to sink putrid fangs into him, the older Stout stuck him to the ground, stabbing him through with the spear he had been wielding.

Syren tried to repeat her striding intimidation as she done before, but it was ineffective amid the throes of combat because of the tumult all around her. Once the battle was on, there was nothing for it but to wade in. Sweeping aside a thrusting spear with her burlap sack, she closed in on the impending Hiddean and skewered him. Employing an unusual tactic, Durast allowed himself to get swarmed by half a dozen of the creatures as a way to get them within reach. Then grasping one with his mighty fists, he used it as a club, pummeling the others with the beast until they fled or perished under his determined onslaught. Braenog dropped one more with a rock as the last of them fled, leaving Syren and her friends panting and scraped but otherwise unharmed and in possession of the camp and its plunder.

Coins, spears, and peddler's wares lay asunder in every direction of the camp, the vegetation matted down by the trampling of the combat, the blood, and the dead bodies. Durast began the task of gathering the plunder while Syren and Braenog dealt with the corpses. After liberating the fallen Hiddeans of anything salvageable, Braenog crossed over to where Syren stood, contemplating what must have been the body of the peddler. There wasn't much left of him, having mostly been eaten raw by the pack.

"I hope he died first," Braenog offered solemnly, tugging his beard gently. Durast came over and stood beside his kinsman. Syren turned away not because she was squeamish but in an attempt to keep at bay the dread imaginings of how her father might have met his fate.

"Shall we bring his remains to Westpost?" the younger Stout asked Syren.

"I don't think anyone should see him like this," she answered. "Let's bury him here. Then we should gather up and get back to town."

An hour later, Syren, Durast, and Braenog crossed through the Wallgate with what remained of the peddler's cart, loaded down with his battered wares and the Hiddean salvage. Syren and Braenog were pulling the cart by the wooden yoke, which had probably held a donkey or a pony at one point. One of the wheels had been destroyed by the Hiddeans, but the axle was intact, so Durast was supporting the small wagon on that side. His great strength and short stature made it easy for him to walk along, functioning as a living left wheel. Together, dirty, scratched, and victorious against the cruel Hiddeans, the trio made quite a scene as they walked down the main road. Stopping first at Syren's house to dispose themselves of gathered coins, they then took their entire load to Oswald's Venture Salvage to report in and get paid. After much haggling with Aglar Grump, they decided to wash up and then celebrate by dining and debriefing over the day's activities at the Crow.

Though somewhat sparsely populated on this particular evening, the Hooded Crow was warm and invitingly lighted. Lively music cavorted cheerfully among the patrons as Syren and her friends entered, escaping the dark and unseasonably cold night outside. Crossing to a table near the stage, she was surprised to be greeted by the smiles and raised mugs of some and by the whispered conversations and flicked glances of others. She, Durast, and Braenog took their seats, enjoying the relaxed atmosphere of the place while they waited for the serving maid to come over. After all the day's trials, terrors, and triumphs, the welcoming smells of crackling firewood and chicken stew with leeks blended amiably with the quiet conversations and occasional laughter of simple folk to produce within Syren a deep sense of satisfaction. Folded in perfectly with all this were the merry tunes of the local folksinger and his troubadours, whose jigs and reels put toes to tapping and tired faces to smiling. Taking it in, Syren noticed that even the flames from the many chimneyed chandeliers that hung from the ceiling seemed to dance about in perfect time to the music, as if there were some kind of enchantment behind the playing, bringing harmony to all.

Tonight the serving maid was Heather, and she brought Syren out of her reverie with steaming bowls full of savory stew and bread. Then taking their drink order and their money, she was off.

"Chicken?" asked Durast, looking at the meat that was poised on his spoon.

"Problem?" inquired Syren. She did not know the Stouts to be picky eaters.

"Nope, nope," assured Braenog, slurping a mouthful of the hot stuff in answer to the call of his rumbling stomach.

"Just wondering," Durast blew on his spoonful gently before eating it.

"The boar we brought in last week has probably been used up by now," Syren speculated between bites, in answer to Durast's implied question. The Stouts nodded in unison, to each other, and to the music. They ate and drank for a while in appreciative silence.

"Durast, how much money do we have toward the amount we owe the Palace?" Syren asked at length. They were keeping the money they were earning from their salvage activities at Syren's house, in the root cellar. She had a pretty good idea of what the total was, but she knew that Durast would know exactly.

"Two hundred two," he pronounced. Braenog belched his approval, slid his bowl away from himself, and ordered another, along with more bread and fresh drinks for all of them.

"Two hundred one," Durast corrected. Of the three of them, even of just the two Stouts, Durast was fascinated by the acquisition of treasure in general and of money in particular. He had insisted on excavating a new little alcove, down in the cellar, in which to hide the coins they were gathering, to keep them safe from theft. Syren had assured him it wasn't necessary, but she granted her permission anyway, and Braenog had helped Durast make the arrangements. Then they concealed the area behind a pile of Syren's stores and showed her where they had done the work, congratulating themselves on the quality of their project and plying Syren for similar compliments. To Syren, it was a hole in the wall and not a terribly large one, but they had had much to say about dimensions and angles, interior wall smoothness, what they had decided the space was, or was not, to be like, and so on. Syren had played along for the sake of her friends, who clearly took pride in a perceived reputation of Stoutish underground construction skills.

All this, thought Syren, for a small hole that was intended not to be seen by anyone. She found herself grinning as she remembered it. Durast, meanwhile, spent a fair portion of his time at Syren's house studying the coins they had collected or been paid, and he counted them frequently. The hobby made him rather adept at figures, at least where money was concerned, which was the skill she was interested in his using for the present conversation.

"Two hundred, say," rounded Syren, glancing over at Braenog, who was eating contentedly. "And today was the fifteenth day of the sixty we were given by the Palace to raise the thousand silvers. Where does that put us, in relation to where we need to be?"

"Behind," Durast admitted after a quick mental calculation, "but better than we were. Today was deep good salvaging." Braenog rolled some *r*'s in agreement.

"More days like today will do us well," he offered.

"Agreed," replied Syren. "And that shouldn't be too hard to do. We seem to be getting better at this. I mean, look how much more easily we tracked them than when we started two weeks ago. Not only that, we're starting to find them in bigger numbers, and we're fighting them more successfully, with less injury to ourselves."

"We would gain faster if we sold our own salvage," Durast proposed.

"Yeah, but we can't. We're under contract. I think we've pushed those terms as far as we dare already. Besides, to sell salvage, one of us would have to remain in town to peddle it. That would make going out much more dangerous than it already is. I say we continue on. After the sixty days, we'll be free of the court and the contract both. Then we'll see. Meanwhile, it seems we're starting to do pretty well."

"Pretty well indeed," came a new voice from the direction of the stage. "All hail to Westpost's new conquering heroes, or so the tales bear."

The music had stopped, and as the troubadours were taking a break between musical sets, Syren and her friends were approached amiably by the troupe's leader, a man known to all the townsfolk as Jessero. He was stocky and middle-aged in appearance, perhaps forty years old. His brown shoulder-length hair was curly and streaked thinly with gray in places. Though he looked as if he had been strong and fit at one time, he was somewhat less so now. Seating himself at their table without their invitation (or objection, really), Syren noted that he bore a faded tattoo of a dragon's head on one hairy forearm—the writhing, snake-like body of which disappeared underneath his three-quarter-length sleeve. Upon the other forearm there was a dove, equally weathered. His right leg was pegged from the knee down so that he hobbled distinctly when he walked, yet his clean-shaven, rugged features and indeed his whole manner were bright and unstrained, and he managed to insert himself seamlessly into their conversation by his intriguing introduction.

"Tales?" Syren inquired. "Conquering heroes?"

"Oh, yes. At least that's the scuttlebutt. You're the new venture salvage artists, I'm told, and a local product, no less. Everyone's talking about you. It seems that congratulations are in order."

Jessero was obviously trying to pay a compliment, but Syren felt uncomfortable with the notoriety. "Why are they talking about us? What have we done that's so heroic? Where do people get these ideas?"

"From Aglar Grump, for one."

"For one?"

"Yes, he's been singing about his merry band of salvagers all over town, drumming up business, trying to gain an edge on the other salvagers. Baron is already locally famous, as you know." He leaned in toward Syren as he said the last part, apparently hoping to get a reaction out of her. Grinning his approval at her sigh of disgust, he went on. "And people are starting to speculate about the wealth and the wounds that you've hauled out of the wilderness these last two weeks. Truly, the tales grow longer and wilder by the day. In fact, there was quite a stir over all the items you three lugged through the gate this afternoon. It seems that something of a popularity contest has arisen among the townsfolk."

"Popularity contest?"

"Indeed."

"Contest over what?"

"Over who is the greatest salvager in Westpost, you or Baron. I tell you, people are taking up sides on the issue."

"It's not like that," Syren objected. She felt a growing frustration, but Jessero seemed entertained by the sheer folly of it all.

"Oh?" he prompted, snapping his fingers sharply at Heather to gain her attention. "Not like what?"

"Well, people seem to think that everyone who does venture salvage is impossibly brave and capable, that for us it's like…berry picking, that it's some rollicking adventure."

"When in fact, peril is your constant companion," Jessero offered pointedly.

"Yes, exactly!" answered Syren.

"Sounds terrifying," Jessero suggested.

"No, it isn't, exactly." The minstrel raised his eyebrows at her. "Well, maybe that's true at first," she corrected, "but I still wouldn't put it quite that way."

"Really? How then?"

"It's more like…like you never know what might be lurking about, and once a battle is joined, it's bedlam. From then on, the risk of dying from something you failed to see is everywhere at once, the whole time." Jessero was nodding knowingly as Syren continued. "The key to surviving it, I think, is not to let your mind get overwhelmed by it. Don't panic and stop thinking. I'd say that the trick is…is…"

"Is keeping it all in front of you, mentally," Jessero finished for her.

"Yeah," she acknowledged. "I guess so." Jessero sat back in his chair, looking curiously reflective.

"I know exactly what you mean," he said, and Syren could tell by his expression that somehow this crippled old lute player did know.

Jessero squared himself eagerly then and leaned toward Syren and her companions attentively.

"So what was 'lurking about' out there today, hmm? Tell me. Leave nothing out. I do so love a good tale." There was a mischievous twinkle in the man's eyes as he spoke. His voice took on a melodic quality, and his smile was so easy and engaging that Syren and the others found themselves almost captivated in recounting for him all the events of their encounter in the forest that day. Jessero listened with a nostalgic interest, asking detailed questions about what the forest looked like in that area, what the Hiddeans sounded like, about the strategy of their attack on the camp, and how their foes acted at various points of the narrative. When Syren described her ability to startle the Hiddeans, how she essentially reduced their numbers by scaring some of them off, Jessero added his insight to the story, for completeness.

"You've learned to speak their language," he said approvingly.

"How's that?" Syren asked, confused.

"The Hiddeans have a dialect of their own, a kind of trade language, if you will, that they share with other savage races and mythical creatures. In a very real sense, fear is a language to them." In response to Syren's dubious expression, he elaborated.

"In any language there is give and take, question and answer, statement and response. The Hiddeans speak that language fluently not only through the yips and yowls they utter but also by their unsettling appearance, by attacking in abundant numbers, and so on. Because of their cruel nature, everything about their appearance and posturing is a communication in fear, the issuing of a challenge. If the response they receive indicates an advantage, then they'll attack and can be ruthless. At the same time, though, they also listen to that language. If you know what to say and how to say it, they are usually unwilling to risk fighting to the death, unless they have much greater numbers, especially if it seems that their adversary is willing to do so."

Encouraged by Jessero's interest and his willingness to share knowledge with them, Syren, Durast, and Braenog described every detail of the day's encounter to their fascinated audience of one. When they described the large burrowing holes they had seen on several occasions, Jessero again offered up a bit of his own information.

"Mammoth ant-crabs," he inserted absently.

"Mammoth...what?" asked Syren, pausing from her account.

"Very dangerous if you stumble upon a nest of them. Not so bad as individuals, but you still have to be wary."

"What are they like?" asked Braenog.

"They look rather like...army ants, I'd say, but sandy-colored and very large, probably four or five feet long. When they attack, they squirt a juice upon you, which is paralyzing. Then they grab you with nasty, pincered beaks and drag you back underground to eat you." Syren thought nervously about all the holes they had seen near Stormwood, but Jessero encouraged them to finish the description of their encounter with the Hiddeans. Afterward, he was interested in knowing how Syren felt about the whole experience. She thought for a moment about the threat to Westpost by Hiddean raiding parties and how she and her friends had fairly easily routed one that day. It had been too late for the poor peddler, of course, but maybe they were in a position, after all, to do more than just get themselves out of debt. Voicing her hopes about her higher ideals was met with approval by Jessero, and he also pinpointed for Syren the aggravation she felt over the senselessness of the debate that was going on in the tavern between her "supporters" and Baron's.

"That's why I don't like this popularity contest," Syren concluded. "It's serious business out there, yet some people make such a sport out of it."

"I wonder where they get such a notion," Jessero prodded. Turning his head purposefully, he directed the table's attention across the room toward the doorway, where Baron had just entered with two of his lackeys. The Crow had been gradually filling as the night progressed, and a brief cheer arose at the salvager's arrival. While acknowledging the crowd, his gaze caught Syren's. Frowning coldly, he instructed his men about his usual table, near the recently repaired window. Chasing the patrons there away gruffly, they sat down, devoting themselves to their own conversations.

Syren turned her attention away from the odious Baron in time to see Heather depositing another mug in front of Jessero without asking for copper. Reaching an arm casually around her waist, he guided her easily onto his good knee so he could whisper something into her ear. Blushing slightly, she giggled at whatever his suggestion had been and smote him playfully upon the front of his shoulder, in mock objection. When she rose immediately to continue her barmaiding duties, however, he didn't prevent her. Then turning back to

Syren and the conversation, his smiling countenance was met by her look of scolding inquiry. Jessero cleared his throat briefly.

"The poor girl's nanny is feeling poorly," he explained sheepishly. "I thought that perhaps I would pay them a visit. Later."

"Indeed," Syren responded dubiously. The Stouts blinked across the table at him.

"Anyway," he redirected, taking up his mug, "whether you want it or not, there does seem to be something of a popularity war going on between you two salvagers, at least as far as the people are concerned." Syren noted that many in the tavern were now engaged in private but nevertheless lively discussions, which included pointing or nodding in her direction or Baron's.

"I can't think why," she speculated. Jessero shrugged.

"Small town, small minds," he conceded, "but in any case, it remains that quite a debate has developed among the villagers over who's the greater salvager: you or Baron." The musician glanced across the room at the other salvager. "He appears to be embracing the challenge. Perhaps it will be to your advantage to do likewise. You can't win a game if you won't play."

"It's not a game!" Syren insisted, but just then Heather returned on her way by to drop off three new mugs for Syren and the Stouts, explaining that they were paid for by a table of villagers across the room. When they searched in that direction, four red-nosed men raised their tankards in happy tribute.

"There, you see?" affirmed Jessero. "The battle ensues. I believe some are even wagering on it."

"Around what does this debate hinge?" asked Durast, lifting his new mug.

"Well, it's clear that there is no love lost between them," Jessero advanced, goading Syren again slightly as he cast a glance subtly at Baron. "That, I'm sure, helps to feed the speculation that some sort of contest exists already. Much of the rest comes from every person's natural desire to rank one thing above another."

"What is this ranking based on," asked Braenog, "and who is ahead?"

"Too close to call at this point, I'd say. Baron is, of course, living on his reputation. That and the fancy sword they say he wields when he ventures out, which, again, makes him look successful. He fits the image, basically. He goes out, he returns unharmed, he swaggers effectively, and it serves him well. You three, on the other hand, are rapidly gaining ground because of the 'what have you accomplished lately' factor." Syren was suddenly listening intently.

"Fancy sword? Of what type? I mean, what does it look like? Where did he get it?"

"I have no idea," Jessero countered. "I have not seen it." Without explanation, Syren rose and turned in Baron's direction.

"Here we go again," Braenog said to his mug, but before she could take a step, Durast was tugging at her arm.

"Syren, look: Jack Frost has returned," he said.

"Yes. Hasn't he?" Jessero agreed somewhat derisively, without looking around. Behind him, the rest of the band were assembling themselves onstage in preparation for their next musical set, which was a cue for Jessero to return to work.

Searching the now crowded room, Syren saw the well-dressed old man standing at the bar, waiting for an order and chatting idly with Stinky Joe.

"Remember our first plan, to ask assistance," Durast prompted.

Syren was torn. On the one hand, she suspected that the sword Baron possessed, if he truly owned one at all, was the sword of her father, lost along with him these long years. If Baron had it now, she wanted it back, salvage or not. Moreover, it probably meant that he knew where her father lay, unburied in the wilderness, and that instead of honoring his remains, the scoundrel had plundered them. Thinking about it made Syren's blood boil. She wanted to go right over there and have it out with him, once and for all. On the other hand, though, Baron was a regular at the Crow. He wasn't going anywhere and Jack Frost probably was. This was the first they had seen of him in over a month. Syren was still eight hundred silvers short of her need, and if there was some chance that Jack would be willing to help her meet even part of that obligation, now might be her only chance to say something. Regretfully, she shelved her wishes to confront Baron for the time being and made her way through the crowd toward old Jack, while Jessero excused himself and returned to the stage. Taking up lute and drum and pipes, the musicians struck tune once again as Syren greeted the old man purposefully.

"Say, good evening, Syren," Jack said amiably. He was dressed in his usual elegant robes and familiar bronze skullcap. "I hear that you and your friends have been prospering while I was away."

"Well, yes and no," she replied. "You may remember that Durast and Braenog got into a bit of a scuffle in here a month or so ago."

"I seem to recall," he acknowledged wryly.

"So the Palace has levied fees and fines upon us. We have sixty days to raise a thousand silvers."

Jack whistled. "That's a lot of wood."

"Right, so we've taken to doing venture salvage, for Aglar Grump."

Jack winced. "Not my favorite choice, but then the good citizens of Westpost seem to approve generally."

"You know, that's something I'm not quite comfortable with."

"What's that?"

"All the people who are comparing our salvage actions to Baron's, like it's some kind of game, debating over it, betting on it even."

Jack shrugged as he lifted his glass. "People will seek their entertainment where they can. Besides, it's right for them to be interested in what's happening in the wilderness. Their safety depends on it. As to their choice, you wouldn't have them root for the Hiddeans, would you?" Syren chuckled.

"No, I suppose not. Anyway, there's a question I want to ask you."

"Ask away."

"Well, frankly, we're eight hundred silvers short of our requirement. I was hoping that you might see your way clear to loaning us the money." Jack pursed his lips. "We would pay you back, of course. It's just that the Palace would never be so understanding if we couldn't come up with the whole amount by the deadline."

"No, I'm sure they wouldn't."

"We intend to honor the obligation," she assured him. "I guess we're looking for a creditor who's a little…easier to work with?" Jack turned to face the young woman and addressed her seriously.

"Syren, I admire what you're trying to accomplish, and I give my admiration most cautiously. There's value in this, for you and for Westpost. I commend you and your friends to continuing on, and I shall support your doing so for a long while." Then he emptied his glass and placed it on the bar. "Well, well," he announced, smiling. "I must be off. I am expected at the Palace and as you know, they are very sticky about deadlines!" Then he flicked the top of his skullcap with his finger so that it made a dull ringing sound, nodded courteously to Syren, and left the Crow. Syren watched him leave while she speculated about what his comments might mean toward the solving of her problem. After his exit, she intended to find Baron and question him about this fancy sword Jessero had spoken of, but when she searched in the direction of his table, she was discouraged to find that he had apparently left the tavern. Having missed that opportunity, she made her way back to where Durast and Braenog sat at their table, chatting with each other, allowing random patrons to buy them drinks, and enjoying the music.

"Well?" asked Durast when Syren at last sat down.

"Is he going to help us?" inquired Braenog.

"Will he lend us trrreasure?"

Syren paused for a moment to consider, turning her head to stare at the door.

"I don't know."

CHAPTER 8

Casualties

The scream had a most terrible and despairing quality, which banished every common thought and halted all other activity, commanding the attention of everyone who heard the sound pronounce its baleful knell. More than simply an exclamation of surprise or cry of pain, it was a curdling of the air that carried it. Syren had been dragged anxiously from her house by the dissonant, inconsolable wail, which had crawled across her skin, penetrated her flesh, and resonated menacingly inside her chest. Calling impatiently for Durast and Braenog, she stood outside amid the collection of modest dwellings and humble folk of her neighborhood, searching about her earnestly for signs of the danger that had provoked such a desperate howl. The expressions she encountered were mostly curious or confounded, people glancing at each other briefly in wonder before resuming their normal activities. Some few began to walk furtively in the direction of the Town Green, from whence the call had come, but Syren recognized the horror within the cry. She had felt something of that same terror herself while facing the vile creatures of the forest and the memory filled her with an ominous dread, for this time it had come from within the town's protective wall.

Joined at last by the hustling Stouts, the trio jogged intently toward the Town Green, unsure of what they might find there but concerned for the safety and well-being of friends who might be involved. Syren knew that the very reason why so few of Westpost's citizens ventured beyond the confines of the town's wall was their fear of suffering violence from the savage races that they knew marauded there. In the absence of any determined and successful attempts to drive them away, only the wall provided any measure of the security, which was critical to the safety and success of the town. If that security had now been breached...It was hard for Syren to imagine the panic that would ensue, but Father had taught her that panic in the face of danger often led to disaster. The last thing she wanted was to see evil ultimately consume what could have been a haven of peaceful civilization simply because the fear caused people to throw their hope (and their lives) away without even putting up a fight.

They hurried on to the site where a nervous crowd had gathered by Othan's butcher shop, on the far side of the Green. Pushing their way through to the front, they beheld a scene of general destruction and chaos. The stockyard beside the shop was a huge jumble of upturned and mounded earth, like an enormous mole hill. Any farm animals that might have been there were nowhere in sight. The disruption had caved in the nearest wall of the butcher shop, resulting in the collapse of the roof over that part of the structure and moderate damage to its contents. A contingent of Prince Hallas's guard had arrived to restore order, to keep the populace at a safe distance from the precarious building and grounds, and ostensibly, to investigate.

Othan was visibly shaken but looked unharmed physically. He was standing near Jack Frost, who was speaking to him while consoling a woman who was weeping hysterically. Syren presumed that she must have been the owner of the scream that alerted the town. All around her, excited people were throwing wild conjectures and asking frantic questions of the guards and each other. The guards were angrily denying every claim and roughly forcing back any who tried approaching the area too closely. The woman caterwauled on. From some more distant place, a man's voice was shrieking about tentacles.

Durast and Braenog took a great interest in the formation of the mounded earth, examining it as closely as they were allowed and comparing opinions in quiet, Stoutish tones. Meanwhile, Syren pressed through the reluctantly dispersing crowd to where Jack stood, the woman sobbing and gasping into his shoulder.

"What happened here, Jack? Did you see anything?"

"A regrettable accident of some sort," he replied soothingly. "I'm sure everything is going to be all right." But when he looked up from the woman to meet Syren's gaze, his silent expression was one of grave concern.

"Of course. What can I do to help?" Syren asked, taking the hint.

"Maude here has had quite a start. Could you take her over to the Crow so she could sit and collect herself, perhaps get her something to calm her nerves?"

"Certainly. Come with me, dear," Syren said soothingly, taking the older woman gently by the elbow. "That's it. Let's wash your face, hmm? Mustn't let people see you this way, must we?" Syren comforted, trying to offer some sense of normalcy to the poor distraught woman. Then turning to Jack, she asked pointedly, "I'll see you there later?"

"As best I'm able," he assured her, and then he walked over to consult with the captain of the guards.

With the company of the Stouts and the help of Marley, the tavern keeper, Syren did her best to settle Maude, eventually delivering her into the care of neighbors, who took her in. At length, Jack returned and joined them, looking not so much worried as contemplative, like he was struggling to solve a difficult riddle.

"How's Maude?" he asked, sitting.

"Fair, I'd say. She took a little brandy and some tea, but she refused to eat."

Jack looked curiously at the empty soup bowl, but before he could form the question, Braenog's stomach rumbled.

"Ah," he said, understanding. "And where is she now?"

"We sent her home with friends," Syren answered. Jack nodded his approval.

"Did she tell you anything?" he asked.

"No, she mostly just stared at the table, though we tried to talk of other things. She must have had quite a fright."

"I daresay."

"So what happened, really?" Syren asked. Jack stroked his goatee thoughtfully.

"I'm not altogether sure at this point. The facts of the matter are that a great rumbling shook the ground near the butcher's place, where Maude and her husband were just delivering a steer. The ground seems to have burst open with enough force to produce the damage we've seen. The cattle, and sadly, Maude's husband, Bert, were lost."

"Lost?" inquired Durast. "No remains were found?"

"Well, not as yet," Jack explained.

"This reminds me of the house that collapsed in one of the neighborhoods a month or so ago," Syren observed.

"Yes, only this time there was a witness, of sorts."

"Of sorts?" Syren asked. Jack shrugged.

"The woman is delirious and in shock. It's difficult to know the accuracy of her report."

"What did she tell you?" asked Braenog.

"In addition to lamenting the loss of her husband, she uttered the word *monster* and kept saying 'I saw it' as though the mere sight of the incident was a promise of her own demise. I'm not sure what *it* was, but she is certainly very disturbed by the event."

"Grief talks," Durast suggested. "She may not be right in the head."

"Perhaps," Jack conceded. "It would be terrible to watch a loved one being devoured, whether by beast or natural phenomenon."

"I saw the alchemist coming over as Maude and I were leaving," Syren observed. "Did he have any ideas?"

"The Palace is calling it an earthquake officially, but I wonder. You two seemed to be forming an opinion before the guards shooed you away. I should very much like to hear it."

"Earthquake is unlikely," Braenog pronounced. "There are Stoutish tales of colossal earthworms, but they are said to delve in the deep places. We have never seen one."

"And if it were natural?" Jack inquired. The Stouts studied each other briefly.

"Groundswell?" offered Durast. "If a bog pocket were near the surface—"

"It might disrupt the earth when it escaped," Braenog finished.

"Possible," Jack conceded. "There is a marsh to the south of here that could account for the phenomenon, though it's still a bit of a stretch because of the distance."

"Nothing quite fits, does it?" mused Syren. Jack sighed before rendering his verdict.

"The mystery remains, I'm afraid," he said. "It would seem that for the sake of the villagers, the best course of action is to accept the decision of the Palace for now, comfort the grieving, and resume our daily lives."

"I guess so," resigned Syren.

"Time is both your ally and your opponent, in a game of riddles," Jack declared, standing. "Best to keep our eyes open, and watch what develops." Then nodding to everyone, he excused himself from their company to check in on the newly made widow.

Whether the dangers of Stormwood were real and pressing or simply implied by reputation was difficult to tell, but Syren could feel the imminent threat of impending violence lurking beneath every broad leaf and behind every vine strangled tree. Compared to the relatively open spaces of the much grassier and tamer Nearwood, the forest to the west of town was altogether denser, taller, and wilder; it closed around a person, as if it had swallowed them. Here, at the farthest point from the security of the Wallgate, the forest crowded the protective wall of Westpost in open defiance of civilization, and while no fierce creatures had yet jumped out to assail them, Syren and her companions nevertheless felt engulfed by a shroud of botanical malice.

Rarely before had Syren ventured this deep into Stormwood. Though it was broad daylight, little of it could be seen from the forest floor as if the sun's rays had been choked off on the way down, unwelcome in this feral place. Despite being a fairly short distance from the town's west wall, a quarter mile perhaps, they would probably have gotten lost had Syren not paid careful attention to certain landmarks and their direction of travel at every necessary turn. (The Stouts confessed that they had no idea where town was from where they were.) Durast and Braenog seemed especially wary of their surroundings, but their focus was more about avoiding an ambush than it was about discerning their way, and that was just fine with Syren. Both kinds of awareness were useful.

The three were searching the foreboding thickets of this part of Stormwood for several reasons. Syren had begun to suspect that the two village tragedies, the so-called earthquake and the sinkhole before that were not, in fact, isolated. She was even entertaining a more dreadful notion that perhaps they were not caused by anything natural at all but were rather the result of an attack by some form of monstrous creature. Since Jack had agreed to the possibility of swamp gas from the marsh, which lay some distance to the south-west, Syren thought that with the help of her Stoutish friends they might confirm or refute the theory. The two events had occurred at this end of town, and Stoutfellows did have the reputation of owning expert knowledge about all things subterranean. Durast and Braenog certainly enjoyed playing the part, to which her root cellar would attest. In addition, if the two unfortunate calamities were caused by some huge and reckless beast of the stark wilderness, this would be a likely place to find it.

Either way, Syren had more confidence to face whatever they might encounter because of the added companionship and sturdy help of Durast and his kinsman, which provided the second reason they were braving the perils of Stormwood: they felt that together they could handle it. Durast and Braenog were remarkably strong, they had demonstrated themselves to be capable fighters when they had to be (and sometimes even when they didn't), and thanks to their racial tendencies, they were largely fearless. Syren marveled at how differently she viewed the wilderness now than when she had endured her first real threat, just a couple of months ago, by herself. As a team, they were much more successful at confronting and routing the Hiddeans than Syren or indeed any of the individual salvagers had been previously. Though she had privately noted a curious lack of the kind of trails and signs that marked the passage of the little imps in this part of the wilderness, she still felt certain that together the three of them were equal of any threat that the deep forest might impose upon them. After all, Syren was becoming an able woodsman and tracker with good general skills. She was a sharp thinker under pressure, and the Stouts were solid and dependable. While it was frustrating, having to chase this debt they'd incurred because of Baron's actions in the Hooded Crow last month, they were nevertheless starting to enjoy success in doing it and in a way that might be a benefit to the entire village. Syren felt for the first time that she was making a difference, that she and her friends were actually beginning to "force back the darkness" as it were. In that way, she was following after the footsteps of her father, which was the third reason they had come to this seldom traveled section of Stormwood.

Syren was determined to learn what had really happened to her father and his patrol. She wanted to find him if she could, return with him to Westpost, and by some means gain closure to that chapter of her life. A thorough and repeated search of the Nearwood, which surrounded most of Westpost, had yielded few clues. Now with the help of Durast and Braenog, they could explore deeper into Stormwood itself. Maybe at last they would find the answers she had long been seeking.

Suddenly, a cry of distress broke through her silent reverie. Its source, though near enough to hear, was nowhere in sight. The three companions, immediately alert, took up positions, which formed an outward facing triangle.

"What was that?" wondered Durast aloud, looking all around him for signs of approaching danger.

"Some wild creature is becoming prey," Braenog offered. From somewhere in their vicinity, the continued but intermittent sounds of desperate exertion, muffled by the dense foliage, suggested the drama of a mortal struggle.

"Perhaps we should leave before we do too."

"No, it sounds like someone's in trouble." Syren strained to discern the direction from which the skirmish was coming.

"It could be a call for aid," suggested Durast.

"To whom? There is no one out here to answer," observed Braenog.

"We're here," said Syren emphatically.

"Yes, but nobody knows that," countered Braenog.

"All the more reason we should answer," assured Durast. The wailing continued, louder and more desperate than before.

"That sounds like Baron's voice," Syren recognized suddenly. "And it's coming from over there. C'mon." Durast, Braenog, and Syren began to move warily in the direction Syren had indicated.

"Why would Baron wander so far from safety that he needs rescue?" Braenog asked.

"Because he is a fool," Durast accused bluntly as he struggled through the thickly tangled undergrowth that in places was fully as tall as he was. "Who else would wander aimlessly in a deep treacherous wilderness with no sense of direction? Who else would blunder into harm, alone, at the hands of...Syren? Nog? Where are you? Where am I? Curse this forest!"

"It already is, I think," suggested Braenog as he pushed through some vines to come within sight of his kinsman.

"Here we are, Durast," announced Syren. She and Braenog crossed over to him from behind a wide tree that was some distance to the left of where he was standing. "Stay close to me," she instructed. "Whatever is happening is back that way, beyond that huge fallen tree, see?"

Advancing cautiously but quickly on that position, Syren took a turn to answer Braenog's question. "I suspect that he's out here trying to win that stupid popularity contest that's going on in town. He's just conceited enough to risk his life over something that petty. Besides that, remember that the Palace levied fees against him too. He needs the money as badly as we do."

"What if he is facing a giant or a dragon?" Durast asked.

"Then we will find one less topsider," Braenog replied sarcastically.

"I mean, how do we then proceed? What is our plan of battle?"

"I think we should barrel in," offered Braenog.

"Of course you do," observed Syren of her fearless friend. "But I doubt it's quite that serious. He wouldn't be out here fighting it if it was, and besides, anything that large and destructive and this close by would have shown itself to the village by now."

"By collapsing houses and devouring their owners, you mean?" reminded Durast. Syren was silenced by the dread that the statement's implication created, but just then they emerged onto the scene.

Syren and her friends beheld a tumult of snarling, imposing creatures that before that moment she had only known by reputation. Taller and more muscular than Hiddeans, these were about the same height as Stouts, though not as robust. From their brutish faces sprouted ugly boar-like snouts and protruding lower jaws with long upward-curving lower fangs. Wild jaundiced eyes leered from beneath oversized brow ridges and coarse black hairs jutted from the hides of their grotesquely hunchbacked but generally humanoid forms. In the midst of the slavering throng, flailing ineffectively, was Baron. He was pale with fright and stumbling. Crying out desperately, his panic shrouded eyes looked everywhere at once but without really seeing anything. If what Jessero had said was true, that fear was an actual language among the savage races, then Baron was screaming "I am dinner!" to these fiends.

"Grrremlin!" Braenog announced angrily. Baron wheeled about at the sound and saw them across the melee.

"Syren! Help me!" he called frantically.

"Even one such as Baron should not be abandoned to their ilk," Durast proposed. Agreeing, Syren began a quick assessment of how best to render aid, and then she recognized the sword that he was waving futilely at his pursuers. Long and lithe, the elegant blade bore engravings near the silvered hilt. She couldn't be absolutely sure, given the amount of time that had passed since she'd seen it, the distance between her and Baron, and the random slashing motions he was making with it, but it seemed likely that the scoundrel was in possession of her father's sword. Worse than that, he was in peril of losing it (along with his life) to the Gremlins!

Not wanting to see even Baron end up as the peddler had the day before, Syren turned toward the Stouts for a quick strategy session. When she did, though, she saw that Braenog's expression was set in a deep and distant anger. It was a kind of pain that could only be spawned by profound and despicable cruelty. Syren recoiled at the idea of simply charging in against untested foes without first making some sort of plan, but there was a promise of wrath in the old Stout's eyes that could not be turned aside, and he was already moving toward the fray. Called forth by the trumpet of some ancient wound, Braenog had mounted a warhorse of vengeance, and Syren knew in an instant that there was nothing for it but to ride that terrible steed into battle.

Ignoring Baron's pitiful pleas, Braenog charged in, roaring, against the Gremlin closest to him. Hearing the enraged shout, his target turned to face him, snorting and snarling, just in time to be plowed into. Momentum and fury carried them both along until they crashed a short distance away, lost from Syren's view in a confused tangle of arms and legs and vines.

Durast rushed in also, but his advance was more calculated than Nog's had been. From the field of battle rose an ancient oak tree that threw down buttress-like roots on two sides of its massive trunk. Crossing determinedly to that spot, Durast set himself into the notch and began calling out challenges to nearby Gremlins in Deepspeech, the ceremonial language of his people. Syren couldn't tell what he was saying, but the accompanying gestures and their general inferences were decidedly insulting and had the desired effect, which was to draw their attention and their attacks. Several Gremlins turned their attention from Braenog or Baron and closed on him, wielding primitive stone hatchets and small shields, which looked to be fashioned out of tree bark and vines.

Syren had only an instant to choose where to lend her support. Durast was clearly outnumbered and could use the help, but he had chosen a defendable location from where he could not easily be outflanked. Braenog, meanwhile, seemed to have the upper hand for the moment but was in a much more vulnerable position overall. Rolling about the ground against his opponent made it difficult for him to see what was going on around him. Despite his strength and tenacity, his chosen tactic (or lack of one) left him open to being ganged up on from behind.

At the same time, though, Baron was still screaming and flailing like a small child who had a disturbed beehive. Of all of them, she was most worried for his survival not only for his sake but for hers. He wasn't a very likable person, but no one deserved to be torn to shreds by Gremlins. In addition to that, she knew that if he died in this skirmish, so did her chance of finding out from him what he knew about her father's fate, and if they made off with the sword, she would probably lose it forever. Despite what she thought of Baron personally, she had to help him. He was in the most danger because he was panicking, and if he got himself killed, she might never find out what happened to Father.

Leaving the Stouts to defend themselves for the moment, she strode as confidently as she could into the midst of the menacing Gremlins who were swarming around Baron, trying her best to communicate doom to them by the way she bore herself upon them. Unlike the smaller, scrawnier Hiddeans, however, these villains were less impressed than she had hoped. Only three of them lost their nerve and fled. Nine others remained and several of them turned their attention from Baron and squared off warily against her. Standing this close to him, Syren became certain that he was indeed swinging her father's sword, but for the time being, surviving the Gremlin's attack was much more important than debating the ownership of weapons. A desperate battle was being lost, but if she and Baron fought together, they could probably come out of this fight alive and run to the Stouts' aid after that.

"Baron!" Syren shouted. "Stand back to back. They're going to surround us. We can't let them attack us from behind!" The salvager's face was white with fear. He didn't seem seriously injured as yet, but he ignored Syren's instruction and continued to swing the sword so wildly that he was more of a danger to her than he was to the Gremlins. Syren realized that, in order to rescue Baron, she needed to adapt her strategy to what he was capable of, which was unfortunately little. Ducking his next wild swing, she slipped behind him, thrusting her Hiddean spear at an encroaching Gremlin. The brute's shield blocked the attack, though, and it countered by swinging its ax at her midsection. Syren tried to redirect the blow with a sweep of her burlap sack as she had done before against the Hiddeans, but the technique proved ineffective against the sturdy stone ax head, and it thudded painfully against her side. In the next hectic minutes, she was outflanked by her opponents, dodging desperately, kicking aggressively, and exchanging one attack for every three of theirs. Baron's shrieking and flailing was at least keeping the rest at bay, though at one point Syren took the flat of the sword against the back of her head. If it had been the edge, she knew, it might well have killed her. It was proving a challenge to stay beyond the reach of Baron's random sword swings and yet close enough to him that it prevented Gremilns from slipping in between them and surrounding them both. Interacting with the man was once again making Syren's life harder than it needed to be, as it always did.

The Gremlins' shields effectively parried her Hiddean spear for the most part, but finally, Syren managed to block an incoming ax blow and stab its owner, snapping her spear in the process. New enemies were stepping in to fill the void, and Baron was moving randomly, causing him to stray from their somewhat defendable position. On impulse, Syren dropped anxiously to the ground and rolled to a new location. This caused her to dodge another wild swing from Baron and also allowed her to pick up the fallen shield and ax. It was more of a bludgeoning weapon, really, which explained why Syren hadn't been slashed despite having been struck a number of times already. As the marauders closed, Syren managed a quick assessment of the Stouts. One Gremlin lay skewered next to Durast, and he must have chased off another because he was defiantly wielding a Gremlin ax in each hand, swinging them with gusto against multiple opponents. Two other Gremlins lay still where she had last seen Braenog, but he was disturbingly absent from view.

Armed now with ax and shield, the battle began to turn in Syren's favor. She discovered an effective tactic of offering a feint, blocking the counterstrike with her shield, and then swinging hard into the opening that the Gremlin's attack created. Sometimes she would have to trade several blows before gaining mortal advantage with her longer reach, but at least this way she wasn't blocking incoming strikes with her body. Just as she was feeling they were gaining the upper hand overall, though, something unexpected happened. One of Baron's frantic swings connected with a Gremlin by chance, and Baron moved through the opening created when the creature fled the scene, leaving Syren's flank unprotected.

"Baron!" Syren called. "Not that way. Stay together!" But it became clear in the next moment that the terrified salvager had no thought of staying with the group, no intention of helping them. Seeing his opportunity, Baron dashed through the gap in the Gremlin lines and fled toward town, taking what salvage he could grab, and the group's best weapon, with him.

In response to Baron's flight, the Gremlins, who had appeared to be on the verge of breaking morale and running, rallied themselves and bore down on Syren, surrounding her and attacking viciously from every side.

"Syrrrin!" Durast called in distress, but Syren was too occupied fighting a losing battle for her life to look around. She couldn't even tell if his concern had been for her situation or his own. Her heart in her throat, all she could do was fight on and hope that they would wear down before she got overwhelmed, which she knew wouldn't take long.

Though she knew she couldn't afford to, Syren began to despair.

"Strong and sure shall Deepfellows endure!"

Suddenly, Braenog appeared from behind a wide tree. Barreling furiously toward the pack surrounding Syren, he crashed headlong into the Gremlin nearest him, driving it into the next one and those two into the next until he had plowed away from Syren a Stout-wide swath of the foul creatures, claiming their reprisals for himself.

Gratefully setting her back to the opening created by Braenog's assault put the remaining six Gremlins generally in front of her. From there, she saw Durast rushing up to attack the group from the rear, so she engaged them as best she could, shouting loudly to cover the sound of his advance. At the moment that her wooden shield split in two and became useless, Durast struck a mighty blow to the head of one Gremlin, collapsing it instantly. The surprise attack cast the other five into disarray. Syren and Durast then pressed their advantage, each wounding one more before the vile troop scattered for the forest.

Turning toward Braenog's last known position, however, they were horrified to see that the last four Gremlins had managed to drag the older Stout off his feet and were gathered around him, clubbing him savagely with their axes. Racing over, Syren grabbed one by its upraised arm and hauled it away from Braenog while Durast cracked the skull of another. Once she had wrestled the ax away from it, the Gremlin fled into the forest, Syren chasing it for a short distance out of anger and frustration. By then, the others had fled also, but when she looked back to where the old Stout lay, she put her hand to her mouth in shock and dismay. Badly beaten and bloodied, he was completely motionless.

Braenog had been killed.

CHAPTER 9

Alchemy

Panting heavily from the exertion and crisis of the combat and reeling from the sight of her fallen friend, Syren stared down at Braenog's grim-looking form with dread-filled eyes. Durast was kneeling over him soberly. Brutally battered by Gremlin axes, perilous-looking gashes had been opened on the Stoutfellow's head and face. While Durast had done his best to staunch them, much blood had already escaped, matting his hair and staining his clothes ominously.

With one hand over his own breast, Durast reached under his kinsman's beard, gently grasping his throat with his other hand. For several tense moments he was silent, with his head bowed and his eyes closed. Syren was unsure whether Durast was paying homage to his dead friend, listening for something, or performing some magic ritual, but at length he withdrew his hand, rested it compassionately on Braenog's chest and sighed.

"Well?" Syren asked anxiously. "What news?"

"He lives yet," replied Durast, "but his wounds are deep. He is very weak."

"We have to get him back to town," Syren observed, looking about her nervously. "It'll be dark before long. We can't be in Stormwood when that happens. Can he be moved?"

Durast poked Braenog's oozing wounds gingerly and panned his gaze across the threatening woods.

"He has no choice," he said.

"We can fashion a litter," Syren determined, gathering herself. "I'll search among the trees nearby for branches to use as poles. We can stretch our burlap sacks across them and carry him back to Westpost on it."

"I will come with you," Durast offered.

"No," Syren responded. "You stay here with Nog. If you wander about in the woods and we get separated, you could get lost. Then what would we do? Besides, if the Gremlins come back and find him unguarded, they might take him to who knows where."

Durast rose to one knee, then pressed himself to his complete height while gazing at Braenog loyally.

"I will stand and watch," he declared resolutely. "If Grrremlin return, they shall not have him."

Syren reached down and clasped Durast on the shoulder, the way she had often seen Braenog do.

"I won't be far, or long," she promised. Durast nodded slowly while studying the spaces between the trees, and then she was off.

Searching the ground for stray branches that might be suitable for use as litter poles, Syren was careful to be as quiet as possible. She wanted to blend in with the forest so that she wouldn't draw the attention of the Gremlins or anything else that might be lurking nearby, yet she also needed to work quickly. The seriousness of her circumstances and the pressure of time, which seemed to be fleeing before her just when she needed it most, were making it hard for Syren to concentrate. Braenog was unconscious and his life was ebbing away, moment by excruciating moment. Syren hated the panic that welled up in her when she thought about it, but she couldn't help it. Unless they could get help for him in town, and soon, he would probably die. In addition, she and Durast were each battered, aching, and exhausted from their battle with the Gremlins, and now they were separated from each other by the need to watch over Nog and find the means to bear him home. If they should be confronted again by any creatures tough enough to dwell in Stormwood, she doubted they could withstand them or even come to each other's aid. Making matters worse was the fact that night was falling on this notoriously dangerous forest, and they were as far from the safety of the Wallgate as they had been since becoming salvagers. The strain of everything at once was almost unbearable.

Frustrated by her inability to find just what she was looking for in short order and worried about what might be happening to Durast, she decided to return to where she had left him, standing guard over Braenog, and devise some other plan. On her way back, she stooped to gather a plant she recognized, which she had learned from Mertie had healing properties. Nearby to it, she spotted a small wooden chest, which by its location had probably belonged to the

Gremlins. Antique and much weathered, it was iron bound at the corners and was missing its latch. Taking it up, she lifted the lid as she walked. Inside were a collection of silver coins, maybe a hundred of them, a similar number of copper coins, and a curious-looking, cream-colored jar with a black lid. What it contained, if anything, would have to remain a mystery, though, Syren thought. This was certainly no time for investigating trivialities. Nog's life was hanging in the balance of how quickly they could get him back to town.

Emerging suddenly, from her thoughts and from her concealment, she barely managed to dodge a rock that came flying at her head from Durast's direction. Crouching defensively, she glared over to find the vigilant Stout shrugging apologetically.

"I thought you were a Gremlin."

"I should have announced myself," Syren conceded. "Here, grind this in your hands and place it over his wounds. It may help to reduce the swelling." Durast did as he was instructed. The plant made something of a chirping sound as the leaves and stems were rubbed together.

"You have long sticks?"

"I couldn't find anything suitable, and I didn't want to wander too far or be gone too long." She considered Braenog's unconscious but not yet lifeless body. "How does he fare?" she asked.

"The same," Durast replied soberly. Syren found the news both hopeful and desperate.

"This is all Baron's fault," she mused, fuming. "If the coward hadn't abandoned us and fled for town at the first opportunity, none of this would have happened!"

"First we see to Braenog," Durast insisted. "*Then* we see to Baron."

"Yes, of course," Syren accepted.

"What have you there?" he asked, indicating the rusty-hinged box.

"I found it among the things left to us by the Gremlins," she creaked back the lid and showed him the contents. For the first time since she'd met him, Durast showed comparatively little interest in the treasure. Nevertheless, he did remind them that they had come for a purpose.

"We should gather the salvage and Nog and make for the Wallgate."

"Agreed, but how are we going to transport him without leaving a blood trail or jostling him to death?" They both thought for a moment. The next suggestion was Durast's.

"We put Nog in his salvage sack. Then I will carry him on my back, like sticks."

"Hmm...Not ideal," mused Syren, "but if we're careful and quick, it just might work." At Durast's admonition, Syren quickly gathered the salvageable items that lay about, putting them in her sack along with the small chest. Then she helped Durast place Braenog gingerly into the burlap sack he had carried with him into the forest. Having done so, they hoisted the broken Stout carefully onto Durast's back. Even for Durast, the weight was burdensome, but together they began the perilous trek back toward civilization.

"Which way walks back to Westpost?" Durast asked, confused. Syren glanced around quickly, getting her bearings.

"It's this way, through those trees. Come on."

The pair made the best speed they could with Durast so heavily laden. Before long, he was puffing from the exertion, but he maintained a determined pace anyway.

"I should have gone the other way, I think," Durast confessed at length. "When will Stormwood become Nearwood? Where is the wall?"

"It can't be far now," Syren assured. "I remember these ferns."

"How can you remember ferns? They are all the same." Syren chuckled at the observation but didn't answer it.

"You are sure we are not lost," Durast stated questioningly when next he spoke.

"I am sure," Syren replied confidently.

"Did Baron come this way? Will we find him in Westpost, or is he lost someplace?"

"I don't know," Syren admitted. "Maybe he's a better woodsman than I give him credit for, or maybe he's just lucky. In any case, he does seem to find his way into and out of the wilderness easily enough."

"I hope he is not lost in Stormwood," Durast puffed after a brief silence. "I hope he comes back to Westpost."

"That's a very generous attitude," Syren congratulated.

"Because I want to pummel him!"

"Oh."

"He is a coward. He has caused us much trouble and harm and for this, he should be pummeled."

"Well, there is that."

As Syren predicted, they eventually found their way out of the tangled depths of Stormwood. They located the protective wall of Westpost, though not exactly where Syren expected to find it, and followed it eastward, toward the Wallgate. On the way, they exchanged strategies about what they would do to defend themselves and Braenog if they should encounter Hiddeans. The sun had already abandoned them, and it was swiftly dragging the twilight with it.

Though she didn't say so openly, Syren worried secretly about how Braenog was faring inside the burlap sack. Would it be too late to find help for him when they got back home? Were they already too late? There was no point in stopping to check. There was little they could do for him out here, and the additional jostling might do him worse. Sorrow and regret were building a mansion for themselves inside Syren's heart. What folly it had all been. What were they thinking, prancing merrily into Stormwood without shields or armors or real weapons of any kind? How sure they had been, how proud of themselves. Now look where that had gotten them! A good man was dead, or might be, and it was all her fault.

Well, not all her fault, she reconsidered. Both Stouts had rushed in against the Gremlins without first making a proper plan. She'd have to talk to them about that, she decided. Even so, they might still have carried the day if Baron hadn't turned tail and fled, and with her father's sword no less! The dirty, thieving coward. Durast was right. The next time she got her hands on him...

Syren was pulled out of her despairing reverie by the distinct sounds of a Hiddean hunting party. By the noise of it, she could tell that it was somewhere nearby.

"Should we stop and defend?" Durast asked. His words were beginning to sound strained by the hard labor of bearing his heavy kinsman on his back this whole way. Syren thought seriously about agreeing, just so Durast could lay down his charge and rest, but it sounded to her like the Hiddeans were already in a struggle of some kind. Hoping they were too occupied to notice, and concerned for Braenog's oozing life, she advised that they move on. Admittedly, there was a risk that they would be charged up on from behind this way, but they were not in the end, even though darkness had fully set by the time they wearily reached the Wallgate.

A quick inquiry of Coran and George told Syren that Baron had come that way some while ago, but that he "seemed in too big a hurry to chat."

"Was he carrying anything with him? A sword? Anything?" she prodded.

"I don't know," was their collective reply. Syren was pretty sure that if a giant should ever come and tear the gates off the wall, Coran and George would fail to notice it. Bypassing Syren's house, they proceeded directly to the home of Mertie, the herbalist widow who lived alone in a neighborhood of the town's southwest side.

"Syren, dear," greeted the old woman in a welcoming voice.

"Mertie, you've got to help us," Syren pleaded. "My friend has been hurt." Syren's urgency and her expression ushered her and Durast inside. They laid Braenog gently on Mertie's table and peeled back the burlap cover far enough to allow the old woman to examine the battered Stout's wounds delicately.

"I crushed up some cricketweed and put it on where I thought it would do the most good," Syren explained. Mertie nodded silently in approval, but her face was dour.

"This is serious, girl." Mertie announced. "Your fellow here needs alchemy. There's naught more I can do."

"Are you sure? I mean, do you think the alchemist will see us at this hour, or at all?"

"I know the best way to find out," Mertie implied. "Waiting till morning may be waiting too late, dear. Your friend is whispering with Death already. Only an alchemist can fix that."

Hurrying to the Palace gate, they bore their fallen companion with them. Mertie had offered the use of her wheeled barrow wagon, but Durast insisted on carrying his kinsman himself.

"Would it help us with the alchemist if you come along, Mertie? You know, as an expert witness?" Syren had asked.

"I rather think the reverse," she answered. "He sees me as something of a meddler. Better you go without me."

Syren wasn't sure they would even be granted an audience with the alchemist of Westpost, but she could think of no other plan if they were denied. Fortunately, the reputation that she had not formerly welcomed as "popular salvagers" came into use with the guards who, when they learned the basics of the tale, ushered them into the Divining Room. There, they set down their charge and were bid to wait. All her hopes for Braenog were placed on this meeting. She had never actually seen the alchemist do anything wondrous, but he did carry that reputation. She figured he must be powerful because he lived at the Palace and was the prince's personal healer.

After what seemed an impossibly long period, the alchemist appeared. Deeply wrinkled, grumbling, and shuffling, he was wearing an ornate and professional-looking robe, which he had obviously donned over his bed clothing without changing. He was looking quite perturbed, and it worried Syren. She felt eager to prove to the powerful old healer that the case was worthy of his time and effort. Without acknowledging her or Durast in any way, the alchemist bent his disheveled white-haired head over Braenog and studied him with a concentration, which made Syren wonder if he knew that she and Durast were even present.

"A Stout," he murmured at length, more to himself than anything.

"Yes, sir," Syren began, hoping to assist in the assessment process and prove herself useful. "You see, we were—"

"Silence!" he growled. "I'm not your grandsire, lass." He went back to his examination, adding absently, "The wounds will tell me what I need to know. When I want your inane babbling, I'll tell you." Syren swallowed hard. The ancient-looking sage removed the remnants of the cricketweed from Braenog's head wounds.

"This is that woman's quackery," he accused disdainfully. Syren winced but said nothing. The alchemist lifted Braenog's eyelids and peered into his blank pupils. Then he shoved him hard.

"Hey! You there. Get up!" the healer exclaimed sharply, but Braenog did not respond. Syren heard Durast begin the deep-throated rumble she had heard before the bar fight, and she quietly placed her hand on his shoulder to quell it. Meanwhile, the alchemist had somehow learned what he wanted to know.

"Two hundred silvers," he announced disinterestedly. Syren gulped.

"That's nearly everything we have," she responded reflexively. She had been so concerned with getting help for her friend that she hadn't even considered what it might cost. The remark just blurted itself out. Shrugging indifferently, the alchemist turned to leave, shuffling in the direction of his chambers.

"Wait!" exclaimed Syren. "We'll pay it." The alchemist turned back, only slightly less indifferently, and glared expectantly at Syren. His stare was more intimidating than anything she had faced that day. She produced the wooden chest they had removed from Stormwood and took out the hundred silvers.

"Here's a hundred," she said. "We have another hundred we can bring you."

"It's one hundred five," Durast said at a glance. Then he pulled a sack from beneath his vest and dumped silver coins onto the bench near Braenog's feet until he was satisfied it equaled the required amount. Syren glared down at him in surprise and mild annoyance.

"Trrreasure calls out to itself," he explained earnestly. "'Tis always well to take some along." Syren sighed resignedly.

"All right?" she asked the alchemist. He snapped his fingers sharply for attendants, who gathered up both the coins and the injured Stout and carried them off. Then he turned again to shuffle from their presence.

"So what happens now?" Syren inquired at him anxiously.

"Now, you go away," the alchemist stated flatly without turning back. "There will be nothing to report before tomorrow." And with that he disappeared. Syren and Durast were escorted without further explanation back to the Palace gate and told that they would be sent for as necessary.

The full weight of the day was bearing down on Syren, and beginning to feel light headed, she realized that she hadn't eaten. Being weary and near to the Hooded Crow, she recommended they eat and drink and rest. If worry had been healing, Braenog would already have been well, but they had done for him all that they could, given Baron's treachery. His fate was out of their hands now. There was nothing they could do but wait and see.

Inside the tavern, they took a table by the hearth. The food was warm, the drink was brisk, and the mood was happy and reassuring. Jessero and his minstrels played songs of cheer and sang ballads of hope, which made Syren feel oddly sad, though no one else seemed to be. Even Stinky Joe spouted his tentacle warnings but seldomly as flute, lute, and timbrel pranced out a lively cadence. Syren looked around at the innocently oblivious villagers. At least here in the

Crow, she thought, life was as it should be. Even if hope was just a specter, she would dance with it tonight.

At the break, she and Durast were joined by Jessero, who was curious about Braenog's absence and eager to hear the news of the day's events. At first, they were reluctant to relive many of the details, but he implored them, and as if compelled by some mischievous spell of his casting, they told him everything.

"So old Nog is with the alchemist," Jessero mused.

Syren was suddenly concerned. "That's okay, isn't it?"

"Probably. I mean, what choice did you have, right?"

"What do you think he will do for Braenog?" Durast asked.

"Fix him if he can, I would wager. He took your money, so that's a good sign. Alchemists are part surgeon and part wizard, as I see it, but more dependable. They can't do everything, but they're pretty handy if you need to be sewed back together. That's provided you have all the parts, of course." He clicked his wooden leg on the floor.

There was an awkward pause in the conversation.

"And what have we there?" he continued, indicating the jar Syren had been toying with absently as she spoke.

"I don't actually know," she confessed. "We found it in Stormwood."

"May I?" Jessero offered easily, holding out his hand. Syren handed it over, whereupon he immediately opened the container. Inside was a glistening, vaguely greenish-colored salve. There was an unusual quality to the stuff. Something within it was almost twinkling. Jessero whistled musically.

"What is it?" Durast asked.

"It's healing salve," Jessero pronounced.

"Healing?" Syren repeated. "Healing of what?"

"Almost anything," he replied.

"Anything?" Durast inquired incredulously.

"Almost," he clarified, casting a quick and regretful glance in Stinky Joe's direction. "This stuff would fetch a handsome price, if you sold it at Potters Pendants and Peculiary."

"How handsome?" Durast inquired, interested.

"Maybe enough to satisfy the Palace or carry you most of the way. You should show it to Maynard Edgeworthy tomorrow."

"We can't," mourned Syren. "We're under contract. We can only deal with Aglar Grump."

"Oh, I see," admitted Jessero sympathetically. "In that case, I would hang onto this if I were you. It could come in handy for salvagers who do much venturing in Stormwood. It's alchemy in a jar." As he handed it back, Syren was suddenly frustrated.

"Wait a minute. You mean we could have healed Braenog with this stuff?"

Jessero shrugged his assent. The implications sent Syren reeling once again. They had exhausted themselves and endured great risk, both to themselves and to Nog, in returning him to town, and had delivered him uncertainly into the hands of the prince's alchemist at great expense. It was by no means sure that their friend would live, yet they had spent most of what they owned on the chance of it, in spite of the tremendous debt that still hung over them. Now they were discovering that here, in this jar, they had possessed the means to revive him the whole time if only they had known it. At that moment a cheer arose, and Baron came swaggering in, arrogantly waving and taking his usual seat.

Overwhelmed by the strain and emotion of the day, Syren stood abruptly upon seeing him, her chair shooting out behind her so violently that it nearly landed in the fire. She moved determinedly in his direction, with Durast following in her ire driven wake, while Jessero grinned and returned to the stage area. Without a word, she pushed past everyone, giving speed to her anger, until at the last moment she leapt upon him. Seeing her approach, his smirking expression turned to one of shame and fear. As Syren drew close, he made to offer her his excuse, and save something of his reputation in front of the crowd.

"Syren! Good to see you. Listen…I…uh—" And she crashed into him, driving him backward over his chair and onto the floor. A roar arose from the imbibed patronage, and they gathered to watch the spectacle as Syren poured out her furious rage and frustration upon him in a wild (and somewhat ineffective) flurry of punches, slaps, and scratches.

"You got him killed, you worthless cur!" she howled. Several of his miscreant followers moved to intervene, but Durast made use of his short stature and great strength to grab up the table Baron had been sitting at by the centerpost underneath. Wielding the entire wooden table like a battering ram, he rushed them with it, pinning them to the wall.

Despite his meager attempts to fend off her attacks, she pressed on until, exhausted by effort and by sorrow, she came around to the point of her assertions.

"Give me back my father's sword!" she demanded.

"Here! Take it!" he conceded, offering it up. Syren knelt on Baron's chest and inspected the weapon briefly. There could be no doubt that the lithe, elegant blade with the dual griffon engraving was indeed the sword she knew, the one that her father had taken with him on his final patrol.

"Where did you find this?" Syren asked, panting and easing up a bit.

"In the wilderness. It was salvage," he justified. "I was just—"

"Where!" she screamed hoarsely, threatening him with her fist.

"All right, all right! There's a ruin in Stormwood to the east and south of here, beyond the Nearwood. It's an old tower or something, surrounded by a stone wall." Syren thought for a moment. She had never been that deep into the forest in that direction.

"Why didn't you bring back his body for burial?" she accused.

"What body? It was just a weathered old corpse." Syren made to pound him again in defense of her father's honor, but he threw his hands before his face in protest. "He was unrecognizable! I didn't know he belonged to anybody! Besides, the place was infested with Orcs. I was lucky to come away with my life. I took what I could and got out of there. I've never been back. Trying to return would be insane!"

Just then, a squad of the prince's guards arrived to restore order. Durast put down the table and tried his best to look innocent. The crowd began to part, and feeling exposed, Syren stood and brushed her hair back out of her face, keeping possession of her father's sword. By the time the guards approached her and Baron suspiciously, he was also standing, wiping away the blood from his nose and patting his scratches tenderly.

"What's all this, then?" one of the guards demanded. Syren braced for the worst.

"Nothing, sir," demurred Baron sheepishly to Syren's surprise. "I...uh...fell. Had a little too much to drink, you see."

"No doubt," the leader of the squad observed disdainfully. Then he looked to Syren.

"Did this man force himself on you, miss?" he asked. Baron's expression changed to one of objection and fear. Realizing suddenly what the whole scene looked like, he knew that it would only take one tearful lie by Syren to land him in irons. Syren took a moment to straighten her rumpled clothes and brush back her hair with both hands before answering. Baron squirmed anxiously over the tense moment, but he was not allowed by the guards to say anything at that point, and he was unable to get Syren to meet his imploring gaze.

"No. It wasn't like that," she said honestly. "We were having an argument about...there was a disagreement," she summarized, after a pause.

The guards seemed unconvinced, but given the man's own testimony and the lack of any formal complaint to act upon, they conceded. "Well, let's keep it civil, hey?" the guard scolded Syren.

"Yes, sir. Sorry," she responded penitently.

"Go on home," he instructed gruffly to Baron, and he slipped away, finally exchanging one bitter glance with Syren as he did so. While the guards spoke briefly with Marley to make sure that he had nothing further to add, Jessero and his players piped up a lively tune just then to lift the mood and encourage everyone to get back to more normal activities, which had the desired effect.

Syren and Durast returned silently to her house and washed up from the ardor of the day, he storing treasure items in the "vault" in the root cellar while Syren went into the yard behind the house to talk with her mother, which she had not done in some while. Taking the sword with her, she found when she sat down that she could do no more than weep softly for the emotion of it all. Though Durast must surely have come up from the cellar by then, he gave her the respect of her privacy, busying himself with other tasks until she gathered herself finally and came inside.

CHAPTER 10

Negotiations

A wild and rampant maelstrom of evil-twisted enchantment, chaos, and cruelty surrounded and permeated the kingdom's western frontier. Within it groaned the forest of Stormwood and all its foreboding malevolence. Cowering fearfully inside the oppressive malice of the forest and ruled by its anarchy was the village settlement of Westpost. Among the meager collection of wood and stone structures that were huddled, there stood a simple three-room dwelling in a northeast neighborhood of the town. Inside the house, a capable and sturdy but forlorn young woman sipped her tea and ignored her breakfast.

Syren sat at the table in the main room of her house. In her hands she held the cream-colored jar with the black lid, the container of alchemical healing salve she had found in Stormwood the day before. As she turned the jar over in her hands, she turned recent events over in her mind. Beside her, to her right, was Durast. His feet not quite touching the floor, he sat with his chin just slightly above the level of the table. Noisily chomping and slurping away, he vanquished his breakfast with the same endearingly hearty gusto that Stouts seemed to apply to everything.

Beside her, to her left, sat no one.

"Durast," Syren asked, knowing that he would know, "how much money do we have?"

"One hundred and ten," he stated, without having to think about it or pause from eating.

"It's been nearly three weeks since the grievance hearing. One hundred and ten is, what? A tenth of what we need to raise?"

"Slightly more than," Durast corrected.

"So we've gained slightly more than a tenth of what we need, and it's taken half the time we've been allowed."

"Slightly less than," Durast corrected again.

"Even so," Syren complained, "we're not making it. That's the point."

"Yep, yep," Durast admitted. "We are behind, but there is still time. Don't forget, we have yet to sell the salvage from our last outing. It is good salvage, and we took it from Grrremlin. It was a deep day, yesterday."

"Yesterday, we got our heads handed to us by the forest!" Syren exploded. For the first time since climbing into his chair that morning, Durast paused to look up at Syren, surprised at her outburst. "It was foolish for us to go out into Stormwood," she lamented. "What were we thinking, blundering around in the forest without any kind of real weapons, rushing into combat without any sort of coordinated plan? We're lucky we didn't all get slaughtered! We let ourselves become sassy and overconfident, and what did we get for it? A sack full of trinkets and a sack full of Stout!" Syren planted her elbows on the table and rested her head in her hands. "We'll never be able to pay our debt to the Palace at this rate," she said, but her real source of discouragement was over Braenog's condition and the uncertainty of what might become of him.

"So we work harder," Durast shrugged. "We go into Stormwood more often. Use strrrategy."

"Just the two of us?" Syren pointed out. "We had all we could handle from the Hiddeans when there were three of us and more than we could handle against the Gremlins."

"But we know them now. When Nog returns, we will be three again, and now Syren has her father's deep good sword," reminded the Stout optimistically.

"*If* Nog returns," Syren corrected gently. Durast searched Syren's face for understanding, and she explained the dire possibilities as compassionately as she could. "We have no promise that the alchemist can heal Nog. His wounds were serious. If he can, there is no way of knowing how long it will take. I have no idea how long he will need after that, to rest and recover his strength before he can venture out with us again, if indeed he will be able to at all. Remember Jessero and his leg?" Syren could see that Durast was beginning to appreciate the weight of their circumstances. "I'm sorry to say it, my friend," she offered, "but I think it wise that we prepare ourselves for the worst."

For the next few moments, they ate in solemn silence. Then Durast spoke. "If Braenog does not endure," he said quietly, not looking up from his plate, "I would like to lay him beneath the earth, next to Syren's mother."

Syren stared at her friend in quiet admiration and sympathy. This wretched wilderness had done what she had known it to do all her life. First, it had taken her mother. Then it had swallowed her father. Now it had claimed Braenog, and soon it would consume the last of their hope. She patted Durast gently on one shoulder to acknowledge his request.

"He may yet recover, eventually," she suggested, sighing. "Meanwhile, I think we should come up with another plan for raising the thousand silvers."

"Is there another plan?" Durast wondered.

"Well, I have an idea, anyway." She hefted the jar of healing salve. "Last night, Jessero told us that this stuff could be worth most of what we owe, and of course we still have the other salvage. If we haggle strongly with Aglar for it, we can add that to the coin we already have. From there, I could try to borrow from people in town. Maybe our so-called popularity will come in handy after all. If we're still short after that, I can try talking to Jack Frost again. He seemed inclined to help us at one point, though he didn't say exactly how or by how much."

"By this plan, we will not find your father," Durast pointed out. "If we sell the salve and all the weapons of the Grrremlin, the two of us will have nothing left to fight with against Stormwood. By this plan, we are giving up venture salvage."

Syren frowned. She knew that Durast was right, and it galled her. She hated the idea of slinking away, of having to admit defeat to the wilderness. It was just all so hard, the cost so high. At first, it seemed that she and her two Stoutish allies were making progress. For the last three weeks, they had been accomplishing more than just making money or even making friends. They had been making a difference. These last three weeks had truly mattered, she thought, right up until yesterday. Then just as they were making their first bold stride against the chaos, it was as if the forest itself had risen up, exerted its evil will against them, and crushed them as easily as one might swat a mosquito. Syren could see in Durast's expression that the Stouts had adopted her quest as their own, and she hated to abandon it. She hated to disappoint them. There just didn't seem to be any better answer, at this point.

"Perhaps another chance will come," she tried to say optimistically, but she didn't believe it, and she knew that Durast didn't either. "Come on," Syren said finally, standing and gathering the dishes, "let's get over to Oswald's. We've got salvage to sell."

A late, dreary morning was already pouring in through the windows as Syren quickly washed out the breakfast dishes and set them on a cloth to dry. Then having convinced her comrade of the unfortunate wisdom of her plan, they gathered up their burlap sack of Gremlin artifacts and the jar of healing salve and bustled resignedly out the door toward their tasks. As they did so, Syren crashed roughly into someone who was just coming to the door from the opposite direction, along the path from town. In a last ditch effort to keep herself from completely trampling the shorter visitor, Syren went sprawling.

"Oh! I'm so sorry," Syren apologized emphatically as she pressed herself up from the ground. "We were in a hurry on our way out, and I wasn't watching where I was going. I wasn't expecting there to be anybody—" Just then a huge hand reached down to help Syren to her feet. Glancing up as she took it, she saw that it was attached to someone she wasn't sure she would ever see again, much less that morning.

"Nog? Nog!" Syren exclaimed in delighted unbelief. "It's you!"

"Quite possibly!" The old Stout beamed through wide, white teeth. In the next instant, she was pushed aggressively aside, again landing unceremoniously in the dirt, as Durast rushed up to his kinsman. Roaring and laughing, the pair stood face to face, slapping each other roughly on both shoulders and tugging each other's beards repeatedly. Picking herself up from the ground, it was Syren's turn to push Durast aside. She was so glad to see Braenog that, crouching slightly, she threw her arms around the portly Stout's rotund middle and hoisted him off the ground.

"Oof!" he exclaimed happily. Then just as Syren was setting Braenog down, Durast squeezed both of them in a hug of his own, and with a joyful yell, lifted both of them off the ground. Afterward, the reunited trio stood together under an overcast sky for a few moments, arms around each other's shoulders, and laughing for joy and relief.

"Strong and sure shall Deepfellows endure!" they all shouted, and Syren did her best to join them in rolling many *r*'s at each other.

Syren stepped back for a moment to take in the sight that her eyes still couldn't quite believe. "How is this possible?" she wondered aloud in amazement. "When we left you at the Palace last night,

I wasn't sure you were going to make it. Now you look as good as new."

"I feel as good as new."

"But what did he actually do? I mean, how did he cause such a transformation as this?" In response to the question, Braenog simply shrugged.

"When I awoke, I was on a table in a workshop of some kind, in the Palace. Whatever he did, by then he had already done it because I was well again."

"Astonishing. And you're feeling completely yourself?"

"Yep, yep." He grinned, adding sincerely, "Alchemists are handy fellows. We should get one." Fascinated, Syren pressed the Stout for details of the alchemical process. Again, he could offer little more than a shrug.

"The room I woke up in looked like a glassworks because of all the tubes, bottles, and vessels. The alchemist was there, but he didn't offer an explanation. By the way he acted, it seemed to me that I was not to ask for one. When I turned my head to look around, he came over and stared at me. He asked me only, 'How do you fare?' Seeing all the glassware and jars filled with liquids of different kinds, I sat up and asked him if there was any beer. Then he sent me home."

"Was there any?" Durast asked earnestly, but Syren cuffed him on the shoulder.

"Alchemy is deep good," Braenog concluded to the group. "We need not worry of injuries in the battle now. As sure as anyone survives, the rest can be brought to the alchemist."

"Yep, yep," agreed Durast enthusiastically.

"Wait, wait," countered Syren, imitating their way of talking. They both looked up at her inquisitively. "Don't forget what we paid for the alchemist's services. I mean, I'm glad it worked, and it was worth every copper, but it cost us almost everything we had. We can't keep that up. Even if we could, we're going a different direction now, remember?"

"Different direction?" asked Braenog, confused. "Every direction is the same. We are surrounded by the forest."

"I mean that we're not going back to Stormwood," Syren announced regretfully. Braenog looked surprised.

"Not going back?" he echoed incredulously. "But the Grrremlin are there!"

"Yes, that's my point exactly," Syren explained. "It's too dangerous."

"Nope, nope, nope!" complained Braenog emphatically. "Not so dangerous. We must return to Stormwood. Durast, we must return. Fight the Grrremlin. Have rrrevenge!" Braenog was agitated, desperate in his opinion, and Syren could see that he had instantly won his kinsman over.

"Yep, yep," Durast responded. After rolling some *r*'s at Braenog, he turned and looked up hopefully at Syren. "Nog is well. See? We will make new strategy now," he insisted, but Syren shook her head.

"It's easy to feel bold now, but you almost died last night. The risks are not worth the reward."

"Not died, though, quite possibly, nope, nope," replied Braenog, his enthusiasm running ahead of his language skills. Syren remained unconvinced.

"I don't think you're understanding how serious our situation was yesterday," Syren argued. "We were being overwhelmed by the Gremlins, and it happened more than once during that fight. We could have all been slain out there." Syren's face became very serious as she concluded her argument. "It's not just about the danger," she confessed. "I've lost so much to the forest already. If I lost you too, I don't know how I would bear it." The Stouts tugged at their beards in quiet appreciation, like they had the night that Syren explained about her parents. Then Durast took Syren gently by the arm with his oversized hand.

"Nope, nope," he suggested, "it is Syren who doesn't understand how serious our situation is. Kinsman Braenog is from the Silvercore Mountains." When that announcement didn't seem to help Syren's understanding, Durast continued patiently on.

"For generations beyond telling, his clans dwelt there and delved there, harvesting the ore. Traders would come from among the lands of men to buy the ore that makes into sliver, silver like the Palace now demands of Syren. Braenog and his clans had purpose and trrreasure. They had their mountain, and their beards grew long." Syren decided not to interrupt the story to ask what certain expressions meant, as Durast continued the tale.

"Then like an avalanche, came the Grrremlin. The Deepfellows were swept away from Silvercore. Many fought bravely in defense of home and treasure, but some were taken into cruelty. They met their end in despair, their chins exposed, not even allowed to fight. Others, like Braenog, were convinced to flee, in hope of a someday to return and drive out the Grrremlin.

"Because he did not stay to face his doom, he could find no home among my clans. Rejected by the Deepfellows, he was forced to live above us, as a topsider, in disgrace. The ways of our people are deep, but I disagree with this decision. He is not the same as some others who have deserved the name. So I have chosen to braid my beard into his. We are topsiders together, in exile until we can prove our worth to our kinsmen." Syren stared at them both in renewed admiration of their kinship, sacrifice, and loyalty.

"This is why we understand about Syren and her father," Braenog said solemnly.

"This is why we must fight on, now that Nog is back among us and well," Durast explained.

"My life was lost to the Grrremlin," Braenog added earnestly, with imploring eyes, "just as Syren's was lost to Stormwood. To fight them is to have it back again."

The Stouts were right, Syren realized. Some things were worth the risk, the sacrifice. The forest must not win. For the memory of her father, for the sake of the town, and for her own honor, this defeat must be answered. Truly, they had two debts to repay. One was with the Palace and the other was with the forest.

"Okay," she announced finally. "We're back in the salvage business." The Stouts cheered in deep-throated voices accompanied by beard tugging and shoulder slapping. "But from now on, we're going to do things differently," she insisted. "Whenever we can, we're going to make plans, use tactics."

"Strrrategy!" approved Durast eagerly.

"No more barreling in," Syren declared, shaking her finger at Braenog. The older Stout stuck out his lower lip prominently, but Syren's scolding expression would not be refused.

"Yep, yep," he conceded begrudgingly. "To the forest then?" he asked, raising his hedge-like eyebrows.

"Not quite yet," Syren clarified. "We were on our way to Oswald's when you arrived. We have salvage to sell, remember? Oh, uh, actually you don't remember that, but we do."

As they walked through the damp air in the direction of Oswald's Venture Salvage, Durast reported to Braenog everything that had happened while he was unconscious and away from them. The story, which was punctuated by many yeps and rolling *r*'s, included an enthusiastic account of Syren's fight with Baron and the recovery of her father's sword, as well as a description of the jar of healing salve and what they had learned about it.

"Syren," Durast suggested once the subject had come up, "since we are salvaging again, we should keep the healing salve, and not show it to Aglar Grump."

"Yes, you're right," she agreed. "Can you hang onto it for now?"

"Yep, yep," he assured her, and taking the jar from her, he placed it inside his shirt and beneath his beard, so the bulge didn't show.

Upon arrival, they encountered Syren's cousin Quig, who was just leaving the shop as the trio were entering.

"Hi, Syren!" the youth exclaimed happily.

"Hi, Quig. What are you doing here?" For a moment, Syren gained a concerned expression. "Don't tell me that you've signed on as a salvager?"

"Oh, goodness no, nothing like that," the boy assured her. "I've just been doing some shopping."

"Shopping?"

"Yeah. Look, I just bought this rare flower. It's a Canabal plant, right from Stormwood! They say it's poisonous, even to touch it. I had to sign a paper and everything!"

"Isn't that the tulip he tried to sell us?" Braenog asked Durast.

"Quig," Syren began, "I don't think that—"

"Did you come to sell some stuff you salvaged? Baron's in there now. That's what he's doing. He's got a black eye. It's a real shiner! Did you give that to him?"

"Listen, there was—"

"He says that he got it fighting with Gremlins yesterday, but I heard this morning that he was in a scuffle at the Hooded Crow last night. Some people are saying that you pounded him! Is that what happened?" Syren didn't want to encourage that kind of thing in Quig, but a grin escaped her face when she recalled the satisfaction of it.

"Wow! You guys must really hate each other! Imagine, my cousin battling to be the best salvager in Westpost!"

"Quig, it's not like that—"

"I bet you showed him a thing or two!"

"People are making more out of it than it was," she managed to say.

"I have to go," the boy apologized, calling back to them as he hurried away, "Gotta put some water on this plant. Mr. Grump said that if I don't, it'll get hungry and eat somebody. See you later!"

Shaking her head, Syren and her companions entered Oswald's Venture Salvage just as Aglar Grump was finishing his transaction with Baron in his usual, fast-talking style.

"What else have you got? That's it? One measly item? How are you going to work off the money you owe me at this rate? You're lucky I don't tear up your contract and call in the debt! Why can't you bring in a wagon full of stuff like Syren does? You're a waste of good burlap! Syren! Good to see you guys. I'll be right with you." Having noticed Syren and company and the sack they were carrying, the cunning businessman changed his manner abruptly. He was still speaking at Baron, but it was clear that most of what he said was aimed at Syren.

"Good work here, Baron, you probably brought me the best salvage item in Westpost. If only Syren could bring me valuable stuff like this. Here's a bonus silver for risking your neck. Buy some raw meat for that eye. Now, get back out there, my man, and by that I mean, go away." Grumbling, Baron gave Syren a wide berth as he left the shop. She did likewise for him as she approached the counter.

"Well, Syren, I hope you guys are as good at salvaging as you are at getting into bar fights. What do you mean, beating up my best salvager like that?"

"I thought we were your best salvagers," Braenog objected.

"It depends on the day," Aglar retorted brusquely. "I thought you were dead. May you rest in peace." He put his hand over his heart.

"We've come with salvage," Durast pointed out. "We want to be paid."

"Of course you do," he complained dryly. "All right, let's see what you've got, but it had better be good. Baron just brought in some real salvage. Look at this!" He held up a Gremlin hand ax for them to see. "It's Gremlin. From Stormwood, no less. The bar is officially raised, my friends. No more paying good silver for rickety old junk. If you want to impress this wily old shopkeeper, you've got to do even better than one of these!"

Syren looked down at Durast expectantly and raised one eyebrow. Without a word, he handed her the burlap sack. When she upended it, a small horde of treasures tumbled out onto the counter top for Aglar to see. Altogether, there were three bracelets and four necklaces, six jerkins made from some coarse and untanned hide, the much weathered (and now empty) wooden box, four small Gremlin shields, and eight stone axes like the one Aglar had just been proudly waving at them. The "jewelry" was all made from small pieces of quartz or agate, combined with the bones or teeth of dead Hiddeans. At the first sight of everything, the proprietor gasped and his eyes went wide with greed, but he quickly recovered himself, feigning a cough. From somewhere outside, Syren thought she could hear music playing.

"By the mysteries...er...that is"—*cough*—"what do you mean, trying to pass off trash like this?"

"Oh, no. No, no, no, no. We saw that look!" Syren accused.

"No, you didn't. What look?"

"The 'I'm about to make a pile of money' look," she described.

"Nonsense!" Aglar claimed, trying to distract them. "My looks are the same as always: poor and dashingly handsome." Syren pressed on, ignoring his excuses.

"This is legitimate salvage from Stormwood. It's valuable. You know it, and we know you know it!" The music was getting louder, like the musicians were walking up the road toward the salvage shop.

"All right, all right," he conceded impatiently. "Since I'm such an old softy, I'll give in to your bullying. Here." He dropped a small pouch onto the counter in front of Durast. It landed with a chink. "I'll give you twenty silvers for the lot."

"Are you crazy?" Syren protested. "Try two hundred."

"Impossible!" he countered. "I'll give you thirty. *Now* I'm crazy." Aglar was getting agitated, like the music was making him nervous. Periodically, he would glance out the front window.

"For genuine Gremlin artifacts from Stormwood?" Syren countered. "One seventy-five."

"What, do you think I'm made out of money?"

"Yes!" they all answered emphatically.

"This stuff won't even sell. You've created a glut in the market."

"We've created?" Syren complained. "A glut? What are you talking about?"

"How do you think I'm going to move eight Gremlin war axes at the price they're worth?"

"Ah-hah!" exclaimed Durast. "So they *are* valuable!" Aglar stabbed his finger in the Stout's direction, speaking more quickly than ever.

"Forget I said that. The point is, there aren't enough buyers in this town. I'd be inventory rich and money poor for months. Then how would I buy the next fabulous thing that wandered out of Stormwood, hmm? I'd have to sell these things at a loss. You should have gotten here before Baron. It was a seller's market ten minutes ago, but things change. That's business for you. I'll give you thirty-five silvers. Last offer."

Exhaling a huff of exasperation, Syren was just about to admit defeat and accept the offer when a noisy parade began to pass in front of the window, outside of Aglar's shop. Turning, she saw a trio of large, covered wagons roll by. Each one was being pulled by four draft horses, and they were accompanied by a group of serious-looking mercenary fighters. The walkers were dressed in long leather coats. They wore short swords at their belts and brandished sturdy cudgels that they also used as walking sticks. Perched alongside each driver was a pair of archers, whose longbows stood at rest beside them as they took in the sights of the village. The whole company was announcing its entrance into Westpost by the troupe of minstrels (pipers, drummers, and lute players) that had jumped out of the wagons to lead the procession from the main gate to the Village

Green. These were the source of the lively music that Syren had heard approaching while she was negotiating with Aglar Grump.

A merchant caravan had come to town from the larger civilized cities of the eastern side of the kingdom.

The uncommon event was causing a stir among the villagers, who were abandoning the routines of their neighborhoods to follow the newcomers to town center. The commotion of curiosity and excitement, which hummed around the slowly moving caravan like bees around a hive, gave Syren the inspiration she needed to solve her dilemma.

"Look!" she commanded at Aglar, gesturing emphatically toward the procession with a sweep of her arm. "A caravan has come to town. Merchants from Centerville or Angloria, or some other big eastern city. This is your big chance! You could sell all this stuff today. Instant profits. One-day turnaround."

Staring out the window as the wagons passed, Aglar was beginning to look like a starving man who got set before a feast.

"I'll give you forty for the sackful," he offered quickly. Donning a smart-looking brown leather cap with a read cloth band, he had begun to place the salvage back into the burlap sack as though the deal was already struck. His mind was on its way to town with the stuff, planning slick salesmanship talk for the big city merchants, but Syren stomped her hand roughly over the sack to stop him and keep his attention.

"You're going to make twenty times that!" she complained.

"Instant profits," he replied. "You said it yourself." He grabbed at the sack to take it away from Syren, but Durast reached up and took hold of the bag with his big hands. A tug of war ensued as Aglar and Syren continued their frantic negotiating.

"I meant for both of us. Give us the two hundred."

"Robbery! Where are the guards when you need them? I'll give you fifty."

"One eighty then," Syren countered. Already, the wagons had moved on from outside the shop. Their music was fading into the distance as they rolled on toward the center of town. Aglar was growing desperate and agitated, and Syren knew that the advantage was hers.

"Sixty. Not a copper more!" He was hauling on the sack, trying aggressively to wrench it from Durast's grasp. Meanwhile, the Stout stood in passive defiance, tugging back just sharply enough to drag Aglar back awkwardly to the counter. Syren spoke smoothly and calmly into Aglar's growing frustration.

"That caravan's going to set up on the Village Green, Aglar. Right next to Laustin's place, probably. They're wealthy merchants, no doubt, but even they only have so much coin. It's a seller's market now, but once they spend their money on Laustin's junk and Edgeworthy's trinkets, well, that's business for you," she reminded, stabbing Aglar with his own words. Then she added, "We'll take one seventy. Then off you go, if you can get there quickly enough, that is."

"You can't sell this stuff to anyone but me!" he warned. "Do you mean to tell me that you would cut off your nose to spite my face?" Syren crossed her arms in front of her, in silent affirmation. Aglar ground his teeth angrily at her as his gaze flicked nervously out the window. Braenog stood in the street with his hand shading his eyes, watching the caravan roll into the distance. The music was all but gone. Releasing his hold on the burlap sack, he retreated briefly to the back room, grumbling to himself, and returned with a small sack of coins.

"One hundred forty," he spat desperately, tossing the bag onto the counter. "And you can have my hat!" Snatching it off his head, he threw it onto the counter in front of them in exasperation. Durast let go of the sack to grab up the bag of coins and peer into it. Syren put one hand down on the counter, looking to Durast for confirmation.

"Ooo!" he said reflexively as he studied its contents. Satisfied, Syren yielded the sack to Aglar, who began hurriedly stuffing it full.

"You can keep your hat," she conceded. Popping it roughly back into place with a glare, he finished gathering the salvage he had just bought, ushered them all impatiently out the door so he could lock it, and bustled off after the caravan.

Syren watched him shrink into the distance until he disappeared among the other villagers who were moving in that direction. Meanwhile, her companions ogled the collection of fourteen gold coins they had received as a result of their haggling.

"Syren, you see?" Durast proclaimed. "All is good again. Nog is well and Syren sells salvage. Now, we return to Stormwood."

"Yep, yep," approved Braenog, and the two Stouts began walking toward the Wallgate, still discussing their plan with each other.

"Fight Grrremlin," suggested Durast.

"Take rrrrevenge!" returned Braenog.

"Get trrreasure!"

"Yep."

"Yep, yep."

"Yep," they said.

"Wait! Hold on," Syren called after them. The Stouts turned and blinked at Syren quizzically. "No barreling in, remember?" she reminded.

"But this is not barreling," Durast assured her. "Syren has her father's sword. The Deepfellows endure. We have alchemy." Durast patted his chest, where he was storing the jar of healing salve. Syren put her hands on her hips.

"Have we discussed strategy," she asked scoldingly, "or are we just marching off to Stormwood again?" The Stouts began to fidget. As they looked to each other for answers, they pointed first to the gate, then to Syren and to each other, then to the gate again, until finally they stood still in the dusty street, tugging their beards sheepishly. Syren walked over to them.

"I understand your eagerness to get back at the Gremlins," she told them earnestly. "I want to as well, but we have an opportunity that doesn't come up every day. We should see to that first." The Stouts blinked up at her, confused, so she explained.

"Those wagons that came to town are a caravan from one of the big cities. They usually carry wares of various kinds that people around here don't have and can't make. Often, merchants will come hoping to sell weapons and armor to the prince for his soldiers. I have a weapon now, but you guys don't. We could buy you each one, and maybe some armor too, or a shield, depending on what things cost." The Stouts considered the idea with interest.

"But are we not trying to save our money, to give to the Palace?" Braenog asked.

"Yes, of course," Syren answered. "Think, though, about how ineffective our Hiddean spears were against the Gremlins and how tragically that almost ended for us. It's like they're experienced in defending against and defeating the Hiddeans. They're tougher creatures. The Hiddeans bully us and they bully the Hiddeans. If we're going to get the better of them without having to leave someone with the alchemist each time, we're going to need something that gives us an advantage. The caravan is our chance to do that, and it doesn't come very often. I think that if we spend some of our money now, we'll save a lot of hardship, injury, and expense later on."

The plan seemed "deep" to the Stouts, so instead of heading straight into the wilderness, Syren and her companions followed the music and the growing crowds toward the Village Green to see what the traveling merchants had brought. On their way, they discussed another mystery that was puzzling them.

"What do you suppose Aglar meant about Baron repaying his debt?" Braenog asked.

"Maybe he paid off what Baron owes the Palace," Syren speculated.

"Why would he do that?"

"He does not seem to be a generous fellow," observed Durast.

"No, he sure doesn't," agreed Syren. "He probably didn't want to lose Baron as a salvager. Annoying as he is, he does keep after it."

"Even so, there must be some gain for Aglar," Braenog supposed.

"Indeed. Maybe Baron is working it off. You know, he brings in salvage, Aglar keeps back a portion of what it's worth and applies it toward what he owes."

"At the rates Aglar pays, Baron will be Aglar's man for the rest of his life." They all chuckled briefly, thinking about the justice of it.

"I wonder why Baron didn't register a complaint after last night's fight at the tavern," Syren observed. "I more than half-expected that another summons would come looking for us when we woke up this morning. It's not like him to be humble in defeat—or otherwise, for that matter."

"It was humiliation, not humility," suggested Durast.

"How do you mean?"

"Jessero says that popularity matters much to Baron. To complain, he would need to admit to everyone that he was trounced by a young lass and that he needed help to get even. Not good for popularity."

"Get even? I thought we were even. That's what last night was about."

"Topsiders like Baron are not *even* unless they are more even than you."

"Yeah, you've got a point there," Syren acknowledged.

As they came upon the Green, they beheld a milling throng engaged in the activities of hopeful chaos. The three merchant wagons had spaced themselves out around the circle. Their canvass covers had been stowed, transforming the travel wagons into peddler's shops, ready for public business. Kept under the watchful eye of their drivers and handlers, the draft horses had been unhitched and were placidly grazing in the center of the Green, while Morgan the blacksmith attended them with an expert hand. The arrangement of the wagons allowed enough room that shoppers and sellers could crowd around all three, which they had.

Everywhere they looked, villagers were happily shouting over each other's conversations and pushing past each other. Some were merely enjoying the excitement and community of the day, browsing the vendors' wares and sharing stories. Among them, Syren caught sight of Jessero, who was chatting amiably with a couple of the mercenary soldiers about their travels and encounters along the way. Most of the people were clamoring for the attention of one merchant or other. Buyers in the crowd waived cloth pouches of coins over their heads, indicating their desire and ability to make a purchase. Others, hoping to sell items of local produce, were also vying for the notice of the merchants. Burke had managed to get close enough to one wagon to hand up one of his clay pots for examination. A cold wind had begun to swirl around them all, a warning of oncoming rains from a darkening sky.

"Where do we begin?" Durast asked. "Which wagon has what we want and how do we get to it?"

"We may as well look at everything," Syren advised. "We know more or less what we're shopping for, so we'll know it when we see it."

Syren worked her way deftly through the jostling crowd, with Stouts in tow, until she had approached the wagon nearest their position. That one, it turned out, belonged to representatives of Pate's Haberdashery and Wardrobe, one of the larger clothing manufacturers in Centerville. From aboard it, the proprietor and several helpers were holding up various articles for the people to see, while the merchant promoted the qualities of each item. There were hats, shirts, dresses, gloves, scarves, skirts, leggings, stockings, and bolts of cloth in a wide range of colors. Some of the articles were made from exotic materials, silks, or fine linen. Others were richly embroidered and elegant in their design.

Syren was fascinated.

"How would you wear a sword with an outfit like that?" Braenog inquired derisively to Durast.

"Hush!" Syren scolded. From the rear gate end of the wagon, a worker was handing down to Jack Frost a variety of skullcaps, which he was examining with great interest. The rush and thrill of everyone's admiration for the fine attire, and the company of people around her who were offering up bags of coin for certain items made Syren want to buy something for herself. Just some small thing, perhaps.

"This is not what we have come to buy," Durast reminded, tugging on Syren's arm. "Our treasure is not deep. If we are to keep some back to pay the Palace and have weapons, we must be careful."

"Yes, yes, of course," Syren agreed reluctantly, without looking away. "I just want to see what they have. Look at that one. Aren't they beautiful? It's like watching a play!" Durast and Braenog stood beside Syren for a short while, arms folded across their barrel-like chests, until boredom overtook them.

"Watch your play," Durast conceded at length. "We will go look for weapons."

"Yep, yep," encouraged Braenog.

"Yeah, sure," Syren acknowledged, waiving absently toward them as they walked away. "I'll catch up with you in a bit," she promised.

Syren sighed. Her life had been devoid of the finer things, for the most part, and it was fun to imagine wearing elegant outfits like the ones being shown. Out here, though, on the western frontier of the kingdom, it was difficult to justify or afford such frivolous luxuries. Anyway, she valued being the capable and practical sort. She didn't really want to be a porcelain doll in a shop window. Perhaps one day, if she could ever get ahead of the daily struggle, there would be room to enjoy just a little bit of frivolity. For now, though, Durast was right. There were certainly more important demands upon her money.

After what seemed like several minutes (she had rather lost track of the time), Syren decided that she ought to find out what was becoming of her Stoutish friends and see what they had discovered. Weaving her way through the crowd, she eventually spotted them. They were standing amid a group of jolly revelers, grinning broadly and exchanging pleasantries with people, as though they had not a care in the world. Nearby them was a wagon from the caravan that was loaded with a great number of crates and barrels. As she approached, Syren could see lettering on one of the kegs that read,

"Specter's Spirits." Most of the people around her were sampling various ales, vintages, and spirits from very small wooden cups. The proprietor appeared to be handing these out for free, along with descriptions of each and encouragements that they should tell the tavern keeper about any sample they liked.

Instead of the tiny sample cups, however, Durast and Braenog were wielding tankards. Just as she arrived on the scene, Braenog hoisted his kinsman awkwardly onto his shoulders. Though somewhat precarious, this arrangement rendered Durast tall enough to get the proprietor's attention, whereupon he handed over both mugs to be filled with ale. For that amount, to Syren's dismay, he was paying a small fee. Then once both Stouts were again at ground level, they clanked their mugs together merrily and lifted them to their mouths.

When they did so, Braenog spotted Syren coming toward them disapprovingly through the crowd. Nudging Durast with his elbow, Braenog tried sheepishly to evade the guilt of his activity by hiding his tankard underneath his beard.

"What do you think you're doing?" Syren demanded. "What happened to all that talk about not spending money frivolously?"

"Thirst is not frivolous," Durast replied simply.

"But they're giving the stuff away!" she argued, gesturing around her.

"Barely enough to wet the tongue," Durast gruffed. "This is a proper taste," he said lifting up his mug.

"Yep, yep," Braenog agreed instructively to Syren, nodding at her and pulling his mug out from beneath his beard. Syren exhaled in resigned frustration.

"I thought we were here shopping for weapons to assail Stormwood with."

"Yep, yep," acknowledged Durast while raking foam from his mustache with his lower lip, "the spirits wagon is also a venture salvage buyer. The owner lady is around the other side."

Circling to the far side of the wagon, Syren and company encountered a fit-looking middle-aged woman with sharp, leathery, tanned features. She was dressed in mauve-colored silks, covered by a leather vest, chaps, and knee length leather boots. Her coarse sand-colored hair was tied behind her head. Unlike the salvage shop owners in Westpost, this woman looked to Syren like she had once been a salvager herself. A number of people were milling about the table she had set up, and as she answered their questions about what various objects were and what they cost, her accent spoke of lands far away, beyond the kingdom's borders.

"Well, there's a hearty troop of salvagers if ever I saw one!" The woman greeted Syren and the Stouts. "I'm Anne, of Anne Teak's Venture Salvage. Are you looking to sell some things? 'Cause I'm buyin'!" As they got close to the table and drew the gregarious woman's attention, they noticed that she wore an eye patch on the left side, the color of which closely matched that of her leathery skin, and she was missing the small finger from her left hand. Syren smiled back at her.

"Actually, we're looking…um, that is, we're hoping to buy some things," Syren stammered, instantly conscious of the eye reference.

"Oh, don't worry about the patch, honey," Anne insisted, dismissing the comment with a wave of her four-fingered hand. "I got over that years ago. *I lost this eye from stealing treasure from a two-headed dragon!*" she proclaimed dramatically to the onlookers, who gasped appreciatively. Then she leaned in toward Syren. "Truth is, I got slashed in a combat against some Orcs, the savages. That was a long time ago. It ended my wilderness career, but I stay in the game by connecting with caravans like this one. By dealing in salvage, I still get to travel about and stay close to the work, and thanks to the eye of a hundred stories"—she tapped herself on the forehead, above the patch—"I practically never buy my own meals in a town! Now then, let's talk shop. I came out all this way expecting more to buy stuff than to sell it, but you never know. I might have what you need. What are you looking for?"

"Cleavage!" Durast announced confidently. Anne raised her eyebrow at him while resting her hands on her hips.

"Are you indeed?" she asked, amused. Syren cleared her throat.

"He's referring to edged weapons, I think," she explained as her face reddened. "You know, like a butcher's cleaver?" Durast was looking confounded.

"That's what I said, was it not?" he defended. Anne chuckled forgivingly while the Stouts looked at each other quizzically.

"Weapons are what we need most right now," Syren affirmed. She scolded Durast again with her gaze, which he returned with an innocent shrug of his own. Then she glanced about at the curiosities Anne had on display.

"See that? You're in luck!" Anne announced, clapping her hands once together and pointing at the trio. "I just got in a supply of weapons today. How about one of these?" The woman reached into a sack she had been keeping behind her. Pulling out a familiar Gremlin hand ax, she presented it to Syren for examination, but Syren declined.

"Thanks, but I think we're in the market for something a little less…rustic. Also, a weapon that extends our reach would be helpful." She flicked her gaze in the Stouts direction, and Anne nodded.

"Ah, of course."

"What is this?" Braenog asked. He was examining a cork-stoppered vial that contained a syrupy, reddish fluid.

"That, my short friend, is a rare alchemical elixir!" All three of the companions paused to wonder at it.

"How can you tell?" Syren asked, hoping to gain some insight. "I mean, you got it from some salvager somewhere, right? How do you know that it's the genuine article?" The old salvager was happy to show off her expertise, by way of explanation.

"Most alchemical compounds, in my experience, fall into one of two categories: salves or elixirs. Salves are for external use, as the name suggests. Elixirs take effect only if you swallow them."

"How do you know which is which and what they are for?" asked Durast.

"As a general rule, salves are thick and elixirs are runny, though that's not always the case. If you know an alchemist, you can just ask them. Otherwise, it's trial and error, pretty much. Get a dab on your finger and spread it on your skin. If it's a salve, that'll tell you what it does. If nothing happens, it's probably an elixir. For those, you have to taste them.

"So what does this one do?" Syren asked.

"It's a potion of forgetfulness!" Anne announced proudly. Then absently she added, "At least I think it is."

"Interesting," Syren encouraged, taking the vial from Braenog and returning it carefully to the table, "but not really what we're looking for."

"No, probably not," Anne agreed. "Say, how about healing salve? I've got some of that." She held up a small jar for their inspection. When Syren opened it, there was a small quantity of the same oily greenish substance that they already owned at least five times as much of. "I can let you have that for a hundred silvers." She offered.

"No thanks," Syren returned, thinking of how much their own jar of the stuff must be worth. "What about this?" she asked, hoisting a chain mail head skirt off the table for investigation. It was rusty and tattered and had clearly been lying on the forest floor for some while before coming into Anne Teak's possession, but Syren thought it worth asking about. Some measure of protective gear would certainly be useful, if they could get it affordably.

"Oh, that's Lucky's headpiece," Anne replied jauntily. "I can part with that for eighty silvers." Syren raised her eyebrows in surprise at the price. Turning the item around, she showed Anne the gaping hole where the head skirt had yielded to some massive blow. Anne shrugged apologetically.

"Yeah, that was Lucky's misfortune," she admitted. "I realize that it's worth less to you because of the damage, but it's worth more to me that way. That's why I have to ask eighty. I know I can get that much for it in Centerville, especially if I slap a story onto it." Syren handed it back to Anne.

"I think we'll pass," she affirmed.

"Like I said, I'm here mostly to buy. That's why I share expenses with Abel Specter. He empties the wagon of his treasures out here, and then I fill it up with mine for the trip home. I should be around for a couple of days. If you gain any salvage, come find me. I pay good money!"

"Thanks, but we can't. We're under contract. We work for one of the local salvage owners, Aglar Grump."

"Oh. I'm sorry," she said earnestly. Then she added, "Hey, if you're looking for new weapons, something with an edge on it, try across the Green, there. Those folks are from Link's Chain Mail Outfitters and Lance's Reach. They're here mainly to sell arms and armor to the Palace, but I'm sure they'd deal with anyone who has coin."

Thanking Anne, they left her telling embellished stories to interested potential buyers, and worked their way through the crowd toward the third great wagon. When they arrived, they saw that workers were arranging sheets of impressive-looking chain mail. The sections had clasps at the edges, which allowed them to be hooked together. Metalsmiths wearing heavy leather aprons wielded specialized tools for the purpose of forming customized suits of armor out of the sheets of interwoven metal ringlets, according to the needs of each of the prince's soldiers. Also on board, in another area of the wagon, was a varied collection of gleaming weaponry. Syren looked down at the Stouts, who were grinning broadly at the spectacle.

"Looks like we've come to the right place," she suggested. Then waving her arm, she called up to one of the busily working craftsmen, to get his attention.

"Hey, how much for a suit of chain mail?" she asked. The bald, burly man called back his answer without looking away from his work.

"Seventeen hundred. Maybe more, depending on how tall." In midsentence, he glanced up from his work to see Durast and Braenog blinking up at him eagerly and checked his answer. "Or maybe a little less," he finished, studying them with an expert eye. Syren, convinced that in any case, armor was not affordable, changed the topic of inquiry.

"We've come shopping for weapons, actually," she said, hoping they wouldn't also turn out to be too expensive.

"Talk to Kadan," he said, jerking his thumb toward the rear of the wagon. "He'll show you around. Hey, Kadan!" A thin man with short black hair and a goatee looked over from where he was, polishing a sword with oil and a cloth. "These people want weapons." The weaponer set his tools down, wiping his hands on a rag as Syren and the Stouts walked over to where he was standing.

"These two men are looking for something shiny and sharp," Syren informed the merchant, indicating Durast and Braenog.

"Okay. How about these, then?" Judging them based on their short stature, the seller, Kadan, handed down a pair of daggers. The blades were about a foot long, and the handles about four inches. Durast and Braenog looked almost offended. Taking hold of them by the hilts with thumb and forefinger, they held them up at arm's length and stared at them, the way one might consider a dead animal.

"We're in the market for something a little larger," Syren explained tactfully. "We do venture salvage in the wilderness. It's fairly aggressive work. Sometimes we need to strike forcefully." Kadan took the daggers back, nodding his head understandingly.

"The best way to defend is to press the attack," he echoed. "Try these."

In the next several minutes, Kadan showed the Stouts a variety of swords of varying lengths and shapes. They were beautiful instruments, gleaming and smooth. Durast and Braenog were partial to heftier blades. Regardless of design, though, they encountered a recurring problem in the grips. None of them fit their oversized hands adequately. Many of the sword hilts came with knuckle guards that were, naturally, made to accommodate human hands. As a result, Durast and Braenog couldn't fit their hands inside of them, and grasping the entire handle from around the outside, guard and all, proved awkward and uncomfortable.

"What about those?" Durast asked. He pointed to a pair of axes that featured large, wide blades that were mounted onto short, thick wooden handles. They were being held onto a wooden placard by brackets. The axes crossed over each other, with the blade edges facing outward.

"What? Those?" Kadan confirmed incredulously. "No, no. You can't use those. They aren't real weapons. I mean, they are, they're steel and oak and sharp, and all that. But they aren't made for wielding. They're just part of the sign that I put up to announce my trade. That's why they're oversized like that, so people can see them from a distance."

Durast was eager to heft them, despite Kadan's disclaimer, waving them toward him with his massive hands.

"You don't understand," the weaponer stressed, taking one down from its perch. "The handles are too short for ax heads of this size. They aren't balanced for swinging. They're overly top heavy. You see?" He handed it down to Durast, to prove his point. As soon as the Stout grasped the fat, sturdy handle in his right hand, though, a broad white-toothed grin broke out on his face. He deftly made a few practice cuts in the air with the item, then asked to have the other one handed down to him.

"Both?" Kadan asked. "I don't see why you'd want one of them, never mind wanting a spare." When Durast got ahold of the other one, he wielded both of the heavy axes about him effortlessly, using one as a counterbalance as he swung the other. Then he chuckled a deep, hearty laugh and rolled some *r*'s at the axes in approval.

Meanwhile, Braenog had settled upon a more conventional poleax. It was a double bladed affair, on a long handle. The weapon was taller than he was, but he found the grip suitably comfortable and declared the balance as well as the reach to be "deep" when he swung it with both hands together.

"Hey, what about that? Is that for sale?" Syren asked, indicating a small, dented shield. It bore a host of scratches and scuffs and had lost its sheen to time and use.

"No, that's my shield," Kadan deferred. "If you want a new shield, though, we've got—"

"Can I see it?" Syren pressed. Kadan threw up his hands.

"Sure. Why not?" He handed it down to her. Hefting it, she found it not too heavy to wield but still large enough to protect her midsection.

"I'll take it!" she announced.

"But that's not, I mean, we didn't even, that is…it's mine," Kadan objected finally.

"Isn't all this stuff yours, essentially?" Syren pushed.

"Well…yes. I suppose so."

"And you're here to sell stuff, right?"

"Yeah."

"So sell us this stuff," she said, motioning to all the items they held. "How much do you want for it?" Kadan stood, scratching his head as he looked down at them.

"Well, let's see. You've got one poleax, my old shield, and a… sign." Durast grinned broadly again at his find. "Two hundred silvers," Kadan concluded.

"For an old shield and a sign?" Syren complained.

"For the only sign your friend can wield, sold by the only weapons maker in town, who will only be in town for a day or two," countered Kadan. Syren considered silently for a pair of moments.

"How about one hundred fifty?" she offered.

"One seventy-five," he returned, "and I'll throw in a whetstone and an oilcloth." Syren looked to Durast, who hefted both axes and then nodded back to her.

"Done," she said. It had begun to drizzle.

CHAPTER 11

Better Mettle

The rain was good because it was good for everyone's garden, but it was bad for businesses. It kept people indoors. The rain was worse for salvagers, far worse than the clingy inconvenience of getting soaked through from head to toe or the risk of getting sick afterward. Heavy raindrops splattering everywhere in the forest at once, combined with the wind howling through the flashing foliage, tended to catch the eye and cover the ear. It became very difficult to discern the difference between that and dangerous creatures that might be moving within the forest nearby. Conditions such as these made it easy for even normally alert salvagers to get ambushed by any of the myriad savages that stalked the wilds around Westpost. Add to that the slippery footing, the thunder that rolled deeply overhead like a chorus of giant Stouts, and the natural tendency to hunch and hunker from the elements during such times instead of being lithe and wary, and it became obvious that attempting venture salvage in the rain was a disaster in the making.

Eager though they were to test their newly acquired weaponry against the evils of Stormwood and begin again to raise the required tribute that they seemed always to be spending instead of saving, Syren, Durast, and Braenog had decided to wait out the inclement weather. The gray threat that had loomed above them the entire day in which the caravan had come to town had finally broken out upon them all, man and beast, house and forest. Two days of steady rain had been followed by two more days of soggy, sloppy ground before Syren and Durast determined that conditions were again favorable for a trip to the wilderness. It was a wiser, though less satisfying, strategy than any of them would have liked, especially Braenog, but at last they were ready.

Leaving the long shadows of the Wallgate behind them, Syren led her Stoutish companions into the Nearwood north of town, with weapons in hand, burlap sacks tucked into their belts, and the encroaching twilight all around them.

"This is the path to the Grrremlin?" Braenog asked eagerly.

"Not directly," Syren confessed.

"Which way, then, to the Grremlin?" he protested, searching around him as if he could find it.

"I understand your wish to have at them," Syren explained sympathetically, searching the surrounding wilderness warily as they walked. Durast rolled some *r*'s. "Keep in mind, though, that these weapons of ours are new to us. They're untested, as is our ability to wield them against actual foes. Practically speaking, Durast's axes aren't even real weapons. It makes sense to break them in against an enemy we have confidence in facing."

"I have confidence against the Gremlin," assured Braenog.

"I'm sure," conceded Syren. "Even so, I am more comfortable trying my sword against the Hiddeans before seeking out heartier targets."

Braenog gruffed his disapproval.

"Besides," Syren went on, "It'll be dark soon, which is a good time to encounter groups of savages, but a bad time to be far from the Wallgate. We can't take on the whole forest, however confident we are."

Braenog seemed poutingly unconvinced by Syren's cautious logic, but Durast crossed over to him.

"Remember that Hiddeans are for Syren as the Grrremlin are for Nog," he explained. Syren didn't fully agree with the comparison, but the truth was in that direction, at least, and she was glad to see that the younger Stout's words had satisfied Braenog's thirst for immediate vengeance entirely.

Suddenly, a volley of stones came flying at the group from behind the grove of trees that surrounded them. The barrage klunked against them and fell among them. No real damage was caused, but it made the trio crouch and cover their heads instinctively with their arms to guard against being stunned by a lucky strike.

"Look out!" Syren called. "They're throwing rocks!"

In the next moments, they found themselves encircled by a small horde of Hiddeans. They were snarling and stinking and advancing on them in a rush, seizing the advantage that the stony hail had provided. Syren drew her father's sword from its scabbard, took up her shield, and set herself nervously against the fetid assault, but before she could devise any sort of tactic, they were upon her. Two of the little fiends tried to grab onto her and set her off her feet, while a third brandished one of the familiar-looking wretched spears, readying it for a disabling thrust.

Syren had never wielded a real sword in combat, and her first attempt at it was awkward and only mildly effective. Ambushed as they were, her first instinct was to defend herself against the charge. Fearfully, she shoved at the nearest of the Hiddeans with her shield. The effect pushed the creature off, and it collapsed into a pile of itself a short distance away, momentarily stunned. At the same time, Syren swept her sword arm somewhat wildly at the encroaching spear wielder. The blade, which had not really been aimed at anything, missed her attacker but knocked the spear aside with sufficient force to send it flying from the creature's hands. Finding itself suddenly disarmed, that Hiddean broke off the attack to go retrieve its weapon from where it landed. Syren's third assailant latched on to her leg as planned and wrenched at it, but without the help of the other, Syren's balance was not upset.

Meanwhile, Durast and Braenog had taken their axes in hand and stridden robustly away from Syren, into the chattering morass that came descending upon the group from behind.

"Strong and sure shall Deepfellows endure!" they both promised aloud. Syren didn't see their initial swings, but the screeches of the enemy told her that the Stouts had begun well.

Syren wanted to vanquish the foe who was attached to her leg, but her sword was so long that she couldn't bring it to bear at such close range. Instead, she banged the creature hard on the head with her shield. The impact caused the Hiddean to let go of its hold on her. Stepping away from it, Syren was accosted by another spear wielder. She couldn't tell if it was the same one as before or a different one, but in any case, she made a sweeping motion with her sword again, effectively turning aside an attack that would otherwise have impaled her thigh.

Another volley of stones came at her, and she hunkered behind her shield to fend them off. Standing, she looked briefly across the battle in time to see Braenog keeping a host of the feral beasts at bay with menacing sweeps of his two-handed poleax. By the looks of it, he had already slain one of the creatures, which was inspiring great caution in several others. Durast, swinging both of his heavy hand axes in alternating succession, was chasing after opponents rather than allow them to throw rocks at him from out of range. Between the sharpness of his new weapons and the great strength he could assign to the blows, any of the Hiddeans who closed on his position to attack fell before him with a single strike.

Of Syren's two companions, only Durast seemed injured. One of the Hiddean spears was protruding from his side, the point sticking out behind him. The wound didn't seem to be slowing the younger Stout down, though. It was possible that the spear was only sticking through his clothes and had not (or not severely) engaged his flesh. Syren's neighborhood had become lively again, however, and since Durast didn't seem to be in distress, she turned her attention away from her friends to address more pressing matters.

Another group of Hiddeans had closed on her. Again, some were trying to haul her off her feet so others could finish her off.

Waving her sword at two of them, to keep them out of reach, she bashed two more with the front of her shield, which made them stagger back from her and her from them. When she moved from the position, though, they pursued, and Syren realized suddenly that she was making two mistakes in this skirmish. Firstly, because of the initial surprise of the ambush and the Hiddeans' chattering, frenzied attack, she had reacted with alarm and fright, and she was still doing so. That was making her look like prey. As a result, she was drawing groups of Hiddeans to her. She was constantly back on her heels, and that was a perilous way to fight a battle.

Secondly, she noticed that she had been thrusting with her shield and parrying with her sword the whole time. That was the opposite of what she should be doing. No wonder she hadn't seriously wounded any of her opponents yet. No wonder they weren't seeing her as dangerous!

This time, when the vile troop rushed her again, she stood her ground. As the nearest one came within reach, Syren cut an arc with the leading edge of her sword, as swiftly as she could, from a point near her left shoulder to the ground near her right foot. Timing it perfectly caused the neck of her attacker to run right into the swing. Not only did the strike wound her opponent, but it severed its mangy head entirely as effortlessly as she might have sliced a potato back home.

The three others, already committed to their plan, rushed at her viciously. Instead of pushing at the two "wrestlers," though, as she had done earlier, she stepped toward the spear wielder and took his attack on her shield. This splintered his pitiful wooden stick, rendering it useless. It also put just enough distance between her and the other two foes that when, she turned on them, she had the space she needed to skewer one of them, killing it on the spot.

Having a Hiddean impaled on her blade made wielding it against another opponent difficult. Syren hadn't anticipated that, and for a moment, she wasn't quite sure how to deal with it. The change in her fighting style (and its effectiveness), however, had overwhelmed what little courage the Hiddeans had. While she wrenched her sword free of the dead Hiddean's body, the rest fled for the forest. Turning, she saw that Durast and Braenog had put the Hiddeans in their vicinity to flight as well. In response, they had taken up the pursuit and were already some distance away, almost out of sight, in fact.

"Don't you get lost from me!" Syren scolded in a loud voice. As she watched, the two Stouts stopped obediently in their tracks, and the surviving Hiddeans disappeared into Stormwood.

"Let's gather the salvage and get on home," she instructed. Durast and Braenog rolled a group of *r*'s at her across the distance to indicate their understanding. Then they began walking in her direction while laughing victoriously and tugging each other's beards.

Searching together, the group found a half dozen each of spears, vests, and necklace-/talisman-type ornaments. One of Durast's strikes had knocked a fanged tooth from its owner, and they decided to take it as salvage also. Briefly, they considered gathering the stones that had been thrown at them by the Hiddeans and trying to sell those to Aglar, but upon close inspection, they turned out to be no different than stones that had not been thrown at them. In the end they chose against the idea, deciding that it was too much like something Baron would do. They also managed to find eighteen silver coins.

By the time they were on the safe side of the wall with their treasures, Oswald's Venture Salvage was closed, and the dark of night had fully come, so they stowed everything but the coins in Syren's root cellar and headed over to the Hooded Crow for supper. Though it was more expensive to do so, Syren found that it was easier to pay for supper than to cook it on days that ended with combat and treasure lugging, even on days that went well, as this one had.

Once they arrived, Syren and her companions took seats at their usual table, near the stage. Though it was completely unnecessary, as far as Syren was concerned, the patrons had designated the spot as "Syren's table" as part of the popularity contest that seemed to exist in everyone's mind but hers. Because of that, it was generally available whenever they came in or not long after. At the table next to theirs, Aglar Grump was trying to recruit new salvagers from among the leather-clad mercenaries that had come in with the caravan in his usual emphatic way.

"Good! It's settled then. Godfrey stays in Westpost to hunt salvage for good old Oswald, may he rest in peace." Syren shook her head, grinning, as Aglar placed his hat over his heart before continuing. "Now then," he said while putting his hat back on his head, "how about you, my fine young lad? What did you say your name was?"

"Tor," answered the young mercenary indifferently. He was tall and scrawny and had deceptively boyish features. He looked like his first shave was still a decade away, though it couldn't have been, given his occupation and the sound of his voice.

"Well, how about it, Tor? Join your pal, here?"

"Who said he was my pal?" he teased, grinning derisively at Godfrey.

"Join your enemy, then. I don't care, just sign here." He thrust paperwork at the young man.

"Why in the world would I want to become a...a...what do you call it?"

"Salvager. Why, for the adventure, for the excitement, for the wealth! There's good money in salvage. Ask anybody!" Just then he glanced over at Syren's table. "Except for them," he advised quickly, jerking his head in her direction. "Some people are just negative."

"Look," Tor countered before anyone at Syren's table could object, "I got me a good thing. It ain't that I'm afraid to risk my neck. I got no problem with that, but the wagons hire enough guards that we all stay safe, mostly without even havin' to fight. I ain't gettin' rich, but I ain't gettin' dead neither. The wagons are leavin' tomorrow, and I'll be leavin' with 'em." Syren could tell from the way he expressed himself that while the mercenary was a thoroughly uneducated and simple man, he at least knew what he wanted. Unlike his friend, he had not been lured by Aglar's brash promises.

"Mark my words," Tor announced to those at his table with finality, "wanderin' the wilderness is the last thing you'll see me do."

Aglar went on arguing his perspective, but Syren, Durast, and Braenog were distracted by new company. At a break between musical sets, Jessero came over to their table and invited himself to join them.

"Well, if it isn't Westpost's most popular salvagers," he greeted amiably as he sat down. The minstrel was always eager to hear about the latest activities from anyone who had ventured into the wilderness. "Nog! You look decidedly perky for a dead guy, I must say. Good for you!" Braenog grinned large white teeth at him.

"So what's the latest, my fine fellows? No more battery against other salvagers, I hope," he teased.

"Nope."

"Nope, nope," the Stouts replied.

"We encountered a band of Hiddeans tonight, in the Nearwood, north of town," Syren explained.

"Indeed?" Jessero exclaimed with interest. "Out fighting for your lives again, were you?" Durast and Braenog shook their coarse bushy-haired heads, and Jessero raised his eyebrows expectantly.

"We made the Hiddeans fight for theirs!" Durast replied.

The troubadour threw back his head and laughed heartily. As he did so, he spotted Molly, the serving maid, passing by with mugs for other patrons. Reaching up, he snatched two of them from the tray she was carrying and set them before the Stouts, who set into them gratefully before Molly could object.

"However did you manage it?" Jessero wondered aloud admiringly, and the trio told him the tale. "Sounds like it was a perilous affair," he judged.

"More than it had to be, for my part," Syren admitted. "There's more technique involved in sword wielding than I had realized, apparently, but I got it figured out by the end."

Jessero nodded his approval. "No one looks wounded. Did you make use of the healing salve?"

"Didn't need to," Durast announced. "Sharp steel makes deep good fighting!"

"Does it now?"

"We really did carry the fight to the enemy this time," Syren asserted. "Sure, having good weapons made a difference, but so did having some experience."

"Yep, yep," agreed Braenog. "When the fight ran against us early on, we recovered."

"We faced them!" Durast attested proudly.

"And we hardly took a scratch doing it. We really are better at this than we were just a month ago," Syren concluded. "We aren't just sneaking and snatching and fleeing, like other salvagers do, like Baron does. We're doing more than outwitting the savages. We're defeating them. We might just be in a position to help this village after all."

Jessero's men had returned to the stage from the bar and various other wanderings and were organizing for another set.

"Fare thee all well, then, brave heroes of Westpost," Jessero bid them jauntily while standing to rejoin his musical troupe. "What brings the morrow, dragons?"

Durast and Braenog stared enthusiastically at each other.

"Grrremlin!"

CHAPTER 12

Revenge

The next morning found Braenog, Durast, and Syren trampling the dense and treacherous foliage of Stormwood, where the forest encroached the protective wall, west of Westpost.

"Durast," Syren complained, "do your feet have to make so much noise?"

"'Tis not my feet but the forest," Durast defended. "These weeds cry out against them!"

"Yep, yep," agreed Braenog while noisily slashing away a path for himself with his two-handed ax. "In the halls of our homeland, our boots are but whisperers."

"But you're going to alert the whole forest to our presence!" Syren argued.

"Is that not the object?" Braenog asked earnestly. Durast rolled some *r*'s in approval.

"Bring the villains to us!" he said.

"Save us the trouble of hunting," added Braenog.

"Yep."

"Yep, yep."

"Yep," they said. Syren sighed in frustration. The Stouts' natural fearlessness was certainly an advantage in the face of savage enemies, but it sometimes made it difficult for them to accept the sensibleness of being cautious. Then a notion came to her.

"Fine," she acknowledged casually. "Let's just stand here and shout until they find us. Of course, they'll hide their treasure before they come. We might find it anyway, though. Right? I mean, I'm sure it'll be somewhere in this...vast, trackless wilderness." The Stouts were silent for several moments as they considered. After the pause, they were much quieter with their voices and more careful about the way that they pushed through brambles and stepped over brittle branches.

When they had come venturing that morning, Syren's goal had been to return to the place in Stormwood where they had faced their only previous encounter with the Gremlins. Unfortunately, the forest looked very much different in the early morning than it had the other day at dusk. For one thing, the small amount of sunlight that did invade the bleakness of Stormwood came from a completely different direction, which cast confounding shadows. In addition, an unexpected and creeping mist permeated this part of the forest at this time of day. It helped conceal Syren and her companions but also hid any violent creatures that might be lurking nearby. Syren didn't relish the thought of being taken by ambush again. Moreover, the wafting mist changed the way the terrain looked. As Syren studied the woods around them, she found it difficult to recognize familiar landmarks. It was as though the forest itself were shifting. Syren stopped and gazed about at her surroundings warily.

"Syren?" Durast inquired. "What are you thinking?"

Stormwood was known as an enchanted forest. Haunted, even. For a moment, she was overwhelmed by the unsettling possibility that Stormwood was, in fact, shifting. Where were they, exactly? Syren wasn't quite sure, and that made her nervous. Was her mind just playing ticks on her, or had the forest itself worked evilly against them? Was it just the swirling mists, or was Stormwood weaving itself into a feral botanical maze as they blundered along, to confuse them, entrap them, and consume them?

Suddenly sweating in the chill morning fog, Syren was just about to recommend that they turn around and try to make their way back to civilization, if even just to make sure that they still could. As she opened her mouth to speak, however, they heard a familiar sound rustling toward them from beyond a nearby cluster of moss-draped oaks. Peering silently in that direction, they could just make out a group of vaguely Stout-sized shapes that seemed to be moving obliviously past their position, from right to left generally.

"Grrremlin!" Braenog hissed quietly to the others. Durast took an oversized ax into each of his massive hands.

"Are you sure?" Syren asked, drawing her sword carefully from its scabbard and squinting into the mist.

"We can hear their speaking," Durast confirmed.

"And their foul smelling," Braenog added. Syren's heart began to race, but she also felt confident that, this time, the advantage was theirs.

"All right then. Where is the best place to strike them?"

"Anywhere!" assured Braenog, and grasping his poleax tightly in both hands, he began to move forward.

"No, wait a minute," Syren asserted. "This will go better if we have a plan."

"Yep, yep," Durast said to Braenog. "By strategy, we will take deep revenge. Without it, they may all flee." Desire and logic wrestled against each other within the old Stout's chest for one tense moment.

"Quickly," he insisted.

"Nog should barrel in from here," Durast suggested. They will gather to him. Then we will barrel in after and strike by surprise." Syren swept a stray lock of her hair from her face with her forearm. It was a risky plan, but it did make intentional use of what Braenog did best, and include the element of surprise.

"I'm going to swing around that way and get ahead of them," she modified, indicating a spot that was some distance off to their left, through the fog. "Count ten breaths before you begin so I can get into position. Then do what you will. That way, we will have surprise from two directions, and you won't get lost from the fight while trying to sneak through the forest."

The idea seemed a fair compromise of striking quickly and seeking the best opportunity. Syren left the Stouts standing ready,

Braenog breathing and Durast counting, while she moved silently to the flank of the Gremlin troop. She still didn't know how many there were, but by the sound, it didn't seem like a huge number. She chose a spot behind a wide tree where, just across the trunk, a small group of the fetid savages were milling about. They seemed to be marking the territory of their group the way dogs or cats would. It was a disgusting picture to imagine, but it also taught Syren how to track the Gremlins in the future.

Just then, Syren heard a roar from her right, which was answered by a chorus of outraged squeals. The fog was starting to lift as the morning warmed on, and though she still couldn't see clearly across the whole distance, she knew that Braenog had gotten to "ten." The Gremlins nearest her turned to move in the direction of the conflict, and her heart was suddenly clutched with the fear that Braenog would be swarmed and overwhelmed before they could enact the rest of their plan. Nevertheless, she resisted the urge to rush in. The plan would work, she told herself. The plan was sound.

Whirling about with a start, Syren set herself behind her shield and pointed her sword threateningly against the sudden, promised onslaught thrashing its way toward her through the underbrush to her immediate right. To her surprise and dismay, the creature who appeared, scowling menacingly but pulling up short at the sight of Syren and her defensive stance, was Durast. He took on a look of concern and confusion, all at once.

"Syren!" he scolded. "What are you doing here?"

"What am I doing here?" she answered, suddenly frantic. "What are you doing here? Where is Nog?"

"He barreled in, as we planned, but the Grrremlin were moving on, so I barreled to the left, to keep up. Now I am here."

"And you missed the Gremlins entirely?"

"They must be nearby somewhere." Durast shrugged. "Nog will be among them if we can find them," he assured.

"Oh, for crying out loud," Syren exclaimed, exasperated. "Just once I'd like to have a plan actually go as planned. He's over that way. Come on!"

With Syren leading to give direction, the pair charged from their hiding place into the open melee of the Gremlin column. To her great relief, she found that most of the Gremlins had stayed away from the fight. Though her friend was hard-pressed by those who were attacking, many others were standing in reserve, guarding something that Syren couldn't make out. The rabid attacks of the rest had forced Braenog back until he was up against an immense tree. From that position, he was trapped and hopelessly outnumbered, but at least they couldn't surround him and club him down from behind. He was swinging his ax furiously and now, with Durast and Syren on the scene, they could attack the vermin on two flanks and rescue him.

This they set in to do.

At their appearance, however, several of the previously unengaged Gremlins moved to intervene against their new adversaries. Durast raked the first Gremlin who charged up to him with both of his axes, cutting it down instantly. Syren blocked a frenzied attack with her shield and counterattacked with her sword, which was also parried by her opponent's shield. The Gremlin roared his outrage at her with his intimidating hoggish features, but Syren remembered about the language of fear and held her ground. They exchanged two more strikes before she managed to draw the creature off balance with a feigned strike, which left it open to a lethal jab from Syren's sword point.

By then more than half of the foes that were pressing against Braenog had turned their vile aggression against Durast and Syren. As they did, Braenog cut one of them down with a long stroke from his poleax. The Stout was battered, breathing hard, and bleeding but seemed not to notice as he pressed his attack. The long reach of his heavy-ended weapon made it slow to wield, and he was taking two attacks for every one that he laid out. The power he could put behind each stroke, however, was devastating, driving through shield and Gremlin alike.

Durast's short but equally heavy axes and his great strength made quick, shattering work of the flimsy Gremlin shields. He waded in with gusto, swinging one hand to the destruction of a shield and the other to the destruction of its owner. Unlike the other day, this battle was not happening in any sort of clearing. The many trees and deep forest cover, combined with the still lingering morning fog, made it difficult to know how they were doing overall, but as each individual skirmish was going well, it seemed to make sense to press the attack and fight on.

Meanwhile, Syren's elegant blade had more difficulty against shield-wielding opponents, but her reach with it was so long and swift that she managed to slash perilous gashes into her enemies, which would drain the fighting spirit (and sometimes the life) out of them. Courage, tenacity, and superior weapons were carrying the day until Syren stepped back from blocking a strike and tripped over a fallen Gremlin that had been slain by Braenog. She went sprawling. Losing her grip on her sword, it went flying and several Gremlins closed on the opportunity.

"Nog! Durast!" she cried out. As she used her shield to protect her head, heavy, blunt stone axes crashed against it and thudded painfully into her midsection. Above her, two Stouts roared into action, swinging axes with catastrophic enthusiasm. On the first moment that Gremlin ax blows were not raining down on her, Syren glanced about quickly for her sword. Finding it just barely out of reach, she rolled in that direction, grabbed it up, and scrambled to her feet again. When she did so, she was accosted by the most severe stabbing pain she had ever experienced. Radiating from the left side of her pounded rib cage, it stole her breath away and made it impossible to even hold her shield, much less wield it in combat. Crying out again in surprise, pain, and frustration, she had no choice but to let the small metal shield drop to the ground. Looking about her desperately, however, she discovered that few combatants were left among the Gremlins. Those that remained were making a guarded retreat to follow the rest of their ilk, which had gathered up whatever it was they were protecting and were trying to sneak off into the deeper forest with it.

Cradling her aching side with her free arm, Syren bore down in long strides against the rear guard of the Gremlins. Carving a wrathful figure eight in the air before her with her sword, she advanced upon them, bearing a determined, sneering grimace. Watching Syren's approach against the background of slain Gremlins, the remnant of the savages turned coward and fled in every direction, leaving the litter bearers unprotected against the Stouts. Dropping their charge, they too fled for their lives. Braenog chased them for a short distance, but they quickly disappeared into the wilderness, and their treasure had not, so he returned to where Durast stood, next to a heavy-looking, badly weathered wooden chest. The locking mechanism being long since disabled, it was tied closed with thick vines from the forest. Grinning to each other, the Stouts readied to use their axes as "vine keys" when they heard Syren's distressed cough and sorrowful cry.

They looked up in alarm simultaneously to find Syren, wincing and struggling for breath, staggering toward a tree. Leaning on it for support, she let the sword drop from her hand weakly.

"Syrrin!" they both called thickly as they ran over to her. She was already pale, her eyes squeezed shut tightly against the pain.

"Did we chase 'em?" she gasped through clenched teeth.

"Yep."

"Yep, yep."

"Yep," they answered, but with great concern in their voice.

"Braenog has avenged the other day," he said of himself, trying to cheer Syren.

"And we have salvage and trrreasure," encouraged Durast. "You see?" Syren tried to laugh, for bravery's sake, but the effort sent waves of wracking pain through her, and it ended in a horrible grimace and a sob.

"Syren must lie down!" Braenog insisted. Untying their travel capes, they arranged a smooth place on the ground and, laying their capes upon it, assisted Syren off her feet as gently as they could, with their large hands. Syren found that as long as she lay still and didn't try to inhale sharply, the pain was less, but that was hard to do because she was exhausted from the rigors of the battle and needed to catch her breath. The dilemma made her feel like she was suffocating.

For a pair of tense moments, Durast and Braenog watched silently as Syren struggled against the impact of her wounds. To cough was an exercise in torture. Durast clenched and opened his mighty fists repeatedly, in grave concern.

"I don't...know if I can make it back...," Syren struggled to say, but the Stouts interrupted her earnestly.

"No. Syren must return to Westpost," Durast required.

"Syren must be well, quite possibly," Braenog instructed, nodding emphatically.

"Yep, yep," Durast agreed seriously. "Syren must walk home and get healing. She will not fit into a sack." They watched her again for an anxious moment, then Durast's bushy eyebrows shot upward.

"Healing!" he blurted, clapping his hands together. "Syren, we have with us the healing salve!" Quickly, he withdrew the cream-colored jar from his burlap sack and carefully unscrewed the black lid. For a moment, he and his kinsman stared at the twinkling greenish ointment.

"How does it work?" Braenog asked, sniffing at it with a frown.

"The salvage lady with the caravan said to rub it onto the skin, probably where the injury is." They looked at Syren sympathetically. Then Durast knelt down beside her.

"We must see the wound," Durast instructed Syren seriously. Nodding, she indicated her rib cage on the left side. Gently, he helped her expose the heavily bruised area.

"The rib bones look broken," Braenog whispered to Durast. Then the younger Stout took a moment to study the salve uncertainly.

"How much to use?" Braenog voiced their mutual concern.

"Until it works," Durast decided with finality. Using two of his large fingers, he scooped out a generous amount of the stuff, about a fifth of the total contents, and spread it gingerly across the area of the injury. Syren did her best to lie still. At first, any contact with the affected area sent shocks of pain across her torso, down her left leg, and up to her throat. As instantly as it started, though, a warm, tingling kind of soothing began to settle in. As if by magic, or perhaps it was by magic, the bruising faded before their astonished eyes as they watched. Syren's stiff, pain wracked body relaxed and her breathing became deep and easy. Only a matter of seconds later, Syren asked to sit up.

"How do you fare?" Durast asked in wonder. Syren prodded her side curiously.

"It's amazing," she gaped. "I feel almost completely well. I mean, it's a little sore if I push on it, but I feel okay. I actually think I could get up and we could walk out of here!"

"Alchemy is deep good stuff!" Braenog proclaimed, grinning his relief broadly. "I told you, we should gain an alchemist of our own!"

When they turned to laugh with him, Durast and Syren noted that the older Stout still had open wounds. Carefully, Durast dabbed the places with smaller amounts of the healing salve. Just as they had witnessed with Syren, the wounds closed and healed instantly and Braenog reported feeling strong again.

"All right, then," Syren decided confidently, "let's gather up our salvage and get back to town!"

That morning's combat, having occurred amid the dense thickets of Stormwood instead of the relatively open grassy spaces of the Nearwood made salvage finding more difficult, but the Stouts were determined.

Especially Durast.

Because of thick vegetation (and because of the early morning fog, which was dissipating as morning drew nigh unto noon), Syren and her companions had not been sure, even while they were fighting in the chaos of the battle, exactly how many Gremlins they had initially rushed in against. When they scoured the area in search of any salvageable items that had been abandoned by their foes, however, they counted ten slain Gremlins. Altogether, they found ten of the Gremlin war axes. Five of the Gremlin shields were more or less intact. Durast's effective skirmish tactics had demolished the rest. They put these items into Syren's burlap sack, along with the vests, talismans, and other trappings that the dead Gremlins no longer had use of. Then they cut the vines that secured the contents of the trunk and peered inside.

Braenog whistled his admiration. The heavy, modest-sized trunk was filled with a mixture of copper and silver coins, and also contained several well-crafted pewter items of tableware. There were at least two goblets, a plate, and some number of forks and spoons.

"Trrreasure!" celebrated Durast.

"It's just like we thought," confirmed Syren. "The old tales are true. Bands of the wild races will move their lairs from place to place, either to avoid detection or because they are basically nomadic and need to move their home base from time to time. Either way, we seem to have intercepted one of those transfers. How much do you think is here, Durast?"

The Stout swept his hands through the jumbled collection of copper and silver coins. He was grinning contentedly, listening carefully to the jingling sound of the coins tumbling against each other, and enjoying the feel of the cold, sparkling metal as the coins flowed through his fingers. At first, Syren assumed this sifting motion to be part of the Stoutish assessment process, but after several such sweeps, she had to remind him that she had asked him a question.

"Um…Durast? Durast!"

"Hm? Yes?"

"How much? I mean, what do we have there?"

"Oh. Yep, yep. Near to a thousand, I would say, mostly of copper."

"Wow. No wonder the box was so heavy. And the silver?"

"Less, certainly. Of course, I will want to spend time to catalog it in detail…"

"Yes, yes, of course," Syren accepted impatiently. "But how many, generally speaking?" Durast frowned at the pressure to give a number. He clearly wanted to sit right down, dump the contents of the trunk on the forest floor, and begin counting right then. Pressed by Syren's expression, however…

"Two hundred, perhaps," he said. Syren nodded as she performed a private calculation of her own.

"Well, we should take this all back to town right away. I can carry the salvage, if you two can manage the trunk."

Indicating that they could, Durast and Braenog divided the spoils among them and the trio made for the Wallgate. On the way, they passed the huge buttressed oak tree, which marked the sight of their previous encounter with the Gremlins. For all of Syren's developing skill at tracking and forestry, the location was not where she had figured it in her mind. This made her wonder again about the difficulty of navigating so tangled a wilderness. It also renewed her uneasy suspicion that the whole forest was enchanted with a malevolent spirit. In any case, they made it successfully out of Stormwood and returned to the village without further encounters of the dangerous sort. As they walked, they congratulated themselves on their victory, revisiting various points of strategy. They also celebrated the benefits of healing salve and speculated about the merit of gaining some armor for themselves as soon as they could afford it, though they agreed that paying off their debt to the Palace remained as their first priority.

Once they were on the secure side of the town wall, they went directly to Syren's house. Depositing most of the coinage in the Stouts' "secret" vault, in the root cellar, they temporarily stored the salvage in a corner of the main room, in the burlap sacks.

"The vault is filled with our treasure," Durast reported happily. "No more will it hold."

"Nope, nope," confirmed Braenog earnestly.

"Now, we should excavate another," advised Durast.

"We can't sell our salvage until we have room for the treasure."

"Yep."

"Yep, yep."

"Yep," they decided, without consulting Syren on the matter. Then they tugged each other's beards and started off in the direction of the root cellar.

"Wait. Hold on a minute," commanded Syren. The Stouts turned, obviously dumbfounded as to why she would question the sense of their plan. "I'm not against the idea, entirely, of the two of you digging more holes in my cellar—"

"Excavating," Durast corrected.

"Fine. Excavating. The point is, there is something else I'd rather we do." The Stouts looked at each other quizzically.

"Rather than make room for treasure?" Durast asked.

"Yes. Listen, we're in great shape, even after thrashing a group of Gremlins in Stormwood." Braenog rolled some *r*'s as she continued, "We seem to be pretty comfortable with our new weapons, and there's still a lot of daylight and healing salve left. I want to search for that ruined tower that Baron told us about. The one where he found Father's sword. After all this time, I think we might be able to find my father today. We might be able to bring him home."

Solemn expressions grew on Stoutish faces. Then they crossed to where Syren stood, each grasping one of her forearms in one large hand.

"That is a worthy 'rather.'" Durast said, and Braenog rolled his *r*'s in quiet affirmation. Having just decided their next course of action, Braenog's stomach rumbled lustily. He looked up at Syren hopefully.

"There is time first for eating?" he inquired. Syren grinned at her portly friend.

"Quite possibly," she said.

Walking into the Hooded Crow at midday, Syren and her Stoutish friendsfound that they had the place was largely to themselves. Marley was having one last conversation with the caravan merchants before the wagons rolled for Centerville. No doubt, they were arranging to buy provisions for the trip. Jessero was at the bar, quietly conversing with Stinky Joe, who did comparatively little talking in return. Sitting alone at his usual table in the corner by the front bay window was Baron, sulking into his mug. As Syren and Durast crossed the room to their usual table, Braenog sidled over to where Baron sat brooding sourly to pay him back for some of the trouble he had caused them.

"Not much popularity these days, eh, topsider?" the wide Stout goaded.

"I'm doing well enough, thank you," the salvager countered wryly.

"Well enough to pay back what you owe to Aglar?" The comment seemed to touch a nerve.

"And I suppose you three are?" Baron fumed.

"As a matter of fact, we pulled a haul of Gremlin treasure from the wilderness this morning," Braenog said proudly. "Don't know how we'll spend it all."

"Doesn't look like it to me," Baron challenged, glaring at the Stout derisively.

"Couldn't drag it all over here," the Stout defended. "We stored it at Syren's house." Baron wagged a sarcastic smile at the Stout, which was really more of a disgruntled sneer.

"So you say," Baron replied incredulously.

"Braenog," called Syren sharply, but by then, he was engaged in battle.

"Funny, we didn't see you fleeing Stormwood this morning," the Stout prodded on. He placed special emphasis on the word *fleeing*. "Why was that, I wonder. Was there no one to abandon?"

"Take care by that window, Punie," Baron growled angrily. "Folks have been known to go out that way."

"Folks have been known to come back in," Braenog challenged. At that, Baron pushed his mug away from in front of him. As he moved to stand up, Braenog squared himself to face him.

"Hey now, hey now!" warned Marley, who had finished his dealing with Abel Specter, the ale merchant.

"Nog! Food!" called Durast in a tone that warned his kinsman not to start trouble. Hesitantly, Braenog backed away from the confrontation, eyeing Baron threateningly until he was at a sufficient distance to turn his back and join his friends. Syren kept her eye on

Baron, but he sat back down after Braenog did. Meanwhile, Jessero patted Stinky Joe on the back amiably and brought the remains of his lunch with him to Syren's table.

"I declare, there is truly no end of excitement when you three are around," he said merrily. "So is it more than a boast between competitors? Have you routed a horde of Gremlins this young day?" Syren and the Stouts set in upon plates of roasted chicken and potatoes as they answered.

"Not without some difficulty," Syren admitted, "but yes."

"Impressive," Jessero admired. "Where did you encounter them, and how did you manage it?" Taking turns in the narrative, they told him their account. Despite her dislike for Baron, or maybe because of it, Syren would occasionally glance in the direction of Baron's table. Whenever she did, she found him watching them, listening in, though he would feign indifference and look away if their eyes met. It made Syren feel vaguely uncomfortable. She wasn't sure if Baron was jealous of their success, or if he was up to something.

"What is he doing here?" she asked Jessero about Baron.

"Lamenting the loss of a sword, so the tune goes," he answered.

"It was never his to begin with!" Syren complained.

Jessero shrugged. "Of course," the troubadour conceded. "Still, every singer interprets the song his own way. In any case, his grander problem, the way I read the score, is the damage to his popularity. You three have cut in quite decidedly on his dance card."

"I don't even care about the stupid popularity contest," Syren objected.

"Nevertheless, your success has put him in a difficult spot. He's going to have to come up with something. Otherwise, he'll end up needing to get a real job." Jessero gave a mock expression of fear, which made everyone at the table chuckle.

"Syren," Braenog asked after a pause, changing the subject, "how do you never get lost in the wilderness? How do you know where the wall is when we are in Stormwood? With so much forest in the way, we can't even see it."

Syren chuckled. "When you spend time in a place it becomes familiar. For example, you've spent enough time in Westpost that you know the way to the Hooded Crow from my house."

"That's because we can smell the beer," admitted Braenog. "Our noses guide us."

"So that's how it's done," Durast concluded seriously. "Syren has a very good nose. She can smell the beer all the way from Stormwood." Jessero grinned and Syren laughed. She was pleased to discover that her side did not hurt when she did so.

"No, that's not what I meant," she explained. "It's about landmarks. Not being lost is really about recognizing where you are and remembering where you have been. That, combined with knowing how to determine what direction we are facing, is the key to finding our way around."

"Are you talking about the wilderness or about life?" Jessero asked, and they were all silent for a minute.

Their collective reverie was interrupted by Stinky Joe, who loudly demanded and received another drink. Slightly startled, they all laughed briefly, in spite of themselves.

"Where does Stinky Joe get his money?" Durast wondered aloud. "He does no work that I can see. He is never anywhere but here."

"He drinks on my tab," Jessero confessed simply without looking over to him.

"Is that a good idea?" Syren asked.

"Yes, it is, in my view," Jessero asserted. "He drinks to forget, you see."

"He drinks an awful lot," observed Braenog.

"He has much to forget," answered Jessero cryptically, but before anyone could probe further, the troubadour was changing the topic.

"So what next for our brave salvaging trio, hmm? Another invigorating negotiation with Aglar Grump?"

"Not just yet," Syren confided. "There's still a good bit of day ahead. We're going back out to look for…" She tossed a quick glance in Baron's direction. "To see what we can find," she finished.

"Indeed?" Jessero replied, intrigued by the pause. "How very jaunty!" he then added, smiling innocently along. Baron glowered at them as they left, but neither side offered any banter.

Syren and her companions walked along the road beyond the Wallgate, following the hard-packed, dusty path that the caravan wagons would soon leave their wheel ruts in as they abandoned Westpost for all points east. On their way out of town, they encountered Syren's cousin Quig once again. The scrawny blond youth was eagerly examining a group of silver coins he had just acquired.

"How did you come by those?" Syren had asked, congratulating him.

"I sold my Canabal plant to one of the caravan mercenaries," he reported. "I didn't really want to, but he made me such a good offer, see? I couldn't turn it down. I guess I could always buy another one sometime."

"Tell you what," Syren offered, "we go out to Stormwood fairly often these days. I'll keep my eyes open for you. If I find another Canabal plant, I'll bring it to you." She hated the thought of Quig wasting hard money on another flower.

"For free? Wow, that would be great, Syren. Thanks!" Then the boy dashed on home with his profits.

"So much money for a flower," Durast wondered aloud as the trio walked on in pursuit of their own priorities.

"Perhaps he has a future in the trading business," Braenog speculated, "like Aglar Grump."

"Not like Aglar, I hope," Syren corrected, and the Stouts rolled their *r*'s in agreement.

After a winding, dipping, forest-encroaching mile of travel along the road, their view of the Wallgate had been smothered by the wilderness. From where they stood, any evidence of civilization's existence in that remote and reckless region of the world had been eradicated, save for the modest but intentionally carved dirt track under their feet. The tenuous, muddy-brown ribbon was all that connected the densely populated, sophisticated, and safe society of the large eastern cities to Syren's humble home and precariously situated village. Here, threatening to sever the cord and swallow them, the rampant defiance of Stormwood's ancient and wild presence exerted itself against mankind's meager attempt to pacify it, turning the road abruptly aside, toward the north.

"Baron said that the tower was somewhere to the east and south of Westpost," Syren remembered. "The road curves away to the north from here and out of Stormwood, so the tower must lie between this point and the village, in the part of the forest that extends to the south from the road."

"It's a lot of forest," Braenog suggested hesitantly.

"We'd better start in, then," replied Syren determinedly, and with that, the three companions strove cautiously into the southern wilderness and vanished from civilized view.

"This part of Stormwood looks different to me than the western side," Syren observed at length as they traveled alertly.

"In what way?" asked Durast. "There are trees and bushes everywhere as before."

"Yes, but here the trees are older, wider, taller, and there are fewer brambles and scrub growth. It almost looks as if the area has been...groomed or something."

"How can a forest be groomed, and what would do such a thing?" Braenog asked incredulously.

"I really don't know," Syren answered over her shoulder. "It looks like maybe a fire swept through this area some while back and cleaned out the smaller stuff. Now it's just starting to recover."

The Stouts shrugged their indifference to the whole topic, but just then, they discovered a curious impression in the ground.

"Syren! You must come and see!" Durast called. The earth was still damp in places from the recent rains, and pressed into the moist loamy soil was an enormous footprint. Nearby to it were the charred and gnawed upon remains of at least one humanoid form. At first glance, it was difficult to tell how many because the bodies had been gnawed upon, the bones scattered. Setting her shield aside, Syren knelt down to inspect the print while the Stouts speculated above her.

"What do you think could have made such a mark?" Durast asked his kinsman.

"Orc?" Braenog suggested. "There are remains just over there."

"Baron told Syren that the place of her father was fair crawling with Orcs," Durast reminded them. "Perhaps we are close to the tower if this is an Orc track."

"It would have to be a very large one," Syren chimed in. "This print is three time the size of ours."

"Agreed," said Braenog, tugging his beard for inspiration.

"Troll, then, or Ogre?" Durast guessed.

"Perhaps, though the trollkind love the stony places of the world."

"True," the younger Stout conceded.

"Aren't they the same thing?" inquired Syren.

"Nope, nope," enlightened Braenog.

"Trolls are bigger and brutish. Ogres are smaller but more clever," Durast explained. "It is said that some wield magic."

"Both are large and cruel and nasty," Braenog added assuredly.

"Well," Syren concluded, standing, "whatever it was, by the look of this print, I'd say that it passed this way since the rains, but not very recently. Before today, anyway. What I can't figure is, where did the creature go? There are some fainter tracks coming from that direction, but the trail ends here. And what caused that poor devil over there to get incinerated?"

Before they could speculate further, they were accosted suddenly by a fearsome and giant-sized lizard. Covered in coarse, brownish hide, the thing was as knobby and corrugated as the bark of the ancient tree that had concealed it. Leaping out at them in a flash, the beast stretched forward with gaping, bony ridged jaws and snatched Durast off his feet. Then turning its twenty foot long, barrel shaped body away from the others, it made to waddle quickly away, in serpentine fashion, on stumpy legs that protruded from its sides and stomped the ground in rapid, alternating strides.

"Durast!" called Syren in alarm.

Reacting quickly, Braenog dropped his ax to the ground and racing over to where the creature was already escaping from view, he grabbed the lizard by its long, slender tail. Clutching it firmly in both arms, he squeezed the tail with his large, Stoutish hands and dug in his heels. Rather than halting the creature's progess, though, he was dragged along by the powerful beast, his heels gouging out trails that got left behind him.

Syren picked up Braenog's poleax and ran to catch the whole company, unsure of what she should do when she did.

In an attempt to lose its unwanted rider, the lizard scampered between a huge boulder and a small tree, turning itself sideways as it ran, to squeeze through the gap. Seeing an opportunity for additional leverage, Braenog let his feet go out from under him and sat himself down on the forest floor as he was dragged bumpingly along. Then rather than letting go or allowing himself to be scraped away from his purchase, he got his feet out in front of him, and braced them against the obstacles as they rushed up at him. This time, the strategy did check the lizard's lumbering movement and, roaring for additional strength, Braenog pulled hard against the creature in a desperate tug of war, the beast's tail serving as the rope.

Clever as his impromptu plan was, it afforded no opportunity for Braenog to do anything except hold onto his foe so that it didn't get away with his kinsman, who was still held fast. Durast, meanwhile, continued thrashing and complaining and hurling threats impotently from within the monster's jaws as Syren dashed up to the scene. Just as she arrived, the creature dropped Durast roughly to the ground and, in a feat of surprising flexibility, curled back on itself in order to free its tail from the other Stout's grasp.

Seeing Braenog imperiled by his own stubborn determination, Syren rushed forward and interposed herself between him and the lizard's head. Raising her shield against its open mouth, Syren set herself to fend off an expected bite attack. Instead, the creature exhaled a shower of flame in a billowing, scorching cloud. The blast would have enveloped Syren, but her shield deflected the worst of it, protecting her as she hunkered behind it. Hardly a conflagration, the effect dissipated nearly as instantly as it had appeared, but it nevertheless heated the metal of the shield so much that Syren was forced to let go of it to prevent being burned. That left both Syren and Braenog exposed to the creature's next exertion of wrath.

At that moment, Durast came barreling forward, shouting. He was covered with leaves and dirt and acorns and twigs, which were stuck to him by the slimy lizard spittle he was coated with. Wielding a heavy ax in each hand, he brought both weapons to bear, swinging hard upon the base of the creature's neck. The simultaneous blows thudded hard against the monster, forcing its head away from Syren just as it lunged at her, but they failed to penetrate the densely calloused hide.

Seeing her opening, Syren plunged her sword at the beast. The thrust missed the swiftly moving head, but the razor sharp point stabbed into the smoother skin on the underside of the fiery lizard's gullet. Recoiling from the strike, the creature convulsed violently, which forced a fatigued and drag battered Braenog to lose hold of its tail and go sprawling. Straightening itself out to its normal length caused the lizard to brush Syren inconsequentially aside, casting her to the turf nearby. By the time she had righted herself, the beast had scurried away from sight among the trees it so easily blended in with. Panting heavily, the three companions ignored the idea of immediate pursuit to help each other up and assess the situation.

"Durast is a bush," Braenog observed.

"Are you hurt?" Syren inquired of him. "We've still got the healing salve, don't we?"

"I am gooey, and got squeezed quite tightly, but I shall endure. You?" Syren and Braenog both shook their heads.

"Singed is all, and Nog will be picking slivers from his seat for a while, but we're okay. What was that thing, anyway?"

"I didn't ask its name," Durast joked, "but it explains the scorched look of the woods hereabouts."

"Indeed," Syren agreed as she studied the terrain around them. "Well, in any case, we survived. We should gather up our equipment and move on from here." The Stouts were incredulous.

"Move on? Nay, we should hunt it and slay it!" Braenog advised.

"Yep, yep," agreed his slime covered kinsman, handing Braenog his ax.

"Nope, nope," imitated Syren. "That thing is huge and fast, and fire breathing and camouflaged, and we are already battered and burned and bruised."

"But now it is wounded," Durast argued.

"Which means we just made it mad. All the more reason to leave the area, and quickly, before it comes back to take its revenge."

"Perhaps we weakened it," Braenog suggested.

"We barely scratched it!" Syren contended. "Besides, let's not lose sight of why we're out here. We're trying to find that tower and retrieve father's body, remember?"

"But we also need treasure for the Palace," appealed Durast. "Do you know what that hide might be worth?"

"Do you know what ours are worth?" countered Syren. "I want us to return home with father, not join him. Now come on, let's get out of here!"

Despite their great strength, tenacity and fearlessness, the Stouts also had a mostly endearing child-like quality about them, which responded amiably to Syren's natural charisma. As a result, the trio reclaimed Syren's shield from where she had been forced to abandon it (by then, it had cooled off sufficiently to be handled again), and soon they were hustling away from the charred territory of the giant fire breathing lizard. As they went, Durast stripped himself of the debris that he had acquired while rolling about on the forest floor.

"The fire beast almost succeeded against the three of us," Braenog observed as they jogged through the wilderness. "Syren's father must have been courageous and deep skilled with his sword not to have been devoured by it."

"He must have had Stoutish blood," Durast reasoned, casually, to which Braenog rolled a few *r*'s in support. Syren grinned broadly, understanding the intended compliment.

"He was a capable swordsman," she recalled fondly, "and a capable woodsman. Remember, though, that it was more than two years ago that he patrolled these woods. The lizard may not have been here then, or if it was, he may not have encountered it."

"The woods are vast," Durast agreed. "There seem to be many paths to every place."

"Yep, yep," Braenog agreed heartily. "That's why it's so easy to get lost. We are on the wrong side of the dirt."

"Wrong side?" Syren inquired.

"Yep, yep," Durast echoed. "Under the deep earth, Stouts are never lost. The stone shows us where we are, tells us how to go. Here, the ground is cluttered with endless trees and bushes. We can't see how to get through the forest from place to place because the growth and shrubbery hides the ground from us and obscures our line of sight."

"Under the earth, one knows exactly where to go," Braenog declared wistfully.

"Yeah, back to the surface!" Syren teased. The Stouts laughed in response.

The group had been traveling in a more or less southwesterly direction, in order to distance themselves from their previous encounter. Despite their initial intention to work their way back toward the village of Westpost, they had been, in fact, traveling away from it, when they happened upon a clearing of sorts. Protruding from the ground across the distance from them was what appeared to be an ancient archway, which was keeping a solitary and obsolete vigil in a wilderness that had grown up around it.

They stepped out warily upon a broad and grassy knoll. The hill was populated by a smattering of chestnut and maple trees whose canopies spread widely but not to the point that they interlaced their branches. As a result, there was much more daylight reaching the ground here than in most of Stormwood. Normally, Syren would have advised caution about the prospect of coming out into the open from the concealment of the surrounding forest. In this location, however, all three of the companions were intrigued by the unusual feature, which was standing amid the tall grass at the crest of the gently rolling hill, near the center of the space. Crossing over to it curiously, they saw that it stood in staunch, if futile, defiance of the ravages of time and weather. With no other buildings in sight, the crumbling ruin remained as the lone vestige of a distant attempt to bridle and tame a wilderness, a monument to some unknown noble antiquity.

Durast and Braenog examined the decrepit structure closely and with great fascination. Composed of head-sized fieldstones that had been mortared together, the archway had clearly once been part of a more extensive and obviously man-made edifice of some kind. Their Stoutish interest piqued, they prodded it carefully with their oversized hands. Running their large fingers along the cracked grooves of the mortar, they would occasionally put a finger to their mouth as if tasting the grout to assess its composition. Eyeing individual stones expertly, they even sniffed at the rocks in certain places with their bulbous Stoutish noses.

"This was built here many lifetimes ago," Braenog concluded admiringly.

"That old? How can you tell?" Syren wondered at him. Looking around, Durast pointed Syren toward one of the tall trees of the knoll, one which rose from an especially wide trunk.

"Syren, how old is that tree, do you say?"

"A hundred years, I would guess," she estimated after studying it for a few moments. "Maybe more, but not more than one hundred fifty. Why do you ask?"

"Trees tell their age to Syren," Durast explained. "Stoneworks tell theirs to Deepfellows."

Nodding her understanding, Syren applied her recollection of Baron's account to their current situation.

"Baron said that the tower where he found father's sword was surrounded by a stone wall," she recalled. "Could this be it?"

"There was likely a wall to go with this arch," acknowledged Braenog, "but it has been gone for deep time past. Baron would not have seen it." Syren crowded her brow at that and thought.

"When I was little," she pondered slowly, at length, "Father taught me that in older times, castles were built within a series of boundary circles. Maybe this is what's left of the outer ring of the tower we're looking for."

"It is possible," Braenog agreed.

"But then, which way to the tower from here?" wondered Durast. Syren stood in the archway and faced each direction.

"This way faces the northeast," she declared. Then spinning an about face, she added, "And that way faces the southwest. Northeast goes back to the road and out of Stormwood. That can't be right. Southwest makes much more sense. I say we go that way." Braenog nodded his agreement, but Durast was busy rooting about among the tall grass that surrounded the base of the arch.

"Syren, I have found treasure!" he exclaimed happily. Licking his discovery and rubbing it on his sleeve to remove the wilderness grime from it, he showed it to his friends. "It is a clasp of some kind." Given how it had been washed, Syren was somewhat reluctant to take it from him, but when she did, she was glad that she had.

"This is a cloak clasp," she said as she examined it closely. "See the design on this side? My father had one like it. So did all the men of his patrol. Look, there's a little piece of fabric here. It's pretty faded, but it might have been the same color as the cloaks they all wore. This means that they must have passed this way! Come on, we have to find that tower!"

Syren's heart was pounding as she dashed eagerly across the far side of the knoll. She had never been so close to finding her father. Finally, his long wait would be over. He was going to come home to mother. At last, he would be at peace. Her mind being filled with the possibility that she might be living in the last day of her uncertain, faltering quest, she was paying little attention to her exact surroundings. Behind her, the Stouts were running to keep up.

"Syren! Watch that hole!" Durast cried out. At the last moment, Syren dodged to her right to avoid falling into a three-foot-wide circular tunnel opening, the rest of which disappeared into the ground. Watching it with a start as it flew past her, she nearly tumbled into a second one, which she came upon as she ran. Jumping over that one, she stumbled on her landing, sending a small avalanche of dirt cascading down the slope of the burrow hole. After nearly falling down the chute, she began to slow her pace. Doing so allowed her to anticipate a third hole a short distance away and jog around it. Suddenly overtaken by an ominous recognition, Syren halted and looked around her.

"Durast, Braenog, stop!" she called to them. The urgency in her voice commanded their attention, and they drew to a standstill. From where they each stood, they were surrounded by clusters of the same large holes that they had seen in isolation in other parts of the forest. They were the tunnels that Jessero had warned them about, the kind that even the Hiddeans avoided, and the knoll was littered with them.

"We must be standing over a nest," Durast whispered.

"Come, this way. Carefully!" Syren whispered back. She wasn't sure that whispering was in any way helpful to their situation, but it seemed the right thing to do. "Let's get off this hill. The tower should be that way," she pointed. The Stouts began a mindful walk toward Syren, with weapons in hand.

Then all at once, with a rumbling, clacketing scrabble, they emerged.

"Mammoth ant-crabs!" Syren called out in alarm as she drew her sword.

There were dozens of them, crawling out of their holes in every direction. Equipped with menacing-looking pincers at their front ends, the horrid, insect-like creatures scuttled repulsively along the ground, their five-foot-long segmented bodies covered in a beige-colored carapace.

"Don't let them grab you!" Syren commanded obviously. As she glanced over concernedly, Durast hopped to his left, narrowly escaping being clamped upon. Then rushing up to the creature's side, he brought his heavy hatchets down hard upon the ant-crab's back. To his surprise, though, the sturdy carapace didn't yield to the blow. The beast was unharmed.

At that moment, Syren felt her shield being tugged away from her firmly. Wheeling around, another of the monsters had grabbed onto it with its powerful pincers and was pulling her forward, toward its burrow. Loath to relinquish her shield, she slashed at the thick, spiny tines with her sword. The sharp, lithe steel severed the pincer arm, and she fell back as it gave way. Instead of retreating, however, the wounded ant-crab scuttled forward at Syren relentlessly. Reacting as best she could, there was only enough time to spring into a crouch, with her shield in front of her, when the creature unexpectedly spewed a stream of foul-smelling ichor at her. The monster seemed to pause its advance then as if waiting hungrily for some effect to take place.

Having inadvertently blocked the spray attack with her shield, Syren seized the opportunity afforded by the ant-crab's hesitation to take her own advice and leap away from the beast's damaged maw. Though large, determined, and unsettlingly ugly, the mammoth ant-crabs were fairly slow movers and not especially agile in their stiff natural armor. That made it easy for Syren to stay to the side of any one foe and slash away at its tough outer shell. The trick was to avoid getting outflanked herself by another of the beasts since they were crawling around everywhere.

In fact, amid the swarm of giant insects, Durast was doing more dancing than striking, as he hopped desperately from place to place to evade the spray and the pincers of various opponents.

Braenog, meanwhile, had managed to use his short stature and compact strength to flip one of the ant-crabs over, onto its back. The maneuver did no damage to the beast, but it did incapacitate it temporarily, and though it eventually righted itself, it lay there for a time, kicking its many legs uselessly. Having discovered the effectiveness of the technique, he then ran from place to place for a time, turning them over like turtles.

Looking around at the chaotic melee, it seemed to Syren after a time that the ant-crab numbers were thinning of their own accord. Apparently, the swarm hadn't come out of their dens solely to attack Syren and company but also in answer to the call of some basal instinct. Many had emerged from their holes only to creep determinedly away, disappearing into the forest in pursuit of some unknowable insect objective. In fact, she had spotted a gap in the clamoring throng. It provided an avenue of escape from the perils of the skirmish, and she was about to point it out to the others when she heard a wail of frustration come from Braenog's last known location.

Turning in that direction, she could see that the Stout had come face to prong with the business end of one particular ant-crab and had gotten thoroughly dowsed by the crippling spray of the creature. He responded by angrily burying his ax into the head area of his opponent. The blow split the carapace but also caused the ax head to become wedged in place. In the few moments required for Braenog to clear his vision, counterattack, and then struggle to free his weapon, the toxin took hold and the Stout went rigid. The wounded foe then clamped onto the conscious but paralyzed Braenog with its jagged, powerful pincers and dragged him helplessly down an ant-crab tunnel and out of sight.

"Nog!" Syren screamed.

His attention drawn to his kinsman's plight by Syren's call, Durast cast his axes to the ground immediately and barreled across the field toward Braenog, leaping fearlessly across the occasional ant-crab on the way. Syren tried to disengage from her own hectic struggle and come to Braenog's aid as well, but her area was more crowded, and she had to move cautiously to prevent succumbing to a similar fate.

From too far away, Syren watched in wide-eyed horror as Durast dove headlong into the ant-crab tunnel and disappeared. For several wretched moments, the hill was deathly quiet, save for the wind and the fading clackety sounds of the last few ant-crabs as they dispersed, meandering away or retreating back into tunnels of their own. When she finally arrived at the edge of the tunnel her friends had vanished into, she searched the opening, with dread clogging her throat.

Gradually, as she was choosing from a variety of possible desperate actions, there appeared in the opening the back of a grungy, earth-encrusted, red-headed Stout. Muscles bulging, he was grunting, puffing, and hauling against some stubbornly heavy body of resistance.

"Durast!" Syren shouted in relief. Her first impulse was to jump into the hole and help pull him from the opening, but she could find no way to do so that wouldn't actually impede the progress he was making. As she watched anxiously, he would bunch himself up and then strain backward, extending his legs. Then he would repeat the process. As he came fully into view, Syren could see that he was clutching Braenog from behind, with his arms under the older Stout's shoulders and his hands clasped across Braenog's chest.

At first, Syren found it curious that Durast was straining so hard to drag his counterpart to safety. In recent days, she had seen him hoist Braenog onto his back and carry him. As the older Stout came fully into view, however, Syren saw that the wounded ant-crab was still attached to Braenog's legs, still scrambling fervently against Durast's defiance of its effort to drag them both back under the ground.

"The gap!" Durast growled through tightly clenched teeth. "Between...segments!"

Staring down at the scene frantically, Syren spotted the chink in the creature's natural armor, the articulation point that connected the damaged head portion of the carapace with the body segment. Grasping her sword hilt in both hands, she drove her blade into the slender gap, putting all her weight behind the thrust and pinning the mammoth insect to the ground. In response, the ant-crab thrashed wildly in place for several moments, after which it quickly grew still, its many legs curling underneath it in death.

Durast released his hold on his kinsman and lay exhaustedly on his back, breathing heavily. Braenog lay perfectly still, bleeding and blinking and breathing shallowly. Finally, Syren was able to jump into the hollow to help her friends.

"Durast!" she cried in exasperated relief and admiration. "That was the most amazing...you're the bravest...what kind of strength... don't ever do that again!" she scolded at last. The younger Stout grinned his appreciation back at Syren, too fatigued even to roll his *r*'s. Syren then gave her attention to the other Stout.

"Braenog, can you hear me? Say something," she instructed.

"Strong and sure shall Deepfellows endure," he said quietly, his lips barely moving. Durast chuckled his relief. Syren inspected Braenog's legs. Still attached to the dead mammoth ant-crab, they had been rent badly and looked unusable. Syren winced as she studied the damage.

"I'm going to get this thing off of you," she instructed. "Try not to move."

“Try not to?” the Stout replied. “I couldn’t if I wanted to. I am numb below the neck.” The news startled Syren into a pause, but then she recovered.

“Well, at least you’re not in pain. Durast, we’ll need the healing salve,” she declared as she forced the large, jagged pincers away from Braenog’s injured legs.

Durast produced the jar of salve and Syren spread it liberally over the affected areas, as necessary. Just as they had seen in the case of Syren’s injury at the hands of the Gremlins, Braenog’s wounds closed and healed before their very eyes. The sight didn’t stop being a wonder for the familiarity of it, though it took significantly more of the stuff to heal Braenog’s lacerations, which were in multiple areas of both legs.

“There,” Syren pronounced, once the healing salve had done its work. “How does that feel?”

“Not at all,” he answered uncertainly. “I still can’t move. Am I well?” Syren and Durast frowned confoundedly.

“It must have worked,” Syren estimated. “He looks as good as new. Maybe we need to use more of the salve.”

“It works quickly,” Durast observed, “so it should have worked by now, if it was going to.”

“Jessero did suggest that not every condition could be fixed with healing salve,” Syren remembered. “Maybe paralysis is one such.”

“Then we must take him back to the alchemist,” decided Durast, and Syren nodded, sighing.

“There’s nothing else to do,” she agreed.

"Yes there is," Braenog objected.

"What?" asked Syren.

"We must take treasure!" he promoted enthusiastically but still without moving.

"He's definitely feeling better," Syren announced to Durast sarcastically.

"Yep."

"Yep, yep."

"Yep," she and Durast said.

"The problem with your plan," Syren corrected Braenog, "is that there is no treasure. I mean, they're bugs," she explained with a shrug. "It's not like they carry coin pouches."

"That hide was hard to crack," Braenog observed about the tough carapace of the mammoth ant-crabs. "It would make handy armor." Syren and Durast looked at each other, inspired by the possibility.

"Nog is right," Durast approved.

"If we can get it back to Westpost and get it fashioned somehow," Syren speculated.

"Is there an armor maker in the village?" Durast asked.

"No," Syren replied. "The blacksmith is probably the closest thing we have to one. He does a lot of work for the Palace. That might include working on the weapons and armor of the prince's guards."

"It does no harm to ask when we get the bug plates home," suggested Durast. Syren studied the huge dead beast, which was lying next to them.

"How are we going to manage that, do you think?" she pondered. "I don't like the idea of dragging that whole thing all the way home through Stormwood. It'll draw too much attention to us."

"Syren's sword is sharp and thin," observed Durast. "Can we cut the shell free from the carcass?" Syren drew her sword and laid it against the ant-crab's body in several places, assessing the possibility.

"You know, it just might work," she said.

"But what of our search for the tower?" Braenog asked from his prone position. "What of Syren's father?" Syren looked down at her concerned, loyal, and paralyzed friend.

"Because of our present circumstances," she said, lifting Braenog's hand and letting it flop back to the ground, "I think we should return to Westpost and heal. We learned a lot about this part of the forest today. That'll make things easier for us next time. I'm anxious to bring Father home, but he's waited this long. A little while longer is probably for the best."

Working carefully, Syren managed to separate the carapace sections from the rest of the creature they had killed. Then she and Durast loaded the lightweight but sturdy sections into Syren's burlap sack. Though he was conscious, Braenog's paralysis prevented his walking back to town on his own, so Durast had to put him in his burlap sack again and carry him back.

Without Braenog's availability to help them in a combat, Syren and Durast were eager to avoid crossing the territory of the giant lizard as they returned home. They also wanted to avoid further encounters with the mammoth ant-crabs, so Syren led them on a course that took them due north, to the road. Along the way, they had to crouch and cover to avoid being detected by a small but vicious-looking group of Orcs, the first Syren had ever personally seen. Other than that, they had no real difficulty finding the road and returning to the Wallgate, except that Braenog was much more inclined to complain about his traveling conditions than he had been previously, when he was unconscious.

"This is not very comfortable!" he groused at one point, and Durast had to repeatedly shush him and instruct him to lie still, so as not to disrupt his balance as he walked. By the time they had crossed the Wallgate, however, everyone was delighted to discover that the paralysis was wearing off. Releasing Braenog from his temporary burlap home, Syren and the Stouts went immediately to the shop of Kollan the blacksmith to talk with him about the feasibility of their idea. As expected, they found him at his forge, pounding out horseshoes in the cooler breezes of the late afternoon. He was a burly man who seemed to be made out of soot and grease and sweat. The hairs of one arm were perpetually singed away because of their frequent proximity to the fire. He worked steadily and loudly at his craft, applying a heavy hammer and an exacting eye to the iron as he heated it, pounded it, and eventually quenched it.

"Hey, Kollan," Syren greeted as they walked into the open forge area.

"Syren," he acknowledged, continuing to concentrate on his work. He was a serious man but not unfriendly.

"I've got...a bit of work...to show you," she said, timing her words to fit between hammer blows.

"I can't say when I'd get to it," he confessed flatly without looking up. "I've got an ore load to do for the Palace already, now that the caravan has come and gone."

"This is something of a specialty project," Syren pressed on. "We'd like some armor made."

"Made or fitted? I'm a blacksmith, not an armorer. I don't have the time, the talent or the materials to custom make a suit. Not unless you want me to just hang a few plates on you. You'd look like a wind chime." He grinned at his own humor, and so did Syren.

"We brought our own materials, out of Stormwood. Take a look at this."

Kollan dunked his finished product into a wooden vat of water, sending a plume of steam loudly into the air. Then he crossed over to where Durast was just pulling one large carapace plate out for inspection. Kollan took it into his hands with wonder.

"What in the forge is this?" Kollan exclaimed, fascinated.

"It's the outer shell from a mammoth ant-crab," Syren replied. She found that there was no way to say that without feeling just a little bit important. Then she explained what that was and, generally speaking, how she knew. Kollan, clearly impressed, pried on the edges of the piece, testing its resiliency and strength.

"It's harder than ax blows," Durast assured him.

"Well, almost," corrected Braenog, who was still slightly wobbly on his feet.

"It's a natural product, then, like a hide?" Kollan asked, and Syren nodded. "It'll probably need to be treated in some way, then, so it doesn't rot. I could talk to Evan the leathersmith about that, I guess. Next it would need to be sized and cut, and of course it will have to fasten in some way..." Syren could see his mind whirling at the idea of working with such an exotic material, and she knew that he had taken on the project before he said it. "You'll have to leave it with me," he said at length. "I really am committed to the jobs Prince Hallas has set before me. You know how that is. In the meantime, let me take some general measurements, and I will also need some coin from you. There will be some expenses, if I am to make this work."

"How much do you need?" Syren asked.

"Give me fifty silvers to get started. I'll let you know when it's finished. We can work out the rest then, but it'll probably be twice that again."

Knowing how impossibly expensive standard armor had been, when they had asked the caravan merchant about it, Kollan's request seemed extremely reasonable, so they struck the deal. Then the blacksmith used a familiar implement, the long-handled tongs that he often used to work his fire with, to gauge the length of each person's torso, arms, and legs. Then having taken their measurements and their money, he bid them good day. They left him studying the carapace sections with interest as they returned to the street.

"Where to now?" Durast asked. Braenog's stomach growled a suggestion.

"Well, before that," Syren said, pointing at Braenog's midsection, "we should gather up the salvage we have at the house and take it over to Oswald's before Aglar closes up shop for the night. It's almost that time."

Always in favor of gaining additional treasure and with Braenog feeling much more like himself again, Syren and the Stouts returned to her house, happily reliving the exciting tales of the day, recounting their victories, and comparing notes regarding lessons learned about successful venturing in Stormwood.

When they went inside, though, they were accosted by a shocking discovery: All the salvage that they had stored in Syren's main room was missing. For several minutes, Syren was completely dumbfounded as to how that could be. Durast and Braenog searched the other rooms of the house, but of course, they found nothing. There was no chance that they had misplaced the items. It wasn't that big of a house, and they had only stowed everything since noon of that same day.

"Is it possible that we were robbed?" Braenog wondered aloud. All at once, the Stouts exchanged wide-eyed gazes and then raced to the root cellar, tripping over each other in their concern for the status of their hidden cache of coins. In their absence, Syren stood by her table, staring at the now vacant corner in disbelief. As she did so, she contemplated Braenog's statement, trying to make sense of the scene.

Theft of any kind was rare in a small and isolated village like Westpost because everyone knew each other. Moreover, the theft of salvage was unheard of. Salvage was serious business and everyone knew it. After all, people had risked their lives against the wilderness to get it. Syren scratched her head in confusion. The whole circumstance was hard to fathom. Just then, the Stouts came running back in to report.

"Everything in the cellar is just as we left it," Durast announced. "The hidden vault has not been unsettled, and not so much as an onion is missing from among the stores."

Syren decided to let the "vault" designation of the Stouts' small alcove go unchallenged in lieu of solving the mystery of their missing possessions.

"It's odd that the salvage items would be the only things taken," Syren mused. "Maybe some kids from the neighborhood came over while we were gone, to ask for something. Then when they didn't find us home, they saw the stuff and decided to play with it."

The idea seemed plausible, so Syren went to her neighbors to inquire while the Stouts stayed back, in case anyone in possession of their salvage should return. Unfortunately, when at last Syren came home, she was empty-handed.

"I can only think of two other possible explanations," Syren speculated. "Either officials from the Palace have taken our salvage—though I don't see why they would—or someone has indeed stolen it from us. Either way, the thing to do is to report the problem to the authorities."

"How do we make such a complaint?" Durast asked.

"Night is coming on," Syren observed. "There should be a patrol wandering the town. Let's register our grievance with them before we go to supper."

Upon leaving Syren's cottage, she and her friends were surprised to encounter the very group they were intending to search for, walking up to them.

"Hey, it's the guard," Syren exclaimed to Durast. "What luck! We were just going to come looking for you," she said to the leader of the squad.

"Indeed," he replied sternly. "Turning yourselves in, were you? That's good. Saves us a lot of trouble in hunting you down."

"Turning ourselves in?" Syren answered in bewilderment. "What are you talking about?"

"Syren of Westpost," the captain announced officially, "on the authority of Prince Hallas, I am arresting you and your two companions here. Come quietly, or we shall take you by force."

"You're arresting us? What's the charge?" Syren demanded.

"A grievance has been registered against you, that you have violated your contract of legitimate salvage operation by selling salvage independently to an outside agent," the captain replied firmly. "I am to take you three into custody until such a time as His Highness can hear the matter. Now come along."

Standing behind the guards, and off to the side slightly, was Aglar Grump. His arms were crossed in front of him, and his face was a portrait of betrayal and outrage.

Standing just behind him in the fading daylight of the early evening, wearing an expression of smug satisfaction, was Baron.

CHAPTER 13

Visitors

Prince Hallas's dungeon, beneath the guardhouse, was a dark and squalid place. It was located near the servant quarters, not far from the kitchens. Syren, Durast, and Braenog had allowed themselves to be escorted more or less peaceably into captivity after being arrested on the previous night. All assurances of their own innocence had fallen on deaf ears, though Syren knew that they would. The guards, after all, were merely discharging their duty and could do little else.

After being marched indifferently down the stairs and past an archway revealing a chamber that contained some ominous-looking equipment, Syren and her friends had each been deposited into a cell of their own, a standard precaution to prevent escape attempts. Syren's cell was an eight-foot-by-eight-foot cubicle of bare stone. Its only features were a musty straw tick sleeping mat and an acrid-smelling toilet hole in one corner. The door to her cell was an iron-bound, heavy wooden affair with one small iron-grated window at face level and a slot at the bottom, where food could be slid through. The entire arrangement was cold and damp and slimy. She assumed that the Stouts' accommodations were the same.

By the time they had been incarcerated it had become early evening, and they were informed by the jailer that they had missed the dinner hour. The duress of the events had chased away Syren's appetite anyway, but Durast and Braenog had complained mightily, accusing the guards of cruel interrogation and confinement practices. Their protests were ignored, however, and when the guards left, they took the lanterns with them, leaving Syren and the Stouts in absolute shivering blackness.

Syren paced her cell furiously for a time while listening to the Stouts grumble about being "intentionally starved to death" through their cell door windows. Eventually, by casting their comments into the hallway, they began to speculate with each other about what was happening to them.

"We have committed no crime," Durast protested. "We should have refused to be arrested."

"I think that would have ended badly," Syren advised. "They were prepared to take us in by force. The captain said so."

In response, Braenog harrumphed derisively. "I agree with Durast," he said. "We should have stood our ground and defended. I doubt they could have taken us."

"Yep, yep."

"Yep."

"Yep," they decided, but Syren was unconvinced.

"With just our fists? Against their clubs and greater numbers?" Syren shook her head, though no one could see it.

"We had superior weapons," Durast pointed out. "If we had drawn ours first, they would not have drawn theirs."

"If we had threatened the prince's guards with lethal weapons, then we really would be guilty of something," Syren explained patiently. "Besides, they might have called our bluff. Then we would have had to hurt somebody. I didn't want that. They were just doing their job."

"They seem to think we are guilty anyway," Braenog observed.

"I suppose," Syren admitted. "But we were promised a hearing. When it comes, we'll be able to tell our side. That will be the time to defend ourselves. With our words, not with our weapons. The truth is on our side, and the law sides with the truth. Well, ideally, anyway. If we're patient and cooperative, this will all work out…I hope."

"When will that be?" Durast inquired.

"Yes, when is the hearing to be held?" asked Braenog. Syren thought for a moment and then sighed.

"I don't know," she said. "The grievance hearing after the fight in the Hooded Crow took three weeks to arrange. I'm afraid that we may be stuck here awhile."

It was difficult to tell when morning came, or even if it had, given the isolation and darkness of their surroundings. Syren had done her best to lie down and sleep, but the dank conditions and the injustice of their situation made it difficult to rest properly, and she was unable to gauge how much time she had passed in the effort.

What seemed like the next several hours crawled by rather boringly. She and the Stouts spent some time in conversation about Baron's supposed tower in the woods. The arch they had found did suggest that the place was out there somewhere, and they tried to infer its location from what they already knew of the area.

Eventually, they heard a distant door creak open and the footfalls of some visitor coming down the stairs. Accompanied by a lantern, the jailer arrived. Syren's eyes rejoiced at the opportunity for use again as the dim light allowed her to see her cell door and the hallway beyond. She crowded the little widow anxiously as he walked past.

"Have you come to let us out?" she asked eagerly.

"No," he answered flatly. "Move away from the door," he instructed. Syren did so even though the jailer was apparently standing at Braenog's door, two cells over. She heard the little hatch slide open. Then she heard it slide shut quickly after.

"Food!" exclaimed Braenog excitedly. Shortly after that, Syren heard a second hatch slide open and then close. Finally, the same happened at her door. By the dim lantern light seeping through the cell door window, she could see a wooden bowl containing some kind of soup.

"We are innocent," Syren assured the jailer. "We have done nothing wrong."

"Not my decision," he replied impersonally as he walked away. Syren picked up her bowl while she could still see it by the light that was retreating methodically up the stairs.

"Can you leave us the lantern?" she called after the jailer, but the door at the top of the stairs creaked shut indifferently.

"Where is the rest?" Syren heard Braenog complain disparagingly as the darkness flooded back in, enveloping them.

The contents of their bowls turned out to be a very thin broth made from chicken. It was neither hearty nor especially warm, but it did have some fat in it to sustain them. It and the jailer were the only visitors they had on what might have been their entire first day in prison.

Marking the passage of days, or even hours, while in the dungeon was nearly impossible. Syren slept only fitfully, so she couldn't trust how much time was passing while she slumbered, and her waking hours dragged along so tediously that she lay down frequently on her straw mat, trying to seek the solace of unconsciousness, just to eschew the boredom. The jailer, in his wretched disinterestedness, provided no information at all about events of the outside world or even what day it was. Given the state of everyone's growing hunger, Syren thought it a fair guess that they were being fed once every day. If that was correct, then it was during the third day of their confinement that Syren was visited by her cousin Quig.

"Hi, Syren, how's it going?" the boy asked innocently. He was holding up the lantern he had been given, so that he and Syren could see each other's faces through the tiny barred window in her cell door.

"I've had better days, honestly," she admitted. "Speaking of which, what day is it, anyway?" His answer confirmed Syren's suspicion of the once-per-day feeding schedule and the general timeline:

"I hadn't seen you around for a while, so I went looking for you," Quig reported in his rambling style. "I stopped by your house and guess what? You weren't there. So I asked around, and your neighbors said that you had been asking them about some salvage stuff you were looking for. Well, not all of them said that. Harold said he hadn't seen you, and Helen told me that she saw you walking toward Nellie and Ishan's house, but when I asked Helen, 'So did you actually talk to her?' Then she said, 'No, I didn't actually talk to her.' Then I went to Nellie and Ishan's house, but they weren't at home. So then I went to the Village Green to see if I could find them, but then I laughed at myself because I thought, 'Wait a minute, Quig, you're looking for Syren, not Nellie and Ishan.' So then I went back to your neighborhood and I asked Runyan if he had seen you, but he didn't say anything because he's, like, two years old. I didn't think he would actually know anything, but he's so cute. You kinda just have to ask him stuff, you know?" Syren grinned.

"Yeah, I know," she stuffed in. She was so glad to hear the conversation of someone friendly and to bathe in the pale light from the lantern that she was barely paying any attention to what he was actually saying. Quig continued his rambling explication.

"So Sarah, you know her, right? That's Runyon's mom—"

"Yes, I know my neighbors, Quig," Syren said quickly.

"She said that you had asked her about some salvage. Why were you looking for salvage in your neighborhood, anyway? Doesn't it usually come from the forest?"

"Well—"

"So none of those people knew where you had gone to, but Sarah said that she thought you looked kinda roughed up, so I thought that maybe you went and visited Mertie, the old herb grower lady, but by then I had to get home to do chores. So the next day when I got there, to Mertie's, I mean, she said she hadn't seen you. I tried to tell her this whole story, but she didn't seem interested for some reason. Anyway, Mertie said I should look for you at the Hooded Crow, so I went there, but I stopped at Othan's place first and played with the new puppies their dog just had. Actually, she didn't just have them. That was, like, two weeks ago, but it was yesterday that I stopped by. They're really cute! They're all soft and floppy eared, you should see 'em! Um…what was the question?"

"What day is it?" Syren repeated.

"Oh yeah, right! So I went to the Crow and there was, like, nobody there. I asked Stinky Joe if he knew where you were, and he said that the tentacles had gotten you. I'm not sure what he meant by that. Do you know what he means?"

Syren shook her head slowly.

"Anyway, after I left there, I decided that you guys would probably show up at Oswald's sooner or later, so I went over there. When I did, I heard Mr. Grump talking to Baron about how you had been arrested by the guards and thrown into prison. So then I knew where you were, so I went home. That was yesterday. Today, Momma said it would be nice if I came by and visited you, so here I am!" He grinned at his cousin.

"Quig," Syren told him earnestly, "I want you to know that we are innocent of what we are being accused of." She didn't want her only relatives believing she was a criminal. To that end, Syren was prepared to lay out her whole case before him, wear down his preconceived notions, and convince him of her innocence. She was relieved and surprisingly deflated to discover that she didn't have to.

"Oh. Okay," he said easily, before moving on to his next topic. "It's still pretty exciting, though. I mean, it was great when you were the best salvager in Westpost. Now I have an aunt who's locked up in the prince's dungeon! It's so much fun. I've been telling everybody about it since I found out."

"I'm glad you approve," she replied sarcastically.

"Boy! Come out!" the jailer hollered gruffly from atop the stairs.

"I have to go," Quig confessed. "See ya!"

"Hey, if you see Jack Frost, tell him where we are. Tell him I need to see him!" Syren called after Quig, but he had bounded up the stairs and disappeared. She couldn't tell if he had paid any attention to her request or not.

A couple of days later (it seemed like a week, but it couldn't have been, judging by the number of times the jailer had fed them), Syren heard someone hopping quickly down the steps of the dungeon. The sound was followed by a regular step-click cadence, which grew louder until another familiar lantern-lit face appeared at Syren's cell door.

"Jessero!"

"So hiding out from the old whistle player, eh?" he chided mildly, trying to lighten their burden by inserting some humor. "Is this what I have to do to hear the tales of your adventures now?" He grinned for a moment and winked at Syren, but then he took on a more serious tone. "Sorry I didn't come sooner. I only just found out last night that they were holding you."

"How did you hear?" Syren asked.

"Baron's been talking it up, making what he can out of it." The minstrel shrugged indifferently.

"Oh. What is he saying, exactly?"

"Well, he—"

"Wait, you know what? Never mind. I don't care how he tells it. I can't do anything about it anyway."

"Good for you," Jessero commended. "I'm sure that his rendition ignores the metronome something terrible."

"I don't know what you may have heard, but we've done nothing wrong."

"Really?" By his expression, the musician seemed almost disappointed. "Well, I have," he went on, "and I've come before you to confess."

"You? Confess? Jessero, what are you—"

"Yes, you see, there's a strict rule against bringing gifts to the prisoners, and yet I somehow couldn't resist the urge." As he spoke, he had been wrestling a paper sack from under his clothing, and when he held it up to the window, Syren could see that it was filled with sausages that had been wrapped in flat bread. When he saw Syren's response forming, he put a finger to his lips to quiet her. Then grinning devilishly, he slid the food hatch open and pushed two of them through. He repeated the procedure for Durast and Braenog.

"How did you get them past the jailer?" Syren asked gratefully as she devoured them.

"You might say that I sang for your supper," he answered with a twinkle in his eye. Syren had suspected for some time that there was something more than natural about the singer's talents, but before she could ask him for details, he was moving the conversation on. "Now tell me heroic tales of your adventures. Where have you been, besides here, since that day we ate lunch together."

Between eager mouthfuls, Syren did her best to inform Jessero about their quest for the wilderness tower and the two encounters that forced them to break off their search.

"Fortunately for you, that was no dragon you got surprised by," he interrupted to correct the story. "That was a dracolisk, a giant, fire-breathing lizard. They blend in extremely well with their environment. That makes them hard to spot but easy to identify. A real dragon would have turned you all into cinders, or melted the flesh from your bones with acid, or stomped you into the ground, or swallowed you whole, or provided any number of grisly deaths. As it is, I'm impressed that you fought a dracolisk and survived, even though you barely wounded the beast. It's been a long time since I've heard an honest report that didn't end with 'and then it ate Cedric.'"

About the mammoth ant-crabs, Braenog's injury, and the paralysis, Jessero's primary comment was, "Well, I did warn you, didn't I?" He did think that trying to have armor made from the carapace was clever, though, and was interested to learn about the existence of the nest.

"The individual holes you've seen scattered around the Nearwood may actually lead back to the nest," he said. "Nobody knows for sure."

"I was surprised at how they kept coming after us," Syren remembered. "I mean, the Hiddeans and the Gremlins would listen to fear. They could be chased off after a point, but not these things."

"Mammoth ant-crabs are just bugs on the inside," Jessero explained. "They don't have any morale to lose. They can't be scared away because they aren't smart enough to know they should quit."

"Yeah, I know what that's like," she said sarcastically, turning her head to look in the direction of the Stouts. Jessero chuckled. Just then, the dungeon door creaked open.

"Musician. Come out!" the jailer commanded.

"I'll return when I can," Jessero promised. "But I have to be careful. If anyone gets suspicious, I could get nabbed for smuggling. That wouldn't go well for any of us." Syren thanked him, and he hobbled back up the stairs, whistling.

Darkness and despondency were Syren's cellmates for the next group of daily soup deliveries. Though she tried counting them, the disorientation that went along with the sensory deprivation of her surroundings had caused her to lose track. Conversation with Durast and Braenog trailed off after a time. The shame and humiliation that enshrouded the Stouts' past made them disinclined to talk about it. Syren didn't want to discuss the present for the same reason, and there didn't seem to be much future to speak of, from where she sat.

Somewhere between the tenth and the fourteenth day of their dreary imprisonment, the door at the top of the stairs creaked open. A pair of footfalls that did not sound like the jailer's descended the steps, and Syren crowded her cell door window at the prospect of having a visitor.

"Quig?" she called before she could make out who it was. "Jack?"

"Well, Syren. Fancy meeting you here," Baron's oily, contemptuous voice was accompanied by the appearance of his smug expression at the window bars. Syren pushed away from the door in repulsion, as if she had been spat upon.

"Go away," she commanded, disgustedly, but he didn't.

"My, what delightful accommodations you have here," he goaded sarcastically as his eyes glanced around at her cell. "I must tell you, though, dear, that you really do look worse for the wear." And he *tsk*, *tsk*ed at her in mocking sympathy.

"Take care, Syren," Durast warned. He was shouting to her from his cell, but it was clear that the comment was meant for their visitor. "It seems that we've been invaded by a giant cockroach!" Syren grinned to hear a faint "Yep, yep" come from Braenog's more distant cell. Baron's face left Syren's tiny window and she heard him walk over to Durast and Braenog's cells.

"And how are the Punies making out, hmm? Languishing comfortably, are you?" he teased.

"These are fine apartments," Braenog offered almost cheerfully.

"Nothing like being surrounded by rock and earth, you know. Eh. kinsman?" Durast chimed in.

"Much like our homeland."

"And dark," Durast added. "I do enjoy the dark."

"Haven't used the tunnel vision in a long time," agreed Braenog.

"Rather nostalgic, really," observed Durast.

"Yep."

"Yep, yep."

"Yep," they agreed.

"Oh, I see," answered Baron. Obviously disappointed by their lack of abject suffering, he returned to Syren's window.

"You know, this is quite like visiting a menagerie," Baron mocked at them. "Look at all the curious beasts in their cages. Mustn't feed them, must we? Special diet and all that. And don't get too close to the cages. The rules are all the same. It really is very entertaining!"

"You're the beast, Baron," Syren scolded bitterly. "I don't know how you managed it, but you're behind all this. Somehow, this is your doing."

"It truly was a stroke of genius, though I say it myself," Baron crowed conceitedly. "My little scheme hatched itself when the fat one told me about all that salvage you had just lying about, cluttering up your house. My first thought was to just relieve you of some of it. By doing so, I could earn a few coins by selling what I took to Aglar, not to mention that it would boost my reputation in town once word got around that I was selling Gremlin artifacts again. It would be easy enough to convince everyone that I got it by salvaging. After all, I'm a salvager!" Syren had begun to pace her cell in frustration as Baron continued.

"The real brilliance, though, was involving that simpleton who was guarding the caravan. You know the one. That kid whom Aglar couldn't talk into signing up? I'm sure you've seen him around. Anyway, it was easy to convince him to do me a favor—excuse me, to do *you* a favor—by selling some Hiddean salvage on your behalf to Maynard Edgeworthy, since you were out of town, risking your neck on another salvage run." Baron paused a moment from his diabolical narrative to admire his own deviousness.

"Can you appreciate the sheer beauty of it, Syren? Edgeworthy will swear that he bought salvage from you. I have the money, but of course, I'll claim that the kid stole it, and he left with the caravan days ago. They'll never catch up with him!"

"You're a worm!" Syren growled.

"I believe *wonder* is the word you're looking for," he corrected. "Anyway, once the caravan had rolled out of town for who knows where, all I had to do was mention casually to Aglar as I was selling my Gremlin salvage—a thing I'm known for—that I thought surely I had seen some of your salvage at the shop of one of his competitors. Why, the pumpkin rolled right down the hill after that."

"You won't get away with this," Syren warned angrily.

"Don't be a fool, of course I will," Baron retorted. "Aglar is pushing his claim with the Palace because you broke your contract. Edgeworthy doesn't want to give the Hiddean salvage back because he paid good money for it, money that is now gone. As far as anybody knows, this matter is between you and the salvage owners.

When the grievance comes before the prince, His Highness will side with business as he always does. You will have to buy your trinkets back from Edgeworthy and hand them over to Grump. You will have to pay a similar sum to him as a penalty for breach of contract, and you will have to pay the tribute for wasting His Highness's precious time by needing to have the whole thing brought before him. You will be ruined, and I will be in the clear. It's perfect."

"But why?" Syren implored. "Why have you done this?"

"Because you crossed me, Syren. You and your...pets were getting far too big for your britches. After all, no one invited you to play my little game, did they? No, but soon, there you were, cutting in on my territory, stealing away my popularity, doing actual salvage missions. I had an easy and carefree existence all set up at the expense of these provincial morons that you call neighbors, and you went and ruined it for me. All because one Punie gets tossed out of a window. You should have left well enough alone, Syren. Now I'm in control of the game. I've reset the board. From now on, we'll be playing by my rules."

"All right, enough," Syren conceded miserably. "You've successfully manipulated us. What's it going to take to get you off our backs? Tell us what you want." Baron laughed in derisive victory.

"Oh, Syren. How wonderfully naive you are! I already have what I want. The Gremlin salvage you once had has been safely squirreled away, so I can 'find' an item or two as occasionally as I require for fame and profit. Meanwhile, the whole time you've been down here, I've been circulating the tale of your dishonest treachery all over town. And by the time the salvage owners get done with you, your reputation will be as putrid as this dung hole you're wallowing in currently. Don't you see? I've taken your salvage, your freedom, your popularity, and your good reputation. You'll never be able to pay off what you owe. I have ruined you utterly. It's been a very gratifying couple of weeks." Just then, the door creaked open at the top of the stairs.

"Salvager! Come out!" came the jailer's command.

"I'd love to stay and chat, but my time is up, it seems. I'm going to leave now because, well, I can," he grinned maliciously. "So long, Syren. I don't expect I'll come visit you again. This place isn't my style, really." And with that, he sauntered away up the stairs.

In the aftermath of Baron's obnoxious visit, Syren stalked about her cell for a time, tearfully raging in the utter blackness. Eventually, Durast came to her rescue.

"The topsider is not worth fatiguing yourself over," he said. "Best to put him from your mind."

"Syren should not be uneasy," Braenog comforted. "Later, when we are not imprisoned, we will tunnel under his house and take him by surprise."

"We will repay him for his treachery," Durast assured.

"He will be pummeled," Braenog decided.

"And we will shave his face," Durast promised.

"And his eyebrows," Braenog added.

"And his head," Durast included, with a chuckle.

"And his legs," Braenog laughed.

"And his arms!"

"And his back!" they exchanged.

"And his cattle!" By this time, the Stouts were roaring with laughter at Baron's expense.

"Guys, we don't have to—"

"And his house!" The Stouts were laughing so hard, they could hardly talk.

"Shave his house?" Syren complained. "That doesn't even make sense!" But by then she was starting to chuckle also, and the worst of her disparagement was abated.

In the perpetual darkness of the dungeon, sleeping and wakefulness followed their own schedule, and came more as an escape from the boredom than from an actual need to rest. Syren tried to take Durast's advice and forget Baron's visit and his annoying comments, but like the man himself, they sometimes followed her unwelcomed into her fitful sleep. On one occasion, she dreamed that she was in Stormwood, searching for her father. She was disoriented and kept calling out for him as if he were still alive. In the dream, Baron had crawled out of an ant-crab hole and stood nearby, sneering and intentionally aggravating her. He poked at her repeatedly with a stick and ran his fingers on her skin just to irritate her. She tried to push him away, but she was unable to. The crawling sensation he was creating bothered her to the extent that it stirred her from the dream into the dark wakefulness of her dungeon cell.

Lying on her uncomfortable straw tick mat, the unsettling feeling of something creeping across her skin lingered on. When she reached out to rub the sensation away, however, she was horrified to discover that she was actually being crawled upon by some number of hard-coated creatures—beetles, probably. Jumping up in repulsion, Syren cried out in distress. Sweeping herself wildly, she stripped them off of her, shaking her limbs violently and combing out her hair with her hands.

"Syren!" Durast called in alarm. "Are you all right?"

"Yeah, I'm fine," she answered, breathing heavily from the shock. "Got surprised is all. Something was crawling on me."

"That would be the dung beetles," Durast explained. "They have found that these rooms are no longer empty."

"Dung beetles?" Syren shivered. "How can you tell?"

"By looking at them," he responded obviously.

"By looking at them?" Syren repeated. "How can you see anything? It's pitch-black down here."

"By using the tunnel vision," he said.

"What's tunnel vision?"

"The Deepfellows have a certain way of seeing. It allows us to find our way about when we are deep under the earth, but it is not exactly like regular seeing, and it only happens when there is no light at all to see by. Do your fellows not have the tunnel vision?"

"No, we don't," Syren answered, feeling slightly envious.

"Oh," Durast replied. "Well, then, they are dung beetles. They are harmless creatures, but you shouldn't eat them," he said earnestly.

"No, I wasn't planning to," she assured him. From the far cell, Braenog was snoring away peacefully.

Another long and lonely period was happily interrupted by Jessero, who again brought them rations and news from the outside world. Not long afterward, they were visited by a slender and elegantly dressed gentleman, a dim light reflecting off his skullcap as he held up his lantern.

"Hello, Syren," Jack Frost said with a sympathetic smile.

"Hey, Jack. Thanks for coming to see us."

"Not at all," he dismissed. "You are looking remarkably well."

"I don't believe a copper's worth of that, but it's kind of you to say so."

"They haven't mistreated you, I hope, during your time here."

"They have largely ignored us," she complained.

"Well," he mused to himself, "that, at least, is an improvement."

"Jack, how long are they going to keep us locked up like this? Isn't there supposed to be a hearing? Did they just decide that we're guilty, and we missed it?"

"Oh, there will be a hearing, no doubt," he assured her. "The difficulty lies in Centerville, actually."

"Centerville? Why?"

"Prince Hallas has been gone there, these several weeks, to attend the celebrations of his father's birthday. The chancellor is loath to adjudicate the matter until he returns."

"When will that be?"

"I have heard that he is already on his way, though it will be several more days at the least before he arrives. When he does, you may expect that hearing this grievance will not be the first thing he does."

"So we're just stuck here?"

"For the time being, I'm afraid so. It does give you time to arrange your defense, however. I have been away some little while myself. Tell me what this is all about."

"We're accused of breaking our salvage contract by selling goods to Maynard Edgeworthy instead of to Aglar Grump."

Jack Frost whistled. "That's a serious offense in this village."

"We didn't do it!" Syren proclaimed. "That scoundrel Baron set this whole thing up. He came down here himself to gloat. He told me that he had contrived the whole thing."

"Of course, he will deny that if confronted."

"Of course."

"And the two salvage owners will side with his story, won't they? Their chief concern is to be repaid by the simplest means available. I don't like this, Syren. People should dispense justice, not dispense with justice."

"As I see it, all I can do is tell my side of it and hope for the best."

"Honesty is a good policy," he assured her. Then he took on a worried expression. "You haven't discussed any plans with Jessero, have you?" he asked.

"Not specifically," she confessed.

"Good. Best to keep it that way, in this case."

"He's been very good to us while we've been in here," Syren offered in his defense. "I've noticed that you two don't seem to get along very smoothly."

"Jessero can be generous to a fault," the old man explained. "Show him a fault, and he'll tend to be generous to it."

"I see what you mean." Syren had recognized some of that quality in the musician herself.

"That being said," Jack conceded, "he does a lot of good for people, if allowed to work in his own way."

"You seem to be well received at the Palace," Syren noted. "Is there any chance that you'd be willing to come to the hearing and intercede for us?"

Jack thought for a moment. "I will if I can," he said, obviously still thinking. "Unfortunately, I have no firsthand information about the events. I'd make a poor eyewitness."

"But an influential one," Syren suggested.

Jack nodded slightly. "Thank you," he acknowledged. "Though I think you overestimate my importance at court. No, what you really need are advocates, those who would testify about your importance to this village and to His Highness Prince Hallas."

"Good luck with that," Syren lamented. "Baron has been making rubbish of my reputation all over town. He's probably been at it for weeks now."

"Oh, I don't know," Jack ventured. "I bet if I beat the bushes, I could round up any number who would advocate on your behalf. Let me try. We have a few days yet to spend on the project."

"Whatever you think is best," Syren approved. "I appreciate your help."

"Good!" Jack confirmed.

"Skullcapper. Come out!" commanded the jailer. With a smile and a wink, Jack *ting*ed his skullcap and returned up the dungeon steps with his lantern. After he did, the gloom seemed to be not quite as gloomy to Syren.

An indeterminate number of days passed after Jack Frost's visit. In the immutable darkness of the prince's dungeon, time seemed to flow more quickly and more slowly at the same time. On one hand, every tediously dull minute dragged on like an hour. On the other hand, while it seemed like months of time should have gone by, Syren would find out from a visitor that it had only been weeks. Jessero paid them a third visit to smuggle food in to them but had no other news to tell, really.

Just when Syren had begun to think that she and her friends might never be delivered from their confinement, they had an unexpected visitor. The familiar creaking of the door at the top of the stairs was followed by the rapid footfalls of several individuals who gathered outside the door to her cell.

"Syren of Westpost?" inquired an urgent voice. To Syren's great surprise, the face associated with it belonged to the chancellor.

"Yes," she said, standing to attention reflexively and brushing her clothes and hair with her hands. The chancellor's stern face turned to look down at someone.

"Open it," he commanded harshly, and Syren heard the jingling of keys.

CHAPTER 14

The Rescue

Upon being released from their cells, Durast, Braenog, and Syren were ushered brusquely and without explanation to the Divining Hall of the Palace. The short walk across the courtyard from the guardhouse revealed that it was well after sunset. Syren wondered as they walked why the prince would choose to hold a grievance hearing in the middle of the night. In her experience, it was unlike him to inconvenience himself in any way. When they arrived in the torch-lit hall, Jack Frost was waiting for them. So were their weapons. The prince, however, was nowhere in sight, and everyone was looking very serious. Jack smiled at them kindly as they approached as though he were about to ask for a favor.

"This had better succeed," the chancellor warned Jack severely. Jack nodded respectfully, then turned to Syren and the Stouts.

"My friends," he began, "we are faced with something of a precarious situation. It would appear that upon returning from the east, the carriage conveying His Highness Prince Hallas, back to Westpost encountered a mechanical difficulty of some sort. Fixing it delayed their arrival until after dark. You are well aware that the savage races feel their boldest during the nighttime hours. I happened to be on the east wall as night fell, and when the carriage failed to come into view as expected, I went out cautiously to investigate. When I did so, I discovered that the carriage and its escort have been waylaid by a horde of Hiddeans. They are less than a mile from the Wallgate but not in sight of it. As I watched, I noted that members of the prince's personal guard had established a defensive perimeter around the coach and achieved a standoff. The Hiddeans have the road blocked, however, and more of the foul beasts slink out of the woods every few minutes, adding strength to their numbers.

"Fearing that soon the balance of power would tilt in favor of the vile wretches, I rushed back to report my findings to the Palace. The challenge is how to rescue Prince Hallas without jeopardizing the security of the village. To rally what remains of the city guard and send them out at night, untrained as they are against fighting Hiddeans directly, might actually put the prince in deeper danger and would leave the good people of Westpost completely vulnerable if there were to be an attack on the town." Jack stared purposefully at Syren during his next statement. "I assured my lord chancellor that the people most experienced in these matters, and therefore most likely to volunteer and succeed in rescuing the prince were locked away in his dungeon. That is why he has summoned you. The village of Westpost needs its sovereign, and its sovereign needs you. Will you help us?"

Syren turned and looked at the Stouts inquiringly. Without hesitation, they reached over to the bench, took up their axes, and turned back toward Syren resolutely.

"Show us where the fiends are gathering," Syren answered Jack determinedly.

Led by Jack Frost, Syren and the Stouts traveled as quickly and as covertly as they could along the road until they came within sight of the conflict. Crouching and moving cautiously, they crept closer to the hectic scene. A large crowd of Hiddeans had surrounded an ornate carriage, and were barking and snarling menacingly. The area was being lit tentatively by some number of torches, but the prince's guards could not be seen clearly through the seething, chattering throng.

"There must be close to a hundred of them," Durast estimated.

"Many more than I saw earlier," said Jack, concerned.

"The carriage has no horses," Braenog observed.

"I imagine the Hiddeans were panicking them," Jack guessed. "They were probably released to prevent them from stomping a guard or upsetting the carriage."

"We have to act fast," Syren pointed out expertly. "See how agitated the Hiddeans are? That means they're ready to attack. First, they'll start throwing rocks, mostly to distract their opponents. Then the mob will charge in."

"The prince's men don't stand a chance against that many," Durast predicted.

"We should barrel in," Braenog said confidently, rising as he gave his opinion.

"Forgive me, but that seems foolhardy," Jack challenged.

"It is," Syren acknowledged, "but then, we're in the wilderness at night, the three of us against a hundred savages."

"And they're about to eat Prince Hallas," Durast added.

"The Hiddeans are expecting that fear will override resistance," Syren explained quickly as she crept forward, "because it would for them. We're going to use that against them."

"And we are barreling in from behind by surprise," Durast added again. "They don't like surprises."

"Don't they, indeed?" mused Jack. Some idea of his own seemed to be rolling around inside his head. "Well, then, by all means, surprise away," he said.

Stepping out from their crouched concealment, Syren strode determinedly toward the fray, an ax-wielding Stout on either side of her, on her rear flanks.

"We're going to engage and then pull back," Syren told her allies. As they advanced, she drew her sword and readied her shield. "I want to draw them to us, away from the prince and his men. So hit 'em hard, but don't get sucked into the hole that our surprise attack will create." Beside her, she heard both Stouts roll their *r*'s enthusiastically. "When they scatter, they'll try to loop around us. We can't afford to get surrounded, or there will be no place to withdraw to."

As predicted, the rocks had just begun to fly from the rear of the agitated mass toward the carriage and the men who were nervously protecting it. In response, Syren, Durast, and Braenog charged in against the unsuspecting periphery of the Hiddean mob, roaring with frenzy as they attacked. The first among them to turn at the sound were cut down effortlessly by sword and ax. The next wave lost any initiative they might have had, to surprise. Syren used her momentum and her shield to drive the nearest of those backward into two others, who were pushed awkwardly, further into the throng, upsetting and distracting still more of them. To her right, Braenog grabbed the sturdy handle of his poleax at both ends and, holding it horizontally, used his girth and his churning legs to plow and trample a swath of the vile creatures. On Syren's left, Durast tucked his right shoulder and was smashing into and over any of the stinking fiends that his barreling barrel-like form encountered. With his left hand he swung his hand ax in an upward motion, catching any of the shorter Hiddeans who tried to collapse onto his flank.

"Veer to the left!" Syren shouted, not wanting to drive too deeply into the throng and get surrounded. Hearing Syren's call over the outraged chattering of the Hiddeans, Durast slowed his advance while Syren and Braenog changed the direction of their push. After several strides in the new direction, their progressed was checked by the congestion of the crowd. As the Hiddeans began to push back, groups of them hopped to the sides of the pack, trying to encircle their attackers.

"Nog, slide left," Syren commanded. "Durast, swing around to Nog's right. We're making a stand here!"

Three of the Hiddeans moved to pursue Durast as he dashed behind Syren to take up his new position to his kinsman's right, but Syren stepped quickly to her left, skewering the nearest of them and engaging the others. Braenog stepped back and left also at the same moment, filling the gap made by Syren's maneuver, and prepared to swing his poleax. By this time, they had drawn the attention of nearly half of the Hiddean besiegers.

"Spread out and keep moving!" Syren hollered. "They like to attack in gangs."

For the next several minutes, Syren and the Stouts were hard-pressed. They had drawn to themselves a large portion of the throng and were separated from the rest by the prince's carriage. Because of that and because of the action around her, Syren couldn't see what was happening on the other side of the coach, but she knew that just dividing the enemy had effectively cut their numbers in half, which would harm the Hiddeans morale. The lithe steel of her father's sword made quick work of attacking foes when she could get a stroke in, though against so many, she was doing more defending than striking. Often, she found it necessary to bash one of the fetid beasts on the head with the pommel of her sword while simultaneously fending off another one with her shield. She was also sprinting from spot to spot, taking advantage of her longer strides to keep herself from being overwhelmed. She had slain several of the fiends already, but in the process, she was gaining for herself numerous scratches, nips, and bruises from the clawed and fanged frenzy she was awash in.

And she was beginning to tire.

Durast was faring better and worse at the same time. His axes, like the Stout himself, were most effective at close range, but so were the Hiddeans. He would allow a group of them to rush him, taking any damage that he had to in order to lay out the punishment he wanted. His tactic was essentially the opposite of Syren's, who was trying her best to keep them off of her, at stabbing range of her sword. She was worried about how long he could hold out, but his natural lack of fear, combined with his short reach and great strength, made it a good strategy for him.

Braenog, meanwhile, was doing the best of all of them, in Syren's estimation, and probably the worst of all of them, in his own. Employing his long poleax in broad, sweeping strokes kept whole groups of Hiddeans at bay. As a result, the old Stout had suffered comparatively little damage. Unfortunately, his weapon was also the slowest to wield, and the agile Hiddeans dodged or danced away from the menacing ax blade fairly easily. Braenog's efforts were keeping many of the Hiddeans busy, scattering and rescattering them as they attempted to form into little attack mobs, but he had hardly slain any, and he was clearly frustrated by that.

On the far side of the carriage there was a bright flash of white light as though broad daylight had suddenly come to a specific area. The flash was accompanied by an intensely loud crack, like thunder. Rather than lighting up the whole region, though, or rolling on, the way thunder and lightning usually do in a storm, the effect was a highly localized and isolated event. As instantly and unexpectedly as it had come, it was gone. The impact, however, caused all the Hiddeans, including those in Syren's area, to jump and scurry about for several moments in shock and alarm. Short-lived as it was, the ensuing chaos gave Syren and her battle partners an opportunity, and she hollered out commands to her friends.

"Durast, Nog, fall back! Fifteen paces, along the road toward Westpost. Quick!"

Running up the middle of the road to their new position, Syren made a hasty, estimated count of fallen Hiddeans. There were perhaps eight or ten. Some others might have run off or rejoined those who were harassing the prince's men. Between the tumult of the battle, the terrain, and the dark of night, it was hard to say, but at any rate, they were making a difference. When she arrived at the place where she intended them to make their next stand and turned around, she discovered that she had forgotten to take into account that the "paces" of the Stouts were naturally shorter than her own. She had left them behind slightly. Nevertheless, her strategy had accomplished what she had hoped. Seeing them retreat had inspired the Hiddeans' natural impulse to chase. The maneuver had drawn many of the Hiddeans even further from the prince's carriage and stretched out the column as they ran along the road in pursuit. Quickly, she glanced upward at the sky to see if she could tell how soon she might expect the downpour that the lightning stroke had portended. A driving, soaking rain at night would make footing and visibility more difficult, and dreading the possibility, she wanted to try and account for it. To her surprise and puzzlement, however, a host of stars twinkled innocently down at her. There was not a cloud in sight.

Without time to ponder the mystery further, Syren charged purposefully into the face of the onrushing, slavering horde. Her flailing sword, the ax-wielding Stouts on either side of her, and the shriek of their battle cries were a harbinger of doom to all they confronted. Syren, Durast, and Braenog laid into their pursuers with eager ferocity, as though they had sprung a trap upon them and all the Hiddeans were soon to be caught in it. The fastest and first of the vile imps to arrive at the location were cut down immediately, without any chance of reinforcement from the mob that was following them. That effect seemed to confirm the idea of ambush in the others. A dozen more of them scattered and fled into the dark of the forest without offering any further resistance.

The trio fought desperately in their new location for several more minutes and then a new thought occurred to Syren as she happened to glance across the battle field/road to where the carriage sat in the distance, illuminated dimly by torchlight and ringed by what was now a smaller group of the rock throwing savages. Despite the initial effectiveness of the company's "retreat, reform, and crash in" combat strategy, they found themselves faced with two significant problems. The first was that while they had thinned the Hiddeans' numbers significantly, two to three dozen of the foul beasts remained. If the three of them couldn't manage to break the hordelings' morale and put the evil troop to flight, they might still get overwhelmed in spite of their efforts. The second was that their strategy was moving Syren and the Stouts further away from Prince Hallas, where a contingent of the Hiddeans were still menacing his increasingly beleaguered personal guard. There was no knowing how much longer they could hold out. The Hiddeans would undoubtedly gain ferocity from seeing their prey weaken, and if they managed to swarm the coach, then all this valiant striving would be for nothing.

"Durast!" Syren called out because she found him fighting nearby to her. "We have to regroup with the prince's men. We're getting too far separated!"

"Rejoin our forces," Durast agreed. "Present a stronger face to the Hiddeans." As he began to move in that direction, he sought after his kinsman.

"Nog! We are barreling to the carriage. We must rally to the prince's aid!"

Together, the three of them fought amid the swirling melee in "strike and move" fashion, as they had before, only now they always moved toward the carriage, and they did so as rapidly as they could without inciting the Hiddeans to reform their troop and chase after them. They didn't want to get caught between two ravenous mobs and become swallowed up by them. Once they came within easy reach of the other Hiddean detachment, whose attention was focused on the carriage and the terrified men who seemed poised to give up their defense of it, Durast and Braenog charged noisily out of the darkness and plunged into their unsuspecting lines, with Syren covering their rear flank from attack by the first group. The surprise and the casualties carved a hole in the enemy ranks that allowed the Stouts and Syren to add themselves to the prince's defense forces. Taking advantage of what was left of their initiative, Syren sprung immediately into action.

"Durast, Nog, spread out. You two," she commanded to the guards nearest to Durast, "grab a torch and go with him. You there and you, take these torches here. You're with Braenog," she said, indicating with a motion who that was. "You two are with me. Get a torch and come on over here. The rest of you," she called loudly to the two remaining guards, the driver, and the footman, "grab a torch and something you can use as a weapon." The men gaped at their impromptu commander, looking decidedly undecided. Bitten, bruised, and exhausted, Syren was in no mood to be doubted by people who had never fought Hiddeans before.

"This is going to be over soon, one way or the other," she promised angrily. "We're going to decide which way. Now look sharp and do as we say!"

Spacing themselves out at triangle points around the carriage, the Stouts reinforced with their group the instructions that Syren was calling out.

"All right, listen! On three, we're going to charge straight at them, wheel to the right for ten paces and then pull back to the coach like we are now. We're going to do that over and over, every time I count three. Get ready." Then she turned to her little group to give final instructions. They were visibly shaken by the events of the night and by the unsettling shrieks and yowls of the intimidating crowd that surrounded them.

"Stop your trembling," she insisted as though they could just turn it off. "Believe me," she added more compassionately, "I understand exactly how you feel, but trust me, if we show them a brave face and bloody a few of their noses, we will all get out of this." They nodded their trust, if not their confidence, in Syren's words, and she turned to face the throng. Stones were beginning to fly again.

Syren counted loudly and hoarsely to three, and all three trios charged the besieging Hiddeans, wailing madly as if they had lost their minds to bloodlust. The torchlight, the frenzy, and Syren's slashing sword killed one foe and drove back many others in alarm before they withdrew to their new position, as planned. This time, Syren was careful to only run eight paces herself so as to maintain her distance from the Stouts. After hearing from her companions that all was well, they repeated the process, always shouting out a casualty report for either side. Soon, they were reporting multiple injuries among the Hiddeans, and the carriage driver was cracking his whip menacingly to add to the group's ferocity and protect his location. Within twenty or thirty grueling minutes, the Hiddeans had given up on their stubbornly resistant quarry and fled back into the woods.

The prince's men slouched to the road in relief. Durast and Braenog walked wearily to the front of the carriage to assess what difficulty there still might be, given the coach's horselessness. They both looked like they had been dragged across two miles of brambles and thicket, but to Syren's amazement, they were not breathing especially hard as she was. Admiring their fortitude for just a moment, Syren then went to the carriage door and opened it to check on the prince. Almost immediately, she was joined by the footman, who would probably have stopped her, had he gotten there quickly enough. Inside, Prince Hallas was looking harried and pale from fright but otherwise unharmed.

"The danger has passed, for now, Your Highness," Syren summarized, panting. "Still, it won't really be safe for you until we get you inside the wall. We're not out of the woods yet, as it were."

"His Highness should not leave the carriage." the footman insisted. "Those savages could return at any time." Syren shook her head.

"The horses are gone," she reminded the footman. "We'd have to haul the carriage by hand. It's too heavy."

"Can't we just send for more horses?" asked the prince.

"Send whom, Your Highness?" Syren objected. "If we split this group and the Hiddeans return, then both groups are in mortal danger, in which case, so are you. We should stay together," she advised thickly. Syren's tongue was clinging to the roof of her mouth from all the exertion. Prince Hallas, meanwhile, was steadying his nerves by lifting a crystal glass of some strong drink from a decanter to his mouth with quivering hands. Seeing Syren's disheveled condition, however, seemed to remind him somewhat of his duty as royal protector of the people of Westpost.

"There is a cask of water in the rear of the carriage," he told the footmen. "Dispense a drink to everyone as they have need."

"Yes, my liege," the footman responded. The promise of water drew Syren like a moth to a flame as it did for all the other combatants, save Durast and Braenog. As they drank thankfully and washed their grimy faces, Syren heard the Stouts grunting and growling earnestly from the front of the coach as if they were struggling against a heavy weight. She and several of the guards walked forward to see that the Stouts had taken up the harnesses where the horses had been hitched and were straining against them through gritted teeth, attempting to haul the massive carriage back to town by themselves. Syren opened her mouth both to stop their bold but futile attempt and also to offer them a drink of water, when suddenly, to everyone's astonishment, the carriage began to creak slowly forward, inch by inch.

After watching them for one forgotten moment in slack jawed awe, Syren commanded everyone to grab onto the carriage anywhere they could and push. Together, with Durast and Braenog in the lead, the battle-weary troop escorted Prince Hallas, carriage and all, safely to the Wallgate of Westpost. Once inside, Coran and George faithfully shut and barred the gate doors, closing out the terrors of the night. Then the gate keepers shook hands with a proud flourish, as though they had rescued the prince single-handedly.

Waiting for them all with a concerned expression was Jack Frost, his bronze skullcap gleaming in the torchlight. Rushing up to the carriage, he implored some of the guards to run to the Palace as best they were able, to return with horses for the coach and the alchemist for His Highness. Assured that the worst of the peril was over, Jack turned to Syren, who had been joined by her two tired Stoutish friends. Squeezing Syren paternally by the arm, he advised the three of them to return to Syren's house, wash up, and rest.

As they turned to leave, Syren heard Prince Hallas inquire of Jack, "That young woman, who is she? What was she doing in the wilderness tonight? Have I not seen her somewhere before?"

CHAPTER 15

Resolutions

Syren sat quietly on the hard wooden bench in the Divining Hall of the Palace, waiting for the chancellor and Prince Hallas to enter, take their places and adjudicate the grievance hearing. On her left, Durast and Braenog sat fidgeting beside her. From the low bench they were all sitting on, even their short legs reached the floor. On her right, Jack Frost sat perfectly still, his eyes closed in silent concentration, or possibly meditation. Syren wasn't sure.

On the other bench, across the aisle, were Aglar Grump, Maynard Edgeworthy, and Baron. They were engaged in a quiet conversation with each other as they awaited the commencement of the grievance hearing. Three days had passed since the night they had battled the Hiddeans and rescued Prince Hallas and his personal guard. Syren turned to address Jack, but he spoke first as she did so.

"I am very glad that you are so well recovered from the exercise of the other night's activities," Jack complimented.

"There's nothing like sleeping in your own bed and eating proper food to fetch a person around," Syren asserted.

"Agreed," replied Jack.

"Not only that, but the alchemist paid us a visit."

"Did he? Perhaps it was gratitude," Jack speculated.

"Perhaps. Hey, thanks for arranging our house arrest," Syren told him quietly. Jack smiled back in response, his eyes still closed meditatively. "That dungeon was an awful place," she continued. "I hated being imprisoned. I never want that to happen again. Not to us, not to anybody."

"As harsh a reality as it may be," Jack responded, "there are some who deserve imprisonment." Finally, he turned and looked at Syren sympathetically. "You were not among them," he said, "and I suspected that several days might pass between the ordeal of the prince's return and the occurrence of this hearing. It's an imperfect system, and I was glad to arrange a remedy, in your case. I'm sure that if you were in charge, you would have chosen differently for your prisoners."

"Yeah, like that would ever happen," Syren scoffed. Jack grinned along.

"Did you see much of the fight?" she asked him.

"A little," he answered. "After a point, I thought it best to alert the gate wardens to be ready when you arrived with the prince."

"That was a good idea," she acknowledged, thinking of Coran and George.

"And as everyone else was occupied, the duty fell to me."

"Did you see the lightning that fell?" she inquired. "I mean, I was pretty busy right then, and on the opposite side of the carriage when it happened, but it was a clear night. Where did that come from?" Jack shifted uncomfortably in his seat.

"There must have been a cloud somewhere," he suggested evasively. "As you say, you were a trifle busy just then to engage in detailed weather forecasting."

"I suppose so," Syren allowed. "So how do you think this hearing will go?" she asked after a pause in their conversation.

"It will go as it must," Jack replied plainly. "The plaintiffs will state their case, we will answer the charges as best we can, and then the prince will render a decision."

"What about these 'advocates' you spoke of when we were in the dungeon? You said there might be some who would talk to the prince about how valuable we were to the village, or whatever."

"I remember," he said.

"How did that work out? Did you find any that would testify on our behalf?"

"Oh, yes indeed. I found dozens of them," he reported simply. Syren looked around the room, which was devoid of anyone but the guards and those directly involved in the grievance.

"Well, where are they?" she asked.

"You slaughtered them the other night," he assured her calmly. "Well done!" he added enthusiastically. Syren was befuddled by Jack's explanation, but before she could inquire further, the chancellor appeared in his official robes of state, complete with the hat with the giant blue feather. He crossed to his lectern and banged his gavel to announce the start of the hearing. With everyone sitting in silent attention, Prince Hallas entered from the other door, as Syren had seen him do once before, and seated himself.

During the testimony portion of the hearing, Aglar Grump was first allowed to describe the exact nature of his grievance, which was that Syren had violated a well-established and binding clause of their contract by selling salvage to Maynard Edgeworthy. He offered his copy of the contract as evidence, which was complete with Syren's signature on it. Edgeworthy then testified that he had spent one hundred silvers to purchase certain items for his store, Potter's Pendants and Peculiary, on Syren's behalf. He provided the items as evidence. When asked to identify them, Syren did so, remembering Jack Frost's advice from his visit to her, that day in the prince's dungeon, that honesty was the best policy. She was hoping to have a chance to give her defense at that time, but she was not allowed. Finally, as a corroborating witness, Baron rose to add his lying subterfuge that he had seen Syren talking with a certain mercenary of the caravan wagons. He said that while he did not hear what they were saying, he saw Syren give the lad a burlap sack that looked to be full of objects. He said that the sack, which was the one Syren had already identified, was exactly like the ones Aglar gives to his salvagers. That part of his story was verified by Aglar.

When Syren was allowed to speak, she denied any knowledge of the events, claiming that the items had been stolen from her house before she could sell them to Aglar. Staring angrily at Baron, she assured the prince that whoever took them was certainly a despicable, lying scoundrel, but as she could offer no tangible proof of her claim, she was instructed to keep to the facts of the case. In that direction, she could only assert that she and her friends were deep in the wilds of Stormwood when the events in question were happening. As proof, she offered to describe the area they were traveling in, but since neither the prince nor the chancellor had any knowledge of that area themselves, the chancellor dismissed the description as irrelevant.

By the time Syren finished her account and sat back down, she was feeling the despair welling up inside her. Compared to the interlacing testimonies of her adversaries and the way they supported each other, her own version of the events sounded suspect, even to her. Nevertheless, when the chancellor asked if there was any other testimony before a decision was rendered, Jack Frost rose calmly to his feet and waited silently to be recognized.

"In evaluating the merit of all the testimonies given today," he began, "I would request that His Highness take into account his own knowledge, which is by direct experience, of the particular courage and valor of those who stand before him, accused. Only these felt so inclined toward His Highness as to voluntarily risk their lives for the sake of his. I have great confidence in the prince's ability to assess the value of such a service. Indeed, their liberty is a continuing value to all Westpost. There is, of course, no need to remind the prince of the conversation he had with me some long while ago, in which I agreed to use my meager resources to assist in keeping this settlement safe. This is a pledge I have honored on occasions past and most recently." In making that last point, he indicated Syren and the Stouts with a wave of his hand. Then after a brief pause, he continued.

"If His Highness now has a wish to refuse such help, he certainly has the authority to do so." Jack bowed his head submissively, but when he raised it again, his gaze upon the prince was sharper than the sword of Syren's father.

"Such a decree, however, cannot be changed, once it is made," Jack concluded, and his calm voice had the slightest edge to it. Then thanking His Highness for the privilege of addressing him, he sat.

As Syren had seen before, the chancellor consulted quietly with the prince at his request. She glanced over at Jack, hoping for some indication of what the outcome might be, but he was patiently serene. At length, the chancellor returned to his podium to announce the prince's verdict.

"His Highness upholds the value of a legitimate contract. The salvage sold to Potter's Pendants and Peculiary belongs to Oswald's Venture Salvage. Syren shall compensate Maynard Edgeworthy the sum of one hundred silver coins for his loss. In accordance with the terms of the contract, she shall also pay a like amount to Aglar Grump." As Syren's heart was deflating into hopelessness, the chancellor finished announcing the prince's decree.

"In recognition for services recently rendered to His Highness Prince Hallas generously forgives the fee of five hundred silver coins, which are the usual tribute for these proceedings. In addition, in the interest of the continued safety and future prosperity of all persons living in Westpost, the prince graciously commutes any sentence of imprisonment that might have been levied against Syren or the persons with her, in relation to the events in question. This matter is now closed."

As Prince Hallas and the chancellor left the chamber, Syren and the other villagers also turned to file out, in two small groups. Of the accusers, Maynard Edgeworthy appeared contentedly indifferent about the prince's decision. For him, the whole affair seemed to be nothing more than a business matter that was now concluded. Baron stomped away angrily, his sour face scowling over the leniency with which Syren and the Stouts were treated. Aglar Grump, always the entrepreneur, snatched up the burlap sack that had been awarded him and hurried to approach Syren as she and the others began to shuffle out.

"Well, Syren," he offered in his fast talking and irritating way, "no hard feelings. A deal is a deal, that's all. I'm just enforcing an honest contract. We both signed it," he pointed out.

Syren sighed. "Yeah, I know," she said.

"Don't take it too hard, it's just a hundred silvers. Okay, two hundred, but anyway, I still think that you folks are decent salvagers. Just to show you what a fair man I am, I wouldn't turn down the idea of having you sign another contract. As a matter of fact, I happen to have one right here." Pulling a set of folded parchments from his vest pocket, he snapped it open with a sharp flick of his wrist and forced them into Syren's hands. In the gloom of all the recent events, the young woman felt like she was being offered the chance to choose which type of torture she wanted: Baron's persecution, the prince's dungeon, or the harsh terms of Aglar's salvage contracts. Life was a weary and miserable business, it seemed just then. Fortunately, Jack came to her rescue just as she was beginning to consider the merit of signing her life away.

"Syren, before you enter into any new engagements, don't you think it wise to honor your current obligations?" The tone of his voice was a warning knell, despite the diplomacy of his words.

"Yes, I suppose so," she acknowledged. She tried to return the contract to Aglar, but he refused.

"You hang on to it," he insisted. "That way, you can sign it anytime. No pressure."

When they reached the iron gate that separated the Palace courtyard from the rest of Westpost, Aglar went on about his business, while Jack paused with Syren and the Stouts to consider their next course of action.

"Well, that ended better than it might have," Jack suggested cheerily. "Baron's treachery has been thwarted, for the most part. Your reputations, damaged though they were, will recover as it becomes known that you rescued the prince from a frightful peril, and in heroic fashion, no less. You escaped the burden of having to pay a severe tribute, and you are released from prison on a beautiful, if cloudy, day, and you are free to pursue other possibilities."

"I don't know what you did, Jack, but thank you. I'm sure that this turned out as good as it did because of you," Syren acknowledged.

Jack bowed humbly. "So what will you do now?" he asked.

"Well, we have to pay the Palace the fines that will go to Maynard and Aglar, and we weren't given any kind of extension, so we should do that first and get it over with. Then we should check in with Kollan."

"The blacksmith?" Jack asked.

"Yes," Syren answered.

"He is making armor for us," Durast volunteered.

"Out of ant-crab shells," Braenog added.

Jack raised his eyebrows, impressed. "Indeed," he said.

"He told us he would try, anyway," Syren qualified. "I want to see how he's making out."

Thanking Jack again, Syren and the Stouts left him to his own agenda and returned to Syren's house. There, they stowed their weapons carefully out of sight and retrieved the large iron-bound chest from the root cellar. Previously, they had emptied it to fill the alcove they had excavated into the wall. Having refilled it, Durast and Braenog carried it between them, holding it by one leather handle at each end as they and Syren walked back toward the Palace. The sight caused something of a stir as they passed among the houses of their neighbors. Treasure from Stormwood often did, but none of the villagers were bold enough to inquire after the contents of the rustic and wilderness-battered box. It was almost as if they feared that if they approached, something dreadful would jump out at them.

Upon arrival, they were ushered by a guard into the Divining Hall, where the chancellor watched Durast count out the money necessary for paying the fines. First, one hundred silver coins were counted out, to be disbursed by the chancellor's servant to Maynard Edgeworthy. Then Durast paid in kind the decreed one-hundred-silver-piece fine for Aglar Grump by meticulously counting out one thousand of the small copper coins.

"They are ten of these, the equal to one of the silver coins, yes?" he asked innocently.

"Yes," the chancellor confirmed impatiently. Syren couldn't help smirking behind her hand as she watched the feigned sincerity with which Durast laboriously laid out the exact amount required. The two sums were gathered into two separate sacks by the chancellor's servant while he recorded the transaction on a large ledger, with quill and ink.

"Just a moment," the chancellor commanded as Syren and her friends turned to leave. The trio stopped and turned around obediently. The chancellor was leafing through previous pages of his ledger as if searching for something. Eventually, he found it.

"I thought so," he confirmed to himself aloud. Then he looked accusingly at Syren through squinted eyes. "The three of you still owe His Highness the sum of one thousand silver pieces. It was the decision of a grievance hearing regarding"—he took a moment to glance down and read his own notes on the subject before continuing—"destructive and disorderly conduct at the tavern, two months ago. Do you remember?"

"Yes, sir. We remember," Syren assured him.

"It seems that you were granted an extension of sixty days in which to pay the fine and tribute."

"Yes, sir," Syren agreed again demurely. "We are hoping, though, that the money we brought in today will apply toward today's affairs, since we still have some time to raise the other." In dubious response, the chancellor frowned.

"You have three days remaining," he warned them sternly. Syren's heart sank as she faced the reality of the chancellor's words and the dreadful promise they implied. She didn't know exactly how much money they had left, but she knew that it wasn't much.

"Remind us again after the next time we save the prince's life," Durast retorted sarcastically. Syren gasped in embarrassment and alarm. He made the irritated remark to himself, but he had made it out loud. Cringing, she cuffed him on the shoulder. The chancellor's face became suddenly red with outrage.

"Get them out!" he growled angrily to the guard as he glared at Syren. Quickly, she hustled herself and her friends away from the chancellor's presence and back to the Village Green.

"Durast," Syren scolded, "don't antagonize the chancellor! He can make our lives miserable anytime he wants. He doesn't even need a reason. Don't give him one."

"He forgets himself under his fine hat," Durast protested. "We are in the right."

"Maybe, but let's not be dead right," Syren countered.

"Syren!" a voice called out from across the road. It was Kollan, calling to her from his blacksmith shop. "Syren, come and see!" he invited eagerly.

The three rushed over in anticipation, bringing their box and the remnant of its contents with them. When they arrived, Kollan proudly brought out the result of his month-long labor on their behalf. It was an enameled-looking, sand-colored breastplate made from the materials they had left with him. Dropping to one knee, he fitted the surprisingly lightweight yet durable-looking piece against Braenog's round chest with a studied eye. Braenog flipped his long, thick beard to the outside of it as the blacksmith did so. Curving convexly around the front half of his torso, the breastplate had a semicircular cutaway at the top to keep it from gouging into the Stout's neck and two more at the upper sides to allow free motion of his arms. Two individual flat rectangles of the carapace material hung down below the lower edge of the main piece. They were connected to it by wide leather straps such that they generally protected Braenog's thighs yet would move freely when he ran. The entire unit was padded slightly on the underside with a layer of cowhide, and it fastened snuggly in place from behind by an array of belts and clasps. Kollan cinched it up himself that first time while he was evaluating the fit. Then he showed Syren and Durast how it worked.

"What do you think?" Kollan asked Braenog. The Stout swung his arms, twisted his upper body, jogged around the anvil, and then bent forward as far as he could. When he straightened back up, he was grinning.

"It is mostly comfortable to wear," he said to Kollan. "I believe I can learn to fight in it, though it is somewhat restricting."

"Well, it's going to be, isn't it?" Kollan replied, shrugging. "It's armor, after all."

"Is it still strong?" Durast asked. Kollan handed him a hammer from his tool supply. Durast banged on the breastplate with it, softly at first, then harder and in various places, until his kinsman was staggered back a step by the force of one of the blows. They laughed then in approval and tugged each other's beards.

"Where's mine?" Durast asked. Grinning, the blacksmith pulled out a second breastplate, much like the first, and began to fit it to the shorter Deepfellow.

"I had to scrub the underside with lye and then scorch that surface to cure it," he told Syren as he worked.

"How did you cut it to size?" Syren asked.

"That was a little tricky," Kollan confessed. "It was a bit of trial and error, really. I experimented on smaller pieces with a variety of tools, but nothing seemed to make an even cut." He spun Durast around to work the fasteners. "Eventually, I discovered that I could shape the edges and make the rivet holes with a very hot poker. In the end, I basically melted it into the shape I needed. It was nice that the pieces you gave me were pretty much Stout-sized to begin with."

"And the straps?" Syren asked.

"Evan the leathersmith," he answered simply. "Same with the cowhide lining." Syren nodded as Durast tested out his new armor and declared it to be satisfactory.

"Okay, what do you have for me?" Syren asked hopefully.

"That's where I ran into trouble," the blacksmith confessed sheepishly. "Or rather, where you did. I used up some of the material learning how to work with it. After that, there was only enough left to make the two breastplates and some smaller pieces. I used most of the smaller stuff to make those thigh guards. This is what I did with what I had left." He presented Syren with two curved, rectangular pieces, about four inches wide and eight inches long, and attached them to her right upper arm and forearm by the leather straps provided.

"I remembered that you carried a shield, so I thought these would protect your sword arm," he said. When he tried them on her, they fit reasonably well.

"Seems good to me," Syren affirmed. "What do we owe you?" Kollan rubbed his stubby hands on his bald head as he thought.

"Can you give me another hundred silvers?" he asked hesitantly. Syren knew that there was no set rate of pay for crafting armor out of mammoth ant-crab carapaces. Haggling over the asking price was the normal way of commerce in Westpost, but Syren was so pleased with the skill, effort, and enthusiasm Kollan had shown for the project that she decided just to give him what he was asking. After paying the blacksmith, there were few enough coins left, just a handful, in fact, that Durast placed them in his belt pouch rather than have them slide around inside the big wooden chest they were carrying with them. Then thanking the blacksmith again, they turned to leave.

"One more thing," Kollan advised.

"What's that?" Syren asked.

"That armor is very hard, but that also means that it's brittle. It won't bend or dent, like steel. It'll take a pounding for a while, but eventually it'll crack. Then shortly after that, it'll shatter and become useless.

"Better it than us," Braenog quipped.

"Okay. We'll keep that in mind," Syren promised.

"Besides that, remember what I did to cut and mold it. Don't let it get exposed to fire or anything that's extremely hot. If you do, no guarantees."

"We understand," Syren said. "Thanks."

Leaving the blacksmith's shop, they walked back to Syren's house to drop off the trunk and pick up their weapons. On the way, they were accompanied by the seriousness of their situation.

"How much money do we have left?" Syren asked.

"Eight silvers," Durast answered plainly.

"So after the original grievance hearing, we were given sixty days to raise a thousand silvers," Syren recalled.

"So it was," confirmed Durast.

"I remember thinking at that time how impossible that seemed."

"Yep, yep," Braenog said, and the words were somehow nostalgic.

"Now, it's fifty-seven days later, and of the thousand silvers we need, we have…eight." The Stouts walked along quietly for a few steps.

"Can we gather salvage from the Hiddeans?" Braenog wondered as they passed the vacant and dilapidating storefront that had once belonged to Drayton, the weaver.

"Which Hiddeans?" asked Durast.

"The ones we slew when we rescued the prince." he clarified.

"That was three days ago," Syren reminded them. "We can look, but I doubt seriously that we'll find anything after this much time." The Stouts rolled their *r*'s regretfully in agreement. After a few more steps, Syren sighed heavily.

"What was the use of all this?" she lamented suddenly. "All the struggling, all the searching, risking our lives out there—Braenog nearly died! All the terror we faced outside the wall, the deception we faced within it—first from Aglar and then from Baron. We slew ourselves day after day, even spent time in that awful dungeon, and for what? We are no closer to the thousand silvers now than we were the day we started, and in three days, they're going to come and take everything away from me: my home, my possessions, my freedom… and then I'll never find Father." The strain and the frustration began to force tears unwillingly from Syren's eyes as she ranted. By this time they had arrived at Syren's modest home, and she threw the door open, stormed inside, and sat down at the table with her head in her hands. She wanted not to cry. It didn't solve any of her problems, but since the whole situation seemed hopeless anyway, then if there was a time for tears, this was as good as any. She felt truly at the end.

Durast and Braenog came and stood beside her, one Stout on either side. From where she sat, they were nearly as tall as she was. For a time, they said nothing, but stood in silent vigil as if they were mourning the severity of Syren's plight. Then it was Durast who spoke. The deep and determined tone in his voice was gentle to his friend, but chastising to the despair.

"We have seen discouraging times," he acknowledged, "but we have seen valiant times also. How often have we faced the Hiddeans and prevailed? Who else has succeeded against the Grrremlin, or fought the dracolisk and lived to tell the tale? All these are the deeds of Syren, and they are mighty!" he said with great conviction.

"With the help of my friends," Syren included, taking each one by the arm gratefully.

"How deep and bravely have we ventured into Stormwood?" Durast continued. "Why, Nog and I can even find our way around, I think. I can find him by the rumble of his stomach!" The comment made Syren laugh, in spite of herself. "Name all the warriors who have rescued a prince and defeated a Baron. They are here!" he announced decidedly, patting her and Braenog on the shoulder.

"Baron has caused a topsider's trouble, to be sure," Braenog added, "but Syren has pummeled him, and the Deepfellows would have. And despite all his treachery, we still belong to ourselves for three days more. Say that it was not deep living, even if it comes to an end." Syren shrugged her acceptance of the description.

"And still there is more," Durast went on, pleading their case. "Syren has regained her father's sword and she wields it well. We have armor, and we own a bit of healing salve. Though we have not yet seen it, we know where to search for Syren's fallen kinsman. We know the forest much deeper than we did at first, and we have good weather and three days' time to find him."

"Syren," Braenog implored, "we may or we may not succeed in gaining our trrreasure or in finding your kinsman father, only let us not end our striving, as topsiders would, not while we yet have strength in us."

Syren sat upright at the table and collected herself. Her friends were right. This was no time for despair and the abandonment of all her dreams. Yes, their circumstances were difficult. Maybe they were as hard as they'd ever been, but she had also never been so close to achieving her goals: finding Father, making a real difference in Westpost, hearing destiny's true call upon her life. As long as she and the Stouts were together, there was hope, and if, in the end, there was nothing for it but to fail, then she would go down fighting. She would make her father proud. Rising, she went to the kitchen and washed her face, then turned determinedly toward Durast and Braenog.

"Well then," she proclaimed, "since the forest of Stormwood can take nothing from us that we wouldn't lose anyway, get the weapons. Let's go find my father.

CHAPTER 16

Reunion

High and sturdy, a thick wooden wall stood in silent immutability at the heart of the treacherous forest of Stormwood. Intended long ago by its founders to be a bastion of a spreading civilization, it defended and also imprisoned those who dwelt within it. Only a single dirt road tethered the gradually shrinking community to the safer and more refined culture of the eastern world. Inside the protective wall of Westpost, peaceful people toiled earnestly day by day, scratching out their meager existence, because they knew no other way and because they dared not venture outside. Beyond it, a malevolent wilderness encroached itself around the wall, resisting every attempt at pacification, wanting always to consume the order and civility that affronted it.

Within that hungry avarice that would blot out any trace of civilization's presence, a perilous force was stalking the forest, just outside of the village. Driven by the hunt and the closeness of its quarry, a three-headed, carapace-covered agent of havoc roamed among the trees, searching diligently, bent on the destruction of any who stood in the way.

It was a force named Syren and Durast and Braenog.

The Westpost trio worked their way methodically through the Nearwood, alert to possible dangers but focused on a place that was as yet unseen by their company, a rumored tower that was waiting for them somewhere deep within Stormwood.

"This is not the way we went before," Durast observed.

"Yes," agreed Braenog. "Last time we searched for the tower, we walked along the road until we entered Stormwood directly. Now we are closer to Westpost, in the Nearwood. Is Syren lost?"

"Not at all," explained Syren confidently. "Last month, the route we took brought us over some very dangerous territory. It may have been more direct, given what we have been told about the tower's general location, and finding that stone archway gave us a pretty good indication of where the tower might be, but we also wore ourselves out trying to fight our way through from that direction. This way is more roundabout but also less risky. The Nearwood is a little more open, a little tamer. It's been cleared, or it was, at any rate. By traveling in it for as long as possible, we're less likely to have the kind of unexpected and ferocious encounters that lurk in Stormwood."

"I am not afraid of the unexpected ferocious," Braenog asserted boldly.

"No, of course not," Syren acknowledged. "We just can't afford to get waylaid like we did last time. We need to make it to the tower without having to deal with other distractions."

"This is good strategy," Durast approved to reassure Braenog. "Even in victory against the ant-crabs, if any of us become paralyzed, we would wait long for the effect to wear off, and time is not our kinsman in this effort."

"Besides that," reminded Syren, "we were warned not to expose the new armor to heat. The dracolisk could melt it before we ever got a chance to use it."

As Braenog was admitting to the wisdom of their overall plan, they were accosted suddenly by a group of Hiddeans. Flushed out into the open by the tramping and conversation of Syren and the Stouts, the fiendish dozen quickly surrounded the three of them, snarling and threatening them with spear-like pointed sticks. Syren drew her sword disgustedly.

"We don't have time for this," she scolded the Hiddeans as if they comprehended. Rocks began to fly from the vile troop, but they clattered harmlessly off of Syren's shield and the carapace breastplates of the Stouts. In response, Durast and Braenog rolled their *r*'s defiantly, took their axes into hand, and eyed their foes eagerly. Then as the three of them were assessing where they should strike first, the despicable assembly retreated cautiously for three or four paces and then scattered abruptly, fleeing into the forest in every direction. The first reaction by Syren and her companions was to look quickly all around them. The Hiddeans had certainly fled from some terrible menace, and they didn't want to be attacked by a greater evil than the one they were already aware of. When they checked, however, they found themselves alone in the wilderness. Slowly, the dawning of a new day began to break upon them.

"Did we really just see that happen?" Syren wondered aloud.

"I think they fled from us," Durast speculated back.

"Yep, yep," Braenog confirmed.

"How did that happen? Why did that happen?" Syren asked.

"Perhaps they were among those who fled from us the other night, when we rescued the prince?" Durast suggested.

"Maybe," Syren began to process the implications of their theory. "Do you realize what that means, if they did?"

"They are smarter than we thought they were," answered Braenog, nodding his head decisively.

"No," Syren countered. "Well okay, maybe, but besides that. It means that they ran away because they were scared of us. Of us!"

"They should be," proclaimed Durast. "We have defeated them a number of times. We take their treasure."

"Exactly! They know us and they fear us, and now they're starting to avoid us. Think about the possibilities that creates. If we were to keep up a patrol in the Nearwood, be visible out here, make sure they could see us, they might begin to leave Westpost and its people alone. Eventually, other patrols could be formed also. That would free us up to expand the circle a little bit. We could patrol the edges of Stormwood, maybe even a little deeper than the edges. Then we could finally begin to push back against the evil that surrounds this place. Just like Father was doing!" The whole idea was exhilarating for Syren to think about. It was almost like rescuing all Westpost from a long and terrible oppression.

"There is deep evil in Stormwood," Durast reminded.

"Granted," Syren conceded. "We would have to be careful, use strategy."

"With strategy, it could be done," Durast agreed.

"First, though, we have important business to finish. Come on."

Syren, Durast, and Braenog worked their way through the trees and grassy spaces, to the southernmost extent of the Nearwood. At several points along the way, they spotted small groups of Hiddeans on the fringes of Stormwood. The savages seemed to be following them, tracking them, but always at a distance. When on one occasion the three tried to draw weapons and engage them, the Hiddeans scampered away, only to reform later and resume their surveillance from further away. Ultimately, Syren stopped to assess their progress and location in the wilderness.

"This is as far as the Nearwood goes in this direction, but it should be enough. Westpost is back that way. From here, that stone archway we found would be west and north of us, so the tower should be due west, maybe a little more south, and about a half mile or so into Stormwood."

It was an arduous half mile. The dense undergrowth and tangled vines seemed to work consciously to ensnare and impede them at every step. Strange and ominous noises threatened them perpetually, from no observable source. Feeling constantly imperiled as they walked, they tended to cast their awareness haphazardly, in every direction at once. Being simultaneously vigilant of everything and of nothing, they were startled by a group of creatures that came crashing through the forest, disturbingly close to their own position.

"Get down!" Syren hissed to Durast and Braenog as she huddled into a crouch. When she glanced at her friends, though, she discovered that they were short enough to have effective cover without having to hunch over in any way. Instead, they carefully parted the leafy brambles and peered through silently as the other group passed by them obliviously.

"Orcs!" whispered Braenog. It was difficult to see them well without betraying their presence, but Syren trusted the old Stout's impression.

"There looks to be four of them," Durast reported. "They seem to be transporting prisoners, probably Grremlin."

"Prisoners?" said Syren, though from her vantage point it certainly looked that way. The larger brutes were surrounding and mistreating the smaller ones as they pushed and prodded them along.

"Yep, yep," assured Durast.

"Orcs are known to be slavers, torturers, even cannibals," explained Braenog. He was talking in a slightly louder voice as the Orcs had moved on, toward the west.

"They did not see us," Durast observed. "We could attack them unaware."

"If we barrel in, we will take them easily," Braenog suggested. Then he and Durast moved to abandon the bush they were hiding behind and pursue, but Syren stopped them.

"Wait a second, hold on," she said. "If they're transporting prisoners, that means they're taking them somewhere, probably to a camp of some sort. Baron told us that the area around the tower was thick with Orcs. I bet that's where they're going."

"Well?" asked Braenog impatiently. "What if that is so?"

"If we follow them instead of attacking them, they might lead us straight to the tower! That's our goal, remember? Not fighting every creature that pops out at us." Braenog forced out his lower lip in a pout, but Durast turned to him and rolled his *r*'s.

"This strategy is deep good," he assured Braenog, tugging his beard. "Alive, they will show us Syren's father. They will show us their trrreasure!"

At that, Braenog was convinced, and with Syren in the lead, the three of them easily followed the trail the orcs were leaving until at length, they encountered a battered stone wall, the remnants of which were about four feet high. Then rather than follow the Orcish squad into unknown danger, they left off their tracking and skulked along the wall in the opposite direction. At various points, Syren rose cautiously from her crouch to peer over the wall and study what lay beyond. The Stouts stood on their tiptoes to do likewise.

From appearances, the stone wall was the inner ring of a small, dilapidated castle of ancient design. The wide space inside the ring was loosely divided into three general areas. In one, a single tall tower of rooms enshrouded with creeping vines rose above the landscape across the distance. From the closed wooden door at its base to the crenellated parapet of its roof, the structure was three stories high. In spite of its obvious age, the tower seemed to be in decent condition. In another area, several low and crumbling stone buildings were clustered together on the far side of the circle from where they were. A large number of the humanoid creatures that Durast and Braenog had identified as Orcs were milling about in that area of the compound. They interacted with each other gruffly, fighting and challenging each other, roaring hoarsely back and forth, and beating the Gremlin prisoners, whom they had tethered to a wooden pole that protruded from the ground.

"What are they doing with those prisoners?" Syren whispered to Durast as they watched.

"Tenderizing them, I would say," he answered, and Syren swallowed hard. Smoke, as from a cook fire, was rising from one of the buildings, or perhaps from just behind it. It was difficult to tell from their vantage point.

Between them and the area where the Orcs had congregated to torment their captives, a field of tall, dry grass had sprouted up, which was reclaiming for the wilderness what had once been a paved stone courtyard. The position of the tower partially obstructed their view of the scene. In addition, the tall swaying grass and the swarming movements of the Orcs, among each other and around, into, and out from the buildings made getting an accurate count of the feral villains impossible, but there was certainly a lot of them.

Syren and the Stouts ducked down behind the wall and scuttled along to another spot, where they hoped to see the compound from a different perspective.

"This must be the place that Baron was talking about," Syren guessed. "I wonder where Father's body is. Could he be inside one of those low buildings?"

"He will be terribly hard to retrieve if he is," suggested Braenog but Durast shook his shaggy red head.

"Baron is a topsider. He would not face so many foes. He would not succeed if he did. The body must be somewhere else. Perhaps by the base of the tower."

"He did specifically mention the tower," Syren remembered. "There's nothing on this side, though. Let's move around to where we can see the other side."

Skulking around the outside of the wall to a spot that was in view of the far side of the tower brought them closer to the orcs and somewhat farther from the tower itself, but when at last they peered carefully over the wall again, Syren was both thrilled and horrified by what she saw.

At various points on the tower, windows had been cut so that the inhabitant liege of ages past could look out upon the countryside and also monitor whatever activities were going on in the courtyard of his castle. From one of these, on the second floor, hung the skeletal remains of a human form. Dressed in the tattered rags of an all too familiar uniform, the dishonored corpse clung together in slack-jawed, gaping anguish by the sun-dried, leathery shreds of skin that time, heat, and neglect had mummified into a tautly shrunken, natural shroud. The pitiful eyeless sentinel hung from the base of the upper story window like a tapestry. Facing the low buildings where the orcish company was encamped, the desiccated and woeful figure was being intentionally and garishly displayed as the emblem and warning of some new and cruelly ruthless taskmaster of the castle.

Syren's heart leapt into her throat at the gruesomely recognizable sight.

"Father," she breathed despondently. She tried not to cry. She wanted to be strong and responsible, but at the sight of him a hundred childhood memories flooded Syren's head, piling up until they overflowed, as water, from her eyes. All at once, she was overpowered by emotion at the idea that the long siege of despair, mystery, and doubt that had assailed her could finally be lifted. At long last, her diligent searching and her fervent striving were near an end. All the frustration, failure, and guilt could now be assuaged. She could finally have closure, and her father could rest in peace and honor, if only she could bring him home and rescue him from the terrible spectacle they had turned him into.

Syren sheathed her sword and stowed her shield. Overcome by the nearness of her goal and the sight of her father, she had become oblivious to the risk. In the next moment, she was climbing the wall.

"We have to get him down from there," she announced, but even as she made to swing her legs over the wall and jump down into the waist high grass of the courtyard, she was grappled by two strong and heavy Stouts, who hauled her back onto their side.

"Syren," Durast scolded, "what are you thinking? You can't just run across open ground, in full view of the enemy."

"But he's right there!" she protested, still struggling to free herself of their grasp so she could rescale the wall.

"The Orcs will bash your brains out before you lay one hand on the tower," Durast assured her. "Besides that, your kinsman is twenty feet in the air. The only way to get to him is from inside the tower, and we have no idea who dwells there or how many guard it from within."

"But what if no one does?" Syren argued desperately. "What if they just hung him there to make people think someone tough lived inside?"

"That is a fool's hope," Durast countered plainly but patiently. "It is one that could get us all killed. Then who would rescue your father?"

"No barreling in!" Braenog instructed her sternly, and while she bristled at the rebuke, she also gained an appreciation for how he must have felt all along, and in the pause, she began to see the sense of what they were saying.

"All right, what do we do then?" she asked. The three peeked carefully over the wall again to assess the situation.

"We need a plan," said Durast.

"We need more healing salve," said Braenog.

"We need to move away from this spot," said Syren. "I think they've seen us."

"Seen you," Braenog corrected. "Still, we should all move on. Some of them are coming this way."

Quickly, the three companions hustled along the wall, back in the direction from which they had come. They had almost returned to their initial point when they were challenged menacingly from in front by a pair of intimidating-looking Orcs. They were each a head taller than Syren, and their deep-set black eyes glared down at her from underneath overly prominent brow ridges. Their lower faces protruded forward, like an ape, so that their wide, dark heads had a generally sloping appearance, yet their expressions suggested an evil and confident intellect.

Through a fang encrusted mouth, one of them growled some sort of command at Syren. Though she couldn't make out what he said, she discerned the word *human*. He said it with a sneer, like it was something contemptible.

"So you can speak, eh?" Syren returned boldly. She was unsure that they could really understand her language, but she decided to try. In any case, she had learned well by experience that backing down against the savage races of Stormwood was never a good idea, and for the time being, she and the Stouts outnumbered them three to two. Drawing her sword and shield, she made them an ultimatum of her own. "Well, you've got my father in there, and I want him back."

Outraged at her insolence, the lead Orc bared his teeth, roared his disapproval, and swung his weapon at Syren's head. The brute had smooth reddish-brown skin, for the most part and was rippling with muscles. The weapon he wielded was a club that was made of dense wood, honed at one end for a handle, and contained numerous sharp spikes at the other. As the war club came at Syren, she raised her shield to block it. When she did, she was protected from serious harm but was also driven backward by the force of the blow. Having been thus staggered, her counterstrike with her long sword went amiss.

Before she could gather herself and prepare for another attack, Durast and Braenog rushed past her and lunged at her assailant, sending all three sprawling to the dirt. While the second Orc strode angrily forward to engage Syren, the first scrambled deftly to his feet and squared off against Durast, who was rising eagerly to face him. As Durast closed to within his short but powerful reach, the Orc tried to crash in Durast's skull with his spiked club. The younger Stout dodged the strike, however, and the blow caromed harmlessly off of his carapace breastplate.

For an instant, both attacker and defender paused in wonder at the armor's rigid competency.

Then chuckling enthusiastically through a wide grin, Durast laid into the Orc with both axes. Unfortunately, the Orcs were also wearing heavy leather vests, and while the suit took some small damage, its wearer was little more than bruised by the strikes.

Syren, aware of the strength of her opponent, jumped into range quickly and slashed his arm with a lightning fast hacking motion from her sword. Then as she danced back, she was able to take the Orc's counterattack as a glancing blow to her shield, which was much less debilitating. The Stormwood bully relied always on his strength to overpower his foe. By being fast and agile, Syren quickly wore him down until she found an opening to run him through and finish him.

By that time, Durast and the other Orc had exchanged frontal assaults again, with the same mostly ineffective results, but then Braenog attacked the Orc from the rear flank. Swinging his poleax in a hard, horizontal sweep, he caught the savage from behind, hamstringing him. The wound toppled the brute over, and once he was the size of the Stouts, they made quick work of dispatching him.

"We should leave this area," Braenog advised afterward, while casting his glance about him. "We should return to Westpost." Both of his friends looked at him incredulously.

"But what about Father?"

"But what about treasure?"

"We can return for both, but only if we live," he answered.

"Nog is right," Durast admitted to Syren with a measure of reluctance and surprise. "This battle was noisy, and we still have no plan. If the Orcs respond in force, we will not endure, not even in armor."

Taking only the two war clubs and two small coin pouches, Syren and the Stouts dashed through the woods in the direction they had come, as fast as they were able. The sounds of Orcish cries rang in Syren's ears, and she was unsure if they were being chased, or if the foul fumes of Stormwood were playing tricks on her, but in any case, they made the best speed they could until they had run nearly the entire way back to the Wallgate, and were safely inside of it.

Winded by their sprint, but exhilarated by what they had found, fought, and evaded, Syren, Durast, and Braenog ignored the inane queries of Coran and George and hustled away to Syren's house to examine their loot and talk strategy. Their only stop on the way was the well and washhouses in Syren's neighborhood for water and a chance to cool down from the afternoon's exertions.

"Planning goes better with a mug and a plate," Braenog suggested. "We should talk at the Hooded Crow."

"Not tonight," Syren advocated. "The last time we were there, we accidently revealed our plans to Baron. That almost ended tragically for us. Now more than ever, time is critical. We can't afford to get waylaid like that again. Not when what we have seen is so important. This has to be kept secret. No one must know. Tonight we stay here until we figure this out."

Durast rolled some *r*'s in agreement as he pulled out the coin pouches he had taken off the orcs they had vanquished and set them on the table in front of them.

"I want to quit telling our plans to just everybody, anyway," Syren finished, and the Stouts agreed.

Durast upended the contents of the two leather coin pouches. Seven gold coins tumbled out of the first one and four from the second. The Stouts instantly scooped them up in their oversized hands. Then Braenog reluctantly offered one for Syren's appraisal. She accepted it in grinning appreciation of the friendship represented by the gesture. The Stouts studied them closely for a few moments. They turned them over in their hands and tried to bend and bite them as a way of checking their authenticity. Syren simply hefted hers a couple of times. It seemed genuine enough.

"Well?" Syren inquired of them easily. They grinned wide white teeth at her.

"Eleven gold coins, from just two Orcs," Braenog observed dreamily.

"Altogether, there must be scads of them," Durast projected.

"Gold coins?" Syren asked.

"Orcs!" Braenog qualified.

"There are probably many more Orcs than we saw," Durast began.

"And we saw plenty," Braenog finished.

"Syren, if we can rrrrout the camp, we can still pay the Palace and have treasure left for ourselves."

"And we can rescue Syren's father," Braenog added. "Then we can return him honorably to the ground." Durast tugged his kinsman's beard in solemn agreement about the necessity of such an activity, and Braenog nodded assuredly to Syren.

"Sounds good to me," Syren approved. "So how do we get that done?" They sat for a few moments in a studied silence, until Braenog's stomach rumbled loudly.

"I'm having trouble thinking," Braenog said sheepishly, and Syren went to the larder for cheese, dried meat, and bread. Bringing sustenance back to the table, they began to build their strategy.

"We cannot barrel in," Durast said apologetically to Braenog. "They are too many and too strong." Even Braenog conceded the wisdom of the statement.

"Don't they answer to the call of fear, as other savages do?" Syren asked.

"Probably," answered Durast, "but not as well as some."

"They are very confident," assured Braenog. Again, they were silent for a moment while they thought.

"Could we make them barrel in to us? Draw them out a few at a time, to thin their numbers?" Durast wondered.

"Maybe," Syren postulated. "The problems I see with that plan are that we don't know how many there are exactly, and we don't have much time. It might take days or even weeks to defeat them in pairs, and we don't have that much time." The Stouts acquiesced to Syren's logic.

"I wish we could get to the tower," Syren lamented. "That's where Father is." Her heart became more desperate as she thought of him hanging there, even as they spoke.

"We cannot sneak," Braenog confessed. "Durast and I would be seen for sure."

"What if we made a diversion?" Syren suggested. "Draw their attention away from the tower, to something else."

"Yes," Durast agreed. "Then we could barrel to the tower and slip inside, in the confusion."

"One of us could barrel from the other side of the compound," Suggested Braenog.

"I think not," Said Durast. "We should not split up against so many. From the tower, we could not come to your aid, and you could not come to ours."

"Yep, yep," Braenog retracted. "It is likely that something strong dwells within the tower, something that the Orcs are afraid of." They wracked their brains again in silence for a minute. Then Durast slammed his wide hand hard upon the table.

"The grass!" he exclaimed joyfully.

"Syren, the grass!" Braenog echoed enthusiastically.

"Um, the grass?" Syren queried, confusedly. When she looked to Braenog for explanation, he was forced to admit that he didn't know what his kinsman meant either.

"The grass of the courtyard is tall and dry," Durast explained excitedly. "It will burn easily, make much smoke and fire. The Orcs will run from the fire but not far. They will wait for it to burn out before they return. The smoke will hide us until we are in the tower."

"We can rush in on whatever Orcs are there, because they'll be distracted by what's going on in the courtyard!" continued Syren.

"We take the tower, rescue Syren's father, and return to Westpost, as we did today," summarized Braenog as though the plan were foolproof.

"After we take trrreasure," Durast negotiated.

"Yes, yes, of course," conceded Syren absently, waving her hand. "You know what? It just might work! So how do we make this brush fire?"

"Start fire with fire," Durast shrugged.

"Well, that makes sense. I know where we can get the supplies for such a thing, now that we have some money again," Syren said, indicating the coins on her table. "How soon can we go back? I mean, can we do this thing tonight?"

"Oh, nope, nope."

"Nope."

"Nope, nope," they said, waving wide palms at Syren.

"Orcs are fiercest in the dark," instructed Durast.

"And they see well at night," Braenog added. "Better than Syren."

"Better that we gather supplies, rest tonight, and go back at first light."

"We'll only have two days, by then," Syren reminded them, but the Stouts were determined, so she agreed.

The next morning they were tromping warily through the forest toward that ancient sentinel in the wilderness, the ruined tower that had been occupied and desecrated by the Orcs. Again, they avoided the more direct and open route they had first used, the day they had discovered the archway. They didn't want to risk encountering more mammoth ant-crabs, another dracolisk, or whatever had left that giant footprint if it was still around. Arriving at the stone wall, they peered cautiously over it, taking reconnaissance of the compound.

"There is the door," Durast pointed out in a low voice. "This is the closest place to barrel from."

"There are still Orcs everywhere," Syren observed nervously. "Including those two at the base of the tower."

"They may defend the entrance," Braenog guessed. "If they don't scatter with the others, we will have to take them."

"And so we shall," assured Durast, hefting one large hand ax, and Braenog rolled some *r*'s quietly.

"Where did the Gremlins go, I wonder," speculated Syren as she studied the layout of the compound, noting the vacant tethering post.

"They went where we must not go," admonished Durast without extrapolation, and Braenog nodded determinedly.

Syren found herself trembling with anticipation. It was not that she was afraid of the Orcs, although she respected what they were capable of. Nor did she doubt the soundness of their plan, though it was, in fact, a little unsettling to rush in against unknown foes with an untried tactic. She was certainly not afraid to fight. These brutes were notoriously ruthless, evil, and insatiable. The world would be better off, being rid of them. No, the source of the uncontrollable quivering was inside her own heart. It was the thrilling dread of being so close, after all this time, to actually reclaiming her father's remains, of having an end of it, and yet being so perilously near to failure. As they hunched behind the low, fallen wall of the decrepit castle, the rewards and the risks of their endeavor were both so great that they blended together to create a moment that was both shockingly real and eerily surreal at the same time. It had almost been easier for Syren when she didn't know what had become of her father. Yet she had to know, and now the moment had come. She took in a deep breathful of the crisp, morning air and let it out slowly, to calm herself.

"Are we ready?" she asked, and her friends nodded once, resolutely. "All right, then. Give me the lamp oil."

While in Westpost the previous afternoon, they had purchased and prepared a half dozen pint-sized flasks of lamp oil, the openings of which they had stuffed with rags. Sloshing about on their way to the wilderness wall, the rags had acted as wicks and become soaked in the lamp oil. It was then a simple matter for Syren to light all of them with the tinder box she had brought from her house. Once they were burning, she targeted six grassy areas within the courtyard to set alight, and hurled them at the locations. When she threw them, she arched them high in the air so they would come down in a more or less directionless fashion, and have a better chance of breaking upon impact. Four of the six struck stone and shattered, and even the two that didn't succeeded in setting the dry sheaves of grass ablaze.

As expected, the Orcs were somewhat sluggish in the morning, after their night long hunting and ravaging expeditions, and their distance vision was not as sharp in the daylight. Their first response to the crashing flasks was to run for cover, protecting themselves from possible attack. That gave the burning oil the chance it needed to catch the grass. Their next response was confusion, jostling and anger, as they dashed hectically from place to place, shouting at each other, bumping into one another, and fighting over who was in charge. Before they could get that all sorted out, a full scale brush fire was in progress. The courtyard was thick with smoke and chaos, and fires were crackling and roaring ominously from a variety of places. That, and the naturally unruly tendencies of the Orcs, combined to create a scene of general panic.

"This is the likeliest chance we're going to get," Syren advised, and the three of them scaled or hopped over the coarse, knobby, fieldstone wall, according to their height.

"We should have saved one oil flask so we could burn the door down, in case it's locked," Syren hollered as they ran through the smoke that was swirling about the open courtyard.

"It would take too long," Braenog puffed. "If that door is locked, we're in deep trouble."

"We might have thought of that yesterday," Durast complained, but by then they had arrived.

Before they could even try the door, a squad of four Orcs, which had been loitering nearby when the fire started, saw them approaching and confronted them defiantly. Drawing weapons, Syren and her companions charged fearlessly into the fray. She didn't like their odds, but she knew that all would be lost if they couldn't get inside the tower, and quickly. For her and the Stouts, the die had been cast as soon as they had jumped the wall. There was nothing left for it now, but to succeed.

Syren's determined bearing, as she raced with her allies through a backdrop of fire and smoke at the villainous squad, was a promise of doom to the Orcs as she advanced upon them. Two of the four wretches seemed to decide that if Syren was so sure that the Orcs stood no chance, then they probably didn't. Abandoning their two comrades to their fate, they ran off to join others of their ilk, who were fleeing harm from fire and smoke inhalation, beyond the stone wall.

The other two stayed, undaunted.

The first slash of Syren's fine steel blade tore open the leather vest that protected her opponent. The foe responded by crashing down on her sword arm with his heavy wooden club. Syren flinched at the anticipation of serious injury, but her ant-crab bracer deflected the attack.

Braenog inflicted a shoulder wound on the other Orc using the long reach of his poleax while Durast closed in. Flailing wildly, the brute retaliated by grabbing the ax by the pole, near the blade end. This resulted in a tug of war between the two combatants. Meanwhile, Durast and the Orc exchanged a flurry of ax and club blows. Most of the Orcish swings were off balance as he tried to maintain his hold of Braenog's weapon, and they bounced harmlessly off of Durast's breastplate. The shorter Stout was then able to disable and finish his foe.

After several lunges and counterattacks that were parried, Syren managed to pierce the Orc she was fighting through the midsection, and it bloodied the vines that covered the base of the tower as it slumped lifelessly to the ground. Amid the raging fire, the choking smoke, and the scrambling Orcs, Syren, Durast, and Braenog crowded the thick wooden door at the tower's base. Grabbing the fat iron handle anxiously, Syren heaved on the bar, preparing in her mind for it not to give way. When the heavy portal began to swing in on rusted hinges, though, the Stouts leaned hard against it, and the three slipped quickly inside.

Closing the door behind them, they threw the sturdy iron bolt that secured it, and took hasty stock of their surroundings. They were standing on the lowest landing of a stone stairwell that spiraled gently up and around the inside of the outer wall of the tower itself. Beside them was a door, lighter and more ornate than the one they had just locked, which separated them from the ground floor room beyond it.

"Up the stairs," Syren compelled them. "Father is hanging from a second story window."

"Wait," said Durast, interrupting Syren as she vaulted up the first three steps. "We should secure each floor as we go. Then we won't risk being attacked from behind."

"Well, that makes sense," Syren admitted regretfully, returning to the landing. "Also, if we take care of each room now, we won't have to fight our way out of the tower later, once we have Father with us."

"Agreed," said Durast.

"Only let us hurry," reminded Braenog. "Foes await us, without and above. It is only a matter of time until they discover our deception and marshal against us."

Weapons at the ready, Durast lifted the door handle gently. Then he threw the door back roughly and the three barged in, prepared for action. Inside, the broad, round chamber was empty, except for its furnishings. By appearances, the room once served as the meeting place for official business between the castle's original owner and his subjects. Corroded pieces of armor were scattered in disarray around the room, and pole arms of various types leaned against the wall in places. An elaborately carved, high backed, throne-like chair addressed the room from atop a low dais. Tapestries hung on the walls, depicting scenes of valor, and a variety of desks, writing equipment, candlesticks and other necessities of state were strewn about the space indifferently, probably by more recent and multiple tenants. Signs of their barbaric occupancy were everywhere.

"I think we know where the tower Orcs were staying." Braenog speculated.

"We secured this room when we slew the ones who attacked us, just outside." Durast concluded. "There is surely much trrreasure to gather," he said, and then he commenced picking through the rubble.

"Not yet," Syren demanded. "We have no idea what lies above us, yet. First, we gain control of the tower. Then we rescue Father. *Then* we gather treasure."

Now it was Durast's turn to pout, and Braenog's turn to come to reason's rescue.

"Those scoundrels outside were not the sort to dominate the rest," he argued. "They would not hoist such a banner as Syren's father, they would bow down to it. Something meaner and more wicked rules the stone above us."

Braenog's words and the desperation of Syren's agenda swayed the younger Stout, and leaving the meeting room as they found it, they ascended the curving staircase to the second landing.

As they had done on the floor below, they threw the door open and rushed in, truly convinced that they were prepared for whatever trouble might await them.

They were wrong.

CHAPTER 17

A Towering Foe

The center room of the tower had been a lavish parlor at one time, by the look of it. It was filled with dusty and degraded, but still elegant paintings, statuary, padded furniture, crystal, and so forth. Though it was glittering with potentially valuable artifacts from a bygone era, everyone's attention was instantly fixed upon the most immense and menacing-looking creature Syren had ever encountered.

Vaguely Orcish in appearance, the behemothic figure was seven feet tall and six feet wide, and would have easily stretched above eight feet except that it was naturally and grotesquely hunchbacked, its bald, boulder-like head seeming to protrude horribly forward, as from its chest, rather than rest above its massively wide shoulders. Covered in bluish-green skin, the crushingly muscular arms of the monster hung nearly to the floor, ending in clawed, powerful hands. With comparatively short, but equally muscular trunk-like legs, it stood upright on wide, bare feet that Syren matched mentally to the imposing footprint of an Ogre, whose trail they had seen in Stormwood, in the vicinity of the dracolisk.

So intimidating was the girth, the strength, and the sight of the beast that in spite of all that Syren had learned about not showing fear to the enemy in a fight, she lowered her sword point reflexively, gaping wide-eyed at the thing that was glaring malevolently back at them. Everything about it exuded the threat of terrible violence to any who tarried there.

Fortunately, the Ogre was also caught by surprise. Apparently, he was not expecting that the visitors who bounded up the steps and burst into his presence would be someone other than his Orcish lackeys from downstairs, and he took that first moment simply to roar his disapproval from across the room.

Syren's instinct was to retreat from the room to a more secure location, where she and the Stouts could share knowledge about the creature and devise a specific plan to defeat it. Two circumstances prevented her acting on that impulse and kept her in the room. The first was that her father's body was hanging from one of the windows of the chamber. Being finally this close to getting him back, she was loath to leave him. The second was that without the capacity to experience emotional fear, the Stouts had charged right in and would undoubtedly need her help.

Durast was the first to engage, axes flailing. Before he could get close enough to bring his weapons to bear on any vital area, however, the Ogre scooped up the diminutive warrior in his two hands and lifted the hefty Stout into the air with disturbingly little effort. Drooling hungrily, the fiend then began to pull on one of Durast's legs painfully, the way one might dismember a roasted quail before eating it.

The next several minutes were a jumbled fury of hacking and dodging and stabbing. Braenog rushed to the rescue of his kinsman, opening a gash on the Ogre's forearm with his poleax. With an ear splitting roar of pain and outrage, the creature tossed Durast aside and slashed at Braenog with his claws. The sweep would have easily disemboweled the Stout, but his armor protected him, the breastplate accepting broad scratches as a souvenir of his narrow escape. Durast, meanwhile, had been dashed carelessly against the stone wall of the tower, striking his head against it in the process. Momentarily stunned, he struggled to his feet.

Syren rushed to the aid of her companions, brandishing her sword and shield. When the Ogre reached out for her as he had for Durast, however, she blocked one hand with her shield and stabbed the other one clean through, the exquisitely sharp steel slicing its way nearly to the hilt. In response, the huge brute recoiled, carrying Syren off her feet entirely. For an instant, she dangled precariously before the beast's furious expression and slavering maw, afraid to release her grip on the sword for fear that she might not get it back. Instead of biting at Syren, though, he thrashed his hand violently, in an attempt to dislodge the sword from it. The effort was successful, because of Syren's added weight at the pommel end, and she tumbled to the floor, sword and all. Rolling away from the action to prevent herself being crushed under foot, she found when she tried to get up that she had been shaken senseless by the Ogre's attempt to rid himself of her. She was too dizzy to rise immediately and until her head cleared itself, she could only watch helplessly as the others fought on.

Braenog again swung his ax in a mighty arc, catching the Ogre in his fleshy side. Howling in pain, the enraged monster clenched his hands into two huge maul-like fists and turned to retaliate. Braenog ducked the first roundhouse swing with surprising alacrity, but when he came up grinning victoriously from the tactic, he was caught full on by the second one. Protected again by his ant-crab breastplate from having every rib broken, the impact of the punch and its follow through propelled the Stout across the room toward the nearest wall and deposited him there, roughly. An overstuffed high-backed chair that he landed in broke his fall, as he tumbled over and behind it.

Durast was just regaining his feet and preparing to rejoin the battle, when the Ogre began to mumble to himself and contort his hands awkwardly. The tone of his guttural, gravelly voice had not changed, but the sounds he was emitting made a horribly repulsive feeling crawl across Syren's mind. As he finished, he spread his hands and the room became suddenly and unnaturally dark. Even though Syren knew that it was midday, and sunlight had been pouring in through the windows just a moment before, the entire chamber had been engulfed in a blackness as deep as a moonless midnight.

"Durast?" Syren called out frantically.

"Ogre mage," the Stout called back, and Syren could hear him pushing his way past a low table that had been near him. "He has created a sphere of darkness around us."

"What do we do?" She hollered.

"Fight on!" he proclaimed resolutely. "Use your tunnel vision." She could hear her friend exerting himself against the Ogre, who was snarling back at him.

"Durast!" she protested simply. "I don't have tunnel vision!"

"Oh, right," he conceded. "Never mind." But he was obviously too busy to advise her further.

Through the magically summoned gloom, Syren could hear that both Stouts had begun harassing the foul brute in turns, which she took as a good sign. Her own faculties, meanwhile, were returning to her, and her eyes were even beginning to adapt somewhat to the darkness. Rising, she encountered an oil lamp on an end table near her, so she brought out her tinder box and lit it quickly. The lamp cast a soft, dim glow about the room, which didn't dissipate the darkness but was just enough for her to see by.

The Ogre's position in the room and his bulk hid Durast from her view. She could see Braenog, however, and by their enemy's motions, she could tell that he was fighting both Deepfellows at once. Seeing the opportunity to attack from the rear flank, Syren took up her sword and rushed back into the fray. Just as she arrived, Braenog blocked an incoming strike with the shaft of his ax. When he tried to counterattack, though, the Ogre grabbed the shaft of the pole arm with both hands. Wrenching it from the old Stout's grasp, the powerful monster then snapped it like dry kindling, rendering it useless. Closing on the beast, Syren could see that it was looking haggard, and bleeding freely from a dozen places, a couple of which seemed serious. Hoping to end the skirmish, she drove the sword point deeply into the Ogre's midsection, then wrenched it out and jumped back a pace to avoid a repeat of her earlier experience.

Though significantly wounded by the puncture, the Ogre mage swept Braenog to the floor as he whirled on Syren and glared at her with wrath filled eyes.

"Now, Durast. Finish him!" Syren cried out in doom coated desperation, but even as the Stout swung both axes, his target clapped his hands together loudly, and uttering a single, unintelligible word of that mind curdling language, transformed himself into a vapor. Durast's axes swept through it harmlessly and clanged against the stone floor. Then as they watched, the cloud floated through the doorway and ascended the stairwell.

"Is everyone all right?" Syren asked, still panting from the terror and exertion of the combat.

"I am well, but my ax has not endured," Braenog answered poutingly.

"There were some downstairs, in that first room," Syren reminded him. "Run down and grab one...and come right back!" she warned him, remembering the Stouts' inclination to stop for treasure gathering.

"We must pursue the Ogre mage," Durast advised Syren as Braenog ran off. "If we do not fight on, while he is weakened, he may use that wizardry of his to become strong again. I do not think we can take him twice, especially if he appears in ambush." Syren looked longingly toward the windows, but nodded her agreement.

"Do you know what all his magic is capable of?" Syren asked. Durast shook his head.

"I do not," he said.

While they were speaking, catching their breath, and waiting for Braenog to return, Syren noticed that Durast was holding his arm gingerly.

"Bring that over here, into the light," she commanded. When he did, she could see that he had several deep gashes where he had been mauled by the Ogre.

"We should put some healing salve on that," Syren suggested, but Durast declined.

"This isn't over yet," he observed. "There isn't much salve left, and we may yet have deeper use for it. Given Stoutish medicine, I shall endure," he promised her.

"Stoutish medicine?" she asked. Then sourly she added, "Oh, don't tell me that you spit on it again." Durast shrugged at her.

"What?" he asked impatiently, but just then Braenog came bounding up the stairwell and appeared in the doorway, carrying an armload of axes.

"I thought it best to bring some this far, in case it happens again," he reported. "Look, this one is even finer than the one we bought!" Throwing down the time worn pole arms of various designs into a pile, he held out a swoop-bladed poleax that, despite the advance of years, looked as sharp as the day it was made.

"We can wait no longer," Durast encouraged, and the three climbed the stairs to the third landing. The noise beyond the door revealed that their quarry was inside and had become corporeal again.

"Is there a best plan?" Syren asked the group as Durast reached for the door handle. The Stouts studied each other for a moment and then looked up at Syren.

"Barrel in," they all agreed at once.

"But spread out, so he cannot attack all of us at once," Durast advised. Then throwing the door open as before, they rushed in.

The upper room of the tower had once been an elaborate bed chamber and private room for the castle's original owner, and many of the trappings and furnishings still remained, albeit in more faded and dilapidated condition than in days of glory past. There were also a fair number of boxes, trunks, and coffers that seemed out of place compared to the furnishings, and it was apparent that the Ogre was using this space as his personal lair. One of the coffers was open upon a writing desk. Two small jars, like the ones with healing salve in them that Anne Teak, the caravan merchant, had been trying to sell, lay empty on the floor, and the Ogre seemed not quite as badly wounded as he had previously been. Syren cursed their luck under her breath as they took positions at triangle points around the vile destroyer.

In the time it took them to enter, assess the situation, and maneuver into their desired positions, the Ogre mage had begun to chant again in that awful language.

"Attack!" Durast commanded. "Don't let him finish the chant!" But as they rushed forward, it was too late. An unnaturally frigid blizzard of ice, snow, and frost leapt from the outstretched hands of the Ogre mage. Because of the companion's strategy, the blast managed to catch only one of them, but Braenog was completely engulfed by the arctic onslaught. Syren and Durast carried through with their attacks, wounding the Ogre seriously as he concentrated his energy on the third of his foes. Turning, Syren paused involuntarily with horror as she looked at Braenog. Smoking vapors of cold wafted off of his rigid form. The Stout was completely covered in a thick layer of frost, as if he were made of snow entirely. For just a breath, she thought that perhaps he might shake off the damage and continue the fight, but he toppled over and fell to the floor, frozen and motionless.

"Nog!" she screamed, racing over to him. She reached out her hand to touch him, and see if he still lived, but the frost was so cold that she was afraid that she might get stuck to it herself. Nearby, there was a blanket that had once been a bedspread. Grabbing it up hastily, she wrapped him in it as best she could.

Durast, meanwhile, had pressed the attack with great ferocity, when he saw his kinsman go down. He was slashing, ducking, and pounding against his much larger opponent, using the great beast's size against it in the somewhat enclosed space.

As Syren ran over angrily to exact vengeance for her fallen friend, she fell in line inadvertently with Durast. The Ogre picked up a love seat from where he was standing and hurled it across the room at both of them. Durast ducked the throw easily, but Syren saw in an instant that she was about to get clobbered by it. Letting her legs go out from under her, she slid onto her back. Laying as flat as she could, she raised her shield to protect her face as the loveseat rolled over her. That proved to be a mistake, as the heavy piece of furniture banged against the shield, roughly forcing the edge of it into her cheek and eye. Somehow managing to bounce over the frozen body of Braenog, the loveseat rolled past and clattered against the far wall, near the door.

Rising, Syren saw that Durast had determinedly backed the Ogre mage into a recess, nearby to where a tall posted, curtain enshrouded bed was standing. Reaching into it, the Ogre drew forth the most enormous sword Syren had ever seen. Not a sharp and elegant thing of beauty like her sword, the eight foot long, dull steel weapon was nevertheless an embodiment of catastrophic woe to any who faced it, because of its sheer size and imposing weight. The Ogre accepted one of Durast's attacks intentionally, so he could force himself into a spot in the room where he could swing it. Then he eyed the Stout dangerously.

"Durast!" Syren yelled as she ran up. "Get out of the way!" but he refused.

"We nearly have him!" he called back, but his attempt to strike a crippling blow to the Ogre was deflected. The massive brute took one step to the side, to improve his position, and then he levied the full force of his demolishing swing into Durast's chest.

The impact shattered Durast's carapace breastplate utterly, and the broken pieces rained down around him like shards of pottery. The Stout himself was driven abruptly to the ground, as if he had been struck by lightning. Syren heard him grunt as he fell. With teeth bared in rage, she launched herself at the Ogre, who was still adjusting his grip on the long and cumbersome weapon he wielded. Syren's impassioned stroke skewered the Ogre's sword arm and plunged deep into his ribs, fastening his arm to his side, as with a carpenter's nail.

With Syren standing just behind the beast on that side, the Ogre was unable to reach Syren to dislodge her or the weapon. As he flailed away at her with his free arm, Syren watched in glad astonishment as Durast dragged himself up, raggedly, from the floor and buried both axes deep into the sorcerous monster's other side. The fiend dropped to his knees, clawed once, defiantly but ineffectively, at Durast, and then fell face down to the floor.

Dead.

CHAPTER 18

Henry's Keep

Syren and Durast reclaimed their weapons and stood over the creature warily for a moment.

"I have this weird feeling that he's going to get back up," she said, but he didn't.

"That would be Trolls," Durast instructed. Then confident that the Ogre had indeed breathed its last, they hurried over to where Braenog lay, to assess his condition.

Kneeling beside him, they unwrapped him from the bedspread, dragged him gently to a spot where the sun shone brightly through a window, and unclasped him from his armor. The warmth of the day and the blanket had begun to thaw the Stout. Clearing away the icy residue, Syren saw that Braenog's nose and finger tips were black with frostbite. To their great relief, however, they discovered that though he was unconscious, he was still alive.

"I think the breastplate protected his heart from the worst of the cold," Syren speculated. "We need to do something about the frostbite, though. Where's that healing salve?"

Syren spread what little of the alchemical wonder they had left on the affected areas while Durast searched the room, in case the Ogre had more of the stuff in reserve than he had already used. Unfortunately, there was none. The last of their own supply reversed the effects of the frostbite admirably, but was insufficient to help Braenog regain consciousness.

"This will be the third time that you've come home in a sack, my friend," Syren scolded him gently. "You really need to cut this out." Then she addressed Durast, who was happily rummaging through boxes of coins, gems stones, and other loot.

"He'll be safe here while we rescue Father," she estimated. "Then we can return and gather everything up."

Though Durast was reluctant to leave the gleaming bounty, he accompanied Syren to the second floor chamber of the tower. When they entered the parlor, they found that the Ogre's magically conjured darkness was gone. Neither Syren nor Durast knew if it had dissipated on its own or if it had been dispelled when the Ogre mage was killed, but in any case they quickly located the window that the body of Syren's father was hanging from and drew it carefully inside.

Syren collapsed onto the floor of the room and cradled her father into her lap. His remains were dried, shrunken and somewhat morose-looking, but they were generally intact. It was definitely him. Gently, she brushed his cheek with her finger tips, remembering who he had been in life. Tears welled up in Syren's eyes and ran down her cheeks abundantly and this time, she let them. As her emotions found their release in the completion of her years long quest, she realized gratefully that tears were not a sign of weakness, after all.

"I found you. I found you," she whispered to him. Durast rested one oversized hand compassionately on her shoulder as she mourned. Then he crossed over to a window that overlooked the courtyard and peered out.

"It's a long way down," he observed absently after a minute, to break the silence. Then his following statement carried a much more concerned tone.

"Syren, we have trouble," he warned. "The grass has burned out, and the Orcs have returned. They will soon see the ones that we slew. They will notice that the banner of your father is gone. Then they will storm the tower," Turning to face Syren, he added ominously, "and they will succeed." Syren was jarred from her reverie by the news.

"We can't let them win," she said. "Not now. Not after all this. What can we do?" Durast thought for a moment.

"It is too late to flee. We would be seen if we tried to sneak away, and we would have to abandon everything, and everyone, if we did." Durast grabbed his thick beard with both hands as he concentrated. The Orcs were still milling about, but they were starting to gather and move toward the tower. Then his dark eyes brightened with sudden inspiration.

"The Ogre!" he blurted out. "Come with me, Syren."

Lifting her father's body carefully, Syren followed Durast up the steps to the third story sleeping chamber, where Braenog and the dead Ogre mage still lay. On the way, he briefly summarized his plan.

"Orcs are bullies. The Ogre mage ruled over them by fear, because he was a bigger bully. We are going to convince the Orcs that we are bigger bullies than the Ogre was."

"How are we going to do that?" Syren asked incredulously. "Hold an assembly?"

"Of a sort," he replied evasively. Without further time to explain, Durast retrieved the fine quality poleax that Braenog had found in the first floor room of the tower. Crossing to where the Ogre lay, he wielded the ax against the dead foe in powerful, executioner style strokes, until he had severed the monster's huge head. Then he dragged the gruesome body part to the window that overlooked the courtyard. Climbing precariously onto the open window ledge, he stood in full view of the Orcs, holding the bloody ax for them to see.

From the ground, the Orcs began congregating where they could see him. Soon, they were shaking their fists and shouting furiously at the Stout's bold insolence in their own guttural dialect. When they had gathered sufficiently for Durast's purpose, he put down the ax, and grabbing the Ogre's head by both ears, he hoisted it up for them to see. It took only a few moments for the Orcs in the courtyard to grow quiet. Then Durast cast the severed head defiantly down at them. It clattered garishly down the tower wall, caromed off the base, and rolled horrifically into their midst. The action and all it implied panicked the evil throng. Scattering frantically, they fled in every direction, not just over the wall, but into the forest, out of sight and beyond earshot, until all was quiet and still.

"That has bought us some time," Durast said, returning from the window with satisfaction.

"How much time, do you think?" asked Syren.

"Because they are bullies, Orcs are not well organized. It will take hours for them to reform and hours more, perhaps a day, before they become brave enough to return. By then, though, we must be gone with everything we can take." Syren looked around her and sighed.

"Do you think we can get any of this home? I mean, we're already going to have Nog and Father to carry, and both of us are pretty banged up."

"I think that we must take it all home," Durast insisted. "Syren, look about you. In the coffers of the Ogre mage are thousands of silver coins, piles of copper, gem stones, enough to pay your debt to the Palace five times over, at least. In addition, the salvage from this place is enough for us to start and stock a Venture Salvage shop of our own. With all this, we could truly go into business for ourselves!"

"We are still under contract with Aglar Grump," Syren reminded him wearily.

"For one more day," Durast pointed out. He paused while the possibility sunk in for Syren and rooted itself in hope. Then as he began to see it sprout on Syren's face, he watered it with a grin and chuckle of his own.

"But how can we transport all this stuff?" Syren asked. "Do you realize how many trips would that would take?"

"I think we will only get one, perhaps two, if we hurry," replied Durast.

"And one of those must be used to carry Nog and Father," Syren thought aloud. Durast rolled his *r*'s in agreement.

"Wait a minute. Transport!" Syren exclaimed suddenly. "What if we took some of this money, ran back to Westpost, and used it to buy or rent a couple of wagons? Then we could get it all back in one trip, or most of it, anyway."

"We should not leave trrreasure unguarded," Durast advised, "and I will not leave Nog undefended."

"I agree," said Syren, "but if we take him and Father with us, it will slow us down significantly. Then we might lose our chance."

"You must go alone," Durast said, giving voice to the obvious solution. "I will stay and defend our people and our treasure. You will be much faster and quieter by yourself."

Syren hated the idea of leaving Durast stranded, alone and injured in the wilderness. The plan did make a certain amount of sense, though, given their predicament. Adding to that, the Stout assured her that however it might end, he would have it no other way, so she agreed.

"Do your best not to tarry," he told her jokingly, "I've run out of Ogre's heads."

Promising to return as soon as possible, she filled a sack with coins. Then she clapped him on both shoulders and headed for

Westpost while he barricaded himself into the tower. Doing her best to blend into the foliage and move silently, the trek through the forest and back to Westpost was still the longest and most nerve wracking of her life. She would rather have faced all the Orcs of Stormwood herself than subject her friends to death and worse, but she felt certain that all would be well if she could just manage this one final plan, and get everybody home safely.

With Stormwood at her back, she moved quickly through the Nearwood until she was challenged by a trio of snarling, defiant Hiddeans. They were a hunting party, bent on fierce mischief, just like the first ones that had accosted her that evening three months ago, while she was gathering sticks. Without pause or fear on her part, Syren drew her father's sword—her sword. In one deft and powerful stroke, she separated the nearest one from its head. As the second lunged at her, she fended it off forcefully with her shield. Then she skewered the third, through and through. Leaving the lone survivor to flee into the forest, she wiped off her blade and moved on intently toward Westpost, without looking back.

After crossing the threshold of the Wallgate, Syren walked anxiously up the main street to town. Oblivious to neighbors and shoppers, her mind was consumed with speculations about where she could find wagons and drivers, and how much she might have to pay to acquire them. As a result, she walked headlong into Baron without seeing him, crashing into him unexpectedly as he exited Oswald's Venture Salvage. Tumbling awkwardly into the dirt, the sack full of coins fell from her hands, some of which spilled out onto the road.

"Well, Syren," Baron exclaimed in his oily, irritating voice, "how disagreeable it is, meeting you here. You're looking as graceful as ever, I see." He leaned over and, making an obvious display of not helping her up, snatched up her burlap sack. Gathering the fallen coins, he pocketed a couple of them for himself.

"Leave me alone, Baron," Syren demanded as she picked herself up from the ground, but he persisted.

"Where'd you get that black eye?" he teased. "From one of your many admirers, no doubt."

"None of your business," she retorted. "Now, give me back that sack."

"Not so fast," he scolded, holding the bag out of reach. "Let's just see what you have here." Baron's eyes went wide when he saw all the coins, and he whistled derisively. Before he could do anything else, however, Syren snatched the burlap sack away from him. She decided not to haggle with him over the few coins he had kept. She tried to walk away, but he followed her, like an annoying dog, nipping at her heels.

"On your way to the Palace, are you?" he ventured. "That's not enough to pay your debt, I think."

"Not your problem," she answered over her shoulder. People around them were beginning to take notice of their interaction.

"The deadline's tomorrow, you know." Syren stalked on, fuming, but didn't answer. She tried to ignore him, hoping that would make him go away, but he continued goading her bitterly. "Face it Syren. You and your little Punies are not going to make it. I don't know how you managed to get out of that more recent business that

I worked so hard to arrange for you, but you won't escape this. You're finished."

Syren couldn't take it any longer. Between all that she and her friends had endured these past months and the urgency of her present circumstances, Baron's dastardly scheming and his childish mocking were too much to bear. Drawing her sword, she wheeled on him and threatened him with it, the sword point coming to rest in the hollow of his neck. Baron pulled up short, in the nick of time, the barest trickle of blood appearing at the place where her sword had scratched the skin.

"Enough!" she commanded, seething. "I don't have time for this, and I sure don't have time for you and your nonsense. You walk away, right now, or I swear I will kill you where you stand!" The small crowd that had assembled gasped. Slaying the inherently vile savages of the wilderness was one thing. Slaying someone who lived in the village, or even promising to, was quite another. Syren felt the red hot anger in her face. She had never threatened a person with deadly force. She had never even wanted to, but with everything at stake, she was pretty sure that if Baron didn't back down, she was going to do something drastic. He must have seen it too because his face became pale. Then he raised quivering hands and slowly stepped back. Syren glared at him for two paces. Then sheathing her sword, she turned and strode angrily away. Behind her, she could hear Baron talking to people in the crowd.

"You saw that, right? She drew steel on me. Look, I'm bleeding!"

Syren was on her way, purposefully, toward the blacksmith's shop to ask Kollan about draft animals and wagons, when her cousin Quig ran up alongside her.

"Hi, Syren! Where ya goin'?" he asked innocently."I heard that you got excused from prison this morning. Congratulations. I don't think you'd like it there."

"Thanks," she replied absently.

"Some people are saying that they saw you in some amazing-looking armor. Can I see it?" Syren extended her right arm as they walked briskly up the street, so he could see the bracer. Quig seemed disappointed.

"By the way they talked about it, it seemed bigger than that."

"That's it," Syren shrugged. She knew that he was referring to the Stouts' armor, but she was too concerned with other matters to explain.

"Say, are you getting a black eye?"

"Apparently."

"How'd you get it? Did Baron give it to you? I heard that—"

"Listen, Quig," Syren stopped to confront the boy, gently but firmly. "I really don't have time for a lot of conversation just now. My friends are stuck…" Abruptly, she changed the description of her problem, for his sake. "We had to leave some salvage in the woods, and I need to find a way to get it back to town before nightfall." She resumed her pace toward the Village Green, with her younger cousin in tow. He made three complete strides in silence before he spoke again.

"Salvage in the wilderness, hey? More than you can tote back in your burlap sacks?"

"Yes."

"So you need a cart, or a wagon, or something," Quig speculated.

"Or something," Syren agreed. "I have money, if I can find somebody who has wagons and animals for sale." Now the boy was searching his mind.

"If you have enough money on you that maybe you could buy a wagon, I bet I can get you what you need a lot cheaper. Come with me."

Changing direction, they ran off together into one of the neighborhoods, behind the Hooded Crow. Quig took them to the home of a local resident.

"This is Drake's house," Quig said. "He's really good with animals. He also works a team for Marley, hauling kegs for the Crow." From the dirt on his clothes, the man was just coming out of his garden, and he smiled merrily at Quig when he saw him.

"Hi, Drake! How's Betsy?"

"That old mare is as sound as a silver. Most dependable puller I've got. Have you come around to groom her again?"

"Not this time. Drake, this is my cousin Syren. She's the best salvager in Westpost, and she has a problem. How'd you like to make a hundred silvers in about two hours?"

Syren, Drake, and the man's eldest son, Hensley, rolled into the compound of the old ruined castle in the late afternoon. Jake and Betsy, Drake's reliable old Cob draft horses, had each pulled a buckboard wagon calmly through the treacherous wilds of Stormwood and up to the base of the tower, as though they did it every day. Drake and Hensley were doing their best to hide their terror, though with only moderate success. Syren was also filled with anxiety, but in her case, it was over whether or not the Orcs had returned and what condition she might find her friends in, but thanks to Quig, she had not been gone more than a couple of hours. Durast had apparently been watching for her return. As she jumped down from the lead wagon, the Stout opened the tower door and came out into the courtyard, greeting Syren with his wide white-toothed smile.

It took another hour of steady work to load the buckboards with all the heavy treasure and bulky salvage from the tower. Durast had placed Braenog and the body of Syren's father into burlap sacks, both for ease of transport and so that their hired drivers/porters wouldn't have to look at them. Syren explained the two bundles merely as "casualties," which needed special care, and that was enough to garner the good villagers' concern, respect and privacy.

"Syren, we should search the smaller buildings for treasure also," Durast recommended.

"Probably," Syren agreed, "but I'm concerned for time. The sun's going down, and the Orcs have already been gone for several hours. There's no knowing when they might return. We need to get back to Westpost with what we have, without getting attacked on the way. Our drivers are getting pretty nervous, and it's not going to be a fast trip, with the wagons loaded down like they are."

Durast gazed at the two heavily laden buckboards with admiration. They were both piled high with artifacts, artwork, weapons, armors, knickknacks, furniture, crystals, tapestries, and of course, the Ogre's huge sword and his treasure boxes. Drake and Hensley were just covering each wagonload with a large tarpaulin. Jake and Betsy stood peacefully in their harnesses, looking like they might be asleep.

"Just as well," Durast conceded. "I doubt there is any more room on the wagons anyway. How will we prevent treasure from falling off, if we have to make a dash for the Wallgate?"

"Not to worry," Syren said, grinning broadly. "While I was in town, I bought some brand new canvass straps!"

Syren rode on Drake's buckboard, with her father's remains tucked up close to her, where she could keep an eye on them. Similarly, Durast rode on Hensley's, where he could watch over Braenog. Both wagons jostled along slowly over the uneven ground, towed by the sturdy and docile Cobs. Traveling side by side as they drew away, Syren watched the tower begin to recede into the distance, feeling a sense of melancholy that approached nostalgia.

"It is noble stone," Durast declared. "It has stood long against the wilderness, and deserves better than these Orcs."

"Indeed," replied Syren. "I wonder what the castle was called, in its day," she said wistfully. "Who lived here? Did this place have a name?"

"It has guarded your father well, kept him, until you could come for him."

"Until *we* could come," Syren corrected gratefully.

"What was your father's name?" Durast asked, after a pause for reflection.

"Henry," she said. "His name was Henry."

"Then this shall be Henry's Keep," pronounced Durast resolutely.

"Henry's Keep," Syren echoed, and a tear formed in her eye.

CHAPTER 19

The Beginning

Syren stood reflectively by the tree in her backyard, feeling content. She was gazing down at the two graves that lay side by side. Sprouting grass was beginning to cover the soft earth, which was gently mounded in front of the new headstone.

"They can speak to each other now," Durast comforted, and Syren nodded.

Nearly a month had passed since the day she and Durast had defeated the Ogre mage, plundered his lair, and returned victoriously to Westpost. With the treasure they had gained, Syren was able to pay the debt she owed to the Palace, on the final morning of their sixty day extension. She and Durast had brought to the Divining Hall the thousand silvers, which covered the cost of the damages to the Hooded Crow from the bar fight and her share of the tribute for the grievance hearing. Baron had appeared, expecting to see Syren groveling before the chancellor and begging for more time, but instead of getting to crow, he went home eating it. It was a very gratifying day for Syren.

Braenog gradually recovered from the affliction that had been showered upon him by the Ogre mage's fiendish magic. He had remained unconscious for two days, and was feverish and weak for several more, but he rallied. Ultimately, the only vestige of the treacherous ailment was a persistent sniffle, which was rarely more noticeable than the daily rumblings of his stomach.

Standing graveside, Syren and the Stouts were joined by Jessero, and by Jack Frost. They had come visiting separately, but had arrived simultaneously.

"There they are," Jack said aloud, to announce his presence as the two individuals approached. Syren smiled back at them.

"Hey, Jack. Hi, Jessero," she greeted.

"Well, if it isn't Westpost's newest independent business owners," Jessero hailed. "I hear that congratulations are in order on that score."

"Thank you very kindly," she said, and she bowed in a playful gesture.

"How precisely did you manage it?" Jack inquired. "I understood that you three were contractually obligated to Aglar Grump, that there was some sort of exclusivity clause."

"The terms of that contract expired after sixty days," Syren explained. "He's been contesting it, but the language in the agreement never actually said that we had to sell him whatever we found. It only said that we couldn't sell stuff to anyone else. When we made

CPSIA information can be obtained
at www.ICGtesting.com
Printed in the USA
FFOW02n0953141115
18517FF

9 781634 175869